The Hidden Eternity
AND THE UNSPOKEN RHYME

BY

GABRIEL J. ERKARD

ILLUSTRATIONS BY DAWN JOELL

~Please, come and imagine with me~

ISBN-13: 978-0692805367
ISBN-10: 0692805362

First American edition, January 2017

Contents

"April through August death is its hottest. December through February replenishes the cemetery. January, July your emotions will die. June turns to March when Jym Reapyr is parched. May hates October cuz' not a soul is sober; while November loves September because time won't remember."

- Veraelle Claverkiss

CHAPTER ONE

MEMORIES OF NOTHING

*W*ith twisted skin and a disfigured face a twelve-year-old, homeless boy awakens. Unsure how he even got there, a foggy cemetery surrounded by hundreds of tomb-stones aligned in triangular rows on a cold, fall afternoon, his light, amber eyes darted wildly from one gravestone to the next. Hoping that he were stuck in a sick dream, he began panting as if something invisible was choking him. Mere survival for this scrawny boy meant more than just the need for food and water. He was in danger.

Seated awkwardly on the cold ground, he scratched his slender head; full of patchy, uncombed, brunette locks and his tight, plastic-looking skin wrinkled with every pull. He was obviously unaware that he'd just been burned in a dream that somehow found its way into reality. A brisk wind rustled the nearby leaves that had fallen from the cemetery's dead trees, all of which were centered in the middle of each triangular formation of tombstones. The boy leapt up from the ground, standing just a few inches taller than a shiny, oversized, black, Marblehead gravestone he was next to, rubbing the sleep out of his round eyes, hoping that they were playing tricks on him.

The nearby tombstone read a woman's name, birthday, and date of death in a rather peculiar order. Etched in bright white it read: Elaine R. Lyborikus; born May 23, 1954; died November 17, 1874. 'This doesn't make sense,' he thought silently and read it once more. After a second look revealed the same thing, he began to wonder if he was losing his mind or growing delusional from thirst and hunger.

It was nearing five o'clock and the unfriendly, grey skies let not even the slightest bit of sunshine fall through all that day. The boy looked at another nearby tombstone to see if it, too, had the deceased person's death date wrong. This one, no taller than a small pile of bricks, was bright red and facing the other way, leaving him unable to see when this person had passed away. He did, however, spot four unopened letters leaning against its base as if loved ones had placed them there gently.

Each read 'P.L.P.S' under bizarre symbols. One envelope was pink with a black, African Ohu symbol that looked like a maze. Two were green with black, hourglass symbols. The fourth was purple with a hooked, bloody fang that looked like one from a large animal. Strangely, the symbol that resembled the maze matched the exact scar under the boy's left eyelid; a scar he didn't know he even had.

Without warning, the four envelopes began violently shaking as if whatever was inside was desperate to escape! He backed away. The four letters shot off to unknown whereabouts in all different directions at light speed! Swallowing a million questions, he looked around to see if anyone else had witnessed this unusual mishap. He was alone. Fixing his eyes on the massive gravestone in front of him for a second time, he thought frightfully, 'I'm in a graveyard with tombstones placed in formation...with death dates saying these people died before they were even born...and now I just saw four letters fly off on their own....' Our story begins when the tombstone right in front of him, began slowly erasing its words before his very eyes.

The day Ms. Elaine Lyborikus had passed away was the first to vanish. Then, her birthday. Finally, her name, leaving the black, Marblehead tombstone cold and barren. His eyes widened as if a knife had pierced him. He ran thinking that it was cursed! Mud; tiny, sharp sticks; grass, and other filth peppered his bare feet. Out of the corner of his eye, he spotted another large gravestone that read: Darla Y. Davodsko; born September 2, 1999; died August 4, 1994. It, too, erased itself in the exact same order as Ms. Elaine's:

The death date.
Birthday. Her name.

The poor child feared the dead were coming back to get him! 'Or am I already dead...encroaching on their territory??' he panicked silently and his swift run became a full-blown sprint. Through the foggy distance, he saw a crowd of about thirteen or so, dressed in hooded black cloaks with their faces concealed by smiling, white, mime masks. Each gang member carried various objects in their gloved hands. The vast distance between he and them, however, made it nearly impossible to make out what they were holding. What he saw, for sure, was a brown sack of bones and an oversized snake skull! He gasped, choking on his spit when the group began marching towards him whispering, "Welcome back, Russell."

Left, right, left right, they stomped in sync; black boots crushing the cemetery grounds with a purpose. Gathering his dwindling strength, he sprinted away escaping untold terror.

Adrenaline had overtaken him like cold to the tundra. He whipped and dashed through more tombstones. The cemetery's tall, jagged exit was in sight through the thickening fog. He stopped to catch his breath, each exhale meeting the frigid air, creating a small cloud of condensation around his lips. He looked around to see if he'd been followed. He was alone.

Seeming almost as if time had sped up from the moment he'd awakened until now, he noticed the sky was significantly darker than even just a few minutes ago. What he didn't notice, however, were a few people in the far distance kneeling beside tall gravestones; taller than the ones he'd awakened next to, as if they were peacefully praying for something — or someone.

At the edge of the cemetery's gate was a small, two-lane road. Down its middle was nothing more than its two yellow stripes and across the street was a deep dark forest. He was trapped. He couldn't go back into the cemetery and knew better than to enter a forest with dusk rapidly approaching. 'Crunch...crunch,' something was coming. With no choice, he crossed the road as frozen grass and icy mud caked between his tiny toes slapped the bumpy cement. Deep within the woods he ran, ran, and ran. Tall trees that once looked as if they'd scratched The Heavens now looked a quarter of their size due to the fog. The sharp sound of him crunching through the branches echoed. He paused every so often, afraid that whatever was after him could hear him running.

After a petrifying five-minute sprint, he reached a center field covered in mounds of dirt and weeds. From it, branched eight trailways and only the second revealed immediate safety. That's when he saw it; a two-story wooden-paneled shack. Barren trees had grown through its hollow windows. Its shackles had fallen due to old age and terrible winters. Next to the abandoned house was a fat, dead tree with only one sturdy branch remaining. From it, hung a noose, whose loop was in the shape of a heart. Unable to believe his eyes, there was no time to even digest the unusual siting. It was still coming.

4

'Snap...pop,' he heard behind him. The boy quickly crept up the three rickety, wooden front porch steps, each one creaking louder than the last. Upon entering the cold, dark shack, a bone-chilling silence enveloped him. The stench of sawdust and old age filled the air. His stomach growled. The slightest scent of anything tricked his mind into fantasizing about food. The house's foyer had two rickety, wooden staircases leading upstairs to dark, eerie-looking bedrooms. In front of him was a long hall with just a sliver of light at the end of it. He licked his craggy lips, hoping that the light was coming from a kitchen. He dashed down the hall as if he'd been shot from a cannon! Faster and faster, he ran. Thick spider webs callused the walls. Plump roaches scurried into the dark corners. Fat rats came out to see who was in their house. The boy didn't care — or seem to notice.

There it was, a dirty kitchenette smelling of animal feces and decades of thawed and refrozen trash. Turning the rusty sink knobs, he waited for an ocean to burst through to quench his terrible thirst. Yet, nothing but a gurgling noise issued from the rusty pipes. Disappointed, rather pissed off actually, he yanked open the nearby cabinets above and below the kitchen sink looking for food, only to find a few chunky rats fighting over crumbs and others having sex. The boy peered into the close-by corner cabinet. Nothing. He jerked his head back to the first cabinet, wondering if he could snatch whatever the rats were fighting over! The crumbs were gone, however, they were now fighting over a piece of cardboard and a shoelace. The boy grew angrier.

Next to the tiny oven was a black refrigerator with no freezer door. Never-minding the god-awful smell, he peered into the freezer to find ice and two frozen peas that had probably been there since before he was born. He popped them in his mouth; old socks and trash juice was their flavor. He was too hungry to even care. Yanking open the refrigerator door, he hoped to find at least a piece of moldy bread or a rotten carrot for a well-balanced meal. At the bottom of the refrigerator were dead flies frozen in egg yolk.

Somehow, he was now even hungrier than before he'd eaten the two peas! Slowly dragging his feet to the other side of the kitchen, he held his head low with death resting at his shoulders. The weakening boy slid to the floor and felt his heart thump through his chest. His vision began to blur. Hearing began to dwindle.

Seconds later, 'creak….creak,' he heard. It was in the house. With barely enough energy to even stand, he used all four quivering limbs to pull himself up a nearby back staircase until he found it — a dark secluded bedroom. Inside, he found a black, wooden dresser, a window, and a few scattered books on the dirty, carpeted floor. Something outside the window caught his attention — the sky. By now, it was nearly dark; just a stroke of greyish-blue in the sky as far away from him as possible. When he looked closely, he could see his reflection in the window. His twisted skin had returned to a near-normal state, which he hadn't noticed was even disfigured to begin with. Ugly, he was; jagged teeth, oblong forehead, sunken cheeks, and painfully thin! Suddenly, he heard a bang as if whatever was inside the house had kicked a heavy box of books against the wall. Forced to stop studying himself, the boy searched around the room for an escape; up, down, left, right. There were none.

In a far corner laid a disgusting, brown-spotted mattress whose unbearable stench was enough to kill you twice. He crawled onto the foul smelling box spring and curled into the fetal position. Without warning, his heart nearly shot through his chest when he saw a white, mime mask on the floor next to him! The haunting sound of footsteps continued down the hallway towards the kitchen downstairs. They grew slower and quieter as if, whomever it was, had become aware that someone else was in their house.

The figure stood at the kitchen's entrance. Terror rippled through the little boy's body. He knew that a single audible breath, one wrong move, a clumsy step would end his life. A thud on the first rickety step sent pins and needles down his spine. His eyes widened as his breath grew heavy.

6

The boy covered his mouth and shut his eyes so tightly that tears streamed down his sunken cheeks. A second thud. He buried his head into the smelly mattress, hoping that the ominous figure would just go away! A third and final step, sounding like a deafening crunch, left the house silent for nearly two whole minutes.

The boy didn't move. He opened his eyes and slowly uncovered his mouth, allowing himself to breathe. Suddenly, he noticed that the mask was gone! It was too late. Hovering two inches from his face was a beefy man wearing a black, hooded cloak. His creepy grunts seeped through the tiny slits of the mask. In his gloved, right hand was a large dagger covered in blood. In that moment, something unexplainable happened.

The blood, itself, began dripping towards the ceiling as if time, for just a moment, was reversing itself! Both of them stood frozen, mouths agape, until every last drop was gone. The sinister man examined his clean knife with a slight grin, raising it to The Heavens and the little boy tried to beg for his life. To a terrible surprise, the boy could not speak! Petrified grunts and moans were all that issued from his throat. He was cornered. No way out. Nothing he, or anyone, could do. "Welcome home, Russell," said the big man. From that night on, the little boy moved no more.

A slight breeze ruffled what few leaves were left on the trees outside the shack, which laid stiffly under the black sky as if nothing had even happened. Yet, something more than just a terrible murder happened that night. The death of this twelve-year-old boy just might've been the key to unlocking the wisdom of many past lives for many people. A murder that might allow this homeless boy to answer the un-answered, himself, or find out if he may have in fact deserved such a horrible death. His name was Samol Doscow and this was his story.

CHAPTER TWO

THE AFTERLIFE AWAITS

"It does not matter how you died, yet how you lived."
– Maven J. Dolus

*S*amol felt it being ripped from his decapitated body; ghostly yet alive, was his soul. He could still see life around him exactly the way it was. The room, his body, his murderer, and the shack were all intact. Strangest of all, there was no blood! Samol was being sucked into a large, black hole. He tried to get away from it, but couldn't! The further he fell, the faster he went. He felt his stomach drop as if he were thrown from a derailed rollercoaster. He kicked and screamed as unimaginable terror rippled through every vein. It looked as if he were in the eye of a dark hurricane.

Winds picked up. Terrible god-like thunder tore through the dark sky. Along the sides of the storm's eye were white-gloved hands holding large daggers. They swung at him viciously, but he could not be touched; as he was no longer dead or alive, flesh nor spirit, yet something in between.

A few knives quickly multiplied into thousands! Samol fought and screamed as hard and as loud as he could! Faster and faster he fell as the thunder and winds continued to hurl. Then, he heard it — the sound of many voices of what might've been children. Without warning, he face-planted onto a pile of jagged, black rocks. The impact, alone, should have killed him again, yet he was now in a world in which such concepts were lunacy.

Samol was in a large forest surrounded by dead trees that were peacefully humming a hymn as the fire-bolt skies welcomed him home. He nearly vomited. Such a whirlwind can do a number on anyone, let alone a twelve-year-old who'd just been murdered! All of a sudden, he felt his caved-in face and body begin to morph into someone else! His knees and back sprouted him a terribly painful six inches. He became significantly stronger. 'What's happening to me??' he thought wildly. His teeth went from gapped to straight; jawline from sunken to strong. The odd-shaped scar under his left eyelid had vanished. The only remaining feature were his eyes; still amber. The new body, in which he found himself, was the body of the first life he ever lived.

He was no longer thirsty or hungry all of a sudden. Fear seemed to come and go. For a second, there, he even felt invincible, thank you very much. From what he could see, the sky looked as if it were made of lightning. The fire-bolts scorched gloomy, high-sitting fog that looked like black clouds. After cyeballing the upper atmosphere Samol felt his stomach disappear, because he realized that the bolts were not lightning, yet souls being emitted to unknown places in every direction! Blues, reds, blacks, pinks, greens, whites, oranges, yellows, and purples scattered about, against what looked like a black mist for miles on up. These souls were the very thing that kept this entire underworld lit. Through the forest's far distance, he began to see hundreds of people migrating towards something, talking and singing with one another as though they were family.

'At least I'm not in hell...' Samol thought rashly, erasing that question from his many. There were more children and teenagers than adults, by far. Samol squinted, catching a glimpse of three teenagers apart from the migrating group. One was mangled beyond recognition. Another, with not a blotch or blemish to be found, looked as if he died peacefully in his sleep. The third had many bullet wounds. Strangely, all three of them had a dark, indistinguishable shadow lurking above their heads! "Where are we?" Samol wanted to shout, but didn't even move his mouth because he knew he couldn't talk.

"Hey, Michael," said the boy who looked like he died in his sleep, "when you were shot in the head, did you...*feel* it?"

The boy with the bullet wounds paused, his eyes fixed to the sky as if he knew exactly what he felt but didn't quite know how to explain it.

"Only for a split-second," he answered hesitantly, a slight squeak in his voice. "It's hard to describe...but it — it — feels more like a sudden shock than anything," he struggled to explain.

Samol tried to actualize what it must feel like to be shot in the head, wondering if it was worse than the death he experienced. He suddenly wondered if he were now in a place where he could ask someone what it felt like to be shot, or drown, or even fall off a cliff. He began to imagine darkly.

Before Samol could finish his somber thoughts, the boy who'd been shot added, "Well, only if you're killed instantly, that is!" he blurted importantly.

Behind the three of them were two more teen boys who appeared to be the best of friends in a past life. "Damn, you stink, James! Get away from me!" said the boy, terribly swollen from fatal bee stings.

"Well, I'm dead, Einstein! What do you expect??" the other joked, smearing his decayed armpits in his face like an older brother. They, too, had large shadows floating over their heads.

10

Feeling strangely as if his body had turned to lead, Samol didn't move. He studied the crowd that seemed to grow larger by the second. By now, there were thousands of happy, dead people migrating towards the center of the forest as though a pot of gold were waiting for each of them as a reward for finishing their last life. Quite naturally, as someone who was new to this weird underworld, Samol couldn't understand their excitement. 'Who in the heck would be happy to be dead?' Samol thought. It occurred to him that in this world, *"death"* was nothing more than a friend who lent a loving hand to bring them home where they belonged.

Samol rested his hands at his hips; exhaling heavily; eyes fixed on a fat, purple lightning bolt soul that shot into the never-ending, black sky. Out of the corner of his eye, he saw a blue piece of paper no bigger than a postcard floating from the sky right towards him as if The Heavens had written him a personal letter. He grabbed it hesitantly. In its top right-hand corner was a glistening, black and white stone the size of a small rock. Below, it read:

Death Certificate

~ *The kingdom of Euphod would like to formally welcome you to a blissful eternity* ~

Name - S.T.R.A.D.O.O.
Birthday -- '..ir… f…. d..'
Death Date: October 30 – 2 min 7 sec
Life purpose – '…s .. …r ..v..t …e, O …..mes. …ife … f … te…r cur…. ..wer …l..ies' r…e…. ca..…ertifica...'
Obstacles/disabilities/challenges – 'M… nx….'
Gifts/talents/capabilities – '…lk ..o ….ea….'
Scar – Ohu scar under left eyelid

Hidden Purpose – Show Elizabeth L. Rosewright The End of Time

Samol studied this weird thing called a "death certif-icate," something he couldn't remember ever seeing before. His mind spun over new unanswered questions. 'Why are the words moving?? *The end of time?* Hidden purpose? Scar? *Kingdom of Euphod?* Is this even for me??' He pondered incessantly, until something tragic almost happened.

Barreling down the black hole, butt-first, was a three-hundred pound man heading straight for Samol's head! It sounded like a freight train coming right at him! Samol dove out of the way seconds before the pale, beefy man cracked the ground in two! A noise that was between a sigh of relief and exasperation issued from Samol's throat. He hadn't been in this world five minutes and already wanted to get the heck out!

Rolling on the ground by a tree stump, the roly-po-ly man screamed obscenities while a group of on looking teens pointed and laughed. Unsure how or even why, Samol seemed to realize that in this world adults felt more pain than children. He stood to his feet, dusting himself of dirt and a few wiggling maggots, when something troubled him yet again — the giggle of what sounded like a toddler and a terrible smell.

The stench was god-awful. Samol covered his whole face, wondering if someone was farting and running away as a sick prank! Or if someone never wiped themselves a single day in their last life! Rotten innards perhaps? Samol jerked his head over his right shoulder to find a hideous, bug-eyed girl staring up at him. He nearly jumped out of his new skin!

The little girl's eyes bulged like tennis bulls. A sulfuric stench cloaked every strand of her unkempt, long, brown hair. Her skin was ghostly looking and falling from her bones. She wore a filthy, grey dress that hung just above her kneecaps, each oozing a pinkish pus. On her withered ring finger, however, was a beautiful, glowing, blue, diamond ring - - brighter than anything Samol had ever seen. Staring wildly at Samol's death certificate, she turned her craggy lips and spoke:

"You've got an interesting one," she said in a nasally, high-pitched voice. Her breath was just as ungodly as her looks.

"An interesting what?" said Samol, clutching his throat, realizing that he could finally talk! Suddenly, he didn't even care about what she was saying or her disastrous breath, for that matter.

"Death certificate!" she said surely. "You're missing stuff."

"This? This is mine?" Samol asked seriously, studying the puzzling, postcard-looking thing once more as if he'd hoped it wasn't his.

The little girl nodded vigorously. If her head went up and down any more, the skin from her neck looked like it would fly off.

"What's it supposed to look like?" he asked, suddenly interested, but still caring just a tad bit more that he could actually hear the sound of his very own voice. It was a silvery voice; clear and pleasant to listen to, as a matter of fact.

"Well, everyone's is different," she said, spitting terribly, "but it's always supposed to have all of the letters and numbers," she said, comparing his to hers as the skin from her elbows and neck swiveled.

"Letters? Numbers?"

"Oh, no!" she said with her big eyes fixed on Samol's hidden purpose.

"Oh, no - - what??" he said, leaning in closely to see what she was reading, secretly holding his breath.

She gave him an odd, stiff glare.

"WHAT??" he hollered stiffly, slowly running out of air.

"You're in *Zebrastone!*" she said, spitting again.

"Zebra-what?" Samol asked, wiping the smelly discharge from his arm.

"Zebrastone!" she repeated herself. "You can tell by the stone at the top of your death certificate," she said, leaning in closely to point.

"Whew!" Samol hurled, no longer able to keep quiet about her doo-doo breath. He fanned ferociously, wanting to ask '*if she ate sewage for breakfast!*' Avoiding the second-hand-stink, he backed away three feet covering his face and asked through widening fingers, "What does it mean? Is Zebrastone bad or something?"

"Zebrastone's not bad...well it can be..." she paused in deep thought, unaware that Samol had even backed away. "Zebrastone is the castle in which you've been sorted into for this afterlife," she explained.

"*This* afterlife? You — how — where am I?" Samol stuttered, jerking his head around in every direction.

"You're home!" she smiled (which she shouldn't have). Her teeth looked like soiled barbwire! Samol quickly averted his face in disgust. Any longer and he feared he might go blind!

Still in her own smelly thoughts — or imagination — or wherever she was, she still didn't notice that he was making faces.

"You're amongst those who've lived thirty, forty...even hundreds of lives!" she shrilled awkwardly, skipping away to the center of the forest, now closer to the crowd.

Pieces of her back and butt fell behind. Samol followed hesitantly, stepping over her butt skin, still covering his nose, craning his neck around a tall, buff man in front of him, trying to get a good listen at the almost "too-friendly" conversations that his dead peers were having. He kept close watch on the little girl, who was still clumsily skipping about. Aside from the way she looked, or the fact that she spat terribly when she spoke, or that she smelled like she'd probably drowned in hot doo-doo in her last life, something about her intrigued Samol.

"What is your name?" he asked almost too carefully, afraid that she'd answer by standing two inches away from him and he would drop dead - - again.

"Galena. Galena Grace. And yours?"

"I — er — don't really know, actually," he stammered.

"What do you mean you don't know??" she spat again.

Samol dodged and began to wonder if she were now doing it on purpose.

"Well, I'm sure I've got a name…but I don't remember what it is," he said more to himself than to her.

"What are you talkin' about?" she asked. Her voice went from a nasally shrill to a soft and silvery tone, almost matching his.

"…I don't even know where to begin. I think I was… cursed or something," he answered glumly. "Up until a few minutes ago, I couldn't even talk! Not to mention, I can't remember anything about — well — anything!"

"Hmmm," she said, immersed in her own thoughts again. "I think you need to see Mada—"

"HURRY UP! EVERYONE!!!" bellowed a rough, monstrous voice that could never be forgotten.

Samol jumped nearly a foot off the ground, wondering if that was a demon, and his false sense of comfortability tricked him into believing he wasn't in hell - - when he actually was! He stretched his neck above the crowd, standing on his tippy-toes to see from where that voice had spawned. Over. Next to. Beside. Behind. Through the trees, he looked. 'What was that?' he pondered (so did many others).

Finally, he saw it. A large, old man, who despite his hunchback, stood taller than a two-story house. From head to toe, he was made of nothing but the ugliest rocks ever; stones that weighed the old man down so much, it looked as if the only way he could walk was by magic! He was missing his left eye and his teeth were made of sharp stones that broke his jaw almost every time he spoke.

He carried a large, brown staff half his height. It had an odd symbol etched in its side that Samol knew he'd seen somewhere before; a hooked, bloody fang that seemed to have come from a large animal. Sloppily forced onto the staff's tip was an enclosed gauntlet filled with a cryptic liquid that the old man would sip every few seconds. Judging by his

15

awkward mannerisms, many assumed it was booze (half the teens already had bets on Vodka — the other half, Whiskey).

"What is *THAT??*" Samol whispered intensely, pointing at the old man.

"That's Maven Dolus," she said, not spitting this time as though she were making a concerted effort to keep all mucus in her mouth.

"It's...gross!" Samol blurted.

"Hey!" Galena hollered, giving him a swift, stern look. *"IT* has a name!"

"Sorry," he said respectfully.

His eyes fell away and were now fixed on the old man's jagged body as he and Galena continued walking towards him. "What exactly...does he do here?"

"He's the guardian of the forest," she said. "He's been here for ages...literally! Rumor has it: *he has better vision in one eye than most people do with two!*"

"Hmm...." Samol grunted shortly, thinking that not only did she need a shower and a heavy-duty toothbrush, but she was crazy too.

"In his left eye, it's believed that he's recorded all of our names since the very beginning of time," she explained, not spitting again this time.

"He — doesn't have a left eye..."

"Exactly," she said with a stiff nod. "Nobody has ever seen it. I heard it's hidden somewhere within our world and has powers!"

"Powers?" he questioned, suddenly more intrigued by the old man.

"I didn't believe it until he helped me with my — well — personal situation," she shuddered slightly. "I think the myth holds true."

Samol wondered if her "personal situation" was getting her hands on a bar of soap and a stick of deodorant.

"You see the top of his head?" she pointed discreetly. "They're tiny white coals, not hair."

Samol outstretched his neck, squinting his eyes as if

he could even see such detail from that far, which he definitely couldn't.

"Whenever he even thinks about telling a lie, they burn bright red and scorch him to no end. If he actually says the lie aloud," she paused dramatically, "the rocks turn to lava and drip from his head to the inside of his body!"

All of this new information was way too much for Samol to ingest in under ten minutes. He was overwhelmed, to say the least!

"I know..." she said submissively, throwing her hands up, noticing that he didn't believe her, imagining a little thought bubble above Samol's head that probably said: 'You're full of it!'

"I didn't believe it either until he helped me with my...predicament," she said sadly.

"Was he cursed in some way?" Samol asked gently, hoping to maybe piece together even just a few things about his own past.

"I don't know," she said honestly. "Needless to say, the truth has become his friend - - *best and only friend!* He's so truthful, actually, he's made quite a few enemies down here!"

The two of them, along with a few other stragglers, had finally reached the center of the forest. Samol was now close enough to get a good look at the old man. He was ugly! His face was made of different-sized, pointed rocks! Not to mention, Samol saw that what sat on top of his head were in fact white coals. Another notch of respect he had for his new, smelly friend, but he wouldn't let her know that. God forbid — she might try and give him a hug or something!

The entire time Samol and Galena had been conversing, the old man had been shouting. Samol caught every fourth or fifth word: *'future, corpse, castle, past life, shut up!'* Other than that, he'd somehow tuned out the old man's thunderous voice, which could be heard for miles. With every movement the old man made, pieces of his body chipped away and fell to the ground. Glaring at everyone with his one bright blue eye, Maven shouted like a drill sergeant:

17

"All right, you festering sack of dead debris! Get over here and join the group! There's a lot of reincarnation that needs to happen and we don't have much time to do it! HURRY UP!!"

More people trickled into the forest. Every one of them stood at attention and dared not to move a muscle. Of course, in life (and in death), there are always exceptions to the rule. Walking towards Samol and Galena were two loud, quarreling teens; a boy and a girl. The boy was handsome; blonde-haired and green-eyed, who sounded as if he had a strange mixture of accents he'd picked up from past lives, but did very well to hide them. Anyone who listened to him carefully might've guessed; Australian, French, Russian, Sudanese, and/or Portuguese.

The blonde boy's opponent was a fiery-tempered tomboy. Her thick, red spirals fell far below the middle of her back, which seemed to accentuate her baby blue eyes and freckles. Her accents resembled a mixture of Swedish, Moroccan, Japanese, Italian, Guyanese, and/or New York. She, too, did well to camouflage her accents.

Samol watched the quarrelsome duo bicker like an old married couple over the insignificant details of what happened in their very last life. 'No, you didn't! Yes, I did!' must have been exchanged a hundred times. The arguing continued until the girl saw him. "SAMOL!" she shouted, not even caring that she was supposed to be quiet. The old man gave her a sharp look, but kept talking anyway.

Samol was truly unaware of who she was talking to, looking at everyone around him and hoped that it was someone else - - anybody else! The last thing he wanted was to draw attention to himself in this strange, new place. With his eyes fixed on the red-headed girl and her blonde friend, who were both excitedly careening towards him, he leaned towards Galena and whispered, "Who are they talking to?" Ten seconds had gone by and there was no response. Galena was gone. He jerked his neck all around looking for her. Gone. The loud strangers had arrived.

"Samol! Oh, my gosh! How was your last life?" asked the red-headed girl, hugging him too tightly.

"Yeah, man! How've you been?" asked the blonde boy, giving him a friendly punch on the shoulder.

Samol stared blankly, wondering if that was really his name — *"Samol."*

"You would have loved my last life!" the girl smiled, her starry eyes fixed to the black sky. "I was a thirty-one year old Italian woman living in Siena, Italy," she reminisced, her Italian accent heavily coming through. The happy girl's face split into a wide smile. "I had the most beautiful husband, too! We were poor, but happy…until SOMEONE hit me with a Pepsi truck!"

"Hey, I died too, *London!*" the boy barked.

"That's because you're dumbass can't drive, *Paul!*" she hissed back.

"I had to get you back here to Euphod any way I could!" the boy roared, his Russian accent coming through a bit. "You-were-breaking-the-law! You know we're not allowed to fall in love with a Vreek! You two had your hands all over each other!"

"We were married! What do you expect??"

"You were two minutes away from getting pregn-!"

"ANYWAYS! How was your last life, Samol?" London quickly interrupted, her eyes shifting between Samol's and Paul's with an *I'm-innocent-grin.* "I've missed you SO much!" she said, bear-hugging him again.

Samol was slightly taller than her and stared confusedly at the top of her head, which was covered in the reddest curls he'd ever seen. London let go of him when she noticed that her embrace was one-sided. She gazed into his eyes and her heart began to break in two. Trying to choke back tears, her voice quivered,

"Sa — Samol?"

"You're never this quiet, man," Paul added.

"…I'm sorry…but do I…do I know you two? And what's a…Vreek?" Samol shuddered awfully.

"Samol!" London barked loudly, her Italian accent roaring through again.

"Samol, it's us," said Paul, masking that he was more hurt than she was. His best buddy was acting like he didn't even know him, Paul thought.

With no warning, London jovially grabbed Samol's hands and began singing and dancing in a circle:

> *"Throw, throw, throw your hope,*
> *In the death machine!*
> *Merrily, merrily, terribly, wearily,*
> *Life...is... but...a....scheme..."*

Her singing came to a rolling stop. Samol, once again, stared at her as though she belonged in a straitjacket. London wailed uncontrollably, like a newborn, which caught the attention of those around them. She didn't care. Paul, who saw her as an embarrassment at times, covered her and mouthed: 'I'm sorry,' repeatedly to everyone around them.

"I — I'm sorry if I've offended you," said Samol, trying to shut her up.

"What happened to you??" she screamed, wiping snot from her nose.

"I think someone cursed his memory!" said Paul.

"YOU GOT CURSED??" she hollered, studying Samol from head to toe.

Samol noticed that the word *"cursed"* seemed to draw a bit of attention in this crowd, because more than a few heads shot around to look at him and his two stranger-friends. A few of them weren't too happy about them talking, either.

"Shhhh!" someone shushed.

"Don't you *shush* me or you'll be cryin' next!" London hollered in the wrong direction, not even knowing where it came from.

Whoever it was fell quiet anyway.

20

"I'm sorry, but I still have to ask — what's a Vreek?" Samol asked curiously.

"People who've only lived one life, unlike us," Paul answered squinting an eye, examining his friend from head to toe, toe to head, three times, as though he thought Samol was an imposter. "What's gotten into you?"

"*SILENCE! EVERYONE!!*" Maven shouted at once, fed up with the chattering. "*You'll have enough time to chit chat about your stupid, little, past lives at that nasty Death Day Ball! Now SHUT IT!!*"

The old man stood up as high as his crooked back would allow, which was still well over thirty feet. His one eye danced around the crowd as though he were looking for someone in particular. By chance, he caught a glimpse of a wide-eyed, frizzy-haired man who couldn't stop wiggling as if ants were biting his balls. Maven could care less about the poor, electrocuted man. He shook his head, gritted his jagged teeth, and spoke:

"*All of you standing before me are here because you're dead!*" he began sharply. Samol was shaken by the old man's brashness. "*You all are among the chosen, select few to be reincarnated and live yet again and we-don't-have-much-TIME!*" he shouted and took a gulp from his gauntlet. He nearly toppled over and the teenagers who betted on Vodka winked at those betting on Whiskey.

"Look up above you," he hollered sloppily. "Those are your dead bodies from your very last life. Some are mangled. I see a few that are diseased. Some are even burned to a crisp, but they are YOUR corpses!" Everyone turned their neck to the sky and gasped when they found the bodies of their last life face-down, floating just a car-length away from their heads. Then, it happened...

Mayhem!

The massive crowd, which was now in the thousands, tried to run from their own bodies, yet it followed them like a balloon on a string. London and Paul kept oddly calm for some reason, even though Samol, too, had begun to panic.

21

"They appear scarier than they look," Maven said hoarsely.

No one listened. The crowd swatted and screamed as if a nest of bees had been dumped on their heads.

"They cannot touch you and you cannot touch them," Maven said, trying to calm them.

Everyone kept panicking.

Maven shook his head, thinking to himself, 'I'm getting too old for this mess.'

"Think of them as peaceful ghosts that show us what kind of life we lived," Maven said with a slight thunder in his voice. "They can even show you things about your future."

Samol froze when he heard the words: *'things about your future.'* He looked up, a lot calmer this time, and studied what was left of his shredded corpse. 'Things about my future? Would my next life end just as horribly??' he wondered. There was nothing he could do but swallow his uncertainties and hope to God that this old man was wrong.

"Now, the reason for the rush…" he paused to take another sip, "You only have from now until the time your body fully decomposes to get to your next life."

Now, Samol <u>really</u> hoped that he was wrong!

A heavyset, middle-aged woman standing in the heart of the crowd rose her hand and nervously asked, "So, uhh…exactly how long do we have before our body decomposes and we're — uh — toast?"

With a terribly sadistic laugh he pointed and mocked, "Well that depends on your size and weight, first of all, madame double dip!"

The fat woman's jaw dropped and her eyes bulged. The crowd laughed. Samol was still trying to swallow the fact that dead people could even talk - - let alone make jokes!

Addressing the whole crowd, Maven explained, "Secondly, it depends on how and where you died. If you suffered the tragic misfortune of dying by fire AND you lived your last life in a hot geographic location, you unfortunately haven't-got-much-time to get to your next life!"

The old man bellowed and his jaw popped in and out of its socket. A few people very close to him squirmed at the terrible sound, yet the old man seemed to have grown almost numb to it for the most part.

"However, if you froze to death in the heart of Siberia, for example, you've got a bit more time on your hands," Maven finished.

Samol rummaged through his memory. 'Where had I died? Was it warm? Wait, no...it was cold in my last life, actually. Thank God!'

Without warning, concerned murmurings of everyone quickly escalated into a quarrelsome violence. Those who'd died in hot places panicked and began shoving their way to the front of the crowd! In Samol's plain view were two diseased-ridden, teenage boys who began pushing and arguing:

"Move! I've got to get to the front of the crowd!"

"No, you move!"

"Listen, dumpster dick, I died in the Everglades! Get the HELL out of my way!"

"Piss off! I died in the Sahara — *you* better move!"

A punch. Two kicks. Suddenly a brawl! London snatched both Paul and Samol away from it all. Next to the tussling boys was a blonde girl with three bullet holes in her chest. She was trapped between the fight and the shifting crowd. Trying to escape, she submissively threw up her hands and said, "Everyone can go in front of me, I died in Finland!" People fled past her with a vengeance. Within seconds more arguments, shoving, punches, and kicks spread like wildfire.

There was a great stampede!

"What's happening??" Samol trembled, his neck jerking left and right as though it had been wound up by a string and let go.

"Don't you remember?" said Paul, dodging three fists and a kick. "This happens all the time with the rookies!"

23

"Just stay by us!" said London, kicking someone from her leg.

"ENOUGHHHHH!" Maven bellowed with a shout that could've been heard on Earth.

Everyone froze, mid-brawl, mid-kick, mid-slap, mid-cussword, mid-hair pull.

"JUST because you all are DEAD does NOT give you the right to act like savages in my presence! Stand to your feet, all of you! NOW!" he roared authoritatively. Thousands angrily dusted themselves off, cutting their eyes at their opponents and snuck in a few more punches, of course.

"Now, this is how it works for all of you who did NOT pay attention in science class or…" he shifted his eye, softening his tone because he saw the most adorable toddler, who was wearing a pink sundress and a bow in her hair and finished, "died too early to even get there."

"Within the first twenty-four to seventy-two hours of your death, the internal organs of the human body begin to decompose. Within three to five days, the body begins to bloat and blood containing foam will ooze from the mouth and nose," Maven explained.

Almost everyone, even Samol, squirmed and scratched themselves, looking at their dead bodies, just floating there, only imagining what this god-awful process must look like.

"Ewwww!!" said everyone.

"Oh, shut up! You're already dead!" Maven bellowed. He continued:

"Eight to ten days after you've passed away is when the massive decomposition of organs in your abdomen accumulate massive gases. The body then turns from green to red, due to blood decomposition," he explained as if he were an anatomy major in a past life. Curdled expressions smeared everyone's faces, but they kept quiet this time. "A few weeks after you've been dead, your nails and teeth begin to fall and approximately a month or so later, your body becomes fluid. NOW — I need every last one of you to listen - - carefully!"

24

Everyone, including Samol, leaned in a few inches closer. Yet, Paul and London did not. They looked as though they didn't give a damn as to what this old man had to say.

"Once your body becomes fluid it will begin to flow in whichever direction your soul is strongest. If your soul leans toward good, your body will begin to drip towards the sky. If it begins dripping downward towards you — well — we'll get to that part later."

Samol grew worried and for a second time, he felt his stomach disappear. Maven, after taking another sip of his feel-good-juice, could see the visible fear that painted nearly every face in the crowd. Feeling the slightest sense of compassion, he did something out of his character - - something nice. He hushed them when he spoke gently:

"It does not matter how you died, yet how you lived. You've been assigned your lives for a reason; a reason in which you may not even understand until your fourth, twelfth, or even one hundredth life. You may never understand!" he said as though he were talking to himself. "Every last one of you are a part of a secret race known as the *Aryamites*. For millenniums now, we've been reincarnated into millions of lives; every type you can imagine," he said, noticing that every eye was glued to him.

He stepped forward as though he were going to give a Presidential Candidate Speech and said, *"'Why am I here?'* some of you might be asking yourselves. It's because every single one of you has died with an unfinished purpose and unopened gifts and talents that you most likely didn't know you even had," he said.

"Some of you didn't use the talents you were given out of fear, laziness, comfortability, or sheer lack of respect for what you were given. In the next couple of hours, you will be reassigned a new life. A new face. A new body. New struggles. However, you will have the same talents and, of course, the same soul. It will be your mission to find out what your talents and purposes are and how to use them <u>properly</u> - - it will not be easy!

25

"Welcome to Euphod; the place where death is life."

A great applause tore through the air.

Everyone for just a moment had put aside their differences and embraced one another as family again. Samol felt at ease for the first time he could remember. The old man's uplifting words gave him the courage to feel bold enough to even want to continue on. Right now, all seemed well…even though the whereabouts of Galena still lingered in the back of his mind. "How could someone just disappear like that?" he almost said aloud, but didn't. Samol turned to his new friends and asked,

"Did you see the little girl I was talking to, by chance?"

"I didn't see anyone," Paul shrugged.

"Me either," said London just as nonchalantly.

Once again, Samol wondered if this was all real. Trying to be subtle, Samol spanned the crowd, looking for Galena, even giving the air a discreet sniff or two. Nothing. He mistakenly locked his eyes on a lonesome, googly-eyed man who was having a one-sided conversation with his own floating corpse. "Dead people are weird," he accidentally said out loud, for the first time blurting his thoughts. However, the whole crowd was screaming as though they'd all just graduated college and no one heard him.

Samol would quickly find out that there was a lot more to being dead than just funerals, caskets, a good life insurance policy, and graveyards. He hoped that his new friends had as much knowledge about this world as Galena. Samol would need them for every unforeseen, eerie twist and turn…a few of which were unknowingly just minutes away.

CHAPTER THREE

OLD FRIENDS AND NEW ENEMIES

"There just aren't enough hours in a death to tell you,"
– Paul

*T*he sky was still shimmering with powerful flashes that were not lightning, yet souls. Samol was still getting used to this. The celestial flares against the black sky reflected off the pale faces of well over six thousand newly deceased Aryamites. Casting a hue of blue across Samol's face was a fat, cobalt beam that looked as if it had spawned from an almost-too-tall dead tree, which resembled a disfigured, human stick-figure. Samol stood next to his two new friends, eyeballing the crowd as if he were still looking for his smelly acquaintance, Galena. All he found were busted lips, broken noses, and black eyes smeared across many faces.

Every so often, Samol would clench his throat with a hearty smile, unbelievably joyous that he could finally talk. And there was another reason for him to smile; for the first time, he knew his own name! The whole crowd was still cheering loudly until Maven suddenly thundered, "All right, enough of this gooey sh — stuff! LISTEN! The main objective is not for you to get comfortable and stay here!" he yelled at once, as though he would only allow himself to be happy for no more than thirty seconds at a time. "You're here to examine the flaws, mistakes, and loopholes of your last life and get to your next one! Understand??"

"Yes!" said thousands while others nodded.

"Good!" he hollered. "Trust me when I tell you, life-will-not-be-easy," he said gritting his teeth, as though he were talking to himself. "Many of you will be assigned to live some of the most difficult lives that life, itself, has to offer."

Samol looked at his two friends as if he wanted to say something. He really didn't, but was only reflecting on the horrors of his last life.

"Failure, unfairness, racism, divorce, disease, murder, rape, loneliness, poverty, and depression could only be the beginning of some of the lives you'll be assigned to live! However, you will NEVER be assigned to live a life more difficult than you can withstand. No-matter-what!" Maven said, who then paused as if he, too, were thinking about his own past lives and began drinking heavily from his shiny gauntlet.

Samol glanced at Paul and London, who both looked bored like they'd heard this many times already and Maven's words were slipping into one ear and out the other.

"I've…been here before, right?" Samol whispered with some uncertainty in his voice.

"Yes," they said simultaneously.

"We were just in Verstandfall together in our last afterlife," said Paul, frowning for only a split second, but Samol caught it.

"Ver-what?"

"Verstandfall," London answered instead. "It's one of the seven castles of the dead, here, in Euphod."

"*Seven??*" Samol howled, sounding almost mistrustful.

"He really isn't joking," Paul said to London as if Samol weren't even standing there.

"Samol, don't you remember what we found in the castle of Bridgelove together?" London asked him, sounding almost as though they were lovers in a past life.

Samol's stare was as blank as a sheet of fresh, loose-leaf paper. Paul's sharp, green eyes darted between the two of them, secretly wanting to know what they found. The three of them fell into an awkward silence. Before they could even think of words to say, Maven bellowed:

"*This is VERY important, so SHUT UP and listen! The one and ONLY thing that will forfeit your rights and/ or citizenship, here, in the kingdom of Euphod is committing suicide. Such a dishonorable act will ban you from ever having a chance at a peaceful eternity.*"

Out of nowhere, six people fell from the sky as if they'd been hurled from a plane and landed just a few feet from Maven! They were pancaked on top of one another, soaking wet with knotted hair and shredded clothes. One of them, Paul could've sworn was his twin. Maven scratched the porcelain coals on his head as if he had hair and quietly mumbled to himself,

"Death's downpour has been exceedingly high these days…what month is it?"

Samol heard what he said, but his friends didn't, because Paul was playing with his plaid shirt and London was checking her hair for worms.

"Get your foot outta my eye!" screamed one of the teens in the pile. "Get your butt outta my face!"

29

Maven was somewhat agitated that they just *couldn't die at a later time,* as though it were an inconvenience for him! He briskly cleared his throat and roared, "Come on, now! Hurry up! Line up like everybody else!"

With wobbly knees, they struggled to stand, ringing their clothes and hair of murky waters, maggots, worms, and debris.

"First time here, all of you?" Maven asked with a piercing look.

"No," they answered, sounding rather irritated as if they, too, wished they could've died at a different time.

"What killed you?" he asked, lacking all respect for their privacy.

"Hurricane," they said.

"Oh…" he paused, "Katrina?"

"Patricia."

"Oh! Well…welcome home!" said Maven, forcing a smile.

Seconds later, all six of their death certificates fell peacefully from the sky. It seemed as though watching them yank the floating, blue parchments from the air jogged Maven's memory. He brazenly addressed the crowd and belted,

"Upon entering Euphod, each and every one of you received your death certificate, right?"

"Yes," everyone said at once.

"Good! Now, I want each of you to examine it closely. Get to know it. Have it get to know you. Your death certificate is very much alive and is what has sorted you into one of Euphod's seven castles."

There were those words again, Samol thought; '*seven castles.*' He examined his death certificate as though he were waiting for something to simply sprout from its crisp edges. He couldn't seem to pull his eyes away from the top right-hand corner, where there was the twisting Zebrastone. 'My death certificate is…alive?' he pondered, already learning to accept the oddity of this underworld since there was no way out.

30

Just a few people behind him stood a small, odd-looking boy with curly red hair, who raised his little hand as though he were in school. His teal blue eyes seemed to tell a story of their own, as he discreetly looked at the butts of those in front of him, while trying to hide a large, blue diamond ring on his middle finger.

"Yes, young man?" Maven called on him, sounding very hoarse again.

"Isn't it true," the boy began, sounding intelligent already, "that your death certificate has the capability of letting you go back in time to a previous life?" he asked, rather confidently for a boy who looked no older than seven.

"Ahh! I see we have a returning Aryamite in the bunch," Maven chuckled. "Yes, yes they can. However, that's a bit more than what you'll need to know for right now."

"Hmm," the little boy grunted, averting his eyes back to a few people's butts in front of him. Samol caught him staring and clenched his own butt tight, as though that would stop him from looking.

Maven cleared his throat as though it were getting dry from not taking a drink. He took a sip and sighed as though it was ice-cold water on a hot summer day. Rather satisfied, he parted his lips and said:

"To all of our new Aryamites, right now we are standing in the Genesis Drewstalk Forest. It sits at the very heart of Euphod," Maven explained. Nearly everyone gazed about the forest as if it were their first time seeing it. The old man continued, "There are many forests within our world. Some are much bigger. Some much smaller. Some can even imitate others."

A short, plump boy who looked no older than ten raised his hand. Without even being called on he blurted, "How will we know the difference between the real forest and one that's *mimicking* it?"

Samol could tell that many expected Maven to beat the poor child for speaking out of turn, because everyone gasped heavily. Actually, Maven seemed rather enthused that

31

the boy had such a thirst to know more about what the large underworld had to offer.

"There are many ways you can tell…" Maven smiled weakly. "The two quickest ways are by paying attention to your death certificate and — OUCH!!" he hollered, holding his jaw because it popped terribly.

Everyone cringed as if nails had been clawed down a chalkboard.

"Damn, that one hurt!" he said to himself, holding his mouth wide-eyed as if he'd chipped a tooth. Realigning his jagged jaw he continued:

"The other way to tell is to keep a close watch on your corpses above you. Both will reveal the same result, yet in totally different ways." With a freshly-fixed jaw, he took another gulp, nearly finishing whatever filled his gauntlet.

Samol glanced at Paul, who was absent-mindedly staring at a short tree, bored out of his mind that he had to hear the "Welcome to Euphod" speech again. London, herself, didn't look to enthused either because she was still playing with her hair and now counting backwards in Arabic from one hundred to one. Samol noticed that the attention of a few others began to drift away as well, that was, until Maven spoke again:

"Branching outward from the Genesis Forest are the pathways to the seven castles of Euphod," Maven said. "They are; ***Verstandfall, Bridgelove, Freedomcorpse, Culomund, Zebrastone, Hyenablood,*** and ***Vypercoff***. The emblem at the top right hand corner of your death certificate is what tells you which castle you belong to in this afterlife."

Maven readjusted his crooked hunchback as straight as it would allow and rested his wooden staff against his rocky stomach. Closing his one eye, he placed both hands over his chest like he were about to say a prayer, but instead whispered, *"Perlucidum potestatem."* Maven's words became a creepy whisper that slithered up and down the spines of nearly everyone long after he'd stopped speaking. Samol twitched as if Maven's words had pierced his balls.

32

"What was that??" Samol whispered loudly, cupping his manhood.

"It's the enchantment that calls all castle rulers to the heart of the forest, no matter where they are," Paul explained, pointing to each of the seven pathways.

"Well, all but —" London began before Paul interrupted.

"Only those who've lived three or more lives can hear it. Those who've lived nine lives or more can use it," Paul elaborated.

Suddenly, the forest trees were ruffled by an abrupt, strong wind. Nearby dirt and piles of plump, pink worms were hurled into a vortex in front of each pathway. The sound of buzzing mosquitoes grew louder. Between two tall and round trees, which were at the edge of each pathway, appeared six misty figures that slowly began to take the shape of something. Samol could've sworn they were beginning to look human. 'But they couldn't be,' he thought. 'They're too tall!...But then again, so is Maven...'

And then Maven spoke, quieting the voice in Samol's head, which still seemed more vocal than he was, even though he could now speak.

"The seven pathways are blocked by an invisible electric barrier in which you can only pass through once you say your castle's corresponding password aloud. You must speak ONLY to the first tree on the left."

"*ONLY-the-first-tree-on-the-left!*" Maven repeated loudly.

"The password for each castle will be provided by its respected rulers momentarily. Three attempts is all you'll get in order to pass through. THREE!"

Samol was growing overwhelmed again. He glanced at his death certificate, hoping for a split-second that perhaps it would reveal the password of his new castle, or even a map to this large and scary underworld that lived before him. Yet, what he found left him troubled.

"Hey, it's gone!" he shrieked.

"What's gone?" asked London.

"The — that stone thing that was at the top of my death certificate!"

"Let me see that!" said London, snatching it from him without even asking.

Not only was Samol bothered that his emblem had disappeared, but he kept hearing something too.

"What's that buzzing sound?" he asked.

"What did the stone look like?" Paul asked, ignoring the fact that Samol was frantically looking all around himself like bugs were crawling on him.

"I think it was some sort of black stone," he said still looking for insects, or whatever could've been making that sound.

"A black stone?" London and Paul said together, looking at each other, utterly confused.

"...What did she say it was?" Samol mumbled to himself, trying to remember what Galena called it.

"Don't worry, Samol. Maven will sort us properly," Paul shrugged as if this sort of thing happened all the time. "Both myself and London haven't been sorted into a castle yet either," he said.

Maven was fidgeting once more with his broken jaw and uttered, "As you can see, st — OUCH!" he screamed, now pissed off. "I'm getting too old for this!!" he hollered, no longer keeping his thoughts to himself.

A few Aryamites in the back snickered quietly.

The old man did his best to gather his composure and said, "Standing before each of the pathways are the castle rulers."

Samol studied them all. Many were tall, some were short, a few were sexy, and one looked older than dirt. Although he found this new world somewhat amusing, it was getting stranger by the minute.

34

Maven began loudly, "To those who wanted nothing more than freedom in all areas of your last life and you did nearly anything to get it, you'll find a black starfish in the top right hand corner of your death certificate. In this afterlife, you belong to the beloved castle of ***Freedomcorpse.*** Congratulations!" said Maven, extending his hand towards the first pathway of the seven. Standing at its opening was an incredibly buff and handsome man who was almost as tall as a power line.

More than seven hundred people rushed towards the stoic beauty.

Maven continued, "Those who lived their last lives well enough to be somewhat righteous, yet not pure enough to enter the only true Holy place, you'll find an hourglass at the top right hand corner of your death certificate. I am delighted to welcome you to the most envied and prestigious castle in all of Euphod; ***Bridgelove.***" Standing at the center of the second opening was a tall, curvaceous beauty who, just like Maven, towered high enough to crane her neck over a two-story building.

Nearly five hundred Aryamites happily flocked to the sexy queen.

Maven further explained, "Aryamites who lived their last lives with the treasured gift of intelligence, one of my favorites," he grinned with his one eye closed, "you are here because you let your ideologies lead you totally astray. You'll find a Rubik's Cube in the top right hand corner of your death certificate. You belong to the castle of ***Verstandfall***. Before you leave Euphod, you must figure out the hidden message inside of the Rubik's Cube. Good luck!" he chuckled heartily, finishing the last of his drink.

Standing before the third opening was a tiny, old, ugly woman. Samol looked at her and curdled his mouth like someone had passed gas nearby. Her irritating and hyper demeanor allowed anyone to see her clear across the forest, jumping from side to side, even dancing manically for no reason as though she needed immediate psychiatric help. Approximately three hundred, or so, Aryamites did a bug-eyed double take to their death certificate, hoping their eyes were playing tricks on them when they found a small, twisting Rubik's Cube at the top right-hand corner. They weren't so lucky. Three hundred heads lowered at once as they slowly walked towards the crazy lady like they'd been given another death sentence.

"Paul," Samol whispered intensely. "You said we were in Verstandfall together. Aside from that weird woman, what's so bad about it?"

"There just aren't enough hours in a death to tell you," Paul said sarcastically.

London laughed a little, as if she, too, had been there once or twice.

"Where is that buzzing coming from??" Samol asked loudly, his voice beginning to lose its pleasant, silvery tone.

"The Ary-" London began to explain before Maven screamed:

*"The Aryamites who have that damn buzzing mosquito on their death certificate, get to the castle of **Culomund**! NOW!"*

A massive group of more than seventeen hundred people migrated towards the fourth opening. It was heavily guarded by a woman with short, spiked hair.

"The Aryamites sorted into the castle of Culomund have the emblem of a noisy mosquito on their death certificate," London revealed, uninterrupted this time, her voice barely above a whisper as if she were telling Samol a secret. "It's the castle for those who had a bad mouth! The constant buzzing is supposed to symbolize how annoying people who run their mouths can be," she said, giving Paul a stern glare like she were talking about him.

"What!" he said in an argumentative tone.

"Finally!" Maven sighed, because the mosquito sounds were gone. "Those of you who have a bloody, hyena tooth at the top of your death certificate, you two-faced devils, you belong to the castle of **Hyenablood!"**

Before the sixth opening stood a tall, ominous-looking man dressed in a long, black cloak, who wasn't quite as tall as Maven or the queen of Bridgelove, but still stood eight feet high. Samol couldn't see his face, only his shoulder-length hair that was black on one side and red on the other. Apparently, more than three thousand people had lived their last lives as backstabbing bastards! Samol stared at them, one by one, as they passed him. Each one of them seemed almost embarrassed about the sins of their last life.

"And those who are in **Vypercoff**…you know what you've done and why you're being sent there. Go!" Maven finished coldly.

Standing before the seventh opening was no one. A cold, uninviting aura lurked in the presence of where an overlord should've been standing. Samol intuitively understood that this was the place that no one wanted to end up. Luckily, there were only fifteen.

Still standing at the center of the forest was a group of nearly fifty, or so, unsorted Aryamites. Samol, Paul, and London were among them. Maven scowled, shaking his head, almost angry that he had more sorting to do. Forcefully unscrewing the bottom half of his large, wooden staff something fell out - - a rolled up black papyrus scroll with all the names of the unsorted Aryamites. When he unrolled it, the scroll was longer than he was tall and it dragged on the ground. Written in red ink on its back read. *"Death Scroll."*

Fear, uncertainty, and quivering stomachs cemented through Samol and the unsorted few.

"The remainder of you must be in the castle of Zebrastone — the tricky one!" he said with his one eye scanning the whole parchment from top to bottom. He etched notes onto it using a large, blue quill that seemed to have appeared out of thin air.

37

"Not Vypercoff...not Vypercoff," Paul prayed softly.

"Vypercoff?" Samol asked, staring wide-eyed at his own death certificate. "I thought we were in Zebrastone!"

"Yes," London answered instead of Paul, "but Zebrastone is the one castle that can mimic any of the other seven castles, here, in Euphod. Usually, it's not for the best either."

"What exactly happens in Vypercoff anyway?" Samol asked with his eyes fixed on the seventh pathway.

"WHAT-HAPPENS-IN-VYPERCOFF??" Paul shrieked. "I know something happened to your memory, *but-come-on!*"

"Paul!" London barked, sounding like an angry mother. A hint of her New York accent came through.

Samol stayed quiet, wanting to say something - - anything - - but didn't know what to say.

London revealed, "Vypercoff is a prison! You could be beaten, raped, stabbed, hung, burned, die a final death, or even worse — be reincarnated to live an eternally horrific life without the possibility of ever dying!"

Samol's eyes widened as if he'd been stabbed again.

London continued, "It's the one and only castle meant for Aryamites who were pure evil in their last life! Vicious murderers, calculated terrorists, rapists, arsonists, and far worse!" she whispered covertly, looking over her shoulder, as if someone behind her was eavesdropping.

"During ancient times, it was one of three torture chambers for Aryamites found guilty of treason or breaking any of the ten Euphod commandments," London continued. "Some were set on fire! Seared with molten steel - - even had the faces of those they'd offended branded onto their own for all of eternity!" London elaborated darkly.

Samol and Paul both cringed.

"Some were put in a cage and submerged into boiling water! Attacked by vicious beasts who were purposely starved for the entertainment of the castle rulers who couldn't wait to see unruly Aryamites eaten alive! It's rumored —" she paused, looking over both shoulders again, as if she knew
38

things she wasn't supposed to and revealed, "In the past millennium, or so, it was converted into a castle for Aryamites who were just one step away from going to hell!"

"Let's just hope and pray that we go to Bridgelove or Freedomcorpse!" said Paul, on the verge of a nervous breakdown.

"This is why Maven has the death scroll," London said seriously. "It tells you what castle you're *actually* going to."

"Uh, oh," said a disheartened Samol, hoping that he, too, were going to Bridgelove or Freedomcorpse (whatever that meant).

Maven continued to closely examine the death scroll, jotting down notes next to names where he saw fit. He parted his lips and spoke:

"Some of you may, in fact, end up being sorted into the castle of Zebrastone, and if you are — please be careful. It'll play tricks on your mind from beginning to end," he said, sounding almost angry as though this had happened to him in his youth. "When I call your name, you will join the group in which you are sorted," he said, not making eye contact with a single person in the crowd. He read aloud:

"AUTUMN LEVINE!" Out stepped a blind, red-headed girl. She was ugly and god-awfully thin. Large, patchy freckles peppered her long nose and protruding chin. Her looks told the story of someone who'd lived a hard life and met an untimely death.

"BRIDGELOVE!" Maven exclaimed. The girl let out a large sigh and her fellow Aryamites helped her join the Bridgelove family.

"JASON ECHO!" Maven shouted. Emerging from the crowd was a tall, thin boy with black hair. His mouth had rotted away from losing the unfortunate battle to oral cancer.

"FREEDOMCORPSE!" Maven said without hesitation and the young man scuttled off to join his new family, which was in the first pathway.

Samol wondered why some people were disfigured when others, like himself, only had a disfigured, floating corpse.

"GASHES GHOUT!" Maven called out. Standing near the center of the crowd was a bald boy with an unrecognizably beaten face. Both eyes were swollen shut; lips plumped like sausages. A nose more crooked than a bad politician. One might've expected those to have sympathy for a boy who'd been beaten to death, yet many were glad.

"Gashes..." London hissed hatefully. "Serves him right!"

"What?" said Samol.

"Don't you remember what he did to you??" London screamed. "He was one of the ones who be—"

"He got what he deserved," Paul interrupted seriously. "Hopefully, we'll never have to deal with him again!"

"VYPERCOFF!" roared Maven and Gashes slowly joined as the sixteenth member.

"What did he do?" Samol asked.

"He told Gavin Medg—" London began before a voice, once again, interrupted her.

"LONDON LUCAS!" Maven yelled abruptly.

Her knees buckled. Eyes bulged. She probably couldn't even tell you her middle name if you asked her right then. Samol, who'd already grown somewhat attached to her, feared for her future. Maven paused for what felt like an eternity until he finally broke the silence and said,

"ZEBRASTONE!"

Elated that he didn't shout *'Vypercoff!'* she exhaled heavily as if she had just bench pressed a house! Samol and Paul glumly eyed one another. They, too, now hoped to be sorted into the same castle.

"JONATHAN HUMBLEFIRE!" Maven called out.

A short, good-looking, stocky young man in his mid-twenties emerged. His ice blue eyes sat sumptuously under his buzzed, black hair. His porcelain skin was so clear that it practically glowed. Samol was almost certain that he had died in his sleep, because he was just too well put together compared to everyone else.

"BRIDGELOVE!" Maven shouted in an instant and a strong cheer from the second pathway tore through the air amongst the Bridgelove Aryamites, like they'd gained a champion.

"HANS-PAUL MIKAELSSON!" shouted Maven in the same breath.

Paul's heart sunk to his toes. He glanced at Samol and wanted to say, "Wish me luck," but was too nervous to say anything. With uncertainty squishing his neck, he couldn't help but to keep his head down. "Not Vypercoff. Please, not Vypercoff!" Paul prayed once more.

"ZEBRASTONE!" Maven shouted at once.

London jumped for joy.

"LUDWIG VON TASSELL!" Maven said rather slowly as if the name meant something to him.

An odd-looking boy emerged. One eye was notice-ably larger than the other and so were one of his nostrils. The left half of his teeth were all rotted while the right side were white as snow. He had no arms and deep, red sores that oozed some sort of black pus from his pores. About him lived a sadness that was beyond his physical misfortunes.

"CULOMUND," Maven said.

Samol felt as though he would faint. The crowd was dwindling away faster than he'd expected and knew he was on the chopping block soon! He glanced at his death certificate again. What he found disturbed him enough to take his mind off the diminishing crowd. Instead of the twisting Zebrastone in its top right-hand corner, it now read:

'He's closer than you think...'

For the third time, Samol felt his stomach evaporate. He stiffly looked around, afraid to make any sudden move-ments, terrified that his murderer had returned to kill him once and for all! He didn't see him, or even find anyone who looked "odd" or "suspicious," except for the man who was still talking to his own floating corpse. He did, however, see a girl with a big, frizzy, long braid that draped over her left shoul-der, who kept staring at him as if she wanted to ask, "Don't I know you from somewhere?" but was perhaps too shy to do so.

The girl's knock-knees were as buckled as her eyes were crossed. She kept looking at Samol and then looking away as though she didn't want him to see her staring. When he looked back at his death certificate, the words were gone and the stone had returned. Maven finally said,

"SAMOL DOSCOW!"

The forest fell amazingly quiet; amazing because for the first time ever, Euphod was totally silent. No one stepped forward. Samol knew that his first name was *"Samol,"* but that was only because that's what his friends had been calling him. He hadn't a clue as to what his last name might've been. He wondered if there was perhaps another Samol. 'Is my last name really *Doscow*? Isn't that a city somewhere?' he wondered naively. A few Aryamites mumbled confusedly, "Who is Samol Doscow?"

"SAMOL DOSCOWWW!!!" Maven belted even louder than the first time.

London waved Samol down crazily and mouthed, *'That's you! Get up there!'* Samol sheepishly stepped to the front of the crowd. Maven, for the first time, glanced up from his scroll. His one eye locked into Samol's as though he wanted to yell, "You don't belong here!" An icy fear smothered Samol like darkness to the night sky. Maven scratched something from the scroll as if whatever had been written was wrong. Shreds of black papyrus fell to the ground as he brushed them away.

There was an unbearably long pause. Maven turned his lips and softly said, "Zebrastone?"

What bothered Samol was that Maven sounded unsure of himself. However, he and his friends, were relieved that he didn't put him into Vypercoff, or any other castle, for that matter. London had every intention of re-teaching him all that he needed to know: the wonders, the woes, and all that Euphod had to offer.

"That was close!" Samol sighed as he joined the friendly outstretched arms of Paul and London.
"I'm so glad you're with us!" said London, flinging her arms around him once again too tightly.

"I'm glad I'm not in Vypercoff!" Samol replied, struggling to breathe.

"That is odd though…" said Paul, scratching his head, his blonde hair slipping through each of his fingers.

"What?"

"All three of us got sorted into the same castle. That never happens," he said.

"Maybe it's…divine intervention?" London said hesitantly, smiling a bit. "Think about it — Samol needs us now more than ever," she said to Paul, knowing that this really wasn't normal.

"I guess so…" Paul said disbelievingly.

Standing before the fifth pathway was the Zebrastone ruler; a seven-foot, androgynous figure. The overlord's upper body was incredibly rugged and muscular. However, below the waist was soft and curvesome. Draping from the ruler's head fell black and white spirals long enough to step on, which nearly covered the beauty's large, black eyes with white slits for irises. The overlord's nose and lips were painfully thin, neck was incredibly muscular, and had terribly scarred hands. In a unisex voice the Zebrastone ruler spoke:

"Your hidden past has opened many curses to a riddled future. I am Harragett Jaede; ruler of Zebrastone and time is running out."

Everybody, even those who'd been previously sorted into Zebrastone, couldn't stop staring at the tall overlord. Whispers of whether Harragett was a man or woman sprinkled throughout the crowd like crickets on a summer night. Even louder was the swelling sound of the electrical barrier they were approaching that spanned between the two entrance trees, which blocked them from entering. Harragett stood just inches from the left black and white tree and said,

"Your mystery is backwards…"

The great barrier vanished.

Everyone began trotting down the dark forest pathway as their dead bodies floated above them. Samol and his two new best friends stayed in the back of the group. He wondered what the insides of the castle would look like. 'Would it be big? Cold? Creepy? Would it be full of blood?' His eyes slinked down the quickly passing dead trees; catching a glimpse of a few large, white worms slithering down their barks. He cringed. "Dead stuff is gross," he almost said aloud, but kept quiet afraid he'd sound like the '*new, dead kid on the block.*'

The dirt crackled beneath their feet as everyone walked. Forcing his neck straight ahead Samol saw her again, the girl with the wide braid peeking at him. She was several feet in front of Samol and kept turning around as if she wanted to tell him something, but couldn't for some reason. Samol turned towards Paul and London to ask if they knew who she was, but the two of them were back to arguing about who did what in their last lives. *'No, you didn't! Yes, I did!'* Samol shook his head, knowing already that death was going to be an adventure with these two!

Samol craned his head over his right shoulder to find that nearly everyone was sorted. Maven was gently holding what appeared to be a small, glowing, red box as though treasures were hidden inside. Speaking to those who were left, he said, "The rest of you belong solely to the castle of Vypercoff. The ruby ring will lead you the rest of the way. Good luck." Maven leaned in close to the red box and whispered something that Samol heard as though he were an inch from his ear: *"Future beware as your past has declared, the hearts in sight are as dark as night."* In an instant, the box evaporated. Samol wondered if Maven could say those same words to the man who murdered him and make him disappear too. Suddenly, the frightening sound of something slithering and buzzing grew audible.

"What was that??" Samol said, who stopped walking, darting his eyes wildly through the forest.

"What was what?" London asked, who was fed up with Paul babbling about *"not falling in love with Vreeks"* in her next life.

"I just heard snakes or something!" said Samol, hoping that he was wrong.

"I don't hear anything…." said London, listening intensely.

"I think you're just on edge from your last life," Paul said, who was still upset that London told him he better get driving lessons in his next life. "We're all a bit *'on edge'* from our last lives. Just relax, man."

The three of them had fallen further behind the group and jogged lightly to catch up. Seconds later, Samol heard it again. This time the buzzing sounds were even louder than before. He realized that for some odd reason, no one else could hear it - - not even Harragett, who was proudly strutting upfront. Samol mulled over the strange affair in his head and carefully placed one foot in front of the other, creeping behind Paul and London like a thief in the night. The dirt and branches crunched beneath his bare feet. With each step, the slithering grew louder. Samol tried his best to tune it out.

The darkening pathway zigzagged and led them further and further underground, as if this were even possible. Even worse — no one noticed! The walkway was now aligned with fractured human skulls. Fat tarantulas crawled in and out of their barren eye sockets, making heavy squealing noises as though they were feeding off the leftovers they'd hidden inside of the motionless craniums. Samol, along with all the other dead rookies, scratched and squirmed impulsively. And then there was an unexpected 'thud' that sounded like a beast had fallen from a tall tree not too far away. It was heard by everyone and the spiders scurried away into the forest.

46

"What was that??" Paul panicked, stopping mid step.

"I don't know…" London said coldly, balling her fists.

"Whatever it was, it sounded bigger than whatever was buzzing!" said a frightened Samol.

"I still don't hear any buzzing!" said London, whose eyes were now hurtling around the forest from tree to tree.

"It sounded like insects or…reptiles or something!" Samol attempted to explain.

"That's not good," said Paul.

The young girl with the braid, however, seemed to have heard the buzzing the very first time too. Now standing by the three of them, she squinted through the forest to see what could've possibly made that sound. A thin, plain-looking girl, she was, and judging by how hard she squinted, probably had eyesight a few notches above blindness. The knock-kneed girl, despite her visual inadequacies, had no problem catching a lustful glimpse at Paul though. She fluffed her braid, making sure that it fell sumptuously over her flat, prepubescent chest like a velvet curtain, dimmed her eyes, and in an almost-too-lascivious tone said to Paul:

"You heard it too?"

"Of course I…heard it," Paul's words trickled unevenly. He looked her up and down wanting to ask, "who the heck are you?"

London took notice.

"I'm Leanna Rosewright," she said, forcefully introducing herself in a contrived Southern accent to sound more charming. "And you are?" Instead of Paul answering, another voice said:

"Paul Mikaelsson," London answered for him, who scowled and folded her arms and continued, "And WE are losing the group!" London said, yanking Paul away, making it very clear that whoever this Leanna girl was must remain as an outcast.

"SAMOL!" Leanna screamed excitedly, not sounding so shy after all. Samol stared at the girl as if her neck had sprouted a second head.

47

"You two know each other?" London asked, sounding all of a sudden intrigued by Leanna.

"No," said Samol the same time Leanna said, "Yes!"

"We were in Bridgelove together two lives ago!" Leanna smiled.

"Bridgelove??" London scowled again, "Samol and I were in Bridgelove together...I never saw yo—"

"It's been too long!" Leanna interrupted quickly.

London hated her already.

"I can't believe I didn't see you standing there!" said Leanna.

"That's because you had your eyes on Paul's dick," London hissed under her breath.

"Excuse me??" Leanna snapped back, definitely not sounding so shy after all.

"We're getting left behind," said Paul, trying to diffuse the growing tension. "We really need to catch up to—"

"Guys, I hear it again!" Samol froze, staring at a big, dead tree in the distance.

"Hear what?" said Paul, looking in the same direction.

"The — the — buzzing and slithering," he said, covering his ears as though it were suddenly too loud to bear. "It's getting closer!"

Suddenly, there was a second 'THUD.' This one was so strong it sent ripples through the forest, knocking everyone to the ground. Even Harragett! The buzzing was now accompanied by the growl of what sounded like a saber-tooth tiger! Nothing was in sight until it was too late. A spider. Not like ones Paul had been chased by in nightmares, or the one that had awakened London by crawling up her neck while asleep in Italy during her last life. This furry creature was as big as a horse and drooled a scorching, hot, poisonous venom that ignited a trail of fire behind it! Samol certainly hadn't expected to see anything like this when he died! The seven hundred pound tarantula hurled towards them with the speed of a cheetah! No one stood a chance.

48

The oversized spider's eleven legs bulked with each stride. Its many red eyes were scattered amongst its body; four spanned across its face, four on top of its head, and two sat high on its fat abdomen. Samol's heart gave a horrible jolt. He never imagined he would see Satan's pet in person, not even in a twisted dream! Then, he saw where the buzzing and slithering had come from.

Behind the freakish tarantula was a family of black, red-eyed, poisonous snakes! Each one was the thickness of a man's thigh. The buzzing was an army of zooming, black hornets the size of baby elephants, flapping their bulky wings wildly! It looked as though the spider was their commander-in-chief, because the snakes and hornets were centered around their plump queen and followed her every twist and turn. Everybody screamed and ran!!

"GET DOWN!" Harragett hollered at the people closest to her who ducked.

Swinging her hair like a whip, which was now hotter than fire, Harragett struck the spider! 'BOOM!' It fell to its knees, letting out an earsplitting squeal that was three voices in one! The infernal creature was wounded, but now enraged! Samol, London, and Leanna ran and hid behind a nearby tree where a large wasp was waiting for them! Its body was almost as wide as the tree bark that it clung to! Leanna was almost stung, but Paul had pelted it with a big rock! The whole crowd was swatting, flicking, screaming, and running! Those who weren't quick enough, or didn't have a friend like Paul, who was a major league baseball pitcher in a past life with a nearby stone to hurl, were bitten and stung repeatedly! Harragett was half terrified and half furious and pulled out a crème-complected, silk cloth no bigger than a wash rag and dangled it in front of the hellish spider. The creatures howled in terror! Strangely, so did someone else. Another scream that sounded as if it had come from a woman living in the sky, tore through the air, bellowing as six voices in one!

49

As Harragett had hoped, the clan of oversized, infernal creatures scurried off into the woods as quickly as they came. She was still dangling that grungy-looking rag in the air. The spider left behind a tall trail of blazing fire. The invisible woman in the sky, however, kept screaming a blood-curdling cry as if she were both wounded and afraid. Samol stood frozen. That scream sounded familiar to him. He somehow remembered that he'd heard it in a past life. Harragett was still staring into the woods, afraid that the creatures would return tenfold. Paul's neck spun around as though it had been released like a wind-up doll and hollered, "WHAT - - WAS - - THAT??" Harragett, who was still looking deep within the forest said sternly, "We need to get to the castle now!"

Luckily, only six Aryamites had suffered severe snake bites and hornet stings. However, the venom was poisonous! Thus, six was six too many. They were being tended to by the care of others. Yet, mere rubs and a few people saying, 'apply pressure!' or 'you're going to be okay!' wasn't good enough. They needed the hospital immediately! Thank God, the castle was in sight.

CHAPTER FOUR

WELCOME TO ZEBRASTONE

"Big things come in little caskets," – Gabriella Mae

The great black castle grew out of the darkness. It was surrounded by a mushroom of fog and even though everyone was about a football field away, they could've sworn they smelled blood, sewer gas, rotten meat, and/or potions. You'd think that everybody would've been squeamish and complaining, and some did, however, most were too traumatized by the spider-hornet-snake attack to even care about the stench. Samol dealt with it like a champ; as this was nothing compared to Galena! Half broken skulls floating in murky waters aligned its pathway. Strangest of all was that it was raining backwards; downpours heading up to the sky as though time was in reverse.

The Zebrastone castle sat perfectly behind a row of dead trees. Samol, a boy who couldn't remember ever being dead before, had nothing to even compare it to. London, Paul, and Leanna didn't seem to mind that the whole castle was hovering a few feet off the ground…or that it was completely upside-down! Samol tilted his head left and right as far as his neck would allow, because he simply couldn't understand how everything inside this bottom-side-up castle hadn't fallen out! His eyes trailed up the backwards-drifting raindrops wondering if he, too, would be magically yanked upside-down if he got too close to the castle.

The closer they got, screams were heard; screams that sounded as if the people inside the castle were being tortured! Samol looked around anxiously and saw that everyone else was terrified too. He could've sworn he overheard London whispering something very fast to Paul about her aunt who might've been inside, but he was distracted by yet another deafening shrill that came from the left tower of the castle. Danger was still at hand.

A large graveyard emerged from the right side of the castle behind a dark thicket. There were hundreds of swaying tombstones covered in the skin of what almost looked like dragons, vipers, and tarantulas! Spider skin was the last thing they wanted to see right now! Some of the ugly gravestones were even covered in the skin of…tiny, albino creatures? Samol wasn't quite sure what he was looking at. Guarding the tombstones were mean-looking, black cats and big bats. Both had blue eyes and hissed angrily at everyone walking by. Samol turned to Paul and London and asked,

"Why is there a graveyard if we're already — well — dead?"

"This is Gullavin's Graveyard," Leanna answered instead, once again butting into their group. "It's believed that this is the graveyard waiting for people to die a second death."

"A second death?" he asked, his head suddenly churning with new questions.

"Well…it's not really a graveyard," London argued,

cutting her eyes sharply at Leanna. "I heard," she began, sounding both combative and proud, pressing her hand against her flat chest, "it's for Aryamites in violation of Euphod's thirteenth amendment."

"Thirteenth amendment?" Samol said confusedly, locking eyes with one of the hissing cats.

"It's...complicated" London hesitated. "In short, it's when you live the life you've been assigned as a slave."

"A slave?"

"Yes," she replied. "Living a life where, for whatever reason, your gifts and/or talents have been hidden or diminished. Euphod deems such a dishonorable act as *'enslaving your talents into solitude'* or *'faking your own life.'*"

"I don't understand," said Samol, now more confused than when he started.

"You know how Vreeks..." London attempted to elaborate, "may try to fake their own death when they've committed a crime?"

"Okay..." he said slowly.

"As an Aryamite, you may be reincarnated into a life that you totally despise and may choose not to even use your talents for whatever reason," she said, biting her lip subtly as though she were guilty of said crime in a past life. "What we may forget is that those who are living terrible lives, often times, have immense gifts and talents — some of which are even meant to get you out of such misfortunes. Not using your gifts and talents is considered faking your own life," she explained with a side-eye fixed on Leanna.

"Hey, the tombstones are moving!" said Paul, pointing to a row of ugly, cracked gravestones that were gently rocking back and forward.

"It's believed that a—" London began to say.

"They're not real by the way," Leanna quickly interrupted.

London wanted to choke her so badly.

"What's not real?" Samol and Paul asked at the same time.

"The tombstones," Leanna said, sure of herself. "Well, I shouldn't say they're not real, but they're more than just tombstones," she babbled incessantly, sounding as though she just wanted to say anything to keep London from talking. "They're actually calendars...alphabetical calendars!"

"Alphabetical calendars?" asked the boys.

If Samol didn't know better, he would've sworn that this was Paul's first time in Euphod.

"Yeah, the Euphod calendar is alphabetical and so are our days of the week," Leanna explained. "Well, except for—"

"That makes so much sense now," Paul interrupted, his mouth agape and his eyes fixed on a bright, red fire bolt in the sky.

"You guys know the song Death's Docket, right?" Leanna said in a singsongy voice, smiling awkwardly.

"Death's what?" asked Samol and Paul at the same time.

Leanna began:
"April through August death is its hottest,
December through February replenishes the cemetery.
January, July your emotions will die,
June turns to March when Jym Reapyr is parched.
May hates October cuz' not a soul is sober,
While November loves September because time won't remember."

She skipped away to the front of the crowd, humming and singing the song to herself. London hated her even more now. Usually, it was at least a good half hour, or so, before she began disliking any girl who came between her and her two boys. With Leanna, she broke a new record at a whopping point five seconds!

"Who the hell is that?" London asked angrily, pointing at the knock-kneed girl.

"I don't know..." said Samol and Paul, more like a question than a response.

"I know one thing for sure — she wants a piece of you, Paul!" said London, jokingly punching him in the arm, which was much harder than expected because she, per usual, forgot how strong she was for a twelve-year-old.

"Hey! What'd you do that for??" Paul howled, holding his arm.

"Well…you broke me up with my Italian husband. Now, we're even!" she said, totally letting her New York accent come through.

"I don't even like her!" Paul jeered. "I don't even — know her!" he finished with a twisted face as if he'd smelled doo-doo, but then realized that it actually was doo-doo! The unbearable stench of sewer gas was coming from the castle, because they'd finally arrived.

The crowd of Zebrastone Aryamites, a couple hundred or so, found themselves standing in front of the castle's sky-scraping, double doors. Samol didn't know how they would enter the large, upside-down fortress. He wondered if they'd have to recite more magic words or if the castle, itself, would flip right-side-up the moment they went inside. He turned around to look at London and Paul, who both absent-mindedly had their eyes fixed on four intertwined, bright souls being shot off into the dark sky like fireworks. Samol figured that if they weren't worried, then he shouldn't be either.

There were many coiled, black trees that were right-side-up, sitting on either side of the large courtyard, which was very close to the castle's right-side-up, entrance doors. Each tree was filled with ravens and vultures who hid themselves between the twisted branches, eyeballing the group to see how many of the new, dead Aryamites they could eat. Yet, Harragett's presence kept them away. Above the entrance doors written in large, shimmering, silver letters, right-side-up read: *'Death's Doorway is life's luck.'*

The doors swung open at once. Harragett, who'd been carrying two badly injured Aryamites on either shoulder, led everyone inside. The wounded teens were now an even paler shade of white, thus Harragett sped up to hurry them to the hospital wing. The sound of shod and bare feet padded across the black and white marble floor. Thick cobwebs hung from the walls. The ceilings were too high to make out, but the castle was somehow right-side-up...for the most part.

There were three hundred and forty-seven staircases: long, spiraling ones; some that were only three steps high; wide, sweeping ones; swaying, upside-down ones; a few that only appeared when you were in a part of the castle that you weren't supposed to be; some that led somewhere different on a Tuesday in March than a Friday in October; some that you had to do math to climb; some that connected to the other six castles; and some that were too unsafe to walk on because it would disappear altogether (depending on your heart's intentions). Samol began to wonder what the other castles looked like inside.

A girl behind him was whispering loudly to her friends. She seemed incredibly annoying, almost like a know-it-all, but he fell suddenly interested in what she was saying: "I've read all about this castle and its other half in 'The Seventeenth Inferno.'" Her friends were obviously not as seasoned in dying as she was, because they asked, "Where did you find this book?" Samol peered over his shoulder, but didn't look all the way at them. "In the Euphod Library, you damn dummies!" Samol made a mental note that Euphod had a library - - and that the dead could actually read!

Then something happened that made him jump about a foot in the air. "What the -- ?" Samol gasped. So did all the Aryamites that were around him. It was a nasty shock when a ghost glided suddenly through a wall pretending to be solid and shouted at a girl, "TWIT!" and flew away. Broad-shouldered with coarse, white hair and slightly transparent was the rude ghost. Samol couldn't believe what just happened!

56

The outburst grabbed the attention of Harragett, who was still upfront, the two injured teens now slipping from her shoulders. "Sorry about her," Harragett began, hoisting the youngsters high up on her shoulders so she could regain a good grip. "That was Bella-Miss Ogyny, a real nasty ghost here in Zebrastone. Fair warning: she doesn't like women — or black people, I've noticed recently..." Harragett said the last six words thinly with a confused look. Samol jerked his head around at Paul and London, who both were just as shocked at what just happened.

The stench of the castle worsened. Everyone plugged their noses. Some choked. A few screamed, *"Screw this!"* and left! All of a sudden, three teenage boys projectile vomited; spitting up slimy, half-digested pizza, burger chunks, beans, and liquor they'd probably stolen from their parents' bar, straight forward like a fire hose! As if they were aiming, it plastered the backs of the three girls in front of them! No chance in Euphod they'd get dates to the annual Death Day Ball anytime soon!

Paul snickered, only happy that it didn't get on him. "Newbies," Harragett mumbled shaking his head, "GET UP!" Samol was worried, by the tone of his voice, that Harragett would beat them for puking on his beloved walls - - oh, and the girls too. Harragett, firmly grabbing the tallest of the three boys, parted his lips to give him a firm talking to when suddenly another 'thump' came from outside. Like many others, Harragett feared that the spider had returned with its army.

Standing upright, Harragett's eyes darted between the two upside-down, red, glass-stained windows that were opposite the castle's front doors. She sternly addressed the whole crowd: "I'm taking the injured Aryamites to the Zebrastone hospital wing. In the meantime, you will be left in the care of one of Euphod's finest." Harragett cleared her throat as though she were about to belt an operatic note. "GABRIELLA!" she screamed instead. Her shout echoed through the walls. Harragett pointed straight ahead and said:

"The Secretary of Death awaits you."

In the twinkle of an eye, Harragett and the wounded Aryamites had fizzled away into a ball of fire. Nobody, not even those who'd been sorted into Zebrastone before, had ever seen such magic! Samol shook his head as though he'd been slapped, disbelieving of what he'd just witnessed. He gave his friends a stiff glare, who were also speechless.

Everyone heard the sound of someone with a tiny voice clearing their throat. Yet, they couldn't see where it was coming from. Samol suddenly remembered what Maven said: *'Zebrastone plays tricks on your mind,'* and assumed that this is what was happening. He averted his eyes to a corner where there were three upside-down, hovering caskets that began shaking violently as though another large, hellish creature would jump out, but nothing happened. Seconds later, he heard that tiny voice again, this time with twice the conviction, "Ahem!"

Every eye in the castle's foyer glanced down further, further, and further until they saw a chubby, five-year-old girl. She was incredibly serious as though all of her past lives were spent in military school instead of on a playground. She wore a tight, grey business suit like a woman in Corporate America with an attitude problem. Two fat, stocking-covered legs met her tiny, shod feet which were in black, work flats. Her silver eyes sat deep behind a pair of red, cat-eye glasses and her curly, red hair was rolled into a French twist. Neatly tucked behind her left ear was a red quill that was bigger than her head. In her right breast pocket was a brown gavel. Clasped in her left hand was a glowing clipboard filled with notes and names of the deceased.

"Who-is-that?" Samol asked, already impressed by the tiny toddler before she even said a word.

"That's Gabriella Mae!" London whispered with the utmost respect in her voice as though she were talking about the President. "She's the Secretary of Death for all seven castles, here, in Euphod!"

"Really?…" Samol said somewhat disbelievingly, "but she's a...*toddler,*" he said, sure to say that last word quietly so that Gabriella didn't hear him.

"She's no ordinary *toddler,*" Paul chimed in. "She's been reincarnated one hundred seventy-one times and elects to stay in the body of a child, in her words: for the element of surprise!"

"Whoa..." said Samol, still staring at the small dignitary.

"You see that gavel in her pocket?" London pointed discreetly.

"Yeah…"

"It's got supernatural strength - - more than a hundred times its size!" London revealed.

Samol swallowed heavily.

Gabriella paced the foyer like a drill sergeant. Hands behind her back. Stomach in. Shoulders back. Chest out. She spotted a young, shy boy who was poorly dressed. In an orotund, matter-of-fact voice that wouldn't typically issue from the throat of a five-year-old, she sternly pointed to him and said,

"You! Up to the front!"

The boy's knees buckled. 'I'm dead meat,' he thought, hoping that Gabriella was pointing to someone next to him.

"Yes! I'm talking to you. *Stand up front!*" she sharply repeated herself.

The boy timidly walked to the front of the crowd. Every last eyeball was glued to him like a magnet.

Gabriella slowly paced the floor. Her sheer presence divided the crowd in two. She strode down the middle with one arm placed strictly behind her back; the other clasping her lips as though she were deciding the fate of everyone's eternity. Samol felt almost nauseous like he were going to vomit - - not because of the horrid smell, but because he didn't know whether she would demand that he go up to the front.

Two Aryamites standing side-by-side caught Gabriella's eye. The one to the left was a meek, young girl wearing a singed, yellow sundress and dainty ballet slippers. Sadly, much of her face had been disfigured by fire. The other was a coy, middle-aged man whose body had been waterlogged from a terrible drowning accident.

"You two, join that young man up front!" Gabriella ordered.

"What's she doing?" Samol whispered.

"I don't know," London said honestly.

A few began to think that she were calling the best of the best to the front and began shoving others out of the way. Samol and Paul were among the few that got pushed by three large, snot-nosed, twelve-year-old boys who looked like a pre-teen biker gang. Everyone could tell that they were used to getting their way in past lives and had mastered the art of instilling fear in those around them. Many cringed and cowered away from them. The bullies puffed out their chests and fell right into it — Gabriella's trap. Standing almost three feet over her head, they stared her down (so they thought).

"Uhh! No," Gabriella snapped. She didn't even look at them as though she didn't have time for such rubbish and kept writing on her clipboard.

"What did you just say to me??" the hefty ring leader threatened, tightening his fists.

"Return to the back of the crowd where you belong, sir…" she said with a bit more gust in her voice, fixing her glasses, still writing.

"PISS OFF! We'll go back there once you're potty trained, little girl!" snarled the shortest of the three.

Her eyes shot up from the clipboard and met his.

"Oh, no!" Paul whispered to Samol, "Here it comes…"

Gabriella giggled innocently. For a second, she looked and sounded — well — like a five-year-old.

The suddenly cute, little girl took off her glasses and hung them around her neck from their silver chain. Primping the red quill behind her ear as though it were a flower, she tilted her head and gently asked the leader of these punks,

"What is your name?"

"Durwin Ebert!" he said proudly, peering over at her clipboard, looking for his name.

"Durwin…Durwin…I don't see a Durwin any-where," she said softly, flipping through her pages quickly. The frown lines between her eyebrows were now sharper than they'd been this whole time. "Wait, I'm sorry…I do see a Durwin Lee Ebert."

"Finally! You rea—"

"Son of that wimpy father of yours, John Jose Ebert and that ugly, tramp Darla Jane Ebert? My god, you are her spitting image!" she jeered, stowing the clipboard under her arm. Every eye was now as big as a billboard. Samol, just hearing the tone in her voice, confirmed in his head what his friends had said: 'she was no one to cross.'

She began, "In your fourth life you lost your job and attempted to become…a gigolo, was it? Please correct me if I'm wrong. You are Durwin Lee Ebert, correct?" she smirked, arching an eyebrow above her glasses, scanning her notes once more to make sure she was correct (even though she knew she was).

A unanimous gasp filled the air. Others clenched together their lips tightly so they wouldn't burst out laughing. Samol looked at London and Paul with his jaw nearly on the floor. A few moved closer to get a better listen at the verbal slaughter of this boy they hated. Durwin wanted to disappear under a sphere of invisibility, but Gabriella was just getting warmed up:

"Your crusty, little gigolo business didn't work out too well, because you couldn't keep it hard if your life de-pended on it! Well, it depended on it - - and you died! In your fifth life, you were so ugly the blind could see you com-ing! Not to mention, you were just as unemployed as your

61

fourth life! Hashtag 'Homeless-as-hell!' And you were forced to do something you said you would never do: beg in the streets. But nobody gave you a dime, did they? DID THEY??" she taunted him.

Durwin blinked heavily, unable to speak.

Gabriella continued, "Or even a sandwich? A candy bar? Cat food, even? You, my dear, are the very reason Vreeks created the sign, *'Do not feed the animals!'*"

The crowd laughed out loud.

"Please correct me if I'm wrong, you are Durwin Lee Ebert, am I correct??" she wheeled even louder.

For a second, there, Samol felt a little sorry for Durwin. The bully squirmed uncomfortably. Gabriella glared at Durwin's friends, who cowered and squirmed just as much.

The no-nonsense toddler pressed on:

"Your IQ in your fifth life sagged lower than your man-boobs! You were the only one stupid enough to get tricked into taking the fall for a drug bust *that you weren't even involved in!* HOW DUMB CAN YOU BE??" she insulted loudly. "In prison, shall we say…*they* found you attractive…" she winked.

Terrible memories of *"Bubba"* came flooding back.

People laughed louder and a few even clapped.

Paul leaned into Samol and whispered in an airy voice, "Told you her temper was bad!"

Durwin was choking back tears.

'Should I intervene?' Samol questioned. 'Create a diversion of some sort?' Before he could even conjure up a plan that probably wouldn't even work, Gabriella cat-walked like a model closer to Durwin. A walk like that was something that she was too young to know how to do, but then again, she'd lived one-hundred-seventy-one times, according to Paul. As if it weren't even humanly possible, Gabriella mercilessly hurled more violently than before:

"You are a failed abortion who should've never even made it out of your mother's crusty, overused lady parts!"

"Gabriella, please don—" Durwin begged.

"SHUT UP, I'M TALKING!!!"

He peed a little.

Every stomach dropped.

"I eat morons like you for breakfast and you're gonna be crying before this is over!" she hollered.

Durwin peed again.

"When you were just three years old, in your first life, you broke your ankle when you fell down your grandmother's steps. Shortly, thereafter, your crusty grandmother got you a puppy to cheer you up. You named him 'Winston,' a fun, energetic dog who was crushed by a semi-truck. Awww, how sad…NOT! In your sixth life, your only talents were lying, stealing, and master bating! In your seventh life you couldn't keep a girlfriend, a pet, or a job if someone paid you! During your eighth life, can we say S-T-D's, you nasty bastard! NEED-I-GO-ON??"

Durwin couldn't hide it any longer. He covered his face and wept like a baby and half the people he'd bullied in the past, broke into a heavy applause. In just minutes, twelve past lives of power had been shattered by a three-foot, no-nonsense toddler.

"MOVE TO THE BACK AS I INSTRUCTED - - NOW!" Gabriella hollered, gritting her teeth.

He sheepishly retreated.

"And I suggest you take your two boyfriends, fugly and crusty, with you!"

They, too, backed away. The shortest of the three was secretly most afraid because he figured that anyone almost eye-level with this tiny tyrant would probably get it even worse!

In that moment, Samol both feared and adored her. He wondered how could a five-year-old do that, but had to once again remind himself that she was actually hundreds of years old. With total control over the crowd now, Gabriella

63

gathered her seven hundred plus years of professionalism like nothing ever happened. She centered her glasses on the bridge of her nose like a school teacher, primped the quill behind her ear, and brushed back a few curls that had escaped. As if she suddenly were a new person, she calmly said:

"Good evening, my fellow Aryamites. My name is Gabriella Mae Doronin; Secretary of Death and the Undersecretary of Unfinished Affairs. I'd like to formally welcome you to the castle of Zebrastone," she smiled gently.

Samol had suddenly wondered if she was bipolar, or if one of the personalities of a past life had just taken over.

"In just a moment, we will begin our grand tour, but before we begin please note — *there is a method to my madness.* Those who are humble will learn the most and go the farthest, in life, and in death," Gabriella said gently, looking at the three individuals she'd called to the front.

Suddenly, her eyes made a sharp visit to the back of the crowd.

"Then again..." she began in a harsh growl, "those who are arrogant, rude, proud, and boastful will fail in life, death, and *in-my-presence!*"

A painful quiet thickened over the castle hall.

"Follow me," she said delicately, leading them out of the grand vestibule.

"Whoa..." Samol said, turning to his friends as everyone began to walk.

"I told you she was intense," said Paul, now afraid to even breathe wrong.

"As the Secretary of Death," London began, "she can command any piece of information on any one of us — from memory! She never forgets anything."

"Anything!" Paul reiterated with a shifty look as if he'd once experienced a similar wrath.

"She lived thirty-four of her past lives as a genius!" London whispered quickly as though she weren't supposed to know that.

"And she's one of three judges in Euphod's Court of Law. Stay on her good side!" Paul warned.

Samol took note to do just that.

Following Gabriella's every move, the crowd was led through a long, tall, dimly lit hallway that was sumptuously decorated. Samol stepped over a gold-rimmed light fixture that was in the ground. He stared at it confusedly, wondering why in the heck it was even there. However, when he looked further down the hall, he saw that the floor was lined with hundreds of them! He shot his neck to the ceiling where he saw a magnificent carpet covering the marble floor. Samol conjured up a million questions, and so did many others who gasped when they realized that they were walking on the ceiling! The hallway weaved in between nine large, spiraling staircases that became right side up when they reached the bottom. Samol was shocked that no one threw up, himself included! And then a terrible scream spawned from the castle walls!

"What was—" Samol began no louder than a whisper.

"That…was Death's denial, Samol," Gabriella interrupted before he could even finish asking his question, as though she already knew what he was going to say, and he'd asked it inches from her ear, but he was at least a hundred feet away.

"How did she hear me?" he whispered to Paul, his eyes bulging as though she'd performed a magic trick.

"Sweetheart, I'm the *sec-re-tar-y of death,*" she sassed, sure to proudly enunciate every syllable of her title. "I hear everything!"

Samol gave Paul a sheepish look.

"For those of you who are wondering, Death's Denial is the insane asylum for the deceased, which is where the screams are coming from," Gabriella explained.

Almost every eye averted to the walls as though they were just waiting for one of the crazy people to burst through; just like that self-hating, rude ghost Bella-Miss Ogyny.

65

"It's typically for Aryamites who've lived tough past lives or those who don't believe they're *actually* dead," Gabriella continued to explain. "Some of you in this very crowd have been there but…I won't say names," she winked sassily with her chin up, still walking ahead of everyone.

Samol swallowed heavily and erased any doubt that he was dead at once!

Gabriella's walk was just a few paces behind a sprint. Her short, stubby legs covered more ground than people twice her size! Mangled bodies struggled to drag along as the corpses of their last lives floated above them. Several large, black, right-side-up, sanctuary-like windows; grey, gothic pillars; and big archways passed by in the blink of an eye. Black candles burning of blue fire were lolled sloppily on the walls. At the baseboards of the walls were wiggling spider legs, flapping bat wings, and other twisting animal body parts. Because spider legs were the last thing that anyone wanted to see right now, to say the least, a few more Aryamites ran out the front door and were never seen again! Not to mention, vacillating between being right-side-up one moment and then upside-down the next was way too much!

"What is —??" shrieked a little girl, pointing at a pair of tarantula legs trying to free themselves.

"That is the other side of Death's Calendar," Gabriella answered before the girl could finish.

It occurred to Samol that Gabriella had grown numb to panicking newbies; the gross, wiggling spider legs; and the castle's strange defiance against gravity.

"What??" howled half the crowd.

And then Samol realized that Leanna, who he just noticed was nowhere to be found, was right all along.

London wasn't too happy about that.

"That's the graveyard you passed before entering the castle," Gabriella explained.

"Oh..." said everyone.

Suddenly, a young boy laid eyes on a large room filled with junk from the floor to the unimaginably, tall sky. For a second, he could've sworn he spotted one of his old porn magazines in there.

"What's in there?" the boy asked curiously, hoping that Gabriella hadn't seen it.

"That's Mumendad," said Gabriella, still walking at the speed of a sprint. "The place of lost and found."

"Lost and found?" asked the boy.

"Lost-and-found," she sassily repeated herself. "Each castle has one. Let's say..." she paused as though she were thinking, "you're living on assignment and something right next to you is suddenly gone — it ends up in the Mumendad corridors of the respected castle in which you were previously sorted."

"How — wait — why would Mumendad just take things from you?" the little boy stuttered with his eyes still fixed on his nasty belongings.

"A few reasons," she began importantly, "first off...we, as Aryamites, hold some of the most precious and important objects, here, in Euphod. If for some reason, they find their way into a life you're living (which they better not), we don't want these objects getting into the hands of Vreeks! Secondly, Mumendad will take things that are distracting an Aryamite from their original purpose; the very reason in which you were reincarnated to fulfill."

Samol was still secretly struggling to believe that all of this was real, but then quickly abandoned any such thoughts, fearing that he'd end up in that wacky "Denial Place" for the dead.

Gabriella turned a crooked, sharp corner. As if she had read his mind she said, "Speaking of uncertainty, your next life has already been planned for you."

"Holdzup! I thawt we got tuh choose the destiny of oah next loyvs?" shouted a sassy, teenage girl with a thick, New Jersey accent.

"Only those in Bridgelove have that luxury, Ms. Jersey Shore!" Gabriella said sharply.

"But, awy went tuh church every Sundzay in my last loyf!" she demanded.

It was apparent to many that she'd shown up late and missed the force of nature that was better known as *'Gabriella's wrath.'*

"Awy even put up with Adilgroff's boring classes while, he-ah, in Euphod! Awy want tuh be reincoarnated into whateva loyf awy want, little girl!"

Her thick accent left many unsure as to what she even said. Gabriella, on the other hand, who'd lived three past lives in Newark and had even indulged in a few drunken Jersey Shore beach parties herself, understood every word. This wasn't good. Gabriella halted mid-step. She turned and glared hotly at the girl, as if her silver eyes, alone, could reprimand anyone more than her harsh words ever could. The Jersey girl began fumbling to find words as though she were suddenly intoxicated, "Oh — er — yeah — we — umm…well…right." Gabriella knew that her scary stare was punishment enough and without missing a beat, she began briskly walking again and explained to the whole crowd:

"The way every one of you will review the flaws of your last life is different for each castle. Here, in Zebrastone, you complete said task by going through a carefully engineered maze of your entire last life that's actually *backwards*. Everything you did, didn't do, said, and didn't say, good or bad, will be in the maze."

Samol swallowed heavily again.

"Every Aryamite and Vreek you've crossed paths with, laughed with…slept with," she said, jerking her head over her left shoulder, giving London a stern look.

London cleared her throat with a fake cough, avoiding eye contact, hoping that Gabriella really didn't know all the things she'd done with her Italian, Vreek husband.

"Fair warning: When you're in the maze, you are not to be seen! Not to be heard! Better not even smell you!

You will be traveling backwards in time, which could be dangerous if spotted by a Vreek," Gabriella said importantly.

Samol noticed a growing excitement painting the faces of everyone, as if they were going to an amusement park. He, too, gave his two friends a wide smile, who still looked as though they could care less because they'd done this a dozen times. On the wall next to the crowd was a marble skull. Half of its disintegrated face, who appeared to be a woman, was covered in a red shawl. The ugly head moved slowly, like she were trying to talk but couldn't.

"What is this??" asked a curious boy, stupidly putting his hand near her face.

At lightning speed, the skull bit his finger in half!

"OUCH!!!" he screamed, holding what was left of his finger.

Everyone shrieked.

"Did you provoke her?" said Gabriella, still walking, not even looking back.

"I just wanted to see what it was!" he screamed, pissed that she didn't seem to care.

"Well, don't." Gabriella said sharply.

Those who were next to the injured boy tended to his missing finger, as if there was something they could even do, which there wasn't.

"What was that??" Samol whispered to London.

"That's Talking Tabitha," London replied, somewhat surprised that Gabriella hadn't interrupted her. "She's been mumbling for centuries, according to Euphod history."

"The Epscovians believe that she will become a talking prophet in the last days!" said Paul, and judging by the tone of his voice, it sounded like he were insulting London by calling her an *"Epscovian,"* - - whatever that meant.

"Will you stop mocking them??" London growled, swatting him with her death certificate. "My aunt happens to be one!"

Samol stared at her confusedly, just as he'd done when she bum-rushed him earlier. "Epscovians?" he asked.

"They're Aryamites who believe in the prophecies of the end times, the thirteen months of Euphod Tribulation, and a bunch of other bull! Coo-coo!" Paul mocked once more.

Gabriella stopped walking as if she'd witnessed a crime.

Paul fell frightfully silent.

"Zebrastone Aryamites, please note: everything here in the kingdom of Euphod is alive, cognizant, and knows how you think!"

Paul exhaled, happy that she didn't send him to the dungeons for his comments.

"Most importantly, it knows your heart," Gabriella finished. She turned to the young boy missing half his finger and said, "There's probably a reason why Talking Tabitha bit your finger. *Shape up or there'll be plenty more where that came from!*"

The boy stared back angrily, wanting to call her a cuss word in every language he knew.

"This way," Gabriella said brightly.

As if it weren't even possible, Gabriella now walked even faster. Samol struggled to keep up. She led them to the end of the hall where there were two doors that were so tall, they would've been in the clouds had they been outside. Samol wondered why she was rushing them. 'Was there another spider-snake-hornet attack on the way?' he thought wildly, wondering if the infernal creatures were now surrounding the castle!

Just outside the sanctuary doors were four fat candles that were as tall as an office building. Fire burned dimly from each of their unusually long wicks. The wax of each candle was deeply engraved with large, symphonic scores. As the candle wax melted away, a choir of invisible ghosts sang along as though this was how they kept their place in the music. *"Mozart's Requiem"* was their welcoming concert that evening. Everybody, including Samol, searched desperately for where the singing voices were coming from.

70

Gabriella shoved the large, black sanctuary doors open at once. Inside the dark church there were massive, black-pillared archways that, just like its doors, would've touched the Gates of Heaven had they been outside. Its ceilings were covered in paintings of ghouls, ghosts, goblins, gravestones, and great Aryamites who'd died a heroic final death. As far as the eye could see were rows of black pews perfectly aligned on either side of the church. A bright blue, velvet carpet trailed down its isle.

"This, ladies and gentleman, is the Zebrastone common room," Gabriella said proudly as if she'd revealed a treasure that she, personally, had created.

"It's a…church," said a disappointed little boy, staring at the crooked, black pulpit upfront.

"Trust me – you're gonna see things here that'll have you praying in no time!" Gabriella said, rolling her neck to every word.

Suddenly, a young, sodden girl shouted, "MY POEM!" She ran almost too excitedly towards a twisting wall where she found her beloved poem, *'Rosevine,'* shimmering bright like fire, which unbeknownst to her, was etched into the wall for the rest of eternity.

"Everyone, look!" she said, grinning ear to ear.

"We can't s—" Paul began.

"See anything?" Gabriella interrupted, jotting something down on her glowing clipboard. "You won't be able to unless you were the one who created it in a past life."

"What??" spat half the crowd (mostly newbies).

"Gets em' every time," Gabriella said softly, peering over her clipboard, winking at the three individuals she'd initially called to the front.

"Everything that any of you," Gabriella said, now addressing everyone, "have ever created, dreamed, thought, or even fantasized, for that matter, resides somewhere within the castle in which you are sorted. However, only you as the sole creator are the only one who can see it," Gabriella revealed.

"What if two people, or even three or four, created something together?" asked a young woman who couldn't stop staring at the massive pipe organ upfront, whose black pipes were as big as a house.

"I think you already know the answer to that, young lady," Gabriella replied sharply, writing in her notes, not even making eye contact.

"I never noticed th–" Paul whispered.

"That before?" Gabriella interrupted once again, still writing. "I know, Paul."

Paul grew eager for a moment, wanting to find where his fantasies were hidden inside the castle. But then, he was struck with a horrible thought:

"How does she know what I'm gonna say before I even say it?" Paul whispered.

Samol, for a second time, wondered if this was Paul's first time in Euphod.

"Because big things come in little caskets, *Samol,*" Gabriella said, neatly stowing away her notes under her arm.

"Wait, I'm…Paul…not Samol," said Paul whose eyes darted between Samol and Gabriella to catch if they'd coconspired something behind his back.

"I know," she said confidently. "Follow me, everyone!"

Samol and London were just as confused as Paul.

The other half of the sanctuary revealed more eerie artwork, scarier than the ghouls and ghosts they'd seen on the other side of the gothic sanctuary. There were beasts, demons, half-human half unrecognizable creatures, covered in black fur painted onto the ceiling. Many couldn't believe their eyes, wondering why such evil-looking creatures would be in a church of all places! Everyone began pointing and chatting nervously. Gabriella hushed them when she spoke:

"While you're here, in the Kingdom of Euphod, among many things you will not do — you will not eat and you will not sleep."

"WHAT??" they squawked (mostly the newbies).

"Not to worry my dead, little angels," Gabriella joked unemotionally. "Right now, all of you exist in the uncharted territory between flesh and spirit, the living and the dead. Such humanly desires will not be required for survival…not right away at least."

"Ms. Gabriella?" called out a humble, young boy, who was pocked with disease.

"Yes, my dear?"

"With all due respect…if we're half flesh and half spirit, won't we get…half hungry and somewhat tired?" he asked honestly.

"Yes. Yes, you will - - *eventually,*" she whispered, giving him a rare smile. "This is why Euphod is designed for you to be here no longer than a month's time. Just before your time here runs out, humanly desires begin to surface — the good and the bad."

"Oh," said the boy as though her words made this perplexing world suddenly make sense.

"Not to mention, you better make sure that your spirit is in good standing if you are, for whatever reason, here longer than a month's time," Gabriella said to the boy, now turning towards everyone, "I trust you've all been warned by Maven as to what happens when your body fully decompos-es?"

"Yes, ma'am," said the crowd with curdled expres-sions.

Gabriella sensed everyone's fear and remembered what it was like when she first died many, many lives ago. She gently took off her glasses and hung them precisely from their silver chain around her neck. And then, she spoke gen-tly:

"Things in Euphod will not always be easy and nei-ther will some of the lives you'll be assigned to live. However, you have the strength to persevere or else you wouldn't be going through it. Although many of you are nowhere near done with your eternal purpose, you all have fulfilled many other purposes of their own, or else you wouldn't be dead!"

"I know it's been tough for several of you - - trust me, I've seen your death certificates - - and for that I am proud of all of you," she said, putting her glasses back on.

Many proudly stiffened their backs, as if receiving such high praise from someone who probably never gave compliments was the confidence boost they needed to get through their next lives. Much like Maven, another one with a seemingly abrupt personality, Samol now saw a hidden layer of warmth underneath her strict "get-it-together-or-else" attitude. His face melted into a delicate smile. She walked to the back of the sanctuary and stood near a set of incredibly large double doors made of shattered mirrors. Samol stared at his reflection. Depending on where he stood, he saw himself three different ways. Yet, he couldn't understand how or why.

"What's with the mirrors?" he said to Paul and London as he twisted and turned like a fashion model.

"What mirror?" said Paul, examining both doors wildly as though his eyes were chasing a fly or something.

"Right there!" Samol pointed.

"Samol, there's no mirror. It's just a door," said London, who'd been growing increasingly alarmed about his mental well-being since the three of them had reunited.

In the broken mirror, farthest to the left, Samol saw a malnourished, curly haired boy, surrounded in white smoke being sliced to death! In the shattered mirror that was bridged between both doors was a figure that moved exactly as he did. In the mirror to the far right, stood an indistinguishable, blackened, mist figure that left Samol void of any clue as to what it could be. Perhaps he was seeing himself in the present, a clouded past, and a blurry future, he thought? But why couldn't anyone else see this? He was afraid that he was losing his mind.

Everyone had grown nervously chatty, pointing at a few beasts on the ceilings they could've sworn were watching their every move. Gabriella swiftly turned to face the crowd. A sudden rush of excitement had raced over her as though someone had just whispered something pleasant in her ear.

"Behind this door is the Zebrastone Maze; the very maze that will reveal your last life," she said, fighting a smile. "It can be beautiful and deadly. It exists but *doesn't* exist. Remember, you are going back in time - - things may get a little...tricky," she paused as though she were searching for the right word.

Gabriella pulled the brown gavel from her pocket, which had a clock face on it. "Oh my, the time has escaped me!" she said, almost leaping in the air. "The Death Day Ball starts in a few minutes! You'll view your lives after the soirée."

"Oh, come on!" the crowd begged pathetically.

"Trust me, you'll have plenty of time to see how many times all of you screwed up!" Gabriella sassed, rolling her neck to every word. "In the meantime, it's time to celebrate!"

A heavy weight was lifted from Samol's shoulders. He could use a good party right now. After being murdered, dealing with a girl's breath that smelled like devil burps, and then almost being attacked by a spider and its army...one could only imagine!

"Everybody's got their death certificate, right?" Gabriella asked.

"Yes," said everyone, waving it in the air like a lottery ticket.

"Good, don't lose it!"

Samol glanced at his death certificate, happy that it hadn't changed again.

Before the crowd, now stood a girl with red hair that was long enough to step on, wearing an unbuttoned business suit. No one recognized Gabriella with this casual look because now, she actually looked more like a...child. Round-faced. Rosy-cheeked. She was actually a cute kid. Hiding such innocent looks behind that corporate get-up should've been a sin!

"Ladies and gentlemen, it's time to have some fun!" she said, laughing loudly. Every face went pale. They stared at her as if a third arm had sprouted from her shoulder.

A few had experienced the rarity of Gabriella chuckling from time to time, but that was only because she were about to verbally annihilate someone. Outright laughter?? No way!

"I SAID COME ON!" Gabriella shouted, exiting the sanctuary.

Even more troublesome than Gabriella's oddly, happy demeanor was that the same hallway from which they'd entered was now different! What was once a dimly lit hall was now bright; lit by hovering balls of fire. Not to mention, the hallway now led seven different ways, all of which seemed to have no ending.

"Follow me," Gabriella said confidently, veering down the second hallway.

"Whoa!" Paul gasped. "Where are we?"

"*Where are we?*" London asked rhetorically. "The better question is *'who is that??'*" she whispered strongly, pointing at Gabriella.

"She seemed like a — like a — tyrant until now!" said Samol as he passed the singing candles.

"Tyrant??" Paul shrieked. "What you saw earlier?? That was nothing! You remember last year when she slapped — oh — sorry..." he said sadly.

Paul felt worse than the time he accidentally asked one of his Vreek friends, "So, how's your mother?" when she, unbeknownst to him, was sucked into a tornado.

Samol grew visibly sad.

"...It's okay, Samol," London said gently. "We will do everything we can to get your memory back. I promise," she said, hugging his shoulder.

The end of the second hall revealed a beige, marble room. Its ceilings were high; though not quite as high as the ones in the entrance foyer. The walls were lit by candles that twisted and swayed on their own, much like the gravestones in Gullavin's Graveyard. At the center of the room was a big fountain that, instead of water, shot fire in every color that one could imagine.

76

Blues, reds, yellows, purples, pinks, greens, black and even clear fire illuminated the glamorous room! Unfortunately, such a magical moment came to a sudden halt when a terrible scream tore through the air!

A decayed hand had emerged through a wall that was pretending to be solid, yanking at a girl with a large braid! The crowd turned wild; a chaotic frenzy even! Gabriella was blocked from seeing the tragedy at hand; as most people stood two or three feet over her head. Samol, London, and Paul ran to pry the tightening grip from Leanna's ankle! She was already halfway into the wall, screaming awfully with one hand clasped to Samol's wrist and the other onto Paul's. Finally, Gabriella managed to shove her way through the hysterical crowd.

She ripped the gavel from her pocket and pounded the wall so hard, it sent a ripple through the room knocking everyone to their knees! The ugly hand still had a firm grip on Leanna. Gabriella struck the wall once more. 'BOOM!' The creature loosened its grip just enough to even out the losing battle of tug-of-war. After the third and final hit, the marble wall cracked in two and Leanna was set free. The creature squealed as though it were either wounded or angry that it couldn't pull her through the wall! Like magic, the wall reconfigured itself as though it had never even been touched.

"WHAT WAS THAT THING??" Leanna begged wildly, clinging to Paul's arm.

"That—" Gabriella heaved, huffing heavily with her hair a mess, and suit jacket hanging from her shoulders as if she'd just gotten into a fight, "was a prisoner of Zebrastone! Take note, all of you, prisoners are trapped in the walls of all seven castles! They're lonely, dangerous creatures incarcerated for all eternity, always looking for their next victim and they tend to strike when you least expect. *Stay alert!*"

Tossing her suit jacket back over her shoulders, she flung her long hair over her left shoulder and led them down the rest of the hallway. Everyone was petrified to say the least! Samol was relieved that Leanna was left unharmed.

But this was the second nasty attack that Samol had witnessed in under an hour! He suddenly didn't feel safe - - those who'd been dead many times before weren't even safe! He felt as though he didn't stand a chance in this strange place.

Growing cheers and laughter began to echo now that they were nearing the end of the long hall. Gabriella's words of caution, however, echoed even louder within their trembling hearts. The Aryamites were greeted by what looked like a red carpet event for the dead. There was music, drunken ghosts, a plethora of drinking games, dancing overlords, even seemingly important people stepping out of hearses as though they were limos! For now, all seemed well…except for who was standing at the entrance of the ball.

CHAPTER FIVE

THE DEATH DAY BALL

"Hans-Paul Mikaelsson, you are drunk!" – London

*I*t was October 30th, a seemingly ordinary day, yet it was a day that the dead indulged in more debauchery than the living could ever imagine. Vreeks, mere mortals who've only lived once, may pride themselves in winning a few games of beer pong, or being a flip cup champ, or boast to their friends how they downed thirteen shots of Tequila in under a minute. That was nothing in comparison to Euphod's Death Day Ball.

Try playing *"never have I ever"* against Aryamites who've lived over three hundred lives. The loser, which in their case is the person who has the most fingers left at the end of the game, has to finish an entire basin of Vodka that sits in a large, black casket measuring thirty feet long and ten feet deep. Consider a drinking game where you're not allowed to stop drinking until Luchianna Pevets, a Euphod opera singer who could easily hold a note for three whole days, runs out of air.

Or perhaps, one of the crudest of games known to Euphod, *Fiona Ramona*, the deceased's version of taboo. In this lewd game, cards with arbitrary words, actions, and/or phrases are pulled, at random, from the belly button of a mystical bronze statue named Fiona Ramona, who has both male and female body parts. Anytime someone says or does whatever is written on the cards throughout the night, they must drink. Of course, from the start, all pulled cards are shown to all playing members so everyone knows what not to say or do. The rules are:

Anyone who commits a forbidden <u>action</u> at any time during the party, which could be something as simple as *scratching your head* or *folding your arms*, another player who catches them must shout, *"Fiona Ramona!"* pointing to the offender who must drink Bacardi 151 from the statue's breasts, which are as large as watermelons, until the liquor stops flowing.

Anyone who says a forbidden <u>word</u> during the game, which could be anything as commonplace as *"ever"* or *"please,"* another player who catches them must call out, *"Fiona Ramona!"* pointing to said offender who must drink Absinthe from its twelve-inch member until it stops flowing, even the boys, who surprisingly weren't nearly as reluctant as one might think after a few drinks!

Third and final, anyone who says a forbidden <u>phrase</u>, which could be as ordinary as, *"I don't know,"* or *"Excuse me,"* and another player hears them, they must holler, *"Fiona Ramona!"* and point to the offender who would then have to drink a horrible mixture of both Bacardi 151 and Absinthe from the statue's rear end until it stops flowing!

For obvious reasons, all Aryamites under the age of twenty-one were banned from this game! Of course, many curious teens played anyway once the higher-ups got too drunk to notice. October 30th was a day in which liquor store owners, had they been on earth, would become billionaires overnight! Having month-long hangovers after The Death Day Ball was not unheard of.

80

Puking for seven days straight was typical. Drunken orgies were as commonplace as the many candles that lined the castle's walls! Aside from the vast selection of drinking games and rampant copulatory acts, there was music and Aryamites from all seven castles dancing wildly in festive costumes.

There were also mounds of delicious food carefully placed buffet-style in hundreds of gold caskets that aligned the walls: seasoned roast beef, mashed potatoes, gravy, curry chicken, Spanish rice and black beans, Jamaican beef patties, the cheesiest macaroni and cheese you could ever dream, pierogies, lasagnas, lamb chops, latkes, steamed vegetables, yams, clams, pumpkin pies, apple pies, apple crêpes, chocolate cakes, just to name a few.

In other caskets, however, lay: fried vulture, dirt cakes, worm pies, roach custard, roasted turkeys with maggots stuffed inside, baked vomit, rotten-egg-sour-spinach quiche, maggot cakes, maggot pies, fried larva, spider-and-beetle-filled egg rolls, white-worm pizza, white-worm pies (a crowd favorite), dead fish tacos, and even a few caskets filled with moldy, vegan options, thank you very much.

Samol and his three friends were now standing near the front of the line. Leanna clung tightly to Paul's arm because of her recent trauma. Samol's eyes floated from every shimmering candle, to festively dressed Aryamite, to drunken ghost, to the golden caskets filled with food. For a second, he tricked himself into believing that he was hungry, but his false desires soon died away when he saw an old man chomping away on a Centipede Pot Pie!

Samol slid his eyes over to a well-dressed, fat man who couldn't've been a day under a thousand, stuffing his face with grilled skunk and a cocktail, with mold floating to the top as though it were ice. Samol was disgusted beyond words! His eyes darted between the old, porky man and a coffin brimmed with golden-fried chicken, wondering why there was food to even begin with. He turned to London with almost a sense of urgency and asked, "I thought Gabriella said we don't eat or drink while we're dead?"

"We don't — " said London, pointing to Samol and herself, "They do," she said, pointing to the rulers and those in the administration.

"These old hags have been stuck down here for millenniums!" Paul said with a boyish grin, staring at a group of adults enjoying a game of Fiona Ramona. "Their humanly desires have more than settled in!" he added, cracking himself up.

Samol found both the game and the adults who were playing it down-right repulsive!

The entrance line hadn't moved in a half hour and the four of them were almost inside. Paul found himself gawking at a pale, leggy, blonde woman wearing a black evening gown and a big, sensual, white fur that draped over one shoulder. She stepped out of a long hearse as though it were a limo, cat-walking and posing down a black carpet, that had she been alive and in Hollywood, would've probably been red. Cameras flashed as she waved pompously and there was a loud cheer as though everyone had been awaiting her arrival — whoever she was.

Samol's eyes fell away from the late celebrity and landed on four bald, well-dressed men who looked not a day under four hundred years of age. The African-American men looked almost transparent like ghosts, and had an air about them that left Samol with the impression that they held much power in Euphod. The foursome clinked their tall glasses of Everclear and began the night.

Samol could overhear many conversations and must've heard: *'So, when did you die?'* at least a hundred times. He found it strange that no one even flinched at such a question, but then again, he had to stop thinking like a Vreek! He saw Aryamites seated in corners, playing horoscope games based on the day they died in their past lives and assumed that in Euphod, said question was just as commonplace as asking, *'So, how's it going?'* Samol was suddenly trying terribly to convince himself that this was all normal.

"So, this is the Death Day Ball?" Samol asked gently, staring at hundreds of floating pumpkin wreaths.

"Yes, sir," London said, who sounded as though she were very proud to be dead in that moment. "Every year, the day before Halloween, Aryamites from all seven castles come together and celebrate their death."

"Hmm..." he said, trying to pull his eyes away from a tall, busty woman wearing a feathered mask, holding a wine glass that was longer than her arm.

"Remember last year when Madame Lyborikus got drunk and puked on Owen Loonaddict??" Paul snickered. "Owen-beat-her-down!!"

"No, Paul. He doesn't," said London, rather irritated at Paul's insensitivity to Samol's memory loss.

Paul kept laughing anyway.

They were now inches away from getting inside. Everyone's happiness came to a halt when two twelve-foot giants suddenly emerged in front of the entrance. Samol was almost certain that this was who he'd spotted when Gabriella led them down the hallway earlier. Both giants were menacing. Bald. Buff. Wearing all black. *"Death certificates! NOW!!"* demanded the giant to the left. His voice bellowed like Maven's. The other hulking man stood with his arms folded.

Paul was up first. Shaking nervously, he handed over his death certificate. The man's hands were as rough as concrete and nearly as big as the hood of a car. As if the giant's job description said, *'be a dick,'* he snatched it rudely! Paul jumped. He examined it in the nearby candlelight as if it were fake; top to bottom, front to back, corner to corner. He even smelled it twice, scowling at Paul as though he were trying to pull a fast one. Lacking any regard for Paul's property, the oversized man carelessly threw his death certificate back in his face.

"NEXT!" belted the giant.

Leanna stepped up, still holding onto Paul's arm. For some reason, the bouncer gently looked at her death certificate for not even a second before letting her through. Leanna wondered if he'd seen that she was almost violated by the prisoner that escaped through the walls! That's a darn good reason to be lenient on someone!

Next was London. With an outstretched hand, he impatiently motioned for London to fork over her death certificate — right now! He snatched it, crinkling the edges. London rolled her neck, folded her arms, and had a few expletives seated at the tip of her tongue, but refrained. He studied it for a few seconds, but then frowned when he saw strange symbols mixed within the letters of her name; a sideways hourglass under a big, red 'x'; a feathered frog; and a cactus.

"What the -- ?" he said.

Whereas *'being mean'* isn't technically illegal in Euphod, any authority figure asking an Aryamite to explain their past lives outside of a job application for employment within the Euphod administration services, or otherwise, in the Euphod Court of Law is one-hundred percent unlawful; as it is deemed as *soul profiling* (according to the 33rd Amendment of the Euphod Constitution). The large man was angry that he couldn't pry into her business and ripped her death certificate in half! It let out an earsplitting squeal as though it were in pain!

"NEXT!" he hollered carelessly.

"HEY!" London screamed. "You just destroyed my death certificate!!"

"Piss off! You'll get another one the next time you die!"

"Excuse me??" London howled with a boiling temper and balled fists. "PISS OFF?? I'm gonna F—"

"London!" Samol stopped her. "Don't!"

The giant man looked at Samol as though he'd offended him. His face twisted as though he'd just downed a dozen lemons at once.

84

"Well, aintchu' a little coward!" the giant insulted, which left Samol confused because it was totally unnecessary. "She's got more balls than you do! Hey, Joe!" he called out to the other bouncer, "I think we just found us a new girlfriend — this, here, little boy toy!"

Joe, whose teeth were as crooked as his eyes were crossed, was dumb as hell. He absent-mindedly laughed with no clue as to what his fellow giant was even chuckling about. Samol, for the death of him, couldn't understand why this man was being so mean. He began wondering if he'd had a feud with this giant in a past life or something.

The big man snatched his death certificate, harder than everyone else's, when all of a sudden a massive holler issued from his throat! Samol's death certificate scorched the man's hand leaving a white scar that read, 'H.O.D.' in shimmering letters! It was a rather hilarious site to see a man over twelve-feet tall hopping down the hall like a bunny rabbit for the hospital wing! Samol stared distrustfully at his death certificate, lying there on the marble floor, and so did his friends. For a second, he thought that it, too, might've been cursed.

"What just happened?" Samol asked hesitantly.

"No idea!" said Paul with bug eyes.

Leanna frowned as though she'd seen something like this before, but kept quiet.

Samol crept towards his death certificate as though it had a disease. He bent to pick it up when a voice hollered:

"Don't touch it!"

"I have to, Paul!" Samol screamed back, hoping to God he wouldn't get burned.

Slowly extending his index finger, he grabbed its corner. Cold as a corpse, it was. For the first time Samol could remember, he was both relieved and confused at the same time. He stuffed it in his back pocket.

"Whew!" Paul sighed as though he were the one having to pick it up.

"Wait…" said London. "Why did it burn that man?"

The four of them stared confusedly at one another.

"Let me see that!" she demanded.

Samol cautiously gave it to her and she, too, found that it wasn't hot when she slowly touched its corner.

"Weird," said London, more to herself than to her friends.

"Guys, should we really be...partying right now?" Samol trembled, stuffing his death certificate back into his pocket. "We've got to get to our next lives and I need to find out if I'm cursed — or even if whatever's wrong with me is <u>worse</u> than a curse!"

"Relax," Paul said rather calmly. "We've got a full month, remember?"

"But what if it gets worse??" Samol wheeled again.

"Just relax," Paul reassured him, this time grinning gingerly.

Samol took a deep breath, making a concerted effort not to worry and scanned the grand, gothic ballroom. Hanging from the dark, red ceilings, which was high enough to fit two stacked Goodyear blimps inside, hung black chandeliers and twenty-seven upside-down staircases in a row, each one more twisted than the last. It was quite a shock when Samol saw the people descending down them, who were also upside-down, hadn't plunged to the ground! Corinthian-style pillars were clothed in black velvet and spanned from the marble floors to its ceilings; which met the long, black carpet where more hearses were parked.

The Death Day Ball seemed to have every social group you'd find in a high school and then some! There were nuns, wall flowers (literally), jocks, ghosts, the pretty people, nerds, the goths, preps, and more! Samol tried to remember the last time he'd seen so many people all at once, but couldn't. Out of nowhere, a red-headed, little boy dressed like a court jester ran towards Samol and his friends, smiling and waving as though he knew them.

"Paul, London, SAMOL!!! Welcome back!" he belted jovially and nodded politely at Leanna since he'd never seen her before.

"Di-Di, bonjour!" Paul smiled brightly, hugging the boy, mistakenly speaking French as though he were an old Parisian friend of Paul's or something. "How are you??"

"Oh, ya know — same old, same old," said the boy, fixing his orange collar. "My friend spent his last life as a New York tap dancer in 1936 and taught me a new dance! Wanna see?" he asked, tap dancing away before they could even answer him.

"You're still just as silly as ever," London joked, shaking her head.

"True to form!" he smiled, finishing his last few taps. "Samol, how've you been, man?"

Samol stared at him blankly as though he were an alien.

"Well, don't just study me like a stranger, give me a hug!" he said, hugging him tightly.

By now, Samol was sick of getting squeezed by strangers. He looked at his friends and mouthed, *"Who is this?"* but before they could answer, the boy let go when he noticed that his embrace was one-sided.

"Oh, no!" the boy gasped. "I hoped the rumors weren't true, but they are!"

"What rumors??" Samol jolted as though this boy knew something else about himself that he didn't.

"Your memory really <u>was</u> cursed! Everyone's been whispering about it!" he said.

All of a sudden, the terribly husky voice of a drunken old man shattered their convivial reunion: "Hey, you...court Jester boy! Get over here and give us a...*tap dance!*"

"I'm sorry, Samol. I have to go," he said sadly, lowering his head. "We really need to ta—"

"I SAID NOW!" demanded the crude drunk and the boy nervously scurried off, dusting his uniform.

"—What was that all about —?" Samol asked, the words fell from his mouth slowly.

"Hey, look!" said Paul, pointing into the crowd, totally ignoring Samol. "Madame Lyborikus is drunk — already?"

"Her tolerance must've dropped since Euphod Solstice! Let's go see who she pukes on this year!" said Paul, running off.

Leanna chased behind him.

"Rude," London said, snapping her neck.

"Who was that guy we were talking to?" Samol asked, who by now learned to pay Paul no mind.

"That was Deitrick McCollens," she answered. "You two have been friends since your second life."

"Hmm...I don't re—"

"Remember, I know," London sighed.

She jerked her head around when she heard a woman with a stupid, high-pitched phony laugh trying desperately to be a part of the in-crowd. Samol turned his head the other way when he heard someone call him by his full name. His face brightened like a child on Christmas morning.

"Deitrick is one of Euphod's performers," she said, sounding almost sad, "and he's never been reincarnated into a life on earth (so they say)."

"Really?" Samol asked slowly.

"He only entertains Aryamites and castle rulers during Euphod holidays and celebrations. The rest of his time is spent digging graves in Chèrevam's Graveyard."

"Digging graves??" Samol belted. "That sounds god-awful!"

"It is!" she said. "But, personally, I'd take digging graves over performing any day! Deitrick, along with a few others, are to perform whenever and wherever they are summoned. Sometimes, it's more than just dancing..." she said sadly. "But, you especially, were always nice to him, unlike some of the other entitled, bratty jackasses down here!" London said angrily, scanning the ballroom.

Samol's eyes followed her's. Although he couldn't remember being nice to Deitrick, he suddenly felt good about himself for doing so.

"Even worse - - he's eternally twelve!" London added.

"Eternally?? How?" Samol asked curiously.

"None of us know how or why. We think he's not allowed to say," she whispered as if she wasn't supposed to know that. "I heard the administration put a spell on him in his very first life, but nobody knows who did it or why. I have my suspicions though…"

"SAMOL!" shouted a group of teenage boys. One of them he could've sworn was Paul's twin. "Glad you're all right, man!"

"You made it!" said a freckle-face boy, standing at the center of the group.

Samol forced an awkward grin.

"Yeah! Good to see you too!" he said.

The group of boys ran off.

"Who are they?" he asked London.

"I don't know, but just stick with me the rest of the night. I'll remind you of who's who and who to stay away from. At these sort of gatherings, people exchange more gossip, plans to attack someone and…bodily fluids more than you'd think," she said, staring at a drunk couple kissing in a corner. "Just do what the grown-ups do."

"Which is…?"

"Play-the-game: Smile. Wave. Be cordial with a hint of phony," she said, mocking the pompous lady with the phony laugh. "Say, 'hi' to those who say, 'hi' to you, even if you don't know who they are or you — *hate…their…guts,*" she growled her last three words nearly an octave lower than her normal voice; eyeballing a pink-faced, busty brunette who stood as the queen bee of three teenage girls.

The blue-eyed girl flipped her hair over her shoulder, giving London a 'bow down and worship me' glare and sashayed by the both of them as if she and Samol were nothing more than peasants. London clenched her teeth. Balled her fists. Gave the three girls a fiery glare.

"What happened to '*play-the-game?*'" Samol sarcastically remarked.

"I <u>AM</u> playing the game," she snapped. "I'm not whoopin' that ass with a sledge hammer!"

"Whoa! What's this all about?" Samol asked, taken-aback by her sudden hostility.

"That's Mary-Beth Bradycoot...more like death's prostitute!" she hissed angrily. "She, her floozy friends, and sleazy mother are all sluts of the underworld! They strategically befriend people, whore around to get what they want, and have even caused some to die final deaths! I lost a good friend of mine four lives ago because of Mary-Beth! Her mother caused all hell to break loose in my aunt's life — literally! They'll do any and everything to get ahead in life <u>and</u> in death!"

"That's cold."

"As their corpses."

"Samol!" yelled a terribly diseased-ridden boy, running awkwardly towards him. With each stride, the boy kicked his knees nearly to his chin, as though he were trying to jog in place.

"It's good to see you!" said the boy, whose pores looked as if black boogers and white boils were growing from them. Samol was relieved that he didn't try to hug him and kept running!

"That's Denn Marq," London whispered, trying not to laugh. "You guys became really good friends after your fourth life, but ever since last year's Death Day Ball he and Paul have been at odds and he's been weird around you."

"What happened?"

"I don't know," she shrugged honestly. "I asked Paul about it, but he gets really defensive so I quit bothering."

Samol's eyes drifted away and they landed on an unattractive girl with ghostly skin.

"Wait, I know that girl!" Samol said loudly and pointed.

"What girl?" London asked, looking around.

"GALENA!" Samol shouted, cupping his lips.

The smelly girl saw him, but acted as though she didn't. "Galena?..." he called again, this time a little quieter, not sure if it was even her.

90

"Who is she?" London asked, twisting her face as if she really wanted to ask, "Who let her out of her casket??"

"She was the first person I met when I got to Euphod - - well - - this time, at least," he said hesitantly, still staring at Galena until she faded into the crowd, which had parted because she smelled so bad.

Above all the strange things he'd seen up until now, this seemed to hurt Samol's feelings most because he thought she was his friend.

"London, I really don't think I should be here at the Death Day Ball," Samol said worriedly. "Something doesn't feel right and I need to get to my next life."

"You can't get to your next life right now. The entire administration is off duty — and/or drunk!"

Samol slipped into an uneasy quiet.

"Although…" she began as though she were up to something, "sometimes in life, and in death, I find that when you need information that's not easily accessible, eavesdropping is always a useful tool."

"Eavesdropping? That's not polite."

"Neither is whatever cursed you!"

Samol said nothing.

"This is what we'll do: I want you to listen to as many conversations as you can to see if anything jogs your memory or if anything stands out. I'll watch your back," she said.

Samol shrugged and agreed. What's the worst that could happen? Being called a *'nosy creep?'* A punch in the face if someone caught him? He'd already been stabbed to death; a punch would be nothing! He crept behind a group of teenagers who were chatting. The loudest one had a mixture of Russian, Brazilian, and a North American southern accent being the strongest. Samol listened:

"…Are you kiddin' me? That's nuthin'! Just last week, I was reincarnated three times! For two days, I lived in Alabama where I was gay, black, and poor in 1944." Although Samol's memory loss prevented him from actualizing what any of this was like, his heart still gave a sudden jolt.

"For three days, I lived as a gor-ge-ous Russian woman in Novosibirsk in the year 2042 (that was interesting). And then, for only a day and a half I was a wealthy, Egyptian pharaoh in 322 B.C.!"

Samol thought that was one heck of a week! He wanted to stay and listen, more interested in the second life of the three, but figured he'd find nothing of importance for his own past lives. He and London stealthily moved away. He spotted a little girl who'd captured the attention of everyone around her. Was it her glowing, blue, feathered mask? The fact that her elbows and knees were ripped sideways? Or was it, in fact, that she was reading from a torn parchment that was twice her size? Samol caught the tail end of whatever it was she was saying.

"...I think it's a part of a riddle," she said in an airy voice: *"Time is to blood as future is to life."*

Samol thought over what he'd just heard, wondering if it would even be useful. 'Nah,' said the voice in his head. His eyes fell away and he saw a group of teens playing spin-the-casket. The tiny, red casket looked like it were made for a rodent and landed opposite two teens who got up and kissed each other. He certainly wouldn't find anything there unless he were looking for tips on how to make-out in his next life! He and London covertly migrated towards another group; a crowd of disfigured and smashed teens that looked as if they'd all died in a 12 car pile-up. They listened:

"...Some believe the locket is in the Verstandfall Illu-sion Room. Nobody has ever made it out alive, but if you do, I heard you have to look into the invisible mirror..."

"Invisible mirror?" said a mangled girl in the center of the group. "How do you even find it??"

"What does it show?" asked another boy, who was missing half his face.

"I don't know how you find it, but according to leg-end, the mirror doesn't show what we actually look like - - so you don't have to worry, Brad!" he joked, pointing at the boy with the ripped face. "It shows the words that describe the

92

gifts that we'll either be given or have been given. The problem is that the words are spelled backwards and only show themselves for three seconds!"

Samol turned to London, who hadn't heard a word of this because Mary-Beth and her crew were close-by again. 'Locket?' He thought to himself. 'What's so important about a stupid locket? And what's this *invisible mirror* they're talking about?' Samol made sure to remember all of this and caught up to London, who'd crept off to eavesdrop on Mary-Beth:

"He's so weird! And probably stupid too!" Mary-Beth began in a condescending tone. Samol began to dislike her even though he didn't know who she was even talking about.

"I heard he sleeps in Jym Reapyr's coffin!"

"Are you serious??" the other girls gasped.

"Am I, or am I not, Mary-Beth Bradycoot? *Mary-Beth* always gets the info she needs!" she said conceitedly. "I heard he died three times in one day...on purpose! We think he's looking for something," she said, making sure to whisper her last six words.

Without saying a word, Samol and London locked eyes, knowing that whoever this Jym Reapyr was, was certainly worth remembering. However, London quickly jerked her head around Samol when she saw a swift movement behind him. He didn't even notice because he was immersed in his own thoughts. 'But where would we find Jym Reapyr?' Samol wondered. What troubled him was that Mary-Beth and her friends were suddenly gone, like they'd all said a few magic words and vanished!

"What the - - ?" said London, looking in every direction.

"Let's just — keep moving," said Samol, who'd hoped that they were finally on to something. The two of them walked passed a short, drunk, elderly man, who was wearing a red and black mask, barely able to stand.

"All right there, Samol? I see you made it back..." grumbled the old man. Samol quickly looked at London, wanting her to quietly mouth this man's name, but she didn't.

"Yes, thank you, sir," he said politely.

The drunk man stumbled away, bumping into a few caskets and said, "Oh, sorry Harold."

"Who was that?" Samol asked.

"I don't know…but you're playing the game well," she grinned proudly.

Just when he began to feel he was mastering this whole 'smile and fit' in business, a drunken ghost on a white horse busted through the walls holding a nearly finished bottle of liquor! Above his head was a fleet of drunken ravens that careened into the windows and walls. With a carefree joy, the misty figure hysterically laughed to himself and repeatedly screamed, "TIFF!!" A few uptight people standing against the wall were very angry that he'd startled them, mostly because they almost soiled themselves! Others who were already loosened by libations laughed heartily.

"Okay, now <u>who</u> is that??" Samol asked, caught in the contagious laughter of the drunken ghost and the audience that surrounded him. "And who's Tiff?"

"That's Whiskey Nick; one of Euphod's many drunken ghosts!" said London, shaking her head, trying not to laugh. "It's rumored that Tiff was an old friend of his many, many lives ago that he cared about deeply but would tease mercilessly — all in good fun of course," London explained, watching the reckless ghost ride his horse like a bull. "You've gotta watch that Whiskey Nick, though. He constantly steals booze from parties and blames it on the kids…or says it's his friend, Tiff!"

Samol laughed even harder.

"I'm serious! He got three Aryamites in hot water with the administration just last year and the jerk did nothing but laugh about it!"

Samol kept laughing.

"It wasn't funny!" London said seriously. "One of the Aryamites was your friend, Neera!"

"Neera?"

"Neera Whodweller - - from two lives ago."

Samol stopped laughing and became serious as if he'd suddenly remembered who Neera was. 'Maybe my memory loss isn't something to laugh about?' he pondered gravely. 'What if I die for all eternity or end up in Vypercoff...or in hell??' he panicked.

"Don't worry, Samol," said London, who could tell he was scared and rested her hand on his shoulder. "We'll get to the bottom of everything after the dance."

He exhaled heavily and said, "Well, I've made it this far..."

Suddenly, Paul returned. The problem was that he was staggering, giggling to himself, and his breath reeked terribly of what smelled like Whiskey. Not to mention, he'd apparently ditched Leanna somewhere.

"Hans-Paul Mikaelsson, you are drunk!" London hollered, sounding like an angry mother.

"London Noel Lucas, you are right!" Paul mocked. "Cah — come with me! I just sawww Graf..haha—" he began uncontrollably laughing.

"PAUL!" London screamed. "Pull yourself together. You are underage and if anyone in the administration catches you like this, you're gonna be in deep doo-doo!"

"SHHHH!" Paul shushed her, still giggling carelessly. "You wor — worry much too, womannn! Look! Gra — gralawful's dancing!!" he said sloppily, pointing at a large, cheering crowd circled around someone.

"Who?"

"Just come on!" said Paul, yanking them both by their wrists.

Paul shoved and kicked anyone in his way. Samol and London were thrown into that awkward position of having to apologize for their drunken friend's behavior. The crowd's cheering grew clearer and louder the closer they got to the circle. "Wah-filma! Mah-tilda! Gra-hilda! Grafilda!!" There she was, the ruler of Verstandfall; Grafilda Weegonok. Her age? Try six-hundred-seventy-seven! The music blared as both she and her polka-dotted cloak soared through the air.

Everyone, young and old, was enthralled by this old woman's dance moves. A few secretly wished they could've been sorted into Verstandfall instead of whatever castle they were in. The old woman shimmied and shook for nearly an hour non-stop!

All the fun came to a halt when a fork loudly clinked the side of a wine glass. The problem wasn't the clink - - but who was doing it. Standing at the top of the staircase was one of Euphod's most hated individuals, by both Aryamites and those in the administration. She was a short, grisly-looking, terribly obese woman with more rolls on her neck than a Thanksgiving feast and a face that could startle the blind. Her large, saggy chest hung sloppily over her massive gut and she had pencil-thin legs. It looked as if the only way her twig-like legs could uphold her huge, goblet-shaped upper body was by a host of angels <u>and</u> a magic trick!

The Death Day Ball was coming to a fast close and all Aryamites were to remain silent. Yet, with Paul's current state of intoxication, this was going to be a disaster! It was no secret, to London, that Paul had lived one of his past lives as a comedian. However, right now was not the time for *'Comedy hour at Caroline's on Broadway!'* She kept a firm grip on this loose cannon. The good news was that they were some-what tucked away in a corner under an upside-down stair-case.

"Who's that woman up there?" Samol carefully whis-pered to London.

"Agetha Bloodwig!" Paul blurted loudly, spitting on both of them. "Her — her saggy tits look like — like Tarzan's been swinging on em'!" Paul began.

A few people nearby turned pink, trying desperately not to laugh, with swollen cheeks and bulging eyes.

"Paul!" London yelled, gritting her teeth and yanking his arm violently.

"Well — it's fu — it's true!" he fumbled. "That sexless twat has got — something deep up her assss!" he laughed. "And you know it…"

"Stop IT!" she said, pinching his arm.

"Ac — actually...she doesn't. That's the problem!" Paul wheeled again.

The people around him couldn't hold it and burst with laughter.

"PAUL!" barked both Samol and London.

"You're gonna get sent to the dungeons if you keep it up!" London warned sternly.

He kept laughing anyway.

"It sounds like there are more rules in death than there are in life," Samol said to London.

"You have no idea," she said in a tight voice, scowling at Agetha.

"If breaking you the rules... it's pup-ishable by life," Paul said, spitting everywhere.

"What?" said Samol, wiping his neck.

"GOD, YOUR BREATH, PAUL!" London hollered, pushing his face away from hers. "What drunk nuts is trying to say is unfortunately true: Breaking the rules, here, is pun-ishable by life."

"Life? What do you mean *life?*"

"The administration could purposely assign you to live some of the cruelest of lives where you'll have incur-able diseases, you'll be raped, tortured, and abused, day and night!" she explained in a way that left Samol wondering if this had happened to her. "They could even assign you to live as something stupid, like a cactus or a — "

"Whatever that evil twit conjures up," Paul snarled, his voice sounding huskier than before.

"PAUL!!" Samol hurled. "Keep it down!"

"I hate to admit it... but he's right," London agreed quietly with some hesitation in her voice. "Bloodwig's mean streak is worse than the devil! She always yells about people not following the rules, when she doesn't follow the rules herself!"

"DO — as I say — not as I do!" said Paul, mimicking the fat tyrant.

"The cactus! Ja — dah — tell him about the cactus!" Paul instigated so quickly that he almost couldn't get the words out.

London sighed, "The cactus is one of her favorites. She used it on me six lives ago. I was reincarnated to live the life of a poisonous cactus for *two-whole-years!* There was no one to talk to or befriend. Thank God for those floods that drowned me!"

"Like-I-said," said Paul, mimicking Bloodwig's voice again, "She's-a-twit!"

Paul's growing audience snickered again a little louder than the first time.

"In 1856, she had someone reincarnated into the body of a man who was actively burning to death in a house fire. When he died, she had him sent right back into the same body and burn to death AGAIN — just-to-teach-him-a-lesson!" London explained angrily.

"What the heck??" Samol scowled harshly, beginning to hate her too.

It was apparent that everyone at the party had their fair share of horror stories about this woman, because fueled chit-chats spread like wildfire.

Agetha Bloodwig clinked her wine glass once more, this time with such force that it shattered! She gave her already too-tight-for-her-size, black blouse a vigorous tug and began:

"Another Death Day Ball has come and gone and I truly hope you all enjoyed yourselves! Newcomers, you couldn't have arrived at a more perfect time!" she began in a horribly-honeyed voice, forcing an untrustworthy grin. "I'm Agetha Bloodwig; head of Unfini—"

"Unfinished Affairs! Yes, we know who you are — Madame…Blubberworks — I mean Bloodwig!" Paul spouted.

Everyone laughed - - even those in the administration!

Agetha went pale. A cold, unhinging anger began to brew behind her piercing, green eyes.

Paul felt something slightly uncomfortable in his side. It was London punching him several times, but of course, being intoxicated has its temporary perks like — feeling little to no pain. He did, however, feel a pair of eyes staring at him; a frail, mean-looking, old man whose spiked, brown teeth looked like a rusty fence, watching him. He wore all black and had a fat, discolored mole beside his bottom lip. Samol also saw the hideous-looking man.

"All right! Trash the manners!" Agetha Bloodwig howled in her real voice, which was thick and tart. "ALL OF YOU, SHUT UP AND LISTEN! NOW!!! I own you - - ALL OF YOU!! Any screwing around while, here, in Euphod or when you get reincarnated and I will punish the hell out of you! GOT IT??"

"Yes ma'am," said the frightened Aryamites (mostly newbies).

"NOW — when you're sent to live another life, you better live it and fulfill your purpose!

NO EXCEPTIONS!

"Disabilities, disfigurements, and diseases do not dismiss you from completing your missions!" she hissed evilly. "You and your smelly, fellow Aryamites have all been sorted into each castle based on how you lived your last life — I'm sure you already know this by now," she growled. Her short-cropped, greasy, greyish-blond hair fell between the bridge of her black, pointy glasses.

"Well, also know this…I hate you. ALL OF YOU! I dream about chopping your little bodies into a thousand pieces and setting them on fire! I want nothing more than to choke you stupid, little, fricks and feed you to my fox! I HATE YOU ALLLL!!!" Bloodwig roared.

Jaws dropped. Eyes were as wide as headlights. A silent shock blanketed the crowd. No one could believe the utter vulgarity of this woman! Samol stared disbelievingly, wide-eyed at London. "I told you," London said with her eyes.

99

"I'll-be-watching-each-and-every-one-of-you!!" Bloodwig hollered as all six chins jiggled to every syllable. "When you breathe. When you don't breathe. *I-will-know*. When you eat. What you eat! *I-will-know*. When you fail, falsify, fester, or fart! When you flourish, defy my laws, or break a Vreek's heart! *I-will-KNOW!! Ignorance-is-no-excuse-for-breaking-my-laws!!!! GOT IT??"* she thundered.

"Okay!" replied many quivering voices.

"GOOD!" she snarled like a witch. "Now, where's my chocolate CHEESECAKEEEEEE!!!"

It was official; she needed to die...horribly... once and for all. Bloodwig's negative energy had a terminating effect on the soirée. Some headed back to their respective castles in poor spirits. Others stood quietly, too afraid to move or say the wrong thing, fearing her terrible wrath. "I told you she was satan," London said to Samol. "Yeah, satan's...leftovers," Paul instigated, who was still nowhere near sober.

Suddenly, the old man who'd been watching Paul this entire time realized something. In a sharp, dirty voice he yelled, *"Hey, you! You're the one who stole my whiskey, boy!"* Samol, London, and a few others were startled, but not Paul who hollered back, *"Hey, you! Kiss — my — asssss!"* and then mooned the old man!

Everyone laughed uproariously. The old man, however, didn't find it so funny and charged at them, pulling a razor from his back pocket! Samol's heart shot to his throat and then he, London, and Paul ran! The problem was that *grandpa* was fast! It was like he'd lived several past lives as an Olympic track star! The three of them scurried down a dark hallway, not knowing where it would lead them...

CHAPTER SIX

THE MAGICAL MAILROOM

"...Can you mail letters to a past life?" – Samol

*T*he noise of three terrified teenagers dashing recklessly echoed through the darkening hall. Samol jerked his head over his shoulder to see if they'd lost the old creep, only to find that he was gaining on them! They hollered as if they'd already been cut! "You just had to do that, didn't you??" London shouted over her shoulder at Paul. "Oh, shut up!" Paul shouted back, only angry that his buzz was wearing off. "Quick!" Samol hollered. "Let's hide through that door!" he said, pointing to the end of the hall. The old man and his knife were now closer! They bursted through a dingy, wooden door and quickly latched it shut behind them. Strangely, the man hadn't tried to tackle through the door.

It was completely silent.

They found themselves in a dark room with small windows along the walls letting in just a sliver of light, filled with hundreds of corpses hanging from meat-hooks!

By the windows were decaying body parts hanging from hooks of their own; eyeballs, tongues, toes, and even hearts. Their mouths fell open in horror, which soon became a ghastly, dry heave because of the stench! Any longer and they'd up-chuck the meals of their last lives!

All of a sudden, there was a terrible bang at the door! The three of them scattered and slinked between the hanging bodies, keeping as quiet as church mice. A single audible breath, one wrong move, a clumsy step would get them stabbed! A second 'BOOM' tore the door off the hinges as if it had been blown off by a bomb. The terrified teens ducked, holding their breath as the killer slowly slid through the carcasses without a trace of expression on his wrinkled face.

It looked as if the old man was familiar with this room, because he seemed to know almost every hiding place that a child might run to; inside the large, brown cabinet that leaned crookedly against the wall; or under the small, black table that was in the middle of the room. Samol couldn't believe how angry this man was. A kid stole his booze, yelled an insult, and mooned him. Was it really this serious?? Perhaps the dead had nothing else better to do — or they were just that serious about their alcohol?...

The wrinkled man slithered about the room almost too quietly. He slid through two disfigured carcasses who looked as though they were once a loving couple, because they were holding hands, facing one another. Samol, Paul, and London kept a close eye on the man, mirroring his maneuvers, doing anything not to be seen. London shot her head in Paul's direction to find him contorted, trying to hide behind a fat, bloody leg.

Unfortunately, it appeared they'd forgotten something...just above their heads were their own floating bodies! A grimacing smile painted the old man's rumpled face when he laid eyes on the floating corpse of a woman who looked as though she'd been crushed by a vehicle, hovering in the corner. He advanced swinging his knife wildly! The nearby corpses he'd mistakenly hacked fell to the ground.

"HELP!!" London screamed. Paul spotted a small rock and picked it up. He peered through a row of suspended limbs, waiting for just the right moment, hoping to have the same precision he'd had during the snake-hornet-spider attack! He hurled the stone — 'BOOM' — and the old man was blinded in his right eye! Surprisingly, this did nothing but send the psycho into a frenzy! He hollered and began swinging his knife savagely as though he were surrounded by hundreds of people who were trying to attack him. Samol hoped they could all escape during his frenzy. Instead, the old man threw a sharp, sideways glance at Paul who clumsily kicked over a pail near the cabinet.

Samol's heart couldn't possibly beat any faster. He looked for anything that could be a weapon. A rock, a pencil, a shoe — anything! As if it were almost too good to be true, leaning against the wall behind him was a wooden log the size of a baseball bat. He picked it up and slinked in between the smelly cadavers like a burglar with the log raised in the air. The old man didn't see him but London did, who was hiding behind a row of decomposing legs, gleaming darkly, ready for Samol to bash his brains out! 'BOOM!' The old man fell unconscious.

The three of them surrounded his wrinkled body. Blood began to ooze from his scalp when all of a sudden something strange happened. The blood was being sucked back into his head as if he were going to suddenly spring up and attack them!

"Uh, oh!" said London, unable to take her fear-filled eyes away from the reversing blood flow.

"What's happening??" Paul hollered.

"Let's get outta here!!" Samol screamed, tossing the log aside.

The three of them dashed for the safest way out - - a black, jagged door at the other end of the room. Samol could feel his insides racing terribly.

"That was close!" Paul sighed heavily, the last one out, slamming the door behind him.

"Well, if YOU would learn to keep your butt in your pants, we wouldn't be here!" London snipped.

"Where exactly are we?" asked Samol, studying the words above the door that read: *'mail, body, and soul.'*

They were standing in a large, bright room with thousands of envelopes that were not only in every color one could dream, but were lightly floating up towards the sky! Hundreds of wooden shelves lined the walls, stacked with thousands of these unopened letters. Some of the mail shook violently as if whatever lived inside was desperate to escape. Others floated as peacefully as a dream.

"Hey, I know this place," Paul said brightly with widening eyes. "This is Gutscreek!"

"Guts-what?" Samol asked.

"Gutscreek!" Paul repeated himself loudly, as though Samol were deaf. "It's the mail of the dead. Some of the letters are thoughts. Some are dreams. Some are even letters from past lives meant for future ones!" Paul explained almost too passionately, as though he were a postal worker in a past life.

"Whoa!" said Samol, studying a floating, blue envelope. "How does it work?"

"Well, for example," Paul cleared his throat importantly, "if you write a letter to yourself or an Aryamite you know, the message will be delivered to that person in their next life — depending on how you address it, of course."

"Wow…" Samol said softly, his eyes still swimming about the magical mailroom.

"But not all letters, or dreams, or thoughts, or memories from a past life are meant for good," Paul revealed and there was a subtle sense of caution in his voice. "Sometimes, their sole purpose is to taunt you, deliver a disease, or even a demon in the form of a powder or a potion!"

"That's lovely," said London, who'd been quiet for a while.

"Some letters are simply a distraction from the original purpose in which you were reincarnated to fulfill. Be careful what you open," Paul warned.

104

"How do you know if it's dangerous or not?" Samol asked with his eyes darting from one envelope to the next.

"By the color of the gravecard," Paul replied.

"Gravecard?"

"That's what we call letters or envelopes, here, in Euphod," Paul explained. "If you're ever unsure what's good or evil, just follow the old Euphod adage:

> 'Red is dead but yellow is mellow,
> Green gives you time and blue's good for you,
> White's for the night and black's for the day,
> If mail is transparent you must stay away!'"

"Wait, I see purple ones!" Samol hollered, pointing to the sky.

"Purple is a wild card," Paul said sternly as if he'd opened one in a past life. "It can become anything — good or bad. It usually depends on who sent it."

"I can't believe we actually found this place," London said quietly with her mouth left open after she'd stopped talking.

"...Maybe I should show my *butt* more often!" Paul mocked, rubbing his backside on her.

"Rude," she sassed, pushing him off.

Paul laughed and revealed, "This is only a portion of Euphod's mailing system; majority of it is centralized in Bridgelove."

"How do you know all this?" London asked curiously.

"A buddy of mine worked for the P.L.P.S," he replied.

"P.L.P.S?" Samol asked.

"Past Lives Postal Service."

"Oh..." Samol laughed. "Where exactly do they mail these letters to, anyway?"

"The tombstone of your last life - - Duh!" Paul affirmed sarcastically. "You've gotta have the first and last name, middle initial, birth day, and death date of the person you're sending it to."

Samol gazed about the mailroom once again. His eyes floated from one flying letter to the next, wondering why the acronym 'P.L.P.S' looked familiar. Just as he turned to Paul to ask him a question, he saw that Paul's lips were already parted as if he were going to ask Samol something, but instead he said,

"One of the privileges as an Aryamite, whether you're living on assignment or temporarily here in Euphod, is that you can always write letters to the dead!"

"Do they write back?" Samol asked eagerly.

"Of course!" Paul answered. "It may not always be an actual 'handwritten letter,' though. Sometimes, it may be a sign, even a person who will say the right thing at the right time."

"…Can you mail letters to a past life?" Samol asked hesitantly.

"It's — well…tricky," Paul said truthfully, thinking thoroughly before he spoke. "But it can be done….I think."

Samol smiled lightly as though he were secretly up to something.

Suddenly, they heard a howling noise in the far left corner of the mailroom.

"What's in that room, back there?" London pointed.

"Oh, that's — that's Tugscreek — Gutscreek's evil twin so-to-speak," Paul stuttered nervously.

"What's the difference between the two?" she asked.

"According to what my friend told me…P.L.P.S is *technically* for the living, or those who will eventually be reincarnated again. Tugscreek is for those who will stay dead for all of eternity! They can only write letters to death, itself!" Paul shivered.

"How — uh — why would anyone write a letter to death, itself?" Samol stuttered, his mind now swirling over many new, gloomy questions.

"Well, from what I've heard…" Paul began carefully, "some believe that death is *alive* and holds much power!" The words "death is alive" couldn't stop ringing in Samol's ears.

"Some, here in Euphod, actually worship death as if it's a god of its own! But Tugscreek is a dangerous medium in our world because we <u>are</u> dead. That's dealing with a death within a death and even time, itself, can die when in that realm!" Paul revealed nervously.

"Let's go in!" said London with a mischievous curiosity lurking behind her big, blue eyes.

"Are you CRAZY??" Samol yelled.

"HELL, NO!" Paul agreed, not even a half second later. "LITERALLY!"

"Oh-come-on!" London said, sounding as though she were annoyed at how boring she thought these boys were. "Who knows - - Samol, you might even learn something about your curse!"

Terror rushed over Paul and Samol like waves to an ocean. Their eyes darted between one another's as if they were trying to say, 'we're not gonna get shown up by a girl!'

London shoved them out of the way and darted for the dark, howling room. "Boys these days...such pansies!" she said to herself.

Samol and Paul swallowed their fear. Stomachs in, chests out, shoulders back, and they began walking. Above the doorway was a black, misty sign that read:

'BEWARE! THOUGHTS BECOME THINGS!'

"I forgot to warn you," said Paul, his voice quivering again. "Be careful what you think in here. Your thoughts can turn into living things, either right inside or in a future life." They were getting closer and closer to the entrance, hesitantly putting one foot in front of the other. The howling room began to sound more like a deadly twister. Samol was listening hardest of the three and noticed that it was actually the sound of trapped souls screaming for mercy! It quickly grew deafening! Samol covered his ears and dropped to the ground.

"What's wrong??" Paul screamed, hunched over him.

"I can't…I can't go in THERE!" Samol hollered.

If the howling got any louder, it would rupture Samol's eardrum!

He heard many voices cry:

"DEATH, I'M SORRY! GIVE-ME-ONE-MORE-CHANCEEEE!"

"NO, PLEASE! NOT MY BOY!!"

"Dear *Death*, we are friends. I long to reign with you."

"FIRE!! HELPPPP!!!!!"

Samol was the only one who heard these terrible voices. To Paul and London, the room sounded like nothing more than a light wind rustling through the trees on a summer night. Samol tried to crawl away, but something invisible had grabbed him and began pulling him further into the room! He dug his fingernails into the ground, screaming awfully, trying to tear free! The vortex of voices continued pulling him closer! However, Paul and London couldn't see or hear any of this because they were distracted by something bright and made of fire, glistening in a light at the very center of Tugscreek. The figure, which looked like a fiery ram, spewed two misty figures from its sides that they couldn't see, but Samol could.

Hovering inches from London's face was the first figure; a menacing, black unicorn with red eyes and teeth made of fire! It snarled as though it were going to attack her, but didn't for some reason. Inches from Paul's neck was a hovering, five-headed viper with wings just as big as the horns on its back! It, too, looked as though it were going to attack, but didn't. Paul and London gazed in a daze peacefully at the fiery ram.

Samol had been dragged to the center of the chamber where it was all of a sudden very peaceful, as though he were in the eye of a hurricane. And then he saw her; a beautiful woman wearing a royal blue gown. This woman, whoever she was, looked almost angelic. Her aura, alone, seemed to melt away all of his troubles for just a moment.

108

Her thick, black curls draped over her brown shoulders down to the sway of her back. She had a smile from The Heavens and her eyes had a kindness in them that could not be experienced in life, or even while dead. They were the brightest, amber eyes Samol had ever seen.

In a soft, celestial voice she spoke: "One...four... five...you've done so well, my dove." Samol stared up at her, mesmerized by her ethereal beauty, but heavily confused too. 'Why is she counting? And did she just call me "her dove"?' he wondered. She spoke again, a little louder this time: "The lives ahead of you will not be easy, and every one of them will be over quicker than a dream, once you understand. You have it within you to be righteous, whom are never forsaken. I love you."

Before Samol could even digest the woman's words, she was shredded into a thousand pieces by the worsening winds. Terrifying voices howled in a deadly whisper:

"Amir - - Amir!"

"AHHHH!!" Samol screamed awfully.

"What's happening??" Paul shouted, his eyes were ripped away from the fiery ram by Samol's scream.

"We have to leave! NOW!" yelled London, grabbing the two of them as if she suddenly knew what would happen if they stayed.

They dashed for the exit, but someone was standing in the doorway. It appeared to be a man…an angry man holding some sort of weapon. They couldn't tell if it was an ax? A club? Actually, it looked more like a…log! The old man!!

His blind, scabby eye was covered in thick pus that dripped into a puddle on the ground. He crunched together his rotted teeth. They were trapped and just knew it was over! The old man charged at them when suddenly the floating body of a young girl appeared behind him. 'BOOM!' He was bashed over the head again, yet this time, with a brick! He fell to the ground and behind him stood a girl with a large, frizzy braid.

109

"Leanna!" Paul shouted, who'd fallen to the ground, coiled in the fetal position, actually happy to see her. "You saved our lives — I mean — our second lives — I mean —"

"I know what you mean...you can thank me later," she winked, dropping the brick to the ground.

"How did you find us??" London asked, still breathing heavily.

"I'm sure even Vreeks on Earth could hear the three of you screaming!" she said. "Besides, I could spot that cute butt from a mile away," she said, looking at Paul's backside, which was facing her on the ground.

"Will you two <u>get</u> a room, <u>get</u> it on, and <u>get</u> it over with!" London hollered disgustedly.

Samol laughed inaudibly, which sounded like nothing more than a heavy breath under a small smirk.

"Oh, no!" Leanna screamed, pointing to the sky in terror. Everyone's eyes followed her finger as though they were bewitched by it and found their floating corpses oozing from the nose and mouth! What Paul forgot to mention was that Tugscreek sped up time!

"We've got to get to our next lives! NOW!!" London screamed.

Paul leapt to his feet and the four of them stepped over the unconscious old man, who now seemed to have more wrinkles on his face than even a few minutes ago. Hurriedly, they raced back to the Zebrastone common room, dashing through the halls as if they were being chased by wild dogs. After ten minutes of sprinting up, down, around, and behind several winding staircases that weren't even there before the Death Day Ball, they arrived to find hundreds of Aryamites chatting nervously in the Zebrastone sanctuary. Samol wondered why everyone looked so scared. Their nervousness was making him nervous! Had Bloodwig terrorized them for laughing at her during the Death Day Ball? Did she have someone else burned to death??

CHAPTER SEVEN

REINCARNATION PREPARATION

*"Onyx, gems, jaspers, golds, are not as loved as priceless souls.
I'll live my life until it's time to leave the past ones all behind!"* ~
Sir James Waldenblotts

*P*aul seemed most terrified of the four. His
eyes shifted to Leanna's, who still clung onto his arm like an
annoying mosquito. London looked at the two of them and
rolled her eyes which fell onto Samol, who was gauging how
he should feel based on how calm or nervous his friends
were. Not much of a confidence boost! Suddenly, a serious,
middle-aged woman appeared. She was almost too thin with
silver eyes that were just as sharp as her spiky, black hair.
Her masculine walk and unwomanly mannerisms left many
wondering…

The woman began, "I am Arabis Bestow, death's life coach for the castle of Zebrastone. I don't repeat myself so listen to me carefully!" she ordered. Her voice was toneless and somewhat deep, as though she'd been a smoker for at least ten of her past lives.

"In the maze, you will be able to see yourself in your last life. You'll be able to see what you did, how you did it, when you did it, and where you did it," she said, sounding as though she'd been giving this speech since the beginning of time, and wanted to quit after day two.

"Your objective is to find out why you did what you did and WHERE YOU SCREWED UP!" she hollered as her eyes went crossed and she began choking, laughing, and crying all at the same time!

Her sudden outburst left everyone stunned as though they'd witnessed someone get run over by a bus! Samol turned stiffly towards London and Paul, hoping they would say something - - anything. They, of course, weren't even paying attention, because they'd heard this speech before many times and were used to her bizarre antics. Before he could even finish his own thoughts Arabis bellowed:

"DON'T BE DUMB!"

The room stayed quiet. Not even a wall creaked, which happened more often than not.

"You make mistakes in life for a reason and you are not to repeat them! UNDERSTAND??" She roared.

"Yes," said everyone, thinking she were schizophrenic.

"Good," she said sternly, walking around the room, shoulders swaying heavily from side to side. "Now — there are three rules you must obey when reviewing your life!" she ordered, holding out three of the boniest fingers Samol had ever seen. "Rule number one - - DON'T GET LOST! Many of you will be going back in time. A select few are going into the future and it will be nearly impossible for Euphod to track down what country, time zone, century, or millennium you're in! DO NOT GET LOST!"

A few faces fell ill-looking. A murmur of concerns began to spread throughout the room. Samol looked at his friends, choked with a million and one horrible thoughts, wondering what could go wrong. He remembered nothing about his past life and was bound to get lost!

"SHUT UP!" Arabis howled manically.

No one was sure if she were talking to them or the voices in her head, but the nervous chatter quieted anyhow.

"Rule number two - - YOU CANNOT BE SEEN OR HEARD! Not only will you be dead, whilst amongst Vreeks, but you will exist in a dimension within a dimension. If a Vreek spots you, to them you may appear as a daemalix (you'll soon learn what that is) and it-could-petrify-them!" she said, sounding somewhat like Bloodwig. "If said criminal offense occurs, you very well could be tried by the Euphod Court of Law and sentenced to life as a Euphod slave, a prisoner, or even a final death!" she said sternly as her eyes moved from one person's to the next. "God forbid Bloodwig finds out about it..." she mumbled under her breath.

Samol was growing more and more worried and so were the others around him. At least he had his best friends near his side. Arabis paused for a second as if she were thinking. Placing both hands behind her bony back, she paced with her eyes fixed to the floor, as though she were waiting for someone in her head to give her permission to speak.

And then, she spoke:

"You know those times in life when you swear you saw something out of the corner of your eye...and you simply dismissed it as 'your eyes playing tricks on you?' Those were most likely Aryamites diving out of the way to not be seen!" she said. Nearly every eye whirled to the sky as though they were reflecting on a time when they'd seen this happen. Samol, too, tried to think back, but couldn't remember anything.

113

"The third and final rule - - DO NOT GET KILLED! As you all already know by now, just because you're already dead does not mean that you're exonerated from dying a final death! If you get yourself killed (again), you will be trapped in a death within a death and there's nothing we can do to bring you back! Understand??"

"Yes…" the crowd said seriously.

Samol gulped, hoping that the murderer of his last life wouldn't be lurking in a bush or behind a corner waiting to kill him again.

Arabis straightened a few spikes that had fallen over her face. "Are there any questions?" she asked loudly.

A little, African-American boy, who looked no older than seven with not a blotch or blemish found anywhere on his body, raised his hand.

"Yes?" Arabis said gently.

"Are we able to see each other in the maze or only ourselves?"

"Excellent question. For those who didn't hear him, he asked: 'Will you be able to see each other in the maze?'" Arabis repeated.

"Yes, you can!" she smiled. "You can see and hear your fellow Aryamites, but I'd recommend keeping all chit-chat to a minimum. You are still racing against time, here. Anymore questions?"

A teenage, Asian girl, who looked as if she'd been mauled to death by some sort of wild animal, raised her hand. Everyone could tell Arabis felt sorry for her, because she clutched her thin hand to her ashy, withered décolletage and said sweetly,

"Yes, my dear?"

"You said that we're still *racing against time.* Is this referring to time inside the maze, here, in Euphod? Or time in our last life?"

"Ahh! Good question, young lady," Arabis said proudly. "For those who didn't hear her, she asked: 'Is time inside the maze going to affect real time, here, in Euphod or

114

time in your last life?' - - "*It affects both!*" Arabis answered. "As you already know, you have, give or take, a month before your body fully decomposes. Going through the maze can alter time depending on two things: Where you lived during your last life and how much your body has already decomposed. Very good question! Anymore?" she asked with her eyes swimming through the crowd.

Aside from a few shifty, nervous looks no one said a word.

Samol looked sideways at his three friends. London and Leanna were both fidgeting with their hair and Paul was licking his thumb to rub a Whiskey stain from his plaid shirt. They still weren't listening.

Arabis stood almost militantly in front of two tall, double doors that were as high as an office tower and wide enough to fit a house through. Samol suddenly realized that this was the door that once had the shattered mirrors in which he saw himself three different ways. Strangely, the mirrors were gone! However, his mind was racing with too many things to even care. Arabis ripped open the great doors at once and before everyone shone a large, silvery mist at the starting line of the maze. The crowd squinted greatly, trying desperately to see or hear anything from their last life — a foot, a voice, a tree - - anything. Yet, all they saw was the coiled, black shrubbery around the edges of the doors.

"Everybody, stand here," Arabis ordered strictly, pointing to the dividing point on the ground where the Zebrastone common room ended and the maze began.

"You will have until I blow my whistle," she said, holding a tiny, black whistle that hung around her neck.

"That small thing??" said a little, blonde boy.

"Oh, put a cork in it, Fletcher!" Arabis said, flexing her shoulders.

She placed the miniature whistle between her tight, wrinkled lips and blew, which sounded squeaky and mouse-like. The little boy chuckled and so did she, for different reasons, of course. Off they went!

A sudden burst of deafening screams filled the air. They were all seeing and hearing how they had died, *backwards*. In front of Samol, however, the mist that once shown as a gentle silver had blackened and began to swirl violently!

He backed away thinking that it would turn into a twister like Tugscreek! By now, Paul, London, and Leanna were already deep in the maze and he couldn't call for help! Samol heard his last life happening; the murder, creeping through the lonely shack, and even crunching through the scary graveyard where he'd first awakened. The memories mulled over him like a train to its tracks. Yet, he still saw nothing. Suddenly, there was a voice.

It sounded like an angry, beast-like creature whispering, "Amir - - Amir!" And then another sound followed; the sound of thousands of people screaming terribly as though they were burning alive! Samol's heart thumped through his chest! "What's happening?" he panicked aloud, "WHAT IS THIS??" And then, there was total silence. The black mist left Samol standing right where he started - - alone.

He tried to remember something -- anything from his past lives. Yet, he couldn't. From afar, he caught a glimpse of Arabis who appeared tired and rather irritable at the moment. She was flipping through a glowing, silver book that was several hundred pages thick. Samol walked briskly towards her, noticing that the front and back of the book had gold, cursive letters that read, *'Life is but a second.'* Although he was now right next to her, she ignored him, pretending to be busier than she really was, squinting harder than normal, flipping through pages faster, the same thing we all do when we don't want to be bothered. He bravely parted his lips and said,

"Sorry to disturb you, Arabis, but I ju—"

"That's MADAME Bestow!" she barked without even looking up.

"Sorry," he said gently. "It's just that when I was trying to review my last life in the maze, I saw nothing but a... black...fog," he said, struggling to describe what he saw.

"Impossible!" she said coldly, still pretending to read.

"Honestly, I couldn't see anything!" he said, shocked at how rude she was. "Bu — but I heard everything," he said, almost as though he were trying to prove himself.

Her silvery eyes shot up from the book. She glared through him as though he were trying to pull a fast one. Arabis loudly slammed the book shut. Dust shot in the air and so did Samol!

"What are you talking about?" she asked hoarsely, her eyes still squinting as if she were getting angrier by the second.

"I could hear everything...but saw nothing," he said, looking to the sky trying to remember every detail. "And some...creature...kept calling me 'Amir!'"

"Look, little boy! I've been reincarnated one hundred fourteen times, myself, and I've never been called by a different name once I returned back to Euphod. That-doesn't-happen!" she yelled, stressing every syllable of her last three words. "You see this??" she hollered, holding up the glowing, silver book. "This book holds all birth certificates for every Zebrastone Aryamite's next life. I know every single one of them and not one has ever been called by another name... especially by some *creature* that they can't even see. That-doesn't-happen!!"

Samol wanted to punch her in the mouth for being so unnecessarily rude. He began noticing that this 'being rude for no reason' thing was a pattern with these dead people! He once again tried to explain:

"In my last life, Madame Bestow," he began weakly, "I had no memory and I —"

"If you had no memory, how can you be sure that 'said creatures' were even talking to you?" she asked condescendingly. He froze for a second, wondering if she were perhaps right. But what was her friggin problem??

"I'm telling you, I know what I heard!" he shouted angrily.

"Don't you raise your voice at me!" she barked.

117

Samol froze wide-eyed.

"Besides, the only way that someone or something could ever call you out of your name was if you — "

Arabis froze mid-sentence as though she'd witnessed a car crash.

"Is if I what??" Samol asked desperately.

Arabis fell into a frightful silence. She all of a sudden placed the black whistle to her lips and said, "Cover your ears," and blew. It was an unpleasant shock to Samol's covered ears that this time, the whistle sounded like a hundred horns, loud enough for an entire city to hear! The entire maze crumbled as if it had been bombed! The ground, right before Samol's eyes, had magically transfigured itself into a brick, maroon trail that led to a large black and white arbor, which was upheld by several pillars in a circle. Above the arbor was a powerful beam of bright blue lightning that hovered inches from the top of its open, arched dome.

All of the Aryamites began flooding back towards Arabis with confused looks. Samol must've heard "what the heck is going on?" at least fifty times. When he was finally able to get a good look at the first thirty, or so, he saw many faces looking as though they were painted with the torment of what they'd figured out in their last lives. Others desperately wanted to go back. Two minutes, or so, had passed when Samol heard two recognizable voices:

"Like I told you — we were married!" said a voice that sounded like London's.

"And like I told YOU, he-was-a-Vreek!" said a voice that sounded just like Paul's.

And Samol finally saw them, glad to see that things were back to the way they were — Paul and London arguing, Leanna clinging to Paul's arm, and London giving the two of them a mean, side-eye every three or four seconds.

"You just couldn't stand that I found love in my last life and you were as lonely as the dust beneath my toes, boo boo!" London sassed.

"Oh, shut up! Your husband was a cross-eyed troll!"

"A crossed-eyed troll with better vision and more drive in one life than you had in twelve!" London hollered.

Paul didn't say anything. He looked rather pathetic, actually.

"Why did Arabis end the maze so early, anyway? London asked. "Something must be wrong."

"Darn right, something's wrong!" Leanna agreed. "I was just gettin' to the part, in my last life, where I was peeking at my cute neighbor!"

No one said anything for a few seconds.

"You've never had any, have you?" London jabbed.

"Had any what?" Leanna asked.

London shook her head.

Before Paul could even think of anything to say, he noticed Samol standing by his lonesome. His mouth fell open and his eyes grew big under his downturned, blonde eyebrows. Paul couldn't even form the words, "Why is he by himself?" Arabis stood seriously, hands placed at her hips, slightly slouched, shoulders flexed and said loudly,

"Welcome back! I trust by now you know that the maze was cut shorter than usual."

"Uhhh, yeah..." said a few annoyed Aryamites.

"It seems that we had an unusual circumstance," Arabis said, giving a tapering, sideways glance at Samol. "We must get you all reincarnated to your next lives - - immediately!" Nervous chatter began in the Zebrastone common room.

"There are a few things you'll need to know as an Aryamite preparing for your next life," she said, her voice sounding a little tauter than before. To some, she even sounded a bit like that fat, goblet-shaped, tyrant Bloodwig! She began quickly:

"First -- As a Zebrastone Aryamite, I have no control over who or what you'll be in your next life. You could be reincarnated as anyone or anything, with the exception of an acclaimed deity, of course. How you live, the hearts you touch, your talents, and what you learn is most important."

119

Samol was tempted with the idea of coming back to life as a big, strong man or someone in power so that he could find his killer and teach him a lesson. Or what if he came back as something stupid...like a plant, or a piece of fruit, or a booger! He wondered if it was even possible to come back as such things. Arabis spoke sharply again:

"Secondly -- When you're living on assignment, you are NOT to tell anyone, especially a Vreek, that you've been reincarnated. Informing Vreeks of our world is an unforgivable sin that will not go unpunished!"

Samol suddenly felt as though he'd been punched in the stomach. What if he came back to life as someone with Tourette's and blurted, "I'm an Aryamite from Euphod!" London, who could sense him worrying with endless terrible thoughts, put her arm around his shoulder and said with her eyes, 'Just relax.'

"Lastly -- With each life that you live, every part of your physical being will be — well — should be different," she said carefully, as though there had been a few mishaps in the past. "All except one feature, that is - - your eyes. Your eyes will stay with you throughout every last life you will live until you draw your very last breath," she said, dimming her own eyes with an almost sinister smirk that left a few people untrusting of her.

Before Samol could even allow himself to be divided with a million and one thoughts again, Arabis spoke loudly, "When you awaken into your new life, the first thing you must do is search your whole body for our scar."

"A SCAR!!" cried at least thirty people.

"Once you see it, you will know exactly what it means and how you must govern yourself in that life," Arabis said importantly. "It will be the first clue to your purpose in that life."

"But how will we just…know?" asked a sweet-looking, little girl towards the front of the crowd.

"Trust me, you'll know," Arabis winked with a half charismatic, half condescending grin.

"What do the scars look like?" shouted a faceless voice from the back of the room.

"The scar will always be the emblem of the castle in which you were previously sorted, here, in Euphod. In our case, it'll be the Zebrastone…and before you ask, 'No the scar won't hurt' — at least it shouldn't," said Arabis, raising an eyebrow, peeking at Samol once again as if she were concerned that his scar might harm him.

Samol fidgeted nervously. In the middle of the room someone raised their hand.

"Yes…?" Arabis said slowly. The way she said, 'yes' was long and almost too drawn out. Her voice raised towards the end of the three-letter-word, sounding half confused and half annoyed that someone would dare raise their hand when she was in a rush.

Every neck suddenly craned to the middle of the room to see who she was talking to. They locked eyes onto, what was to some, a familiar-faced, red-headed boy, approximately eight years of age who lowered his hand once he saw that every eye was on him. Samol, too, had seen him somewhere, but couldn't remember where exactly.

"Don't we get to choose which life we relive?" he asked, speaking with the articulation of a forty-year-old newscaster. "Let's say, for example, if we wanted to go back to a previous life?"

"Ahhh!" said Arabis with a long pause, giving him a rare half smile that pushed her lips tightly to one side. "We've got a returning Aryamite, I see! To answer your question, 'technically' you can. However, only those who were sorted into the castle of Bridgelove have that privilege." Many necks spun around, waiting for him to reply.

"Okay…" the little boy said softly, in an almost too-cool-manner for a child who didn't get what he asked for.

Many people in the room, including Samol and London, wanted to know who this boy was. Paul was too busy trying to pull Leanna off of his arm and probably missed the whole conversation.

"When I call your name, you will step forward under the Zebrastone arbor," Arabis said largely. "You will say the universal Euphod reincarnation enchantment:

'Onyx, gems, jaspers, golds, are not as loved as priceless souls. I'll live my life until it's time to leave the past ones all behind!'

The sound of nearly a hundred people attempting to repeat the incantation sprinkled all over the room. "Onyx gold — Priceless life — Leave the soul — Jasper's behind." They quickly gave up and began making immature, fart noises, messing it up on purpose. Arabis shook her head irritably.

"You don't have to remember it —" she hollered. "I'll say it with you when it's your turn."

The silly sounds tapered away.

"This incantation must be taken seriously! It is used as one of Euphod's seven universal enchantments of reincarnation," Arabis said sternly, the frown lines between her eyebrows now very wrinkled.

Samol's nerves choked him. 'What'll happen if I say it wrong? What'll happen if I say it right and my next life is still bad??' he wondered wildly. He reverted back to the tempting idea that he would come back as someone powerful, but maybe he'd use his power for good, not evil. Arabis cracked open the silver book, which had been stowed under her left arm. A powerful gust whirled from its pages as though it were alive. She coughed loudly and rubbed her eyes. A few seconds after that she parted her lips and called out,

"JEFFREY JOHN BLACK!"

A nervous, frizzy-haired, little boy, who looked no older than six, missing both front teeth, stepped to the center of the arbor.

"You will be living as Topfer Autenburg; a wealthy, German genius who has engineered the sciences of time, mathematics, nature, and music together as one," she explained. "I must warn you — you will be loved by some and hated by many. I find such things tend to happen when people who think ahead of their time come along."

The frightened, little boy studied the beam of blue lightning that swirled above his head. Samol watched intensely. In a voice just above a whisper he quivered,

"On — onyx, g — gems, ja—"

"No! No! NO!" Arabis roared. "With conviction! You're going to be a GENIUS in your next life! And WEALTHY! It's a far cry from your last life where you got beaten up every day!" she said, lacking any regard for his privacy. "BE PROUD!" she hollered with her chin up, shoulders straight, flattening her already-too-thin stomach.

Her words seemed to give him a boost in confidence - - better do it now before it wore off, the boy thought. He stood up straight and proudly called out, *"Onyx, gems, jaspers, golds, are not as loved as priceless souls! I'll live my life until it's time to leave the past ones all behind!"* - - 'BOOM!' - - There was a deafening sound and he was gone in an instant. Many, including Arabis, turned their faces away. Samol stared wide-eyed at Paul and London (almost messing his pants).

"Does it hurt?" Samol whispered worriedly.

"It's only a first…maybe second degree burn," Paul answered.

"Stop IT!" London hollered, punching him in the stomach. "No, Samol. It doesn't hurt. It's like being kissed by an angel."

Samol sighed heavily. He, too, wanted to give Paul a good punch, who was still holding his stomach and laughing at the same time.

"DELIVIA JANE O'CONNER!" Arabis called out.

A stoic-looking, middle-aged woman with curly, red hair emerged. Truth be told, she looked like a cousin to London. Arabis sighed as if she were a doctor about to deliver horrible news and explained:

"You will be living as Nadia Wae Crimpston, a woman who just mysteriously died after being committed to an insane asylum. For some reason, Euphod…" she paused, flipping through the pages in the book as if she were suddenly confused, but then found what she was looking for and continued, "Has matched your soul with hers. I'm not at liberty to tell you why - - only that you're meant to change something *calculated* that Nadia has done. She was committed fourteen times and has escaped sixteen (have fun figuring that out). She was violent, homicidal, suicidal, and had nine warrants out for her arrest…"

Samol felt his toes go numb. He worried that his next life would be as difficult as hers.

"There are only two people as of yet," said Arabis, looking at her thin, bare wrist as though a watch was there, "who know she's dead and I'll be damned if I let it get to three!" she said hurriedly, pointing to the center of the great arbor.

Delivia put on a brave face and stepped up.

"On the plus side, she's very-very-VERY gorgeous from what I see," said Arabis, raising an eyebrow. "Remember, you are strong enough to handle such a terrible life, or else you wouldn't be living it."

Arabis's last words of wisdom gave her the confidence boost she needed. Delivia repeated the enchantment, "Onyx, gems, jaspers, golds, are not as loved as priceless souls! I'll live my life until it's time to leave the past ones all behind!"

There was a terribly bright light for a fraction of a second and she, too, was gone.

"ALEXANDER IGOR MIKOVA!" Arabis said quickly.

A pale, black-haired, blue-eyed gentleman with a strong jawline stepped forward.

"The usual," Arabis said to him, lacking any emotion whatsoever.

Alexander snarled.

"You'll stop living lives with the same exact problems once you learn to accept responsibility for your actions and *learn-to-forgive*!" Arabis blustered back as if they'd talked about this a hundred times before.

Alexander sulked and stomped to the center of the arbor. He shouted the incantation angrily and instead of being shot upward like everyone before him, he was shot off diagonally followed by three loud, painful-sounding fire bolts! 'BAM! BOOM! POW!'

"What just happened??" Samol asked, covering his ears.

"I don't know!" Paul said honestly.

"That's...not good," said Leanna.

"DRISCOL PHILLIPS!" Arabis continued, not even caring.

A tall, caramel-complected boy with green eyes stepped forward. He stood strong as though many past lives had toughened him up. Arabis explained,

"You will be living your next life as Sean Myles and I, personally, am so sorry," she said with her eyes glued to the large book and her mouth was agape.

"What is it?" he asked nervously.

Arabis revealed, "You will come back to life as someone who's just been beaten to death...filthy pigs!" she snarled her last two words under her breath. "You will be an impoverished, biracial, gay man, living in Georgia in 1949." Every obstacle will be stacked against you," she said, picking her eyes up from the book, making sure he was acutely aware of her last sentence.

125

"Through your many hardships, however, you will prove that being gay is not a choice; as you will struggle with it all throughout this life!" she said. "You will experience hunger, racism, and discrimination from blacks for being "too white" and whites for being "too black" — let's not talk about the immense hatred you'll receive because of your sexual desires," she said pensively. "Remember, you are to learn from this life. Leave people better than how you found them, even when it will seem impossible! I will see you in twenty-six days, Driscol."

Not knowing what his treacherous future held, the light-skinned, black boy faithfully stood at the center of the arbor and said the incantation. In an instant, he was beamed off. Samol, along with the remaining Aryamites who'd been paying close attention were growing nervous, because they noticed that the lives seemed to be getting harder and harder.

"LEANNA ROSEWRIGHT!" Arabis called.

Finally, Paul's arm was free. He gave it a good shake as if Leanna was clasping it so tightly that it had fallen asleep. London rolled her eyes, trying not to laugh. Samol felt almost unbalanced when he realized that their group of four had returned to its original trio. He swallowed heavily knowing that he, London, and Paul were getting closer to the chopping block. Leanna stood nervously at the center of the arbor. Her bony knees were visibly shaking. Her hands were rattling more than her teeth were chattering.

"You will live your next life as Dasha Ninascova," Arabis said, lifting an eyebrow as if someone she knew had a run-in with this *Dasha*. "…She's a fraudulent, Russian woman who was just shot to death because of her many acts of extortion." Leanna stiffened her neck as if she, herself, had been shot. "In life as Dasha, you will face; three sexual assaults, twelve cases of physical abuse, and two horrendous diseases. Yet, you will live surprisingly longer than expected for someone living a life this hard," Arabis said, studying the
126

page for a second time, squinting as if she couldn't believe what she was reading. "It appears that in this life, you're meant to learn six things that will be used for your future lives. Wild, wacky, and wired with passion will become you, my dear. By the end of this life, you will be stained with the eternal fear of heights," she said with almost a flicker of fear in her voice. "Control yourself!"

Leanna gulped heavily, giving her three friends a swift glance. She closed her eyes tightly like she'd been pinched, parted her lips, and recited the incantation. In an instant, she was gone.

"TIMOTHY STOUT!" Arabis called out.

Who stepped forward was a salt-and-pepper haired, middle-aged man who looked wise at first glance, judging by the way he carried himself. Samol could've sworn he saw him at the Death Day Ball. The man and Arabis exchanged smiles as though they were long-time friends.

"You'll be reincarnated as a seventy-seven year old man," Arabis said gently, not even reading from the book anymore, talking to him rather casually as though she was aware that he knew how this whole 'reincarnation thing' worked.

"He and his wife just died in a car crash and the moment you awaken, *the car will still be on fire! Get yourself out immediately!* I gotta tell ya, Tim, this is when the real trouble begins..."

"Both of your children have died and you've lost all your memory to Alzheimer's disease. I wish that there was something I could do to change this," she said softly, frantically flipping through the pages again as if she had the power to trade the lives of others like nothing more than baseball cards. "I'll see you in fifty-seven Wednesdays," she said. Timothy, who seemed oddly calm, kept a slight grin on his face the entire time. He said the incantation and was whisked away at once.

All of a sudden, Samol got shoved by someone standing behind him. The blur of a blonde boy rushed by him, racing wildly towards Arabis. 'Paul couldn't even say excuse me?' Samol thought angrily. 'What's he up to anyhow?' Paul whispered something in her ear. She suddenly went paler than she already was and began skipping wildly through the pages in her book. Both Samol and London looked at each other, utterly confused.

"LONDON NOEL LUCAS!" Arabis blurted, fumbling to find her words first.

"What did you say to her??" London whispered intensely when Paul came running back.

"Nothing, just go!" he said.

London walked hesitantly, shooting Paul a mistrustful look over her shoulder every few seconds.

"Six!" Arabis blurted confusedly.

"What?"

"I mean…you'll be reincarnated as a six-year-old boy attending a school for the gifted," Arabis corrected herself. It was evident that she was still rattled by whatever Paul had told her.

"The school, however, is corrupt and dangerous. In this life, keep your mouth shut…eyes and ears open at all times?" she said, questioning what was written in the book. "I think you're meant to see something that no one else has."

London's eyes darted between Arabis and Paul, trying to catch one of them in a lie or a flicker of deceit. She didn't trust either of them, but began anyway.

"Onyx, gems, jaspers, golds…." London paused as though she'd forgotten the incantation, but then continued, *"I'll see the truth when lies unfold. The secret spirits are bad if bright and'll burn in hell both day and night!"* The deafening bolt shot to the sky as a powerful purple, knocking everyone to the ground. Nearly everyone was temporarily deafened! Some were nearly blinded! London was gone.

"LONDON!" Samol hurled fearfully. "What happened to her??"

"WHAT??" Paul shouted, who couldn't hear him.

"WHAT HAPPENED TO LONDON??"

"I-don't-know!!" Paul screamed, who'd read his lips.

The crowd stood to their feet, hands still clasping their ears. Arabis screamed at the top of her lungs, "Settle down! SETTLE DOWN!" which sounded like a mere muffle to many. "There is nothing we can do about her! Truth be told, if she knows that incantation, she knows enough to take care of herself up there!"

Arabis re-opened the book and rustled through the pages. For a few seconds, she stared confusedly at whatever was before her.

"Victoria?... No, wait!... SAMOL....DOSCOW!" she hollered, still barely able to hear herself.

Samol's heart sank to his crotch. His knees buckled. Stomach evaporated. It was apparent that Arabis still couldn't understand what she was reading. She flipped the book upside-down. Sideways, even. Diagonally. Left to right! Face down!

"What's wrong?" Samol asked, hoping that whatever was bothering her was nothing more than perhaps a few spelling errors.

"I can't...I can't seem to read anything about your next life," she said. "Everything on your next life's birth certificate keeps...moving."

Samol was too afraid to mention that his death certificate was doing the same thing.

"The only name that I can read is...Victoria," she said.

"Am I going to be a woman in my next life?" he asked sheepishly.

"I don't...know," she hesitated, still flipping the book around recklessly. "I don't think I've ever seen this before."

129

Samol fixed his eyes to the floor, wondering if this, too, had something to do with his curse. He began mentally preparing himself for a life that may not be the greatest when suddenly, Arabis gave him hope...

"One hundred thirty-nine days!" she blurted with a bright face.

"What does that m–" Samol began to ask when it dawned on him.

"I'm sorry, Samol," she said, filled with the utmost condolences. "But, it could be for the best. Life will never give you more than you can handle. Good luck, Samol."

He headed towards the arbor way and each step felt like he were trudging through mud. 'Well, one hundred-thirty nine days beats Driscol's twenty-six' he thought. Samol parted his lips and began, *"Onyx, gems, jaspers, golds, are not as loved as priceless souls! I'll live my life until it's time to leave the past ones all behind!"* Quicker than he imagined, he was engulfed from head to toe by a blinding bolt that felt like being caressed by a wild angel. He was gone. Samol Doscow left Euphod not knowing if he'd awaken as a man or woman, black or white, a plant or a booger, or if he'd awaken at all.

CHAPTER EIGHT

A NEW BEGINNING

"You are two inches away from me setting you on fire, boy."
– Victoria

*S*amol opened his eyes. He was breathing heavi-
er by the second because he noticed that he couldn't see or
move. Darkness was around him and his arms and legs were
pinned down by something! Air seemed to be growing scarc-
er by the second! Now that he was living in the flesh, he was
suddenly bombarded with every humanly desire that seemed
to be just waiting on pause from his last life: thirst, hunger,
and tiresome being the three strongest. Even the subtle desire
for freedom, that we as human beings have, began to settle in.
Seconds after that, a sudden understanding of math, music,
physics, and time seemed to whirl into his head as though a
magic spell was placed on his mind that increased his IQ in
under three seconds! If only he could use his heightened IQ
to wiggle free from whatever had him pinned...

"HELP!" he shouted. "Somebody, ANYBODY! PLEASE! I CAN'T BREATHE!" By the sound of his own voice, he could tell that he was most likely a prepubescent boy. He'd mentally checked that off of his list and thought to himself, 'Well, I'm still a boy in this life.' And then, there was a noise.

Vicious-sounding, quick footsteps that sounded like they were coming from an upper floor thumped towards him; the kind you might hear when you've pissed your parents off and they were coming to get you! Samol didn't know if he were in a torture chamber, the basement of a pedophile's candy shop, or if this was all just a sick prank and once he could see, he'd be staring at the smiling faces of Leanna, London, and Paul again who would scream, "GOTCHA!!" Suddenly, it was ripped from his head - - a plastic bag that must've been used to suffocate him. Whoever tore it off his head, did it with such force that it nearly snapped his neck!

"OUCH!!!" he hollered, hoping that this person was there to rescue him.

Trouble struck yet again when he realized that he still could not see.

"WHAT THE HELL??" shrilled a woman with a despicable voice, staring wildly at the boy tied to a chair in the basement of her house, who was surprised to see him alive.

"I can't — I can't see!" he screamed, still trying to wiggle free.

"Ryan?? How are you...alive??" screamed the thin, unattractive, gapped-tooth, black-haired woman, examining him as though seeing him alive was a sick joke from God.

"Why can't I see??" he hollered again.

"What happened to your eyes??" she screamed, grabbing a handful of his now blonde, curly locks, violently yanking his head back. "They used to be blue!!"

"I can't s—" he froze. Her last five words gave him a terrible shock. He suddenly remembered that Arabis told him that all Aryamite's eyes would remain the same in every life that they live.

132

"What...color are they now?" he asked timidly.

An abrupt, bony fist pounded him in the face, fracturing his nose!

"OUCH!!" he screamed. "What did I do??"

"Don't you EVER back talk me, you little, ugly, degenerate, TWIT!" she thundered.

His blood splattered onto the walls! Oddly, within seconds it evaporated into nothing. The woman didn't see this happen.

"I'm not sure what color my eyes are in this li—" he stopped himself, because he remembered that he mustn't reveal anything about Euphod, or being an Aryamite to Vreeks. "Am I blind?" he asked, almost choking back tears as though he'd been sentenced to an eternity in Vypercoff.

"Yes," she smiled evilly. One of the straps from her baggy, jean overalls fell from her shoulder. "You're blind, you've always been blind — you'll always be blind, you little, visionless twit!" she insulted. "What does it matter to you what color your eyes are, anyhow??"

"I'm sorry!" he said, suddenly afraid that he would get hit again. "You said...they were different, that's all."

"I don't think I like your tone," she said as she began circling him like a bully. "Not only are your eyes some weird hazel...or honey...or some ugly color, but you're more...bold now," she paused as though she were reflecting back on the boy who was once Ryan, still circling him imperiously.

Samol knew this wasn't good. He grew worried that she would figure out that he'd been reincarnated! She leaned in closely, hovering two inches from his face. Her god-forsaken breath nearly made him vomit — even though he'd just endured the stench of well over ten-thousand dead people... and Galena! Hot garbage. Skunk butt. Demon breath! Anything would have smelled better than the terrible waft that fell from her mouth! Inches from his pinkish ear she said, "You weren't nearly as talkative before I killed you....or at least when I *thought* I killed you..." Another rush of malice had flooded her despicable eyes.

133

He was frightened beyond words. He somehow instinctively knew that the only way to rebuild the pieces of his past lives was to maneuver through this one. A thick quiet laid over the air. She kept circling him. Not only was she terribly puzzled as to how he came back to life, but she also needed to know what was different about the boy...

Unable to see where she was, he nervously turned his lips and said, "Umm… ma'am?"

'BAM!' She punched him in the face a second time!

"OUCH!!!" he shouted. "WHAT DID I DO??"

Without answering, she kicked him in the ribs and he fell to the dusty, cement floor, still pinned to the chair! Helpless, on the ground, she repeatedly kicked the poor boy until he could no longer breathe! He begged for mercy, but she didn't stop! He screamed terribly, knowing that she was trying to beat him to death! Blind, confused, and in unbearable pain was the unfortunate welcome to his new life. This nasty woman leaned in closely to his ear again, breathing heavily as though she'd done an hour of cardio and whispered, *"Mama loves you..."*

Barely cognizant, a million and one thoughts raced through his mind. 'Was I truly this woman's son in this life?? Why would a mother treat her own son so horribly?? What did Ryan do before I got stuck being reincarnated into this stupid body of his??'

Someone else came into the house.

There was a second set of footsteps thumping across the floor above them. Samol hoped that whoever it was would save him. She grabbed a handful of his messy, blonde spirals with her eyes fastened to the corner of the basement as though whoever was in the house was coming quickly. She whispered sharply, "You're father's home. Not a word about any of this or I will set you on fire! Understand??" Samol felt a lump in his throat. His stomach tightened and he said softly, "…Okay…"

She untied him. He was black and blue, much weaker, and practically unable to move.

"GET UP!!" she screamed, snatching him by the arm up the stairs, covering his mouth so that he wouldn't scream.

Her hand smelled like she'd been wiping her butt with it for the past ten years. Just before they got upstairs, she softened her grip and gently placed her sticky, disgusting arm around his neck to appear as an affectionate, loving mother in front of Ryan's father.

This was Victoria Palmer. She was dangerous, violent, manipulative, soulless, and somewhat intelligent — the recipe of a true witch.

In the open-floor-plan kitchen were windows at every corner of its white walls. There, stood a tall, handsome, blue-eyed man sorting through mail. He seemed gentle and kind with a sort of magnetism to him; everything that Victoria and his fellow Chicago Trading Floor bankers were not. The dapper, middle-aged man, Christian Palmer, hadn't a clue that just ten minutes prior, his only son was tied to a chair and suffocated in the basement by his ugly spouse. Suddenly, the malevolent woman broke into an abrupt heap of fake tears:

"My poor boy! My baby! Look at what they did to our child!"

Christian, who hadn't seen them standing there yet, dropped the mail as if he'd witnessed a train wreck. His eyes bulged and his mouth fell open in horror.

"WHAT HAPPENED??" he yelled.

Victoria's hand, which still cloaked the boy's neck, gave him a subtle pinch, reminding him that he better not say a word.

Samol squirmed. "I was — um —" he struggled.

"And look at his eyes!" Victoria quickly interrupted.

"What happened to…your eyes? Son??" Christian said, suddenly wondering if he'd been calling the wrong boy 'son' for the past eight years. "They're hazel now?? Wait — I — what happened to you??" he studied him from head to toe.

135

"Remember when we tried to tell him that his friends, Charlie and Jeff, were jealous of how smart he is? Well...they beat him up again!" Victoria lied disgustingly, coughing up another heave of fake tears. "This is what?...the fifth time this week??"

Samol was torn. He hadn't a clue as to who Charlie and Jeff were, but based on Victoria's track record he figured it was all lies.

"Son, you've got to stand up for yourself!" Christian said strongly. "You still remember those jujitsu moves I taught you?" he asked, kneeling gently beside his son.

"Better yet...he doesn't need to be hanging with those friends, anyway," said Victoria. "They keep bullying my baby!" she said, about to '*sob*' again. "Why don't you stay home with mama, she'll take good care of you," she said in a horribly honeyed voice.

"No...he needs to be out with boys his age," said Christian, talking to Victoria but examining his son's fractured nose and busted lip. "We can't let his disabilities stifle him, Victoria. It's not healthy to—"

"Christian..." she interrupted. The way she said his name was somewhat provocative and she used what little feminine power she had. "We've tried things your way," she said, gently clasping her veiny fingers over his large, smooth hands. "*Let mama have hers,*" she said softly, winking with a provocative curtsy, which looked more like she was having a stroke.

Christian surrendered. Not a word or even a blip of dissatisfaction trickled from his lips. Samol, or Ryan if you will, wished that he could see in that moment. 'What did this demented, Vreek mother of his look like? What if she was an Aryamite, herself? A bad one?? He just wanted to see her eyes so he would know what to watch out for in a future life...just in case she wasn't just some evil Vreek!

Making sure that Christian couldn't hear, she leaned in closely to Ryan and said, "You are two inches away from me setting you on fire, boy."

136

Terror thickened through him. He began wondering if he was happier dead or alive! 'Please be wrong, Arabis,' he prayed silently. 'Could I really survive one hundred thirty-nine more days of this? He already wanted to die so badly.

"I'll look after the boy while you're hard at work, honey," she said, caressing her flat hips, still struggling to be sexy.

"If you say so," said Christian.

"Ryan, my sweet child," she said almost too lovingly, "let's get you to bed. Mama'll tuck you in," she said, forcing a smile.

The boy curdled his face.

Christian kissed him on the forehead and said, "I love you so much, son. Get some rest. You look…dead tired."

Samol wondered if he knew.

Victoria led the boy upstairs. The moment they were out of Christian's sight, she covered his mouth and punched him in the ribs with her sharp, diamond wedding ring. She kicked open his bedroom door and threw him to the floor. "Get in there you little, blind twit!" she barked.

"You're supposed to be <u>dead</u>!" she hissed, spitting in his face, grabbing him by his hair. "I don't know how you did it, but-dontchu-worry. Tomorrow, mama's gonna fix that! Sweet dreams."

For a moment he laid on the floor, wondering if she were still there, just hovering, waiting for him to try and get up so she could kick him back down. When he didn't hear anything for three minutes, he knew she was gone. As tired as he was, he was too afraid to go to sleep. He wondered how a woman could be so horrible to her own child. Any child, for that matter?? 'She must've known me from a past life, I know it!' he thought impossibly. He cried on the floor the whole night through.

The next morning when he awakened, he was somehow fast asleep in his bed. Even stranger was what he smelled …a hearty, home-cooked breakfast! 'The living people sure do know how to cook!' he thought.

'Maybe I'll somehow sneak over to the neighbors and steal some,' he plotted because he hadn't eaten in nearly two lives! There was: mouth-watering, cheesy eggs; delicious French toast; spicy, succulent sausages; savory, smoked ham; beans; tomatoes; and large, brown pancakes smothered in syrup. Little did he know, this was all Victoria's cooking!

It was ten minutes after five and just a sliver of sunlight came through the sky on this already muggy, summer morning. Christian, per usual, was rushing out the door to the office. However, something was different about this day. His firm was preparing for a large IPO, so nothing better go wrong! Victoria helped tidy him up, brushed the bread crumbs from his suit jacket, fixed his pant legs, inspected every inch of his shoes, and pushed back a few of his unruly, brunette locks that the humidity took joy in messing up.

"You're gonna do great today, sweetheart," she said, fixing his collar.

"Thank you…" said Christian, not making eye contact. "I'm worried about Ryan, though. What in the world happened to his eyes?? And he's — ju — there's something different about him!"

"Shhh," she said lightly. "Don't you worry about Ryan. I'll take good care of him," she winked. "You just worry about that IPO, sweet cheeks," she said, giving his backside a nice squeeze.

He pulled away slightly as though he found it inappropriate. Christian smiled weakly and rushed for the door as she handed him yesterday's Chicago Tribune that he forgot to brief for the big meeting. She stood at the door, waving as he sped off in his silver Mercedes. Victoria was alone with the boy - - just the way she liked it. She tilted her head, almost childlike, peeking upstairs looking at Ryan's bedroom door where he laid awake. In a voice just above a whisper, she began to sing:

"Hush, little baby don't you cry, mama's gonna stab you till you die. And if you make it out alive, I'll strike a match and watch you fry."

A terrible laugh issued from her throat as she walked to the knife drawer in the kitchen. She pulled it out...a hidden stash of cigarettes and a lighter. Earlier that morning, she set aside Ryan's plate, which had gone cold by now. Victoria lit up her cigarette and sprinkled a large heap of cigarette ashes into the boy's food! Her face split into an evil smile. Out of the pocket of her silk robe, she pulled out a black pill inscribed with a baby's face underneath a skull and crossbones. She stirred the pill in with the ashes in his food! She let out a second terrible laugh, this one was cold and high.

Victoria crept upstairs to his room, entering slowly like a pedophile. Samol shut his eyes tightly when he heard the door open. For a second, Victoria looked almost angry that he was comfortably sleeping in his bed, as though she wanted him to still be on the floor. She inched close enough for her sewage breath to make his face curdle.

"Good morning, my love. Breakfast is ready," she said gently.

He made sure to stay perfectly still.

"Ryan, get up. I've made you breakfast," she said a little more forcefully.

He turned away and let out a fake yawn.

"*I said get up, you blind bag of pus!*" she roared, gritting her unbrushed teeth, yanking him out of bed by his hair, that was flat on one side from sleeping on it.

"*You're gonna learn to respect me before I kill you again!*"

He kicked and screamed as she dragged him, banging his head on the small, wooden bedpost and a few braille books on the floor.

"I SAID GET UP!!! NOWWWWWW! Your-food-is-ready!!" she hollered, sounding like a cousin to Bloodwig.

With weak knees, he slowly stood to his feet holding the side of his head.

Feeling along the walls, he followed his nose to the dining room. Ryan nearly fell down the stairs, even twisted his ankle a few times and Victoria, who'd been watching him at the bottom of the stairs, smirked the whole time. He made it to the table and sat down, ready to put something...anything into his mouth! Feeling around savagely for his food, Victoria watched him coldly and sat with her elbow resting on her knee, cigarette in her mouth, nose in the air, hairy legs crossed, and her usual sinister grin. His food was at the opposite end of the table.

"Other side," she whispered cruelly.

He raced hastily, feeling for it and at last...substance. He swallowed a forkful of French toast drenched in more cigarette ash than syrup and gagged horribly!

"What's wrong, dear?" Victoria smiled irritatingly.

"What is this??" he asked, wiping his mouth.

"That's not very nice, dear," she said sarcastically. "Your mother slaved over your breakfast. *Slaved,*" she reiterated coldly. "Therefore, you will eat what I tell you to eat — when I tell you to eat it," she grinned evilly.

Uncrossing her shapeless, hairy legs, she spoke, "You see...*I own you.* You should be grateful that I've even allowed you to HAVE food! Now, eat it or I'll starve you, you ungrateful slut!"

His mouth flew open in disbelief. He hated this invisible freak and couldn't wait for the moment of sweet revenge (if that was even possible). Reluctantly, he swallowed another forkful of his ash-covered breakfast; this one was beans, syrup, pancakes, cigarette-ash, and what felt like a chewy pill of some sort.

Victoria smiled again.

Suddenly, it didn't matter that he hadn't eaten in two lives, enough was enough! He angrily spat it out and shot up from the table and left.

She snapped her finger.

"No, no, no, no, no!" she said, sounding like a condescending school teacher, "You will sit down and finish the delicious breakfast that your mother has prepared for you. NOW!!"

"It tastes horrible!" he yelled, trying not to cry.

"It tastes horrible," she mocked him in a high-pitched, irritating voice. "So does your father's dick! In life…" she began and cold chills tore down his spine because he thought she'd finish with "Or in Death," like they say in Euphod, but instead said, "…We all have to do things we don't want to do. And if I can put up with your father's small, smelly package three times a week, you can eat a little cigarette ash every now and then. Now, do as your mother has to do and eat it!"

The disgusting thought of her doing such a thing with any human being made it nearly impossible to eat anything. Not to mention, he now realized why the food tasted so bad! "NO!" was all he could shout.

Victoria leapt up from the table and charged! He heard her coming, but couldn't see from where! 'BOOM!' She wound back and pummeled him in the face! His head flew back as though it had been hit by a semi-truck! Blood splattered the walls. She shoved his face in the food, pressing his head as hard as she could, like she were trying to drown him! "YOU WILL DO AS I COMMANDDDDD! LIKE I SAY! WHEN I SAYYYY! EAT ITTTTTTT!" she screamed, sounding like a demon.

He fought and flailed as she held his face in the messy food. She began laughing again. When she finally let him up; beans, syrup, egg yolk, and cigarette ash caked every inch of his face and hair. With an irritating grin, she said softly, "You see, Ryan, *I control you.* If I want you to eat, *you will eat.* If I want you to drink, *you will drink…*If I want you to die, *you-will-die!!"*

He began to cry.

As if she couldn't be any more evil, she slapped him in the face for crying, splattering more blood, beans, and eggs all over the walls and floor. "EAT!" she hollered, plopping another heap of ashes into his plate. Tears cascaded down his face with every bite. He was helpless. Trapped. Not even death was an escape, at least not for another one hundred thirty-eight days.

He wondered if Bloodwig had something to do with this. Victoria sat down in front of him, puffing on her shortening, red-hot cigarette with a smirk. Angling sideways as though she were posing in a mirror, she turned her crusty lips and explained,

"I know you cannot see me, but I want you to know that all of this is for your own good. You're a terrible child, Ryan. Terrible! You're filthy, nasty, retarded! Better off dead, if you ask me!"

'She knows!' he thought rashly. 'SHE KNOWS!'

"And speaking of death…" she stirred, "…Let's talk about your biological mother, shall we?"

Her words gave way to many thoughts. First, thank God this woman wasn't his real mother in this life! But then who was? He wondered if she was trapped in another life somewhere…or if this crazy woman had killed her too!

Victoria scooted close. Her morning breath made his face twist again. Her cruel mouth spoke, "Even if your mother was still living, she wouldn't have wanted you anyway," she grinned. Strangely, the boy didn't seem nearly as affected by her words as one would think because he'd began angrily plotting. Samol was growing stronger with every insult, because he knew that suicide, as an Aryamite, was totally forbidden and he must fight his way through. However, he began pondering what the laws were on homicide? 'I'm sure I could pull it off…no, I can't even see…' he continued thinking. Victoria could tell he was up to something - - something that wouldn't work.

"You can't even see — so don't try it!" she taunted. "How many fingers am I holding up?"

She held up three.

"How many millions have I stolen from your father??"

She held up seven.

"You wouldn't even be a challenge for me with 20/20 vision," she said and began slapping both of his cheeks alternately like an irritating, older sibling.

He tried to block, but it didn't work. She played this aggravating game of patty-cake with his face for nearly ten minutes, until he finally broke down and cried. It was a weep that shook his shoulders and made breathing an impossible task. Tripping clumsily, he ran to his room letting out a blood-curdling scream. Victoria smiled brightly as though she'd done a good deed. She grabbed the car keys and left. Samol cried himself to sleep.

Later that evening, he was awakened by a dream; one filled with beautiful music that he'd never heard before. The true beauty was that neither had anyone else in the world. He rushed out of bed, hunting for anything to write with. He just had to get this on paper somehow (even though he was blind). Grabbing a broken pencil and an old piece of braille he found on the floor, he somehow blindly scribbled music in the form of equations! He, himself, didn't know if he was lucid or if something from another life had overtaken him. He emphatically sang and stomped his feet to the music in his head. Unfortunately, Victoria had returned.

His boisterous passion caught her ear from the moment she walked through the front door. Victoria slithered upstairs like a snake, cracking open his door to find her stepson writing music like Beethoven; wildly and lacking one of his senses! Her face twisted, shoulders slumped, and stomach went numb. She tip-toed behind him to study his ingenious ways of unknowingly converting equations into music and music back into equations! It was certainly above her head (which she did not like). Arching closely to his ear she screamed,

"HOW ARE YOU DOING THAT??"

"OUCH!" he hollered, shooting from his seat like a cannon, holding his left ear. The ringing in his eardrum felt like pins and needles slicing through his ear canal.

"WHAT IS WRONG WITH YOU??" he shouted at once.

"You watch your tone with me or I'll drown you in a pool of Charlie and Jeff's blood!" she threatened.

He fell silent, afraid she'd strike.

"HOW ARE YOU WRITING THAT MUSIC??" she demanded once more, "YOU-ARE-BLIND!"

He wanted to shout back, 'How are you not in hell yet?? YOU-ARE-EVIL!' but didn't. The truth was, he honestly didn't know how he was doing it. How could he explain that in this life he might've been given a certain set of gifts or perhaps these were leftover gifts from a past life? Even if he were allowed to explain this, he would probably be committed! His lips moved as if he were about to say something, but he didn't. The only noise was the ringing in his ears.

Victoria got closer and shouted in the other ear, "ANSWER MY QUESTION OR I WILL KILL YOUUUUU!"

"OUCCHHH!" he screamed, dropping to the floor, covering both ears. "I don't know!" he shouted. "I...think it's just a...talent of mine or something!"

"A talent? Of yours?" she mocked in a plummy tone, as though such things were impossible. "Oh, so we're Mozart now, are we?" she insulted. "The Ryan that I raised couldn't hold a tune if his life depended on it - - and suddenly we're a child prodigy now, are we?"

He lied on the floor massaging his ears.

"Tell me," she began, sounding as if she already knew the answer to whatever it was she was going to ask, "How does the ringing sound in your ears? What pitch is it, Mr. Mozart? Is it… 'music to your ears?'" she laughed terribly.

Tears bottled behind his eyes.

"Speaking of music, guess what I just learned yesterday…" she smiled. "Did you know that mothers who sing to their babies, while holding them, improves the baby's heart rate? And it helps the mother not feel as anxious? Did you know that?" she asked in a high-pitched voice, "Oh, I'm sorry…you don't," she said, snarling with her eyes.

"Never again will your mother be able to 'hold you,'" she said, motioning a mother rocking a baby. "Never again will your filthy mother be able to 'sing you a lullaby,'" she said in a singsongy tone. "Never will she read you a bedtime
144

story or cook your favorite meal!" she said, grinning ear to ear. He didn't know whether to cry or pinch himself. This couldn't be real life! It just couldn't! She walked towards his desk to get a closer look at his strange manuscript of math and music, which was a string of four musical melodies connected over a series of algebraic equations that somehow created the picture of a three-legged-face with wings!

As if the page glared back at her she shrieked, "WHAT IS THIS?" sounding more afraid than angry, like she'd seen it before.

"What's what??" he said stiffly, sensing the panic in her voice.

"OH, NO!" she howled, pointing in terror at the page, "You can't be here! I — we can't be around this!" she screamed as if she were talking to someone else in the bedroom.

"Who are you tal...No! DON'T!!" he screamed, chasing the sound of her voice.

She picked up the manuscript. The boy was getting closer to her, when suddenly he was tripped by a hairy leg. He fell to the ground and banged his head (thank God it was carpet)! Victoria shredded it and threw it in his face like confetti.

"There you go..." she smiled, looking at him on the floor.

He once again fought back tears.

"Hey..." she said softly, slouching down to his eye-level, "Why are you crying, sweet pea?...I gave it back."

He sobbed louder and she began to laugh.

"Glue it back together — if you can find the pieces."

Proud of the pain she inflicted, she left. He wept longingly. Victoria peeked her head back into his room and reiterated, "It's for your own good."

The boy wept flat on the floor. He didn't want food even though he was hungry, or water even though he was thirsty, or love even though he needed it. He simply wished to be left alone. Forever.

145

His hopeful views toward life were being chipped away by this terrible woman. That night, just three minutes till nine, he began to slip into one of life's worst places to be; numbness. Lying in that space between sleep and awake, just thirty-three miles above Euphod's surface, it seemed most opportune that Maven's words would slip into his memory:

"You will never live a life more difficult than you can withstand, no-matter-what. Many of you will experience failure, unfairness, racism, divorce, disease, murder, rape, loneliness, poverty, and depression for starters! However, you will NEVER be assigned to live a life more difficult than you can withstand. No-matter-what!"

Samol fell into an uneasy sleep.

CHAPTER NINE

THE VENOMOUS BEAST

"The boy cut off my hair, broke my two front teeth, and look..." – Victoria

*A*fter enduring the worst day ever, it's no wonder that he slept for nearly twenty-four hours. When he awakened, there was an even bigger problem...a smoke-filled bedroom! 'Did Victoria set the house on fire??' he panicked. He shot out of bed as though he'd been catapulted! He couldn't feel any heat, yet the smoke was thickening by the second! He scurried for his bedroom door, hands outstretched so that he wouldn't bash his face and then his foot met a thin, unshaven leg. Puffing on her twenty-seventh cigarette, she sat there. As if he'd stepped on a land mine, he backed away slowly. "Don't move," Victoria ordered coldly.

His heart skipped a beat. She stood up and circled him like a bully for a second time, puffing on her cigarette. He grew nervous at the lingering silence and began to back away.

"Why are you doing this to me?" he quivered.

Victoria drew back and punched him in the stomach, dropping him to the floor! "I said don't move!" she barked, gritting her teeth.

'One hundred thirty-seven more days — One hundred thirty-seven more days!' He thought repeatedly, picking himself up from the carpeted floor.

She blew a mouthful of grey smoke in his face while circling him. He fanned it and coughed, but was sure not to move, knowing that another step would be another strike. Snickering at the fact that she could manipulate an eight-year-old child, one would hate to know what else was spinning in that hateful head of hers!

"Awww, you don't like the smoke?" she pestered sweetly, "...If you don't like it, then you should move, sweetheart..."

He thought with his eyes, darting them back and forward hurriedly. 'What kind of game was this?' he thought when she continued,

"Go on, honey — I can see that the smoke is bothering you," she said tenderly.

There was another terrible silence. He didn't move. Maybe she left the room or better yet - - maybe she suddenly dropped dead! Slowly, he crept back two steps. It was a trap! He was pummeled in the back of the head and knocked to the ground.

"WHY – ARE – YOU – MOVING?? YOU WERE INSTRUCTED NOT TO MOVEEEEEE!!!" screamed the psycho woman.

The boy, with still some fight in him, struggled to stand and hollered, "You said I could!"

'POW!' A fist split his bottom lip in two and he was knocked to the ground again!

148

"You ever talk back to me again and I will kill you in your sleep!" For a second time, he thought to himself this simply could not be real life.

She puffed on her cigarette, blowing enough smoke to make the room look as though it were a small chimney. The cigarette was red hot. Like she was possessed by the devil, himself, she sat on him, with a demented anger boiling behind her black, beady eyes and pressed her hot cigarette onto the back of his neck, searing through his skin! His awful scream could be heard three houses down! She laughed as he squirmed. The bully from hell then scorched his right elbow and forearm, chuckling as though she believed she was earning points the more places she could burn!

Finally, he snapped.

His blindness and second degree burns suddenly didn't matter. He flipped her off of him and followed the sound of her demented laugh. His fist met her face and the tussle began! Clothes were torn. Hair ripped out. Eyes were gouged. Private parts were kicked. This sick woman found it humorous to repeatedly punch the blind eight-year-old in the face, ribs, and neck and even fractured one of his fingers! Yet, he kept fighting. In one hand, he had a patch of her greasy, black hair he'd ripped out. His other grazed across a plump scar on her right arm. For a second, he wondered if it was the scar from one of Euphod's castles!

Hatred. Adrenaline. A slight nervous breakdown. He suddenly felt no pain. Punching aimlessly, his knuckles shattered something...both of her front teeth! Her eyes were as wide as headlights with both hands, clasping her mouth. The two of them stood still. The boy knew he'd permanently disfigured her face in some way. Arabis was wrong. He wasn't going to die in one hundred thirty-seven days but in three… two…. one…

He dashed for the door, relying solely on memory, and ran down the stairs as fast as he could. Victoria raced towards his desk, grabbing the first weapon she could find. She chased him violently with a pair of black scissors in her right hand! A five second head-start was all he had, but he got to the living room just as someone came through the front door and grabbed him. Ryan screamed, punched, and kicked with everything he had left.

"What's going on??" Christian asked, restraining him. "And what happened to your....FACE??" he paused, looking at his son's black eye and busted lip. A displeasing look grew over Christian's face. "Did the neighborhood kids beat you up again??"

"It's that woman!" the boy hollered. "She's after me!!"

Victoria was stooping at the top of the stairs. She heard the two of them talking, but Christian hadn't seen her yet. She squatted low like a burglar, watching Christian tend to the injuries of his battered son. Unfortunately, Ryan was disheveled and began babbling incoherently. His nervous breakdown had gotten the best of him. An evil smirk painted her face, because she knew that she could now manipulate Christian into believing that their son was *"clinically insane."*

'Let the games begin,' she thought to herself as she began conjuring a plan.

The devil's daughter tiptoed into Ryan's bedroom pulling a picture from the wall. It wasn't just any picture, but a photograph of Ryan, Christian, and his biological mother, Cindy, three days before she mysteriously passed away. Victoria stuffed the picture underneath a pillow to muffle the sound of her next despicable act. She shattered it with the scissors and tip-toed with the remains under her arm into the master bedroom.

Running past the master bathroom mirror, she caught a glimpse of her snaggletoothed face. Never again did she want to smile, or even talk without covering her mouth.

150

She was now stuck with an even uglier version of herself (as if that were even possible). Christian and Ryan were coming!

"How will I make my story believable?" she said quickly under her breath. She looked at the scissors, then at herself. Then at the scissors, then at her clothes. Then at the scissors...then at her hair? Yes, the hair, she thought, grabbing an uneven plunk of her hair and chopped it off! She then grabbed another section of hair on the other side of her head and hacked away. She smiled evilly, sure not to open her mouth.

"Okay...what's my story," she quickly whispered to herself. They were still coming up the stairs. She rehearsed the lie in her head and placed the clippings of hair onto her pillow to make whatever story she were about to conjure up, believable. She ruffled her clothes and ran to the top of the steps, slumping over like an old woman, making sure to squish a few fake tears down her ugly face. Christian and Ryan hadn't made it all the way up the stairs because Christian was tending to the boy's swollen lip midway up.

Victoria began by dramatically pointing at Ryan with a quivering, outstretched finger and cried, *"That child! That child has gone mad!"*

Christian nearly fell down the stairs when he saw her! Victoria hobbled down the stairs, limping for dramatic effect. Truthfully, she could've won an Oscar.

"Christian, darling, look at me!" she pled, hiding something behind her back. "Look at what he did to my teeth!" she smiled widely and Christian cringed. "And...he cut off my hair while I was sleeping!"

"What??" said Ryan, whose stomach contracted.

"He's become so violent and angry when all I..." she stopped to wipe her fake tears, "...When all I try to do is love and support our child!"

Christian was confused. Long hours at the office left him a fantastic trader, but clueless to the fact that his son was at home with a monster everyday!

His eyes darted between Victoria's and Ryan's, as if he were suddenly forced to pick a side. He noticed that something was behind her back and tried to see what it was, but couldn't.

"I made an oath to you," Victoria begged, noticing that Christian didn't know who to believe yet. "You lost your wife and he lost a mother," she began persuasively. "I promised to step in and help raise him and support you, Christian…and look at what he's done to me!" she begged dramatically. *We have to do something! Please!! I'm scared for my life!"* she hollered.

"That's a lie!!" Ryan shouted angrily.

Victoria cowered away from the boy, attempting to make her story more believable. Unfortunately, it was working. The Ryan that Christian knew would never raise his voice in a million years. Christian gave his son an odd, stiff glare as though he didn't know him anymore.

"Sweetheart," she begged pathetically, "you've got to believe me!"

"THAT-IS-A-LIE!" Ryan hollered.

"Hey!" Christian said sternly, removing his hand from his shoulder. "Stop it, right now!"

Victoria knew she was winning and limped feebly towards Christian. "You know that picture of the three of you?" she instigated.

"The three of whom?" said Christian in a frightening tone.

"The very last picture you, Ryan, and your dearly departed wife took before she died?"

"Okay…" said Christian, whose tone sounded like 'you better not say what I think you're gonna say.'

"HE BROKE IT!" she screamed at once, finally revealing what was behind her back. "HE BROKE IT!! I tried to stop him, but — he — he stabbed it with a pair of scissors in one of his manic fits! I SAW HIM DO IT!!!" she said, forcing a hysterical cry, covering her face.

"Wait, what??" Ryan said confusedly, not knowing what picture she was even talking about.

Christian stared at the shattered photograph. The last memories of he, his wife, and child were gone. He was speechless! After a long, stressful day at the office, the man's fuse was short and his face turned red as a slab of beets. As if Victoria had placed some sort of voodoo spell on him, he turned towards his son, enraged with clenched fists! Victoria's mouth cracked open with a terrible grin.

"He said he did it on purpose, Christian!" she pressed on.

"I didn't do anything!" the boy cried defensively.

"SHUT UP!" Christian hollered, gritting his teeth tighter than his fists.

"He said he wants you dead too, just like his mother!" Victoria continued.

"Dad! That's not tr—"

"I SAID SHUT UPPP!!" Christian bellowed loud enough for neighbors to begin peeking through their blinds.

Victoria ruffled her clothes again and spoke:

"Christian, in my humble opinion, coming from an outsider looking in," she began gently, "I can certainly tell you that this is not the same sweet-faced, little boy that I once knew. He's violent, vile, rude, arrogant, nasty, and mentally insane, Christian!" she said, listing all six of his *unfavorable qualities* on her fingers as she spoke.

"He's been expelled from school and — and — he made you lose your job!" she said, searching for more reasons to get Christian on her side. "How many times are you going to let him use his blindness as a crutch??"

The room fell silent.

Samol didn't know if what she'd said about Ryan were true, but figured she was twisting things.

"And now he's become violent towards me - - the woman who has loved and nurtured him into the young man that YOU wanted, Christian," she said.

"He has failed himself, me, and most importantly, you and his dearly departed mother," she added.

There was another terrible silence.

"Christian, you are his father! And now he wants to kill you!! You must not let this behavior slide!"

Christian marinated on her every word, just as she planned. Samol still wished he could see, just so he could have the pleasure of watching her die when he killed her one day. Christian was torn between hurt, confusion, and anger. He opened his mouth several times, but nothing could come out. To further sway Christian to her side, Victoria repeated in a frenzy:

"The boy cut off my hair! Broke my two front teeth! And look…the pièce de résistance — he has taken away the last memory of you three as a family before you said your final goodbye to your lovely wife."

Christian fumed. His face grew redder by the second. Fists balled. Teeth tightened.

"Dad, I never—"

"Don't say another word…" Christian growled in a scary whisper.

"Dad, she's ly—"

"I-SAID-DON'T-SPEAK!!!!" Christian hollered, yanking him by the collar.

Victoria spotted a metal baseball bat to the left of the front door (one of the things she picked up on her errands earlier that day as though she'd planned this whole thing). She handed it to Christian, giving his arm a slight nudge, mustering up more fake tears and added:

"He hurts me so bad when you're not home, Christian. I love that boy with all my heart, but he just won't stop! He told me that he's coming for you next, Christian…"

"Dad, she's lying!" Ryan pled.

Christian's eyes swam around the room as though he were looking for something.

"I simply do everything that I can for the boy and he mistreats me," Victoria pressed on.

154

"Dad, she beat me and burned me with cigarettes!" Ryan said, about to cry.

"See?" she said. "Now, he's become a liar. I just don't know what to do with him anymore," she said, covering her face, forcing herself to cry again.

"Dad, that's not true!" Ryan begged once more.

"He needs to be punished for what he's done, Christian. You can't keep letting him get away with things because he's blind," said Victoria, again nudging the arm that held the bat.

"Dad, no!" he said, sensing that something was about to happen.

"It's for his own good," she whispered.

"Dad, please!"

"Play ball, my love!"

Christian snapped. Right about now, many would've hoped that he would've turned on her. However, life isn't fair. He beat his poor son with the baseball bat for a full minute. Victoria smiled the entire time until she suddenly saw a tiny black and white scar on his arm that looked like some sort of stone. She could've sworn she saw it yesterday, but thought nothing of it.

"That's enough, sweetheart. That's enough," she said, stopping him. "You did good, my love. Very, very, good," she smiled, studying the motionless boy on the ground and patted Christian on the back as if he were a dog who'd just learned how to pee outside. "You go on upstairs and cool off, and — well — I'll — I'll take it from here," she said thirstily.

The boy was beaten beyond recognition. Swollen in places where the human body should not swell. Strangely, there was no blood, which understandably left Victoria perplexed. Making sure Christian was well out of sight, she dragged his body to the garage, and into the car. Something about that scar on his arm (and the picture he drew yesterday) left her spooked out. To make sure he was dead, she kicked him in the side of the neck. There was a terrible crack and she threw his lifeless body into the backseat.

155

It was eleven minutes till seven. Victoria drove for forty minutes (thirty miles over the speed limit) as though she were racing against time. This nasty woman found a secluded alleyway in a quaint town where there weren't very many people. Aside from a group of obnoxious teens smoking on the sidewalk, Victoria and Ryan were alone. She got out of the car quickly as if she felt someone was watching her. When she yanked him out of the backseat, he fell to the ground and cracked his skull. Victoria made another shifty-eyed glance from left to right - - coast was clear. For a second time, she left Ryan for dead and sped off never to be seen again.

Seconds later, one of the teens heard a howling whisper. The glassy-eyed girl looked all around until she laid eyes on Ryan's lifeless body across the street.

"Oh, my gosh!" she yelled, pointing and running towards him as the others followed.

"WHAT IS THAT??" shouted one of the boys who was pointing at something.

"It's HUGE!!" hollered another one of the teenage boys who saw the same thing.

"She's beautiful," said the girl who initially heard the howling whisper.

"She??" asked the boys.

"IT'S ANGRY! RUNNN!!"

Unsure if their reefer had been laced with something, a few of the mischievous teens saw what looked like an angelic figure hovering over Samol's body. They ran, screaming like banshees, catching the attention of a few onlookers who, then spotted Ryan's body. Within seconds, the police were called and a crowd had formed around him. Both eyes were black, blue, and swollen shut. His lips had ballooned like sausages. His nose, neck, back, left shoulder, right ankle, and right leg were all broken. The paramedics couldn't understand how there was no blood.

At the hospital, doctors tried to immediately resuscitate. Three heart shocks became four. Nothing. Four turned to five. Nothing. On the sixth shock, there was a flicker of heart activity. They shocked his heart a seventh time and another spike showed up on the heart monitor. An eighth shock stabilized his heart rate, but he didn't move. Had Arabis misread that he would live a total of one hundred thirty-nine days? If she were wrong, that would've been fine. This wasn't much of a life anyhow. Sadly, she wasn't. The boy remained comatose for one hundred thirty-seven days until death was kind enough to greet him as an old friend.

Why did Victoria hate him so much? Better yet, how did she manipulate Christian into beating his own son with a bat?? Or convince the seemingly intelligent man that a blind child could stab specific pictures, without braille enscribed on it, with malicious intent? Did she have dirt on Christian? Voodoo? Or had he always masked his true colors behind his pretty smile and polite conversations?...Such things are a mystery. For obvious reasons, Samol was happy to get back to Euphod. Unfortunately, it wasn't quite like how he remembered it…

CHAPTER TEN

FREEDOMCORPSE

"Every Aryamite exists in the invisible body of death, the heart of the living, and the mind of the forbidden," – Silas Dottfried

$\mathcal{S}$amol was dead again. Just as before, he felt his soul being pulled from his body. He could see life around him exactly the way it was; the hospital bed, Ryan's body lying there on the white sheets in blue garments, the nurse who'd just covered his face because the heart monitor flat lined, all there, intact. Exactly like before, he was pulled into the large, swirling, black hole. This time, however, instead of knives swinging at him, he heard the sound of Victoria's laughter with an arm swinging a baseball bat. He felt at peace because he remembered that he could not be touched. A few bats multiplied into thousands. Thousands became hundreds of thousands. He closed his eyes and took a deep breath, bracing for impact. Suddenly, he face-planted into the thick shrubbery of the Genesis Forest. The second he landed, his body began to morph. His hair went from curly, blonde locks to straight and dark brown. His skin went from a pink-ish-complexion to somewhat olive. He grew a painful seven inches and the Zebrastone scar on his arm had vanished. The only remaining feature were his eyes; still amber. Just as before, he now stood in the physical presence of the first life he ever lived - - the original body of Samol Doscow.

Forming over his head was the terribly beaten, float-ing corpse of his last life, which unmistakably did its job of reminding him of what had happened one hundred thir-ty-seven days prior. An ice-cold wind tore through him. He shivered as he stared at his own hovering body, as though he were waiting for it to talk to him or something. Suddenly, he saw something other than snow falling from the sky; a blue piece of paper no bigger than a five-by-seven postcard that read:

Death Certificate

~ The kingdom of Euphod would like to formally welcome you to a blissful eternity ~

Name - S.T.R.A.D.O.O.R.
Birthday –– '..ir... f.. d...'
Death Date: December 17 – 16 sec
Life purpose – T..s ..s y.... e...th ...e, Ry.. A.e...d.. De...l. T... li.. ..s l..e .. w.... ..u .ere m...t ... f....t ...der than you... e..ar had ... .. w.. m.... to p..pa.. you f.. ... b....e .. t.. end. T.. answ.. .. y..r .... ..ves' myst....s ... be fou.. .. th. l...

Obstacles/disabilities/challenges – Victoria Palmer
Gifts/talents/capabilities – m..., m...c, p..s..s, a.. ...e
Scar – Zebrastone scar on arm

Hidden Purpose – Show Elizabeth L. Rosewright The End of Time

"Here we go again," he said aloud, because once again the only thing that made sense was his death date and that the obstacle of his last life certainly was Victoria! He, yet again, wondered who this Elizabeth L. Rosewright was and what this end-of-time business was about! At the top right-hand corner of his new death certificate was a twisting, black starfish. He was acutely aware that this meant that he was sorted into the castle of Freedomcorpse in this afterlife.

Samol wondered if time stood still and if everything in Euphod was exactly the way it was from the last time he was there. Yet, this was definitely not the case! Since he'd been living as Ryan, Samol missed: Euphod's Labor Day, Euphod's Veteran's Day, Euphod's Thanksgiving (which had cuisine very similar to what was served at the Death Day Ball, yet very different festivities), and biggest of all was Euphod's New Year.

Euphod was experiencing the dead of winter and Samol was totally alone, unlike last time, where he couldn't move without bumping into someone. He wondered how Paul and London's lives were going or if they were back here in Euphod arguing again. How was Leanna? Was she still in love with Paul? His eyes drifted to the sky and he noticed that he was in a different part of the forest that he'd never seen before.

One half of the forest was backwards! Up was down. Left was right. White was dark. Black was bright! Trees hung upside down as though their roots were attached to the sky. The tips of a vast, upside-down mountain ridge off in the far distance hung just below a blanket of clouds as bright souls fired into the air through the gently falling snow. The other half of the forest was both pitch black and bright orange at the same time, and everything was on its side! Samol had never seen such a thing and it was almost making him nauseous to look at!

All of a sudden, a sound issued from a nearby bush. Without warning, he projectile vomited thirty feet! The smell was ungodly and something was moving inside of his spew, struggling to lift its head. Samol stared at the twisting figure and backed away thinking that it was a bug or rodent, yet it was the head of what looked like an infant! It rolled around slimily, shaking violently, growing bigger by the second. Samol's body iced over with terror.

The creature's asymmetrical, black, beady eyes and shriveled nose were not as ugly as the spikes on the edges of its face. Its lips were perched tightly as if they were sewn shut. The creature kept growing taller and taller. Its skin was scabbed and its body had formed into a gargoyle. Abruptly, it spoke, sounding as three voices in one: *"Freedom, beware!"* Samol, yet again, felt nauseous and weak in the knees.

From its eyes spewed a strong, black mist with a horrible stench! Samol quickly stepped back. It had now grown three times his height and twice as wide! The gargoyle creature let out a terrible scream and charged at him! As if something from a past life had taken control of Samol's mouth, he involuntarily hollered, "FREEDOM, BEWARE!" The monster splattered instantly leaving behind its putrid, black mist.

Absorbed in a million emotions at once, Samol looked around to see if anyone else had witnessed this terrible mishap. He was alone. The poor boy couldn't seem to get a break in life...or in death! Afraid that something else would jump out at him, or emerge from his vomit again, he nervously looked to find a pathway to a castle - - any castle! Just over ten feet away from him were two blue and white dead trees, which was a side entrance to the Freedomcorpse pathway.

Samol remembered from the last time he died, that between the trees spanned an invisible wall of high voltage and that he must speak only to the left tree. What troubled him, was that unlike last time, no one was there to give him the password! He shook nervously, thinking of random words from his last life, wondering if they would work: Cigarette burns? Demon breath? Vreek-under-cover? Devil woman? And then he said it….

"Freedom, beware."

161

He began to sweat. His eyes darted between both trees to see if their physical presence had changed. Nothing. He inched his leg just slightly beyond the trees like a toddler testing their limits. Because his leg hadn't been zapped off, he knew that it was the correct password! He sighed heavily. His breath met the icy air, making puffs of white fog around his mouth. And then something happened.

Right before his almond-shaped, amber eyes the forest changed as though a Divine Power had done so with the wave of a wand. The forest, which was once divided in two, had become a strange configuration of all four seasons in one, funneling around an oversized, swirling, green bush! The leaves on the new trees bore light that sang in four-part harmony! There was sunshine, hail, a blizzard, rain, and wind, all-in-one! At the very end of the pathway was the great, dark, blue castle of Freedomcorpse.

Samol crept through the twisting shrubbery, ducking and dodging, because it seemed like the branches were trying to slap him in the face! All the while, its leaves were still singing, which began to rapidly sound like a million prayers the closer he got to the center of the pathway! Samol heard:

"Freedom, I know you can hear me. I need you right now."

"Please, rescue me. He beats me!"

"Help me come to power. Yours truly, E. Jaede."

"Let the recludet from our past work," H.P.M.

By now, Samol was feeling like a pro in the field of dealing with unusual mishaps and listened numbly. No, actually — he was numb because it was getting cold. Very cold! There was a tall, beefy man, who appeared out of nowhere, standing at the end of the whirling pathway. He seemed unaffected by the chaotic weather. Samol squinted heavily through the snow, winds, and sunshine to see his face, but couldn't. After a few more steps he got a better look at the man. The muscular man stood humble and strong, claiming total authority over all that was around him even before he spoke.

162

As if the big man knew Samol, personally, he rushed towards him. He was almost as tall as a power line and Samol could finally make out his facial features. He was striking and had a mountain of icy-blonde hair that was long enough to sit on. Emerging from his somewhat pointy ears were two monstrous, nine-strand braids that fell far below his legs, yet their tips were invisible as though they continued into another dimension. His eyes were a gentle green and he wore black breechcloths, which exposed his thick, porcelain legs.

"You are in grave danger!" said the man in a deep, sultry voice.

"Danger?" Samol asked seriously.

"Yes," said the man, nodding glumly. "I am Silas Dottfried, ruler of Freedomcorpse and we don't have much time," he said, walking towards the castle. Samol followed.

"I don't understand," said Samol.

"I trust by now, you know you're not like the other Aryamites."

"What do you mean?" Samol grunted, staring at the ropes wrapped around Silas's wrists.

"From the moment you entered the Freedomcorpse Estate, you could probably hear the singing tulips? Or saw the black rain? Or you might've even heard the prayers of those who seek freedom?"

Samol averted his eyes. He knew nothing about the singing tulips or the black rain, but he heard voices. He wondered if he should tell him that he was also nearly eaten by a gargoyle-creature-thing too! Suddenly, he realized that this was the second time he'd almost been attacked by a large, strange creature right after he died. He grew suddenly choked by his nerves and didn't say a word.

"The voices that you might've heard were prayers of the past, present, and...the unfortunate future," Silas said sadly. "Very few people can hear them, Samol."

Samol's heart dropped and wondered how he knew that he only heard the voices! "Why can I hear them?" he asked.

163

"Well…" Silas paused, picking up the pace a bit as though he were suddenly pressed for time, "Aryamites who are extremely talented, extremely driven, and knowledgeable have more spirits after them — good and bad."

"Talents? Knowledge??" Samol squealed as though Silas were making fun of him. "I was tortured in my last life (to put it lightly) and in the life before that I was homeless and woke up in a cemetery!"

Silas stared at him oddly with his large arms crossed at his back and then said, "Every Aryamite exists in the invisible body of death, the heart of the living, and the mind of the forbidden."

"What?" said Samol, giving his body a wild shiver through the frigid air.

"I would be scared if you *did* understand what that meant, Samol."

Finally, they'd arrived. The frozen Freedomcorpse castle sat lonely on top of an icy mountain. The surrounding trees had blue leaves with snow resting gently on their tips. The castle's roses, which surrounded the foyer's outer edges, were bluer than any ocean Samol could've ever imagined. Next to the castle doors was a grey statue of a little boy, who was covered in ice holding a blue violin. Strangely, his instrument had not a drop of ice or snow on it.

There were three winding, cement staircases at the entrance of the Freedomcorpse castle. Silas took Samol up the middle one. He explained, "We're all sent through a funnel of uncanny horrors, mishaps, joys, and trials better known as *life*. Within each life, we've been provided a set of hidden talents, gifts, and knowledge to combat the obstacles that are to come. The problem is that we often don't use our talents like we're supposed to," he said, sounding as though he were kicking himself for doing this in a past life.

Samol didn't say anything. He reflected on the travesties of his last life and all he could say was, "But…why?"

"I don't know," Silas shrugged honestly. "That's the problem with life!"

164

"But shouldn't we, as Aryamites, know more about life than someone who has lived only once?" Samol asked, studying the brightening, grey sky.

"Yes, we should - - shouldn't we?" Silas asked rhetorically, chuckling a bit. "You'll find, however, that we as Aryamites are just as confused, if not more, than Vreeks."

Samol stopped walking. He couldn't believe what he'd just heard. Silas gave him a slight nudge forward and they kept walking.

"It's because Vreeks don't know to be confused," the giant man said softly. "No one can see a pattern after 'just one' of something."

By now, they'd reached the top of the stairs. Silas pointed above the large frozen entrance that read:

'To whom much is given much is required.'

Silas pushed open the double doors. A wintry gust whirled heavily, smacking them both in the face with snow and ice. Silas's hair blew wildly. They brushed the snow from their faces and shoulders and then Samol studied the inside of the castle. Unlike anything he'd ever seen, everything was frozen; from its white floors to its high ceilings! Frozen candles burned with blue flames. Icy grandfather clocks ticked away. Huge windows were glazed with hundreds of ice figurines carved into it. Large chandeliers that looked as though they'd been dipped in ice crystals hung elegantly over the foyer. For just a second, Samol fell in love with the cold until another wintry gust pelted him in the face.

Inches from their toes lived a wide problem. There was a large, gaping hole barring them from entering the castle. The hole was as wide as a house, as long as a bus, and dropped as deep as a large lake. In the cold pit below were frozen cinder blocks, jagged icicles, and a second death waiting to happen! Terror ripped through Samol. He sensed that the only way across was going to be something dumb or dangerous...or both.

"The only way to get inside is to swing across," Silas said as though he read Samol's mind, handing him one of two fat, blue ropes that hung on either side of the castle's doors.

"Come again?" Samol said, barely holding the rope because he was looking for a different answer.

"It's a test of faith," Silas said, gripping the rope firmly as though he were gearing up for a bungee jump.

"Test of faith??" Samol hurled. "TEST OF FAITH?? In my last life, I went through things that could probably scare the devil, himself! The life before that, I couldn't tell you who I was or where I was! And now you're telling me in order to get to my next life, my only hope at freedom, is to leap over some wide, stupid hole?? NO!" Samol hollered, throwing the rope at the big man and walked away.

Silas stared at him gently. He cautiously inched up to him, rather unsure of what to say to the fragile boy. He began anyway, "Samol...in life...and in death, there are — are obstacles that we all must overcome. The reason for the leap across the hole is not to harm you, but to strengthen you. If you want freedom you need faith."

Samol sulked in the blistering wind with his arms folded not wanting to hear another word. The big man spoke again:

"I know it's been tough for you, I've seen your death certificate!" Silas joked, forcing a hesitant smile from Samol's face. "The truth is, if you're going through such monstrosities, not only do you have a big calling, but it means that you are strong enough to endure it."

As much as Samol tried to let his words slip into one ear and out the other, they rang heavily in his heart and mind. He knew he had no choice but to go on.

"But why is it so bad?" Samol begged in an airy voice.

Silas knew by the tone of his voice that this was a boy who hadn't given up yet.

Another blustering wind ripped through them.

"You can do it," Silas said lovingly. Samol gripped the rope, nervously scurrying from side to side.
166

"I'll go first," Silas instructed.

"Your rope better not break or else I'm outta here!" Samol wanted to say, but didn't.

Silas walked back a few feet to get a running start and effortlessly cleared the hole. Samol's confidence level plummeted! How would he, himself, soar over a gaping hole like that?? The man's legs, alone, were twice as long as Samol was tall!

"You can do it!" Silas shouted from the other side, which was so big he had to cup his mouth to be heard.

Samol sighed heavily again. He doubled back as far as the rope would allow and he wheeled off like a plane, leaping from the edge, kicking up a whirlwind of snow behind him.

Midway over the ungodly drop, he looked down, catching a sharp glance of the jagged ice hundreds of feet below him! He hollered terribly and almost let go, but shut his eyes tightly. Before he could open them, he hit something! He was covered in frozen banana peels, a piece of an old stove handle, several cold socks, and ice-cold trash juice! "Where the heck did this come from?" he wanted to scream as though Silas had tricked him. Samol landed in a big pile of waste that looked and smelled like death's landfill! Somehow, he didn't see this from all the way on the other side. He was just happy that he'd made it across.

"Where is everyone?" Samol asked, draining cold slime from his ears.

"On the other side of the castle," said Silas. "It's a little warmer there."

"Hmm…" Samol grunted, staring at a portrait of someone who looked like an older version of Silas, frozen to the wall. Samol began to worry about his curse again. He only seemed to think about it when he was dead. Perhaps he did while he was living, but his lives were so bad that he didn't care. He wondered if Silas even knew that he was cursed since he'd already seen his death certificate. Maybe Silas could give him the magical cure that he needed.

"Can you help me solve the riddle to my curse, Mr. Dottfried?" he asked gently.

"…Yes… and no…" Silas said honestly. "As I told you before, you are not like the rest of your fellow Aryamites and what may have happened to you seems rather complex… based on your death certificates."

Once again, Samol's confidence plummeted.

"I can only help you figure out where you're supposed to be in your future lives to come and this will help you unlock the horrors of your past," Silas said, once again sounding as though he were reading Samol's thoughts.

Suddenly, the slight sound of voices grew from afar. Silas and Samol had reached a tall room that looked like a high-ceilinged, colorful mosque where hundreds of Aryamites were praying for freedom. Above the entrance were shimmering, white letters that read: *'When one life ends, another one begins.'*

"Where are we?" Samol asked, still wiping debris from his pants.

"This is the Freedomcorpse Spiritual Room," Silas replied. "Aryamites have been coming here for the past three hundred seventeen years to prepare for their next lives. You've got to be careful in here, though. Any place where religious activities take place can be where some of the most violent things happen!"

Samol eyeballed everyone there. He felt a sudden rush of wooziness buckle his knees. His eyes began to feel as heavy as sandbags. His knees were as flimsy as cooked noodles. He was dizzy like he'd been tossed through ten twisters! And then there was a voice; a creepy-sounding, familiar voice that began taunting him and called out, "Amir - - Amir!" Samol fainted and didn't awaken for three days.

On the third day, his eyes flickered open slowly as if something was trying to hold them shut. He saw just a sliver of bright lights firing off in every direction from the windows of the Freedomcorpse hospital wing, which is where he was. It was a nasty shock when he saw his beaten corpse floating just a few feet above his face. He nearly catapulted himself out of bed! Now that he was sitting up-right he saw everyone who'd been surrounding him this entire time.

There were many nuns, all of whom were nurses tending to the other sick people in the beds next to him. Samol's vision was a bit blurry and he saw three people standing very close to him.

"Paul, you have my mother's eyes," said a flirty voice that sounded like Leanna's.

"Samol!" shouted a girl with flaming, red curls.

"I'm so glad you're all right, man!" said a blonde-haired boy with a familiar voice.

"What happened to me?" Samol asked in a raspy voice that hadn't been used in days, now fully aware who these three jokesters were.

"You fainted!" Paul answered.

"Has this ever happened to you before?" Leanna asked, the frown lines between her eyebrows now more furrowed than they'd been in the past three days.

"Ye — No — I don't remember," Samol said, unsure of himself.

"Good thing we all finished our last lives within a day of each other so we could find you!" said Leanna.

"How did you all find me anyhow?" Samol asked, readjusting himself on the bed.

"Silas told us," said London. "We came running as soon as we heard the news!"

"Let's get you up," said Paul, hoisting his buddy out of bed to his feet. "We don't have a lot of time."

"Why does everybody keep saying that?" Samol asked himself quietly.

Paul hobbled through the Freedomcorpse hallways, practically carrying Samol because it seemed that he'd lost a lot of feeling in his legs when he fainted. The howling sound of creatures lurking through the cold, castle walls were everywhere! Samol asked his friends, "Where are we going anyw—"

"AHHH!" Leanna screamed as if she'd seen a ghost.

"What!!" shouted London and Paul who'd turned to face her.

"I thought I saw — I thought I saw — something," said Leanna, trying to find something to say.

"He-doesn't-want-you!!" London barked.

"Maybe he WOULD if you'd quit blocking, ginger crotch!" Leanna clawed back.

"Aren't you supposed to be somewhere in Bridg—" London began to howl.

"Will you two shut up??" Paul screamed. "Samol doesn't need the extra stress!"

"See, now you've pissed him off," Leanna whispered loudly to London.

"Die - - again!" London hissed coldly.

After fifteen minutes of walking in silence that was colder than the castle's floors, they'd reached it. The Free-domcorpse maze was rather similar to the one in Zebrastone; large, daunting, and filled with the unknown. Before them was a big and seemingly harmless, grey mist in the al-ready-opened doorway of the maze, which was wide enough to fit an ocean-liner through! The mist seemed as though it were alive and could think. After staring at it, Samol even thought that it might've recognized them from a previous life.

"Ready?" London whispered, pulling a big, blue, starfish-shaped whistle from around her neck that she'd been hiding in her shirt as though she weren't supposed to have it.

"Hey, where'd you get that?" Paul asked, sounding almost jealous.

"Nipped it from Klaire Voyance's chamber!" London whispered as if whoever this Klaire was, was looking for both her and her whistle.

"Together, on three," London said. "One…Two…Three!"

London blew the whistle, and out came the sound of a terribly out of tune choir and full orchestra! The four of them jumped terribly. Just like before, in the castle of Zebrastone, they heard the sounds of their last lives and the great mist brightened the further the three of them walked through. Yet, around Samol grew a terrible, black wind that barred him from seeing anything in his last life. He backed away looking for another way in. There were none.

By now, his friends were too far in the maze to hear him if he even screamed for help. He stepped away from it wondering why the mazes were doing this to him. 'Maybe Silas was right' he thought. 'Maybe I am different from the other Aryamites. What if there's another maze somewhere in Euphod that is made for people just like me??'

Samol experienced the loneliest two hours ever. He was so close to his friends, yet so far away. He and the black-ened mist stared at each other like they were sworn enemies. If it could speak, it probably would've said, 'stay away or I'll rip you to shreds!' Samol thought. Silas's words suddenly struck him: *"The truth is, if you're going through such mon-strosities, not only do you have a big calling, but it means you're strong enough to endure it."*

Before Samol could see his friends, he heard their voices. As though it were a tradition, Paul and London were arguing like an old married couple about the stupid mis-takes they'd made in their last lives. And then, he saw them. Strangely, it seemed as if Leanna and London had almost be-come...friends? Every few seconds, they would smile at each other, but maybe Samol was just imagining things. He felt unimportant; like they'd forgotten all about him and began to cry. And then, something strange happened...

When the first tear hit the icy floor, a figure of Vic-toria arose in a thick, blue mist! She was screaming, point-ing, and laughing at what had become of him. The second tear drop landed on the ground and the spirit of loneliness arose, which looked like an infinite, open, black field. It, too, was surrounded in a bright blue mist of its own. The third teardrop revealed the spirit of confusion, which were grey, fast-moving swirls around the top of a woman's head. The fourth teardrop was the spirit of despair, which was a thin, male figure lost in a thick, darkening forest. Fluttering in the corner away from the rest of the figures was a hazel-eyed, weeping dove.

Samol didn't see any of these figures and kept crying. When his friends finally emerged, their mouths fell open when they saw him sitting on the floor in a puddle of tears surrounded by blue figures.

"Samol!" London screamed, dashing towards him. "What happened?"

"Are you okay? And what are those?" Paul asked, staring at the blue, ghostly figures.

"What are what??" Leanna asked loudly, rubbing her eyes. "This friggin' double vision! I can't see squat!"

"What?" Samol asked, drying his tears.

Suddenly Leanna saw them and gasped as if she knew what they were.

"Those are Lixaedyms!" she blurted. "They're figures that show why someone is crying. The person who's crying can't see them — only others can."

"Whoa…" said Paul who seemed rather amazed.

"Figures? Are there ghosts around me??" Samol began to panic, swatting at his arms and legs as though bugs were crawling on him.

"Relax!" said Leanna. "It looks like they can't even touch you," she said, staring at the figure of Victoria.

"Samol, what happened to you?" London asked softly.

"I don't know," he answered honestly. "I entered the maze just like you guys and then everything got windy and dark — it was like I was in a tornado or something!"

Leanna began stroking her chin like she were a detective trying to solve a case.

"What ghost — figure — things do you see around me??" Samol asked again, looking everywhere wildly, pulling away from the walls as though one would jump through and attack him the way Leanna had been attacked before the Death Day Ball.

"I see a really, really…ugly and evil-looking woman who's screaming something!" said Leanna trying to describe Victoria.

"Beside her are three figure-looking things…" London added, who wasn't afraid of them, but was sure not to get too close to them either. "There's a man who's trapped in a forest who looks like he's ready to give up. And the middle one is a girl who looks like she's in a — in a daze…or lost or something. And the last one is just an open, dark field," she struggled to explain.

"Wait, there's another one!" said Paul, pointing to the corner. "There's a parakeet who's crying!"

"That's a dove, Paul!" London sighed, covering her face, wanting to tell him that his intelligence matched his hair color.

"I'm scared," Samol whimpered, trying to choke back tears.

"Samol, it's okay," said London, who didn't know what else to say.

"No, it's NOT okay!" Leanna shouted angrily. "And you're not doing him any good by sugar-coating it!"

Leanna knelt down next to Samol and said, "This is not good. That's the second time you weren't able to view your life in the maze and I don't think it's a coincidence."

"WHAT-ARE-YOU-SAYING??" Samol snapped.

"What I'm saying…" Leanna paused, trying to be understanding, "is that all of this is probably tied to whatever cursed you. We need to figure out a way around this."

"Is there??" he asked desperately.

"…I think so…" Leanna hesitated. "But — it's against nearly every Euphod rule and we would run the risk of getting caught by Bloodwig! But if it works..."

"Oh, hell no!" London barked, rolling her neck to all three words. "Looky here, hussy! You better come up with something a lot better than '…uhhh… I think so… It might work,' if you're putting us all at risk of dealing with Bloodwig!"

"Well, I didn't hear you come up with anything!" Leanna groaned devilishly.

"You haven't said anything, either!" London howled with hatred.

"Because YOU interrupted me!"

"ENOUGH YOU TWO!!" Paul hollered. "Geez! Were you two lovers in a past life or something?"

"Ugh, puh-leaze!" London insulted. "I could do better than this knock-kneed thot!"

"GUYS! What's the plan already??" Samol shouted desperately.

"It's going to involve magic," Leanna began, ignoring London's insult.

"MAGIC??" the three of them howled.

"Bloodwig will have our heads before we can say '*casket!*'" London hollered.

"No way. It's too dangerous!" Paul agreed nervously, jolting his head from left to right.

"Unsupervised magic is against Euphod rules!" London pressed on.

"Do you wanna help Samol or not??" Leanna belted.

Paul and London fell silent and their eyes darted between one another as though they were trying to communicate non-verbally.

"It's the only way we can even begin to figure out what happened to him," Leanna said, eyeballing Samol as though he were terminally ill. "And unless either of you can offer a better solution, I suggest you speak up now!!" she said, glaring only at London. No one said a word.

"That's what I *thot!*" Leanna gloated. "Follow me!"

Off they went into the deep, forbidden part of the Freedomcorpse castle. One wrong turn, too much noise, getting spotted by that two-faced, Freedomcorpse psychic, Madame Twolips, whose had a serious grudge towards Paul ever since the Death Day Ball that took place three years ago, and they'd catch Bloodwig's wrath! Samol was petrified to say the least. But, it seemed that this was the only way.

174

CHAPTER ELEVEN

DEADLY MAGIC IN THE MAKING

"Mind over matter is the ultimate way. You'll break your neck twice if you touch blue or grey... It's the little ones to watch; as they can be mean. Touch only the green and not a color in between..." ~ Felicks Phlaps

℘he four of them hurled for the pits of the castle. Each step grew darker and colder. The walls in the lower depths of the Freedomcorpse castle were barely lit by black and blue candles, whose wax was frozen. Now, sixty stories below the castle's surface, the awful stench and ominous silence left them fearing that they were nearing the gates of hell! Large spiders and their children sat clothed in webs, waiting to pounce on their next meals. An occasional howling voice seeped from the walls. Leanna, who'd done this before, seemed most frightened of all because the underground fixtures had changed since the last time! However, she hid it well and kept her eyes closed tight, feeling along the walls as if she were in search of something — or someone.

"What are you doing?" London asked, sounding annoyed already. "SHHH!!" said Leanna, hugging the dusty, cold, grey, brick wall until she finally came across a smooth surface that they would've missed unless they were looking for it.

"Mystery is my maker," Leanna whispered in a cold, airy voice.

The wall cracked open revealing a large, deranged, spiraling staircase with no railing and a large, flat mirror lying at its bottom as though it were a window in the floor. The stairs crossed over one another like a helix. Some went sideways. A few were coiled as though they'd been twisted by a whirlwind. Others looped around like rollercoasters. Samol, London, and Paul found the looped stairwells odd and wondered how someone would walk on them - - and where they even led to!

"I'm not going down there!" said Paul, who took one look at the staircase and tried to run away.

"There's no going back now!" Samol said, yanking him back by the arm.

"I won't let anything happen to you, Paul," Leanna said flirtatiously.

"I'm gonna throw this tramp THROUGH the steps!" London said to herself.

"Whatever you do — DO NOT look up or down! Look only straight ahead when walking down the staircase," Leanna instructed.

"What?? We'll fall!" Paul shrieked, gazing down at the bottomless pit.

176

"No, we won't! AND STOP LOOKING DOWN!!" Leanna said once more, who had already began walking down the winding, cement stairs. "We'll have to hold onto each other!" she said, extending her hand.

"Great...now we'll all fall!" Paul said to himself, looking at her knocked knees, which bashed into each other as though they were playing patty-cake.

"Why can't we look up or down?" Samol asked curiously, grabbing London's hand.

"This is the Double Helicks Stairwell — don't ask where it got its name from..." Leanna began. "In this stairwell, when you look down you'll see your past. Depending on how bad it may have been, it could stifle you and cause you to plunge to a final death! If you look upward, you may see your future which, especially for you, Samol, could be confusing. We're not meant to understand or even see it yet."

Samol grew riddled with curiosity and thought about sneaking an upward peak for just a second or two. He quickly shot his eyes to the sky for not even a second, when he saw just as many stairs above him as there were below. 'Would it kill me to look?' he thought. 'What if it only showed me a nice, hot meal in my next life? If this hunger streak continues, that'll be three lives with barely any food!' he thought to himself. Yet, he exercised self-control and didn't look.

"What happens if you look sideways, Leanna?" London sassed, just looking for a fight.

"...How about you do it and tell me what happens!" Leanna argued back.

"Will you two stop for God's sake?" Paul yelled. Just when he thought he couldn't be more annoyed by the two of them, he was. "Where are you taking us anyway, Leanna?"

"I'm taking Samol to see Madame Levine, Queen of Freedomcorpse spells and incantations," she said, pulling a spider web from her face. "Each of the seven castles have an appointed witch, wizard, or sorcerer. However, they're hidden because they're technically not supposed to be there."

"Does the administration know?" Samol asked.

177

"...*Yes*..." Leanna replied hesitantly, her voice sounding more like she were asking a question than giving an answer. "But according to Euphod history, three hundred-seventeen years ago, they decided that having an appointed witch, wizard, or sorcerer placed within each castle was a necessary evil that they would turn a 'blind eye' to. It was originally for people who needed it, with situations like yours or even worse."

"Hmm," Samol grunted shortly, almost tripping on a cracked step he just passed over, still fighting the urge to peak upward.

"Truth be told, a few of the rulers, themselves, have been known to use a spell or two! Still, to this day, the only one who doesn't know about the whole operation is Bloodwig," said Leanna with a sense of relief in her voice.

"Thank God," Paul said softly.

"How does it — well — work if it's forbidden?" Samol stammered.

"Each spell, potion, or incantation that an Aryamite wishes to use must be checked out...kinda like a library book. This allows the administration to keep track of who's using what spell, for how long, and why," Leanna explained. "You'll only be given a spell or incantation for an allotted amount of time and the next person who needs it must wait until you're done."

"Oh..." he said.

"You leave your death certificate, a signature, and/ or some sort of collateral with the appointed witch or wizard of the castle until you return to Euphod from your next life. Madame Levine can further explain," Leanna said, who'd finally reached the bottom of the tall stairwell and the massive mirror was out of sight.

The dungeon in which they found themselves was frigidly cold; colder than even one of Paul's previous lives in Verkhoyansk, Russia. Samol felt his own breath catch in his chest. He was drowning in cold. The dungeon was black as night and almost too still. In the far distance were the faint sounds of what might've been tortured souls trying to escape from the walls just for a bit of warmth. Samol made sure to stay close to his friends for body heat, but the frigid air still tore through them all. All of a sudden, Leanna stopped walking. Paul, who was still holding her hand, wondered if she'd frozen to death while standing up!

"Leanna?" Paul shivered terribly.

"Everything's fine," she said softly. "It's just — I'm just — fre — cold!"

London, who'd been a detective in two of her past lives, could tell from the tone of her voice that she wasn't just cold, but she was also hiding something.

"You got us lost, didn't you??" London accused loudly, her jaw shivered with every syllable.

"I…I don't know what happened!" Leanna admitted. "The last time she…I mean I did this, the Freedomcorpse castle was different!"

Suddenly, a terrible growl that sounded like a beast from the gates of hell riveted throughout the dungeon. Samol grew weak in the knees as though he were going to faint again. Unfortunately, a Euphod dungeon was no place to pass out!

"Oh, shoot!" Paul screamed, running for the stairs.

"GET BACK HERE!" said London, yanking his arm. "We've got to stick together!"

The invisible beast snarled even louder than before as if they were getting close to one of its babies…whatever its babies might've been! No one moved.

"….If 'Ms. Thing' gets us mauled…I swear I will come back in another life and beat that ass!" London threatened under her breath as the four of them began carefully inching through the dark room.

An unpleasant gust of arctic air rushed through them once again. They shivered terribly. The only good thing was that it froze their floating corpses, giving them extra time in Euphod.

Leanna tried to get her bearings once more and began sniffing the air.

"What are you doing?" London asked.

"Where the hell are we??" Paul whispered, sounding very scared.

"This is getting ridiculous!" London accused furiously.

"Shhh!" said Leanna, wanting them to keep as quiet as possible.

And then, it happened.

London spotted a pair of big, red eyes in the corner! She gasped quietly, giving Samol a swift tug on the hand. His mouth, too, fell open when he saw it. He quietly tugged on Paul's hand, who finally jerked Leanna's. The four of them stood paralyzed as the creature's growl grew louder.

Out of nowhere, a bright starfish hovering in blue smoke emerged, startling the four of them. Just when they thought that the creature had found its four-in-one dinner special, it retreated when it saw the hovering starfish as though the beast were afraid of it.

"What is it?" Samol asked, eyeballing the hovering, blue figure.

"I…don't know," Leanna said truthfully, cutting her eyes at the creature in the corner every few seconds.

"Wait a minute," Paul said brightly as if he'd had an epiphany. "That's a spero!!"

"SHHH!!" London shushed him, averting her eyes to the beast in the corner. "A what?" she whispered again when she saw that it hadn't moved.

"Each castle has one," Paul explained. "The Freedom-corpse spero is a starfish. I overheard someone at the Death Day Ball say that if the corresponding spero of a castle ever presents itself, it means that you're in great danger and the spero will protect you."

"Paul, you were drunk!" London accused in a hot whisper.

180

"I KNOW what I heard!" Paul squawked, not caring that he was supposed to be quiet.

"And I know what I saw!" London argued back.

"Yeah — that cute butt of yours," Leanna said quietly, still wanting a piece of him.

"Will you get off his nuts for once, woman??" London hollered as though she'd forgotten about the creature in the corner. "Check your pulse because your whore-mones are RAGING!"

"You know what…I can't wait to f—" Leanna tried to argue back.

"GUYS, CAN WE KEEP FOCUSED??" Paul said in the quietest holler possible.

Both girls fell quiet, but exchanged more hate with their eyes than they ever could with words.

The four of them huddled together, slowly creeping towards the hovering starfish until they were close enough to see the small, zigzagged patterns etched within it. Suddenly, the starfish vanished. They were once again in total darkness and could hear the creature's footsteps thumping towards them! Samol was reminded of Victoria's footsteps and feared he were going to get attacked! Suddenly, another starfish appeared a few feet ahead of them.

They ran desperately towards it and it, too, vanished when they got too close. No one said a word, but they knew to keep going. A third blue starfish appeared and then vanished in the same fashion. They realized that the speros were leading them out of the dungeon. Twenty-three starfish later, they saw the tiniest sliver of light coming from a lit, gold candle on the wall in the far distance. It was another dungeon, but to them it looked like the Pearly Gates of Heaven!

"Told you!" said Paul, sounding like a toddler.

"I guess it's true," Samol mumbled.

"Of course it's true," Paul said proudly.

"Not you!" Samol jeered. "Freedom relies on faith. When life…or death brings you to a situation, you are strong enough to get through it!"

Paul bitterly ruffled his plaid shirt, pissed that something stupid like Silas's words of wisdom had stolen his moment of shine.

They ended up in a long hall. Hundreds of gold framed portraits aligned the candlelit walls as high as the eye could see. The four of them studied the photographs and occasionally looked over their shoulder to make sure the beast hadn't followed them.

"Where are we?" Samol asked, staring at a distant picture of a beautiful black woman.

"This looks like the Freedomcorpse Memorial Hall..." said Leanna, who sounded more confused than thrilled.

"Do you think all seven castles have similar portraits hidden in their dungeons?" Paul asked timidly.

"I don't know," Leanna shrugged.

Samol stood before the first portrait. It was a handsome, serious-looking, olive-complected man. He read aloud:

"Zedcov Symone
Prime minister of Freedomcorpse
1957 A.D. – 1685 B.C.

As a respectable and well-loved Aryamite, Zedcov lived eight hundred seventy-four lives before assuming his one hundred thirty-three year reign as Freedomcorpse Prime minister."

"Whoa!" Paul said, who was more impressed at how many lives he'd lived than anything. He fixed his eyes on two small, practically illegible paragraphs below that and asked, "What's in the fine print?"

"Beats me," said Leanna, who before Samol read his name aloud, couldn't tell whether Zedcov's first name was "Redcop" or "Tupac."

London squinted and read aloud:

" '~Wealth, poverty, genius, handicapped, all races, re-ligions, sexualities, and struggles. Not only have I seen it all, but I've lived it all! Everything you will ever encounter in life breaks down to freedom and love~ "

'Onyx, gems, jaspers, golds,
What is this your heart beholds?
They'll be your friend like they are told,
By now too late your heart's gone cold.' "

"I've never heard of such an incantation," said Leanna.

"Me either," said London.

"Wait a minute!" Paul beckoned. "London, what happened during your last reincarnation?"

"What are you talking about?" she said, almost annoyed that he'd distracted her from studying the portrait of a fat man in a wig next to Zedcov.

"You didn't say the usual incantation for your last life. You said...something different," he said, trying to recall what she said.

"*THAT* is personal business and none of it is yours, thank you very much!!" she snapped.

"Whoa!" Paul said sheepishly. "Sorry I troubled you, *Ms. Personal business,*" he mocked, hiding the fact that she'd hurt his feelings.

Her words were harsh, unnecessary even, but Paul seemed to have the emotional range of a gnat, because he let her words roll off his shoulders not even three seconds later. He stood gazing at the portrait of an ugly Englishman, whose nose was almost beak-like, his dentures were noticeably made of bones, and both eyes were facing in opposite directions. Underneath was a caption that Paul read aloud:

' "Wyllm Roustram
Member of the Freedomcorpse Secret Society
Recipient of the 1883 Death's Trophy Award
Born 1191 A.D. died 1163 A.D.' "

Paul's friends gave him a strange glare, all for different reasons. Leanna was confused by the dates of his life. Samol wanted to know what the 'Freedomcorpse Secret Society' was.

"What's the Death's Trophy Award?" London asked.

Leanna and Paul shrugged.

"What's the Freedomcorpse Secret Society?" Samol asked.

"Never heard of it," said Paul, whose voice suddenly sounded hoarse, as though his mouth had gone dry.

"What's the–" London began again.

"Will you let my Paul finish!" Leanna hollered, her brown eyes angrily fixed into London's.

"YOUR Paul??" London answered sassily, both hands placed at her hips.

"Come on you two!" Samol finally yelled, who just like Paul, was getting fed up.

"Whore-mones," said London, clearing her throat.

Paul tuned them out and finished reading aloud: *"'Wyllm Roustram was last seen naked on the west corridor of the Freedomcorpse castle, covered in dirty tissue paper in the summer of 1884...'"*

"Naked??" the three of them howled with twisted faces as though they'd actually seen this terrible image.

"'That's what it says...' said Paul, re-reading the fine print.

"Guys — I just noticed something," Samol said weakly, examining two more portraits that were side by side.

"What?" they asked collectedly.

"Every last one of these Aryamites died before they were even born...according to these dates."

No one said a word.

"I, myself, have never been able to see any of my past lives yet," Samol said, who was clearly trying to piece things together. "I remember Arabis saying that when you review your lives, you go back in time, right?"

Again, no one spoke, but stared nervously at one another like they were all coming to the same conclusion, but hoped they were wrong.

"I bet every one of these Aryamites died a final death when they were looking at what happened in their past lives!" Samol panicked. "Perhaps these Aryamites are all great because whatever was in their past was only large enough to be conquered while living — not while they were dead!" Samol said as his eyes darted from portrait to portrait.

Paul's eyes followed.

"What if not being able to see any of my past lives is — well — a protection rather than a curse?" Samol asked intuitively.

"You might be right, Samol," London said sadly. "Silas once told me that when you've been reincarnated into a life, you can't see many things by design. Yet, when you go backwards in time to review your life, everything that you couldn't see while alive, is revealed..." she said, looking as though she'd just solved a restless riddle to one of her very own past lives. "Maybe it is a good thing that you can't review any of your past lives. None of them have ever been — exactly — 'a walk in the park'... and if all that's been revealed during *life* has been absolute hell...there's no telling what you might find when you go backwards!"

"Guys, look at this!" Leanna howled, who was now standing at the end of the huge hallway pointing to another hall.

"What is it??" they screamed, running towards her. The three of them turned the corner to find an infinitely, high wall of more gold-framed portraits next to more lit candles.

"It's the Wall of Lunacy," Leanna revealed, looking at the googly-eyed faces staring back at her.

"Wall-of-what??" everyone said together as if they were reading from a teleprompter.

"Are you guys serious?" Leanna said sassily. "Haven't you three ever been dead before??" Leanna said as if they'd committed a Euphod crime for not knowing what it was.

"The Wall of Lunacy has portraits of all Aryamites who lost their minds while living a past life. Most of them were never seen again," Leanna said, who suddenly looked almost unsettled as if she saw a portrait of one of her friends on the top row. "According to Euphod history, the further down the wall you go, the more insane the Aryamites become."

For a second, Samol didn't feel so bad about his past life. He was proud that he didn't end up there after dealing with Victoria! Every pale, googly-eyed face sitting behind the gold-framed portrait told the tale of many wild and uncanny past lives. Some had terribly crooked teeth while others looked like they'd been dragged through hell and back! Surprisingly, the further they walked down the hall, the more Aryamites began to look normal, even plain-looking, like an everyday person you'd pass in the streets.

"Wait," said Paul with a confused look. "You said they're supposed to be crazier the further you go down the wall, right?"

"Yes, according to Euphodology," Leanna answered, who was now preoccupied with studying other portraits.

"But they look so...normal," he said to himself, but loud enough for everyone to hear.

"Well...that's what happens when you try to live a life that isn't meant for you," Leanna replied. "On the outside you look 'normal.' But on the inside..."

"Hmm…" Paul grunted shortly, as though he were guilty of doing this in a past life.

The four of them absent-mindedly studied the portraits, almost as if they'd forgotten the real reason why they were now seventy stories underneath the Freedomcorpse castle.

"Theonardo Va Linci??" Paul howled, staring wide-eyed at the portrait of a man whose bushy beard was long enough to tuck into his black overcoat.

"Who?" asked Samol.

"I didn't know Va Linci was an Aryamite!" said London, staring surprisedly at the painting.

186

"Well, of course he was!" Leanna replied passionately. "You don't suppose all his genius simply spawned from living only one life, do you??"

"I don't understand," said Paul, scratching his head, tugging at his plaid shirt almost at the same time. "Theonardo Va Linci wasn't crazy. He was one of Euphod's more 'normal' geniuses, I thought."

"His case was a bit different but…I do believe that he lived his first life in a time when being a homosexual was deemed as having a mental illness. Thus, he was condemned," Leanna explained.

"WHAT??" shouted London and Paul.

"Mental illness??" London said wildly. "But he invented Bridgelove's first parachute, Euphod's fighting armored cars and vehicles for times of war, and even created our very first diving suit so that we could explore Euphod's Purple Dead Sea!"

"It's sad how ignorant people can be sometimes," said Paul.

"Purple Dead Sea? Samol asked, giving London a slight scowl as though she misspoke.

"Well…I've never seen it. But apparently Euphod's Dead Sea is bright lavender. They say it's from tiny fragments of Aryamite souls who have died a final death. *Some say it's a myth,"* said London, whispering her last five words as though saying this out loud was a sin.

"Mother, your eyesight is terrible!" Leanna said softly, rubbing her eyes.

"What?"

"Oh — er — I — was just looking for a photograph of someone - - I got my mother's awful eyesight," she laughed nervously.

Everyone fell quiet and watched Leanna's eyes dart between three side-by-side portraits and her feet.

"What are you doing?" Samol asked.

"Stand right here," Leanna said, pointing to the ground.

187

"When you look at the wall of lunacy and you stand-right-here," she said exactly, her voice stretching high as though she were reaching for something, "the portraits show them as the world saw them. But, if you stand here..." she shuffled over three steps, "it shows them as they truly were."

"What are you talking about??" said an irritated London, looking to see the difference. "They're all the same!"

"Stand here. Look improperly," said Leanna, nudging London almost too forcefully, as if this was her chance to finally shove her like she'd always wanted to.

London stared strongly. A slight pause followed — and then she spoke, her words tumbled from her mouth as though she'd seen the face of God.

"WHOA!!" she said with a gleam.

"What do you see??" Samol begged.

"I do see crazy people…"

"See! If you ju—" Leanna began.

"YOU, Leanna! UGH! You're so full of it!" London stormed.

"Wait, move over!" said Paul, shoving London out of the way.

He placed his feet exactly where London had placed hers and stood silent for a few seconds. He gave a rather unusual stare at a curly-haired, old woman as if he were waiting for her to leap from the portrait. Samol's eyes bounced between Paul and the old, plump lady as though he were afraid he'd miss something if he even blinked for a second. Sure enough, Paul saw it! Right before his eyes, the old woman morphed from a face to a manuscript of music! The portraits next to her became literature, some became extensive architecture, and a few even morphed into food!

"*Deadly!*" Paul said with an excited smile.

Samol saw that he was captivated by something and he couldn't wait to get a turn.

"Hey, let me see!" said Samol, pushing the dazed Paul aside. Samol carefully placed both feet exactly where Paul's were. Nothing happened.

188

He stared at the hundreds of faces before him intensely as if he were trying to perform a magic trick with his mind or something. Still, nothing happened...until it did. Every lit candle went out. Every gold portrait frame turned black. The faces in the portraits became distorted and turned into an enraged beast that began spitting hot mucus at the four of them, which melted through the brick floors as though it were paper, leaving behind potholes of ascending, black smoke!

"RUN!" Leanna shouted at the top of her lungs.

The ground was beginning to look like Swiss cheese. The four of them ducked and dodged the hurling phlegm and the crumbling bricks that were actively falling from the ceiling! A large loogie landed on London's shoulder, singeing away nearly a quarter of her hair! She screamed terribly.

"LONDON!" shrieked Samol and Paul.

The two of them doubled back to grab her. Leanna was the only one who knew the way out, but she was gone! The boys carried her, still dodging the deadly spit pellets! She quivered as the odorous steam arose from her charred scalp and shoulder. At the end of the hall was a small, rickety staircase. The entire dungeon was beginning to flood with the nasty mucus! The three of them ran up the stairs only to find that the doorway was boarded shut!

"OH, NO!" Samol shrieked, eyeballing the door to see if he could kick through it.

"There's no way out!" Paul panicked.

The spit reached the bottom of the metal stairwell and began buckling the steel, causing the three of them to jolt forward.

"AHHHH!" they hollered, hoping that someone - - anyone seventy stories above them could hear.

"It's over!" Paul screamed.

The smell was awful! They continued screaming, yet no one came to rescue them! Panicked and hopeless, they saw a final death flash before their very eyes.

"Samol, if you can find it in your heart, please forgive me," Paul said strangely.

"I love you boys," London said gently, ready to die a final death, shutting her eyes tightly.

Suddenly, the boiling mucus cracked the ground in two and everything drained! Samol hugged his two best friends, letting out a thoroughly relieved sigh, so did Paul — but, he unfortunately soiled himself! The three of them stared at the ruins of the darkened corridor. It was terribly smoky. Charred gold dripped down the walls. The floors looked as though they'd been bombed! With only two lit candles left, the dungeon was incredibly dark and looked as though they were in a foggy cage from hell. Breathing heavily, they waited at the top of the staircase for the ground to cool.

"Is everyone all right?" Samol asked, his arms still tightly squeezing London.

"No," screamed Paul. "I'm still waiting for my balls to descend! And I had — an accident!"

"Hello?? My shoulder is blistering and my hair is burned off!" London screamed.

"Sorry!" they said.

Glad to know that she still had her feisty spirit, Samol and Paul knew that she would survive. They carefully carried her down the stairs, which wiggled terribly like a loose tooth. Smoke continued to rise from the ground and the lingering stench was still strong. Practically playing hop-scotch over the ruins with an injured girl on their shoulders, they reached another door at the other end of the hall. Paul yanked it open, not even giving a second thought as to what might be lurking on the other side.

They were in a bright room with many windows, which was quite the opposite of the dungeon. White pillars extending to The Heavens lined the walls. Its ceiling swirled above them as if it were alive with thoughts and feelings, yet the three of them didn't even notice. Samol jerked his head around when he suddenly spotted the floating body of someone hiding behind a large pillar in a corner.

"Who's there??" Samol said boldly, afraid that it was another beast or something.

A knock-kneed figure with big hair emerged.

"Leanna! Thank God you're all right!" Samol sighed heavily.

"Thank God you're all right??" Paul mocked as if Samol belonged on the Wall of Lunacy. "YOU LEFT US IN THERE TO DIE!!" shouted Paul.

"I'm sorry!" Leanna said submissively. "What was I supposed to do??"

"Uh — maybe tell us where the hell to go??" Paul belted. "You were the one who led us down here in the first place!"

"Yeah! To help Samol!" Leanna whirled back defensively.

"AND-YOU-LEFT-US!!" Paul wheeled angrily once again.

"Guys, ENOUGH!" said Samol, who was now more fed up with the constant bickering than any of them.

"Look, I'm sorry, OKAY??" Leanna surrendered. "I panicked! The important thing is that we're all fine now."

Surprisingly, the three of them hadn't reacted as badly as Leanna thought they would. One could only imagine what she really thought they would do to her! She studied London's horrible injuries and made the worst mistake she could've ever made and said:

"Nice haircut," she winked.

"You...BITCH!" London hollered, charging at her.

"London! NO!" Paul and Samol shouted together.

London's fist met Leanna's face knocking her to the ground. 'BOOM!' One punch became six...twelve...twenty! The terrible tussle began! Leanna, a girly girl who seemed to have never been in a fight in any of her past lives was no match.

London was on top of her, pounding her head into the concrete! She spat, bit, choked, punched, slapped, and cussed her out in every language she knew! Samol and Paul ran to help the poor girl.

Leanna screamed for help, throwing aimless, flimsy swats in the air! "MOM!!" she screamed. "Mom, your FACE!!!" Leanna howled as if London was beating all the sense out of her! The boys scuffled back and forward around them, figuring out how to get London off of her without getting hit! London was a wild animal. She hit harder than any man Paul had ever seen and cursed worse than any construction worker he'd ever talked to!

What was left of London's red locks flew wildly through the air. Paul went to pull London off of her and she punched him in the balls! He dropped to the ground in the fetal position, cupping his manhood, screaming even louder than Leanna! Samol, who couldn't believe his eyes, stepped over his nearly-crippled friend, cupping his own manhood, and attempted to pull her off Leanna. With cat-like reflexes, a fist met the hand covering his groin, which doubled him over! After a second attempt, he was able to pull her off.

London was still swinging, swearing, spitting, and kicking! Samol restrained her the best he could, but couldn't take his eyes off the unrecognizable, motionless girl that laid on the ground. Leanna's face was beaten inward. Her nose was broken. Both eyes were blackened. Her left ear was torn. Parts of her hair were ripped out (she and London were now even). Both lips were swollen like overcooked Bratwursts. And Paul, not to mention, was still rolling on the ground holding his shaft and berries!

Samol was still restraining the fuming force of nature and said, "Guys, I hate to break up our little love fest, here, but we really need to keep going!" The problem was that Leanna was the only one who knew how to get them out! She struggled to stand to her feet and fell back to the ground like toothpicks under a house. Leaning sloppily on a nearby pillar, she tried once more.

192

Her knees quivered as if they were going to give out any second, but thankfully didn't. Paul stood up and hobbled with a wide gait as though he had a terrible STD! Samol couldn't believe this: he was the one with the curse, but was in better shape than everyone in the room!

"Let's — d — jah — Madame Levine," Leanna babbled incoherently, her busted lips flapped as if they would fall from her face any second. Samol feared that London had beaten all the directions out of her head! Or what if she would purposely lead them astray only to be ambushed by some deadly creature?? After five minutes of attempting to master the task of walking, Leanna led them through the second door on the opposite side of the room and they continued their journey.

Tensions were high and no one said a word.

For nearly an hour, they'd traveled up and down more hidden stairwells, a few more pitch black dungeons - - some with growling beasts and some without. Finally, they reached a long, thin crawlspace that would've been the death of anyone with claustrophobia. The rusty pipe was as long as a football field, but barely wide enough to fit a dog through! Not to mention the kinds of bugs that might've been hiding in there — and the ungodly smell!! All four of them shimmied through the tight, rusty pipe. There were a few times where Paul, the biggest of the four, panicked because he got stuck. Samol once again wondered if this was a part of Leanna's secret ambush plan to get back at London.

"Madame Levine better be a goddess! This is torture!" Paul screamed, pulling his foot a loose from an unexpected twist in the pipe, "How much further??"

"I don't like this either!" London hollered, who was farthest in the back. "Get me out of here! I can't breathe!!"

"Relax, we're almost there!" said Leanna, who seemed rather calm and sounded much better than she looked.

Leanna was in front of everyone in the crawl space. She reached the end of the tunnel only to find that they were trapped! A steel cap was enclosed over the exit as though Bloodwig knew what they were up to! There was only a slight crack, but it wasn't wide enough for the four of them to slip through.

"Why've we stopped moving?" asked Paul with a growing panic in his voice. "Are we stuck?? WE'RE STUCK, AREN'T WE?? HELP! HELPPP!!!!"

"Calm down…" said Leanna, pushing on the steel cap.

"You wait till I get outta here! You're getting another ass-whoopin'!!!" London hollered, wiggling wildly, her voice echoing through the whole pipe.

"Wait-a-minute!" Leanna hollered sharply, only being bold because the barrier between Leanna and said 'ass-whooping' was Samol and Paul, who were both sand-wiched tightly in between the two girls.

Leanna was pushing at the metal seal, now twice as hard, afraid that if she didn't get it open she'd lose some teeth! She punched through the rusty metal enclosing with three hits! Samol was impressed, thinking that if only she'd used half that strength during the fight….

The opening revealed a large circular room with three doors on the other side. The floor was checkered like a colorful chessboard with tiles that were: red, blue, green, and grey. Leanna carefully stepped down and said to herself, "That's not good."

"There's more??" Paul screamed, trying to crane his neck around Samol.

"More what?" shouted London, who was still stuck behind Paul. "Hurry up, Paul! Get your butt outta my face! Damn, did you mess your pants or something??"

"I'm going as fast as I can, woman!" he howled back, not answering her question.

At last, everyone was out of that tight, rusty, god-for-saken pipe.

They stood at the edge of the checkered floor and Paul began to walk across.

"NO! Don't move!" Leanna shouted as though it were a trap.

"What?" Paul froze mid-step, his eyes darting left to right as he stood still. "Is it a bug?? IS IT A BUG?? Get it off me! GET IT OFF ME!!"

"There's no bugs, Paul!" said Leanna. "Calm down!"

Paul almost soiled himself again.

"In order to get across…in order to get across…." Leanna mumbled softly to herself, fingers clasped over her swollen, bloody lips, thinking heavily.

"What is she mumbling about?" Samol whispered to London.

"I don't know," London shrugged.

"I think you hit her one too many times!" he said.

"Mind over matter is the ultimate way. You'll break your neck twice if you touch blue or grey… It's the little ones to watch; as they can be mean. Touch only the green and not a color in between!" Leanna said to herself.

"That's it! Only let your feet touch the green tiles!" Leanna leapt.

She carefully placed her left foot on the closest green tile. Once situated, she extended a hand to Paul, who extended his hand to Samol, and Samol to London. Secretly, Leanna hoped that London would fall on her face or inadvertently step on a blue or grey tile! Within seconds, the four of them were each scattered amongst the floor, still holding hands, moving across as a mangled group. They were nearing the end when all of a sudden, Paul stumbled and fell face forward! Because they were all holding hands, he pulled everyone down with him!

Samol was the closest to him and felt the brunt of his body weight. Paul's face dangled inches from touching two blue tiles. "HELP!" he screamed and everyone pulled. Unfortunately, their efforts were of no use. He kept sinking. The distance between his face and the floor was as thin as a veil.

Everyone else was twisted like a contortionist, trying to hold on! Out of nowhere, the raspy voice of an old woman beckoned, *"Death be tamed! His soul benign! The day you were born changed Euphodkind!"* Like magic, the four of them suddenly found themselves standing in the chamber of a strange, elderly woman...unsure if they were now safe or in danger.

CHAPTER TWELVE

MADAME LEVINE

"Many people in your shoes have not made it out alive, Samol." – Madame Levine

There she stood; a heavy-set, old woman who was shorter than a stack of books and uglier than a vampire bat. She wore a black babushka over her long, stringy, white hair and a black cloak exposing her wooden, left leg. She only had one eye, which was unusually large with a black mole sprouting discolored hairs beneath it. She wore a black patch over the other barren eye socket. Samol and his friends tried not to stare, but couldn't help it because the eye patch kept moving as though a rodent were trying to burst through it! Her nose was longer than a loaf of garlic bread and her chin wasn't too far behind. Her rotted teeth hid themselves behind tiny, wrinkled lips.

Samol and his friends, who were covered in soot and still smelled like mucus, were in an odd, dimly lit chamber. Its velvet, maroon curtains draped over hundreds of crooked shelves, which were stacked with thousands of shimmering, liquid potions.

In the corner was a tiny window, which led to nowhere but a cement wall. It looked as though this very chamber was once a holding cell and the small window was put there as a cruel joke, giving prisoners a false hope of an escape. In the center of the room was a large, crystal ball on a table that was held in a gold encasing.

The old woman was stirring a potion of some sort in a rusty cauldron, humming to herself with her one eye closed. In a deep, airy voice she spoke:

"I am Madame Levine, keeper of spells and incantations within the castle of Freedomcorpse. I can give you the — Oh, dear!" she belted, clutching her wrinkled neck when she opened her eye and saw Leanna. "What happened to you??"

"I — I just —" Leanna stuttered embarrassingly.

"She crossed the wrong person," London smirked.

Fearing a second altercation, Paul quickly interjected, "Madame Levine, we are here because we think our friend, Samol, has been cursed."

"Cursed?" asked the old woman. "What kind of curse?"

"I don't know," said Samol, who was trying not to stare at that nasty mole or her eyepatch that moved every time she spoke. "When I was in the life before my last life, I couldn't talk or remember anything."

"You had no memory??" the old woman scowled, who'd stopped stirring her potion.

"None," Samol reiterated.

"We're his best friends — well — at least Paul and myself are," London said, glaring at Leanna, "and he didn't even recognize us!"

Madame Levine fell quiet and had dark thoughts expressed all over her face. She opened the brown cabinet below her workspace table and began rummaging through it. The clinking of dingy, half-filled glass bottles echoed throughout the eerie chamber.

"What is your name, young man?" asked Madame Levine without even looking at him.

"Samol," he said. "Samol Doscow."

"Any hard drug use in any of your past lives, Samol?" she asked, still rummaging.

"No!" he said, furrowing his brow. "At least…not that I can remember."

"Any booze? Black magic? Whores?"

"NO!" he shouted at once.

"Just checking," she said, pulling a lime green potion in a dirty, glass bottle from her cabinet.

"What does sex have to do with memory loss?" London asked honestly.

"Oh, sweetheart - - we women possess more power in a single swish in the hip than men do in their you-know-what. It'll make a man stupid…even forget his name!" the old woman chuckled a bit.

"Gross," Paul mumbled, almost vomiting at the mere thought of Madame Levine in the bedroom.

"Samol, give me your death certificate," said the old woman with an outstretched hand.

From his back pocket, he pried his crinkled, blue death certificate and gently placed it on the dusty table. She grabbed a pair of thick, silver-rimmed glasses from her bottom drawer and placed them on the tip of her lengthy nose. She swirled the brew and a shimmering mist emerged from its brim. The four of them gathered around her to watch.

"Excuse me, Miss Levine, but what are you doing?" Samol asked curiously.

"This is Phossil Ghoul Memory Juice. It unlocks the memories of your last three lives," Madame Levine explained.

"Whoa…" said Samol and Paul at the same time.

"If your curse is as simple as a memory block, this potion will allow you to actually be reincarnated as the memories of your past three lives!" The old woman adjusted her eye patch and studied the potion, making sure it wasn't too lumpy, or too smooth, not too green, yet just right.

199

"Are there any side effects?" Samol asked.

"There are two...*possible* side effects," the old woman said hesitantly. "The first: the spell could violently disagree with a particular memory of your past, causing the curse to, in fact, multiply itself."

"MULTIPLY ITSELF??" Paul and London hollered simultaneously.

"What do I do if that happens??" asked a frightened Samol.

"Well…" Madame Levine paused, "this potion is like an equation, if you will. If something is not balanced, it will need to balance itself and the only way to do that is…"

"Is what??" Samol begged.

"Suicide?" Paul and London said at the same time.

"…It's the only way, I'm afraid," she said. "But that's only if the spell goes bad."

"I don't like the sound of this already," Samol said, looking at his friends. "What is the other possible side effect?"

"The other downside is if memory loss is merely a symptom of a bigger problem, using this potion could wreak havoc on your next life! Even on those who love you!"

"That's too dangerous!" shouted Paul.

"Samol, this woman is a crook!" London whispered, pulling him aside. "Can't you see that?? Let's get outta here!"

Samol swallowed his fear and knew that this old woman might be the only chance of finding a cure.

"Madame Levine?" Samol quivered with a politeness in his voice. "This is very, very ris—"

"It may be the only way," the old woman coldly interrupted. He glanced sideways at his friends, who were just as much at a loss of words as he was.

"Fine," he sighed.

"Excellent," said Madame Levine, almost a little too excitedly. "I'm going to pour the solution onto the back of your death certificate. If it reacts positively, we've found a cure. If not, well…you four might want to step back a little."

She poured slowly. When the first drop touched, it shot off a violent, white fireball! It bounced from wall to wall, shattering nearly every one of her beloved potions! Surprisingly, not one of them burst into flames! After a minute of terrible destruction, it evaporated into thin air as if the fireball had a mind of its own.

"Apparently not!" said Madame Levine, gazing about the ruins.

She hobbled between the shattered glass on the floor, using her wooden leg like a broom to sweep aside the rubble. Pulling a ladder from behind a maroon curtain, she climbed to the top of her shattered shelf. Madame Levine brushed the broken glass from the shelves and pulled out one of the only potions left; a snow-white potion with small, flaming figures floating inside.

The potion was alluring - - so bright that if you stared at it for more than just a few seconds it would temporarily blind you. Sadly, like many beautiful things in life (and in death), the four of them couldn't stop staring at the blinding concoction as she climbed from the ladder.

"DON'T STARE AT IT!" Madame Levine hollered, hiding it under her cloak. "YOU'LL GO BLIND!!"

"What is it?" asked Leanna, who'd been quiet until now.

"This is Sunbone Juice. It's a special potion that gets to the root of one's unhappiness," she explained.

"Unhappiness?" Samol asked as though she'd offended him.

"Depression. Anxiety. Stress. All forms of negative en—" Madame Levine began.

"I know what unhappiness is, but I'm not unhappy!" Samol screamed, sounding ironically unhappy in that moment.

"How can you be sure <u>what</u> you are if you can't even remember <u>who</u> you are?" Madame Levine asked with an irritating grin. Samol gently scratched his arm, wondering if maybe she were right.

201

She further explained, "If you drink this potion, its effects can be felt in your next life. Even Vreeks can sense when someone is living under the effects of this potion!"

"It's so beau—" Paul began.

"I said DON'T LOOK AT IT!" Madame Levine hollered, popping him upside the head.

The old woman closed her eye for a few seconds as though she were praying that nothing would go wrong this time and then began to pour. The four of them turned their faces away. When the first drop touched, the deafening scream of a little girl tore through the air! It was louder than when London's death certificate got ripped by that mean giant at the Death Day Ball! What was even stranger was that only Samol, Paul, and Madame Levine could hear it. The three of them dropped to the ground, covering their ears. Leanna and London stared blankly at each other. After an agonizing thirty seconds, the piercing scream had silenced.

"WHAT WAS THAT??" Samol screamed, slowly parting his hands from his ears.

"WHAT??" screamed Paul, who was temporarily deafened.

"What happened?" London asked confusedly.

"You didn't hear that nasty noise??" Paul barked angrily, who only knew what she said because he'd read her lips.

"That's not good," Leanna mumbled under her breath.

"What's not good?" London asked Leanna.

"*Five people are standing in the same room. There's a scream that only three people hear! You tell me what's good about that!!*" Leanna belted condescendingly, only being snippy because she knew that London couldn't pop her in front of Madame Levine.

"Maybe you were deaf in a past life," London sneered.

"You didn't hear it either!" Leanna clawed back.

"ENOUGH!!" yelled Madame Levine. "It appears that perhaps we've been asking the wrong questions on behalf of Samol's curse diagnosis."

"What do you mean?" Samol asked, still massaging his ears.

"It seems that your curse is much more complicated than I anticipated; one that is rare and may only be diagnosable by exclusion," said the old woman.

"Maybe if we —" Paul began nervously.

"These two potions imply that your symptoms have symptoms, Samol," Madame Levine interrupted, her fingers clasped over her shriveled lips and her one eye was fixed piercingly into his.

Samol felt his stomach curdle as if Madame Levine were about to tell him that he had the dead person's version of cancer!

"Let's start from the very beginning, shall we," said the old lady, tightening her babushka. "When you've gone to review your past lives in the maze, what do you see?"

"He can't," his friends answered for him.

"What do you mean 'he can't?'" she said, almost as though she were angry.

"After each life, I try to review it in the maze, like everybody else. But all I see is a — a black, shadowy mist like something doesn't want me to see what happened," Samol struggled to explain.

"Were you…at all sensitive to light and/or water during any of your past lives?" she asked, rummaging through more potions in the cabinet below her workspace.

"No, not that I can recall," he said honestly, thinking that question was a bit odd.

"Okay…" she said. "Umm…let's go back to either your first, second, or third life and see what happened to you."

"He doesn't remember it," Paul heaved impatiently. "Is there another way?"

"Paul, shhh!" said London, pinching his arm.

"Have you ever…had anybody who was in love with you and wanted to harm you?" she asked, still rummaging through her plethora of potions, now with her big butt in their faces.

"What does this have to do with anything?" Paul hurled madly, who'd moved away from the awful site.

"Let me work!" she ordered, still rummaging in her cupboard with her butt now shifted the other way, even closer to Paul's face like she were doing it on purpose. "Samol, do you get woozy or feel faint during Euphod Solstice or Daynight Savings?" she asked.

"I don't know what any of those things are so I couldn't tell you, ma'am."

"Okay...umm...have you...lost any pets in a past life? Particularly a cat?" she asked, finally standing up, holding three potions in her plump arms.

"Not that I can remember."

"Why cats?" asked Leanna, who seemed suddenly interested.

"Well, with nine lives they're a viable commodity in our world!" Madame Levine said brightly.

Samol and his friends stared at one another as if they were going to say something, but didn't.

"Samol, have you ever been in love or has someone ever been in love with you who wanted to harm you?" the old woman asked, raising an eyebrow.

"You already asked me that!" he howled.

"And you didn't answer me, dear," she smiled irritatingly.

"No!" Samol shouted, "...At least, I don't think so... no!"

"He really doesn't have time for all of these stupid questions!" Paul spouted angrily.

"PAUL! Quit talkin' or I'm gonna leave you bloodied up worse than Leanna!" London yelled with drawn fists.

A light bulb went off in Madame Levine's head.

"Blood," she softly mumbled to herself.

"What?" said everyone.

"Blood," she said again, this time a little louder. "Samol, I need to know if you're able to see blood...or even be around it," Madame Levine asked, glaring at him through the top of her tiny, silver glasses, looking more serious than the four of them had seen her since they'd gotten there.

"See blood? What are you talking about?" Samol asked, sounding rather caught off guard.

"What does blood have to do with anything?" Paul asked loudly.

"Shut IT!" London said, slapping him on the chest.

"I need to know if you have the capability of seeing or being around blood. If you are, I need to know what blood actually does anytime it's in your presence," the old woman asked seriously.

Samol sensed that she was onto something. He thought back as far as his memory would permit. He remembered being stabbed to death, beaten by Victoria and Christian, burned by cigarettes. Yet, no memories of…blood. Wait a minute!...

He forced himself to think harder. Somehow, he managed to remember a glimpse of a past life! Which one? He didn't know. How he could suddenly remember it? He didn't know that either. In this particular life, he recalled stumbling upon a woman's dead body suspended in midair in a forest. However, when he walked towards her the woman's splattered blood…

"Receded the closer I got to her," he whispered to himself.

"What did you say?" said Madame Levine, who was glued to his every word.

"Her blood receded back into her body when I walked towards her! But it came back out once I backed away as if her blood was…running from me," Samol explained, surprised that he could even remember anything before his past two lives!

"Whose blood??" Madame Levine demanded. "What woman??"

"I don't know exactly which life it was or who this woman is...but I found her body in the woods, suspended in midair, but –"

"Like our bodies floating above us now?" Paul inter-rupted, pointing to his floating corpse.

"No," Samol said quickly. "This was different. Her body didn't move, as if it were…stuck in time or something."

"Did her body recede away from you or just her blood?" Madame Levine asked seriously.

"Just her blood," Samol said surely.

Madame Levine's ugly face grew pale as if she'd died again.

"Strange," she muttered. "Do you recall ever seeing blood in any of your dreams?"

"Ye – I don't know actually," he hesitated, still proud of himself for remembering even that much.

The five of them stood in a spine-chilling quiet. Madame Levine closed her eye and began thinking deeply. Suddenly, she was hit with an epiphany and widened her large eye so much that it nearly shot from its socket! Something in the back corner of the room had caught her attention; a brown, wooden encasement tied shut by a thick, black rope.

"I wonder," Madame Levine muttered solemnly.

She hobbled towards the secluded chest and carefully untied it with her long, witch-like fingernails, coiling the rope around her fat wrist. When she slowly opened the chest, a faceless, shadowy figure with bright white eyes forced its way out, sending a ripple throughout the room, knocking everyone to the ground! "Someone grab it!" shouted Madame Levine, hastily trying to get up. "I'm not touching that thing!" Paul shouted, crawling away. Leanna and London got up and fought to grab it.

The large, ominous creature dashed about the room as quickly as the fireball! Yet, it seemed harmless. The moment it was between Leanna and London, who were racing towards each other to grab it, the creature vanished and they head-butted! The girls were back on the ground right where they started.

206

"Watch where you're going, tramp!" London shouted, holding her head.

"YOU ran into ME!" Leanna hollered back almost as loud as when she was getting that beatdown.

"No, I'm sure YOU had your eyes on Paul again! He doesn't want you — you dense, irritating, piece of sh—!"

"ENOUGH!" interrupted Madame Levine, finally getting to her feet.

The girls sighed angrily.

"Why did you have us chasing that thing anyway?" London asked, standing to her feet.

"Because once it vanishes, it goes into another dimension and can taunt Aryamites in either a past or future life," Madame Levine explained.

"Was that…a daemalix?" Paul asked as though he'd seen one before.

"What do you know about daemali?" asked the old woman, giving him a terrible look.

"I could have sworn I saw one in a past life," said Paul. "They are…"

"Frightened in the presence of Vreeks," Paul and Madame Levine said at the same time.

The two of them gave each other a long, wide-eyed stare. Madame Levine seemed rather shocked that he knew what it was. The awkward silence lingered in the room. Samol hadn't a clue as to what they were talking about. The old woman hobbled over to the chest and peeked inside to find seven tiny, glass beacons filled with potions. Some were liquid. Some were smoky. Some were both. One, in particular, caught her attention - - a lonely, murky, maroon potion that bubbled gently in the back of the chest. With slight anxiety creeping through her old veins, she carefully brought it to the table.

Curiosity enveloped them all. Samol knew that whatever happened next could be it! Madame Levine stood over Samol's death certificate without moving for nearly a full minute. It looked as though she were praying again.

"...I need you all to center yourselves on all four corners of this table," she said seriously.

"Why? What's going on?" Samol began to panic.

"Just do as I say!" Madame Levine coerced.

The four of them took a corner, per her request.

"This is Gehiamese Fire Potion; one of the most dangerous potions known to our kind," said the old woman. "When I pour this potion onto Samol's death certificate, it will reveal seven of something...it could be different places, memories, or people. And they will be shown in one of seven colors. I need you all to watch closely and accurately. Understand?"

"Yes," they complied.

"Depending on where you stand, more than one image may reveal itself to you," she said.

"What are we looking for?" Leanna asked.

"If I knew that, we wouldn't be here," said the old woman. "If whatever you see turns green it means that the curse must be undone by altering *time* in some way. If whatever you see burns yellow that means that something or someone *peaceful* has been trying to protect Samol from a dark force. If the person, place, or memory burns clear, black, red, or white you must immediately shout the incantation *'Probaris!'*"

"Pro-what??" said all four of them, wondering how in the world they'd remember all of this.

Paul snickered immaturely.

"This is serious!" shouted Madame Levine. "Pro-bar-is! Say it with me!"

"Pro-bar-is!" they said slowly, the syllables trickling from their mouths all at different times.

"Good! It's an incantation that makes all spirits; good, bad, or indifferent, reveal themselves. If they're good, they'll tell you. If they're of evil, they will vanish!" the old woman explained.

"Got it!" said everyone.

"One more thing," she paused, "if it burns purple...

call me. Purple could be *anything* and in our case anything could be dangerous."

"Purple is the mystery," Leanna gasped quietly under her breath.

"What?" said Samol and London.

"Nothing," Leanna said quickly.

"And none of you, except for maybe Samol, should see anything burning blue - - blue means that it has something to do with you, personally. Remember, when we're done you must tell me everything you saw — exactly the way you saw it!" Madame Levine instructed.

"Okay," said the four of them, hoping there was nothing else she'd forgotten to say.

Samol's thumping heart could've been heard a mile away. The old woman carefully tipped the glass beacon and the murky potion began to fall. It touched his death certificate and right before everyone's eyes arose seven mists:

In front of London was a bright, fiery, green haze that revealed a sinister-looking, baldheaded, snaggletooth man. His terribly, green eyes matched the mist, making it hard to see the details of his facial features. He was trapped behind bars reaching for something outside his jail cell and looked as though he were screaming but she could not hear him.

In front of Madame Levine was a dove in a peaceful, bright, yellow mist. She could tell that it was a loving spirit in disguise, one that was both familiar, yet foreign to Samol. The dove had always been with him no matter what life he was living, but was barred from getting too close to him for some reason.

Before Leanna arose two mists that were side by side. To the left was a hovering, blue diamond ring bathed in a green mist. To her right was a blue quill that was floating in a swirling, white mist that suddenly grew arms and tried to reach for her neck! "PROBARIS!" she quickly shouted. The quill suddenly turned into a spiked skull and crossbones and burst into ashes! She backed away, breathing heavily, fearing that she would die again.

Arising before Paul were also two mists. To the left was an angry, caged demon missing its right eye encased in green smoke. To his right, however, was a red-eyed, blonde man that was first enveloped in a swirling purple smoke that quickly became blue. He was confused and stared intensely, unable to speak.

Finally, before Samol arose a single mist revealing a black scroll with names written in glistening blood. It reminded him of the scroll Maven pulled out when he'd sorted them. Suddenly, the script was melted away by something invisible and hotter than fire! He could feel an intensifying heat but saw nothing when suddenly he realized that there was a mist — a clear one! "PROBARIS!" he screamed, turning away his face. His death certificate had returned to its original state as if it had never been touched. Samol's rattled nerves left him on the brink of another nervous breakdown and he began to cry.

"What happened? What did you see?" Madame Levine asked Samol worriedly.

"I saw a black scroll with names written in blood. What does all of this mean??" he said, now crying almost uncontrollably.

"No, no, no, my dear," Madame Levine said softly. "Feeling sorry for yourself will not get you through this - - fighting will."

"We're going to get to the bottom of this, Samol," said London, giving him a friendly grab on his shoulder. "We're not leaving your side."

"But what does all of this mean??" he begged again, wiping snot from his nose, feeling the weight of both life and death on his shoulders.

"If my Aryamology studies serve me correct, this is a curse that must've been brought upon you early on — maybe even your first or second life," said the old lady, stroking her long chin.

"Okay…well, what is it? And how do we go back in time to undo it??" Samol said strongly.

"There have only been six other Aryamites in the history of reincarnation that I know of who've had similar symptoms," she said. "And I'm afraid there's no way around it. You have to let the curse go its course and go through it."

"What??" shouted Samol. "You're joking, right?"

The old woman didn't respond.

"But, you're the — the voodoo queen witch lady! Can't you just do some abrah-ka-dabrahs or something??" Samol asked frantically.

"I'm afraid it doesn't work like that," she said. "The only way to unlock your curse is to get to your past lives; the only way to get to your past lives is to live the future ones that lie ahead and I have to be honest…the lives of the six people with your symptoms tend to get worse."

"WORSE??" Samol howled. "No! No! NO! You don't understand! My — my last life was torture and the life before that was — was —" he paused and threw his hands over his face as though this couldn't be happening. "There has to be another way!!"

"Maybe…you weren't a nice person in a past life?" Leanna asked honestly, but with terrible timing.

"SHUT UP, Leanna!" shouted Samol, Paul, and London loudest of all.

"Actually, she might not be totally incorrect," Madame Levine agreed. "Four out of the six people with this curse were absolutely horrendous in at least one of their past lives."

"Samol was never like that!!" London spouted passionately, hands pressed at her hips.

"I'm simply telling you what I know," said the old woman, putting away the potions. "Do you all know the tale of Jym Reapyr?"

"No," said the three of them with the exception of Leanna.

"He was an Aryamite who lived his first life from 1556 – 1619. He mastered the art of thievery; breaking into the spell chambers and taking what he wanted!"

211

"I remember him like it was yesterday and I must say, 'mischief' was his middle name."

The four of them leaned in closer to her.

"One night, he broke into Nyabis's spell chamber and —"

"Who's Nyabis?" Paul asked.

"The appointed sorcerer for Bridgelove," said Madame Levine and Leanna at the same time.

"He stole the 'Hooping Trough' spell which allowed him to be reincarnated as time, itself!" the wrinkled woman explained.

"You can do that?" Paul whispered to London.

"Jym Reaper altered time and he changed the course of many things at the expense of those around him," Madame Levine revealed, sounding as though she were personally affected by this scandal.

"Did he ever get caught?" London asked.

"Well, it was — and still is an unsolved Euphod mystery because authorities couldn't track him. The reason, in part, being: he wasn't even sorted into the castle of Bridgelove when he broke into Nyabis's spell chamber."

"What castle was he sorted into?" Samol asked.

"The very castle in which we stand."

Samol went cold. Chills shot up and down his spine.

"And what ever happened to Jym Reapyr?" Paul asked.

"Well…" the old woman began with a heavy sigh, "he was dangerous - - a murderous thief! Many during that time knew that if they killed him they would also kill time and essentially…themselves."

"Wasn't he killed?" Leanna asked as if she'd heard the myth before, but was told a different version.

"…Yes and no…" Madame Levine answered hesitantly. "Many died during that time and those who survived believed that he was dead too. But it was more complicated than that," she said. "Time for many centuries was thrown off course, which was the very reason why Veraelle Claverkiss

212

reorganized the Euphod calendar alphabetically (through the use of a potion, of course).

"Death's docket," Leanna said softly as though the old woman had just unknowingly solved a mystery that had been bothering her for centuries.

"Yes, death's docket," Madame Levine reiterated with an impressed tone in her voice.

"But wait…" Leanna said loudly all of a sudden, "Any Aryamite who drinks the Hooping Trough potion has never lived past the third day, according to Aryamology."

The room fell silent. Madame Levine went flush as though Leanna weren't supposed to know that.

"Only certain types of Aryamites can drink of the Hooping Trough potion and live. If Jym Reapyr drank that potion, but didn't die...and he and Samol share the same curse…that means that Samol might be an hei-"

"THAT is not for you to decide!" Madame Levine sternly interrupted.

"What types of Aryamites? I'm a what??" Samol hollered in a thickening panic.

"But it can't be true. This wasn't supposed to happen until—" Leanna froze.

"What wasn't supposed to happen?? WHAT'S GOING ON??" Samol hollered.

Madame Levine began quickly rummaging through her bottom drawer again. She was in desperate search of something other than a potion because she was brushing them all aside. She pulled out a large, black, snake-skinned book along with a glowing, red quill with a black tip.

The front of this book was blank. Yet, the back was filled with random names with birthdays and death dates below them that disappeared and reappeared in the order of death date, birthday, and then name. Once old names vanished, new ones appeared. Samol, who had a close view, knew he'd seen something similar to this before, but couldn't remember where. The four of them gathered around the table. Madame Levine began:

"I need each of you to tell me exactly what you saw in detail when I poured the Gehiamese Fire Potion onto Samol's death certificate. Let's start with you, London."

"I saw green smoke that showed an evil looking man," she explained.

"What did he look like - - in detail?" Madame Levine asked, quickly sketching something in her book.

"He was...ugly. Missing both front teeth. Bald. And had a mustache that circled his face," London elaborated to the best of her abilities.

"Hmm," said Madame Levine, still drawing away.

"He was really, really, really sinister-looking and had green eyes that almost matched the smoke around him," London added.

"Ahhh! I wondered why I saw the dove," said Madame Levine.

"Dove?" Samol asked.

"A dove, in most cases is a loving and protective figure in our world that only reveals itself when something or someone with bad intentions is nearby," the old lady explained. "What did this man seem to want, London?"

"Umm...he seemed to be trapped somewhere behind bars...like he was in jail and was reaching for something," London explained honestly.

"Hmm," said an unsure Madame Levine, who kept sketching away anyhow.

"Leanna, what did you see?"

Leanna paused for a moment as though she were thinking.

"I saw two mists," she said. "The one to the left was a blue diamond in a green mist. No one was wearing the ring, it was just floating there and it was one of the most beautiful rings we'd ever...I mean...I'd ever seen. The mist to the right showed a blue quill floating in a purple mist."

"Purple?" asked Madame Levine, who stopped drawing. "Why did you use the Probaris incantation?"

"Because I could tell it was morphing into a white mist which you said was bad," Leanna explained.

"Quick thinking," said a highly impressed Madame Levine. "Paul, your turn."

"I saw two different mists too. The one on the left was an ugly, beast-looking thing in a green fog. And…the one on my right was some sort of male figure."

"What did the male figure look like?" asked Madame Levine, who was now circling and dotting something in her sketchbook.

"He was tall, had blonde-hair, and red eyes," said Paul.

"Red eyes??" shrieked everyone.

"Red," he said. "I know this will sound strange, but I really don't think that this man had any malicious intent."

"What color was his mist?" asked Madame Levine.

"Green," he said.

The old woman sketched away with her tongue drooping from the corner of her mouth.

"Okay and finally you, Samol. You said you saw a scroll of some sort?"

"I saw a black scroll with names written in — what looked like blood. Within seconds, the long script was melted away by something really hot."

"Hmmm…" said Madame Levine, squinting her eye at the painting as if something was wrong.

"The mist was clear and I didn't even know there was one, at first! Once I knew, I shouted 'PROBARIS!'" said Samol.

Madame Levine finished her drawing and slammed it on the table at once. It was a half animal, half-human figurine surrounded by a bunch of strange looking shapes and plants. She glared closely at the drawing as though it still didn't make sense.

"Every one of you is telling me the truth, right?" she sternly demanded.

"Of course! Yes!" the four of them shouted intermittently.

"Well, if my calculations serve me correct…you have the Roscarian Hoggenspit Curse, Samol. Luckily, it is curable over time…"

"Well, that's — good news?" Samol asked, shrugging his shoulders slightly.

"IT'S CURABLE??" London leapt with delight, smiling ear to ear. "See, Samol. It's not so bad after all," she said, hugging him tightly as if she hadn't seen him in centuries.

"Not so fast!" Madame Levine said briskly. "Many people in your shoes have not made it out alive, Samol. Are you sure you want to go through with this?"

"What other alternative do I have?" Samol asked as though there was another way out.

"Well, you could always let the curse take its natural course in which it could either go away completely or it could–" Madame Levine stopped herself.

Samol grew sad when he knew what she was going to say.

"We are here for you every step of the way, Samol," London guaranteed him once more.

"All right," Samol sighed, who realized that he had nothing to lose.

"Excellent!" said Madame Levine, clasping her hands together a little too excitedly. "To counteract the Roscarian Hoggenspit Curse, I'm going to give you the Assyoorum Potion," she said, pulling out a small, beige book and an empty, glass cauldron from her drawer. "I need your signature," she said, opening up the book. "As I'm sure you all know; magic, sorcery, spells, and potions are strictly forbidden, here, in Euphod unless under the supervision of the administration," she said.

She turned the book to page three-hundred seventy-eight, handing Samol the large, red quill, which stiffened when he grabbed it as though it recognized him.

"The quill is reading your heart - - it won't hurt you," Madame Levine said, noticing that Samol was nervous.

She pointed to the fourth line, which unlike the three lines above it, was blank and said in a deep voice, "Sign your name here."

The names read:

1. S.A.D. -   никогда не простится
2. Galena Sis Grace – fourteenth life
3. Sedgeryck Lee Heras - third life
4. _____

He stared at the names with visible concern on his face. For some reason, all three names seemed familiar.

"What's wrong, dear?" asked Madame Levine, staring at him strangely.

"These names. They all look...familiar," he replied with a distrusting eye.

"Really??" said London, peering over his shoulder, shocked that he knew these people (whoever they were).

"Go on," Madame Levine said curiously.

"The first name...well, initials I should say, are the same as mine – S.A.D.," he said, sounding almost manic, because he remembered that someone had called him by his full name at the Death Day Ball - - *Samol Amos Doscow*.

"Was I framed in a past life??" Samol shouted, sounding very paranoid. "What if someone was pretending to be me? What if THAT'S the reason I'm cursed??"

"Impossible!" said the old woman, folding her arms. "I would know if someone entered my chamber as a perpetrator or was DUI."

"DUI?" asked the four of them.

"Dead under the influence," she said. "Listen, I can assure you that this person was just someone who must've coincidentally had the same initials as you. Now, just sign here, please..."

"Wait a minute," said Samol, still looking at the names with skepticism. "...Galena Grace...Gale – I REMEMBER HER! She was actually....the very first person I met when I got to Euphod! Well...that I can remember."

"I understand that, but just sign h–"

"And Sedgeryck Heras. Why does that name ring a bell?" Samol pondered. "Do you guys know a Sedgeryck Lee Heras?" Samol asked his friends.

"I don't think so..." they said together.

"SIGN YOUR NAME! NOW!!" Madame Levine screeched at the top of her leathery lungs.

Everyone fell silent. Samol was distrusting of her sudden outburst, but knew he had no choice. The old lady broke the silence and softly said,

"Please, Samol. It's for your own good and you don't have a lot of time."

"I think she's right, man. Just sign so we can go," Paul agreed.

"We've all already come this far," said Leanna. "She's here to help you."

"...Fine," Samol sighed coldly after a long pause.

"Perfect," Madame Levine grinned as if she'd secretly won the lottery.

From the moment he began to sign his name, the empty cauldron began magically filling itself to the brim. Once complete, a bright pink potion was ready for his consumption.

"Now, drink," said Madame Levine with a dark, thirsty grin.

"What will happen?" he asked, regretting that he didn't ask this question before he signed his name.

"Once you drink the potion, you'll have thirteen days to go back in time to find out what cursed you. Once you find it, you'll know exactly what to do," she said.

"How will I know?"

"Trust me...if you were able to find my chamber, a little curse should be no problem!" Madame Levine chuckled.
218

"When the clock strikes twelve on the eve of the thirteenth night, the effects of the spell will wear off. If you do not accomplish what you were supposed to, you will die a final death."

"WHAT??" they all hollered.

"Don't worry. You'll be fine..." she said with a sneaky-looking grin.

"That's bull!" London screamed, ready to beat her down like she'd done Leanna.

"The potion works differently for everybody due to the fact that we all have different missions in life," Madame Levine explained cunningly. "However, once you drink the potion you will begin to feel its effects in one to three days. I must warn you, the potion is a bit tart."

"THREE DAYS??" London belted, ready to knock out the rest of her rotted teeth. "What if he can't find what he needs in the remaining ten days??"

"That's too bad. He already signed his name," she smiled aggravatingly.

"Woman! I'm gonna kick you in the coo—"

"London, stop it!" Paul stepped in, somewhat afraid that she'd kick his privates instead of Madame Levine's. "Samol, we've come all this way, man. Just drink the potion. We have your back."

Samol felt as if all hope had been sucked from his soul. He stood over the thick, bubbling concoction, which smelled like someone had bottled the stench of every rotting corpse from the beginning of time and poured it into this cauldron - - but made it pink to appear "not-so-nasty" as a sick joke.

"What's in it?" Leanna asked, peering into the glass with a curdled face.

"Three cups of witch blood, two cups of white pus, two teaspoons of sulfuric extract, three tablespoons of Vreek vomit, a half cup of cat pee, three Euphod rose petals, four leaves of saddle weed, and an olive. Bottoms up!" the old woman smiled.

Samol felt as though he died again just from hearing that! So did the others. He turned the glass beacon against his lips and endured thirty seconds of absolute torture! Finally, it was over.

"WHEW!! THAT'S NASTY!!!!!!" Samol hurled, wiping the entire bottom half of his face.

"Whoa! And so is your BREATH!!" said Paul, pushing him away.

"What's that?" London asked, pointing at a tiny, white piece of paper at the bottom of the empty cauldron that was no bigger than the slip you'd find inside a fortune cookie. Samol pulled out the wet, slimy piece of paper and squinted to read it, but the writing was too small to decipher.

"What is it?" Paul asked.

"Maybe it's the instructions?" Leanna guessed.

"...Or maybe it's a contract," London said dubiously, turning to face the old woman.

"Your time has begun now, Samol," said Madame Levine, who was quickly packing away her things. "You have till the eve of the thirteenth night — oh, and seek her like silver," said the canny old woman, pointing to the tiny piece of paper.

"Seek who like silver? And what is this thing anyway?" Samol asked, trying to read the imperceptible fine print.

When he looked up, Madame Levine was gone. His friends were speechless and desperately searched around the chamber for her. "I hate dead people!" Samol almost blurted angrily, but didn't when he remembered that he, himself, was dead and so were his best friends. Once again, he felt his stomach contract. Time was ticking. He had thirteen days to complete a mission that he didn't even know how to start.

CHAPTER THIRTEEN

THE UNLUCKY ESCAPE

"One minute, you were fine. And then you — you said you were hearing voices - -" London

"Where did she go??" Samol asked, his eyes darting wildly throughout the chamber.

"We've gotta get outta here!" Paul shouted, running for the door.

"That's not good," said Samol, stuffing his death certificate and the tiny, wet paper in his back pocket.

"WHOA!!" London screamed. "What's 'not good' is your breath!

Samol and his friends yanked open Madame Levine's door. What troubled them was that everything on the other side had completely changed! The floor was no longer a colorful chessboard, yet a room with many staircases that somehow looked both young and old at the same time. The walls were aligned with ugly, boil-ridden candles that burned bright pink.

"Which staircase do we take?" Paul asked as his eyes hurtled from one staircase to the next (because they weren't there before).

"Let's think logically," said London. "Which door did Madame Levine bring us through?"

"I dunno," said Paul. "We just sort of appeared there the same way she sort of — disappeared."

"This way!" said Leanna, standing closest to a massive, winding staircase on the left side of the wall.

The four of them dashed up the staircase, which led to a dark, narrow hall.

"I don't like the looks of this!" said Paul, who began backing away.

From the end of the hallway came a sound, which was almost like a tiny squeak.

Everyone froze and listened stiffly.

"What was that?" London whispered.

"I don't know," said Samol.

And a second squeak grew out of the darkness. Was it a bat? A really big bug? A rodent? Suddenly, Samol saw tiny, beige paws. It was a small, rosy-cheeked, light-brown mouse, who was scurrying from one side of the hallway to the other in desperate search of food. The little guy was homeless and probably hadn't eaten in days. For just a second, Samol wanted to cuddle the cute critter because he was reminded of the mice fighting over food in that rickety shack two lives ago.

"Let's go!" Leanna whispered, leading them down the hall.

Suddenly, the mouse began to panic. Something was coming! Something ferocious. Something cold. His squeaking intensified, as did his pace. Any faster and his little heart would beat out of his little chest! Out of nowhere, there was the sound of a hundred tiny critters and before their very eyes grew an army of large, glowing, snow-white beetles that crawled out of the abyss!

"What the heck??" Paul hollered, cowardly shoving London in front of him.

"What are those?" Samol yelped.

"I think I know what those are, but they usually

move…a lot quicker," London gulped, who was shoving Paul off of her.

The poor mouse was trapped between the beetles and four harmless humans, unsure of which species would try to kill him first! Without warning, the beetles began violently shaking their large, bulky backs as though they were communicating.

"Oh, no!" said London. "THOSE ARE —"

Before she could finish, the vicious vermin darted towards them ready for the kill! Sadly, the mouse was devoured within three seconds. They left behind nothing more than a pile of rat bones! The four of them dashed down the stairs faster than they ever had while alive or dead! When they reached the bottom of the staircase, so did the hungry, white beetles, who were rapidly gaining on them! Many of the bugs climbed down the walls and ceilings, determined to eat them as if they'd been pining for an entrée of humans for years now.

"WHAT ARE THESE!!" Paul screamed, checking his hair and clothes for the critters.

"They're Blister-wick Albino Beetles!" said London, who also frantically checked her hair and shoulders for the bugs. "We need to get as far away from these things as possible!!! They can follow you into your next life if they smell your scent! And they'll never forget it!!!!!"

"AHHHH!!!" everyone screamed.

Their adrenaline shoved them into light speed as they ran towards a second staircase.

"Please God, let there be a way out! No dead ends! PLEASE!" Paul prayed loudly.

They ran up the winding staircase as the beetles covered the dungeon floor, which now looked like a sea of crawling, white pus. They reached the top of the staircase and immediately saw a dead end!

"OH, NO!!" screamed Samol.

"This way!" yelled London, who happened to spot the tiniest sliver of light coming from an offset, diagonal hallway.

They raced for it like a bat out of hell.

"FASTER, GUYS! FASTER!!" shouted London, looking over her shoulder, noticing that the bugs were gaining on them.

Finally, they reached the opening of a dimly lit elevator shaft with no doors. The slightest bit of light revealed hundreds of feet above them. There were several thick ropes hanging in the middle of the shaft. Without even thinking, Samol, Paul, and London leapt for the ropes not knowing if it would even support their weight! Below them were the barely visible tops of human heads, and they realized that they were holding onto nooses! Unfortunately, Leanna stood crippled with fear at the edge and was unable to jump.

"Leanna, JUMP!" Paul screamed, who saw that the bugs had raced around the corner like they were on fire. "NOW!!" he panicked. "HURRY UP!!" Little did they know, Leanna was thrown off a cliff in her last life which scarred her with the fear of heights for the rest of her existence (which was why her floating corpse was practically unrecognizable). However, now was not the time to be afraid!

She leapt crookedly from the edge and missed the rope! London reached out and grabbed hold of her hand seconds before she plunged to a final death! Thankfully, London was strong; as she was able to hold Leanna with one hand and herself with the other. Leanna clasped onto the rope and was okay. Many of the beetles stopped at the edge, scurrying from side to side, pissed that they just lost a meal! Some had even fallen into the elevator shaft.

It was then that an unspoken establishment of sisterhood had formed between the two young ladies. Leanna forgave London for that emphatic beat down and London forgave her for forcing herself into her circle of friends where she was used to being the only girl. Samol and Paul, who were on separate ropes, began climbing up towards the opening on the next floor. Once there, they dropped to the ground because their muscles were exhausted as if they'd just finished an Olympic competition. They were in a dark blue room that looked like a gothic church. Blue fire burned from white candles, which gave the room an icy tint.

"Where are we?" asked Samol, looking around the room.

"I don't know," Paul said softly.

"AHHHH!" Leanna screamed as soon as London helped pull her up from the elevator shaft.

"What? What is it??" Samol hollered, who found Leanna violently slapping herself all over her body.

"It got in my hair!!" Leanna screamed, still scratching manically.

A single glowing beetle dropped from her long, frizzy braid and ran in between everyone's legs. The four of them hopped in the air repeatedly as if someone was shooting at their feet. The bug ran along the edges of the room until it was out of sight. Everyone backed away from Leanna like she had a disease, as though they were just waiting for more critters to crawl out of her ears or something.

"That's not good," Paul said softly.

"We all have to get outta here!" said Samol, looking at the floor for more bugs.

"Where do we go??" Paul asked. "And we still haven't figured out your curse!"

"Let's go to Silas!" London suggested.

"Silas?" said Paul as though she'd offended him.

"He's the *ruler of Freedomcorpse*," London said in a swatty tone.

"No…" Samol said hesitantly as though he were thinking. "I think that what both Leanna and I need is bigger than what can be found in just Freedomcorpse alone. We need someone who's knowledgeable about all seven castles, spells, curses, and — well — beetles!" he finished, giving Leanna a worried look.

"What about Gabriella?" Leanna suggested.

"That tiny tyrant? Are you crazy??" Paul wheeled. *"She's-the-sec-re-tary-of-death!"* he said, sure to enunciate every syllable of her title. "If she ever found out we went to see Madame Levine..."

"What about Harragett??" Leanna proposed, now sounding almost desperate for help.

"The ruler of Zebrastone??" said London. "No. There's something — something I don't trust about him... her..."

"Well, then who??" Leanna roared.

"...What about Maven!" Samol finally suggested.

"MAVEN??" shouted the three of them with disgust.

"You're better off going to Bloodwig!" Paul hurled.

"What's wrong with Maven?" Samol asked innocently. "Think about it," he said, holding out three fingers as though he were about to count the reasons why Maven was the best choice. "Maven's the one who initially sorted us all into our castles. Surely, he knows something about all seven of them and maybe a curse or two! And you guys know about his missing eye, right?"

"What about it?..." his three friends asked slowly, suddenly interested.

"His missing eye has powers! And the one eye that he does have, has better vision than people do with two eyes!" he said.

"Powers?" London frowned, only interested in that part. "What kind of powers? And who told you this?"

"Well...I don't know exactly what powers for sure — something to do with recording names," Samol tried to recall. "Galena Grace told me AND I saw her name in Madame Levine's spell book! She must know something..."

"Samol, this Galena woman sounds like bad news," London said mistrustfully.

"Where is she now?" Leanna asked quickly, still scratching herself.

"I don't know. After we talked, she — sort of vanished," Samol tried to explain.

226

"*Sort of vanished??*" London howled. "And you trust what this girl has to say? She might've very well been the one who cursed you!"

"WE-ARE-WASTING-TIME!!! Samol hollered at once. "Let's just go see Maven! Besides, he has to tell us the truth - - no matter what!"

"How do you know?" they all asked simultaneously.

"Because he can't lie," said Samol, innocently slumping his shoulders. "Galena told me that if he lies, his head will burn!"

His frustrated friends looked at him as though he belonged on the Wall of Lunacy.

"Listen, I think you–" Paul began, already sounding a bit condescending.

"NO, <u>YOU</u> LISTEN!" Samol screamed with an anger that filled the room. "None of you got cursed! I DID! None of you woke up in a cemetery unable to remember who you are! I DID! None of you have a problem going back to review your lives in the maze! I DO! And unless ANY of you have any better ideas, then I suggest you STOP TALKING and FOLLOW ME!"

You could hear a pin drop.

No one had ever seen Samol so angry. He, himself, didn't even know he had that much pent-up anger. But, who could blame the boy (just from dealing with Victoria alone)! Paul exhaled heavily, resting his hands on his hips and looked to the sky like he wanted to say something to fill the awkward silence, but couldn't form words. Suddenly, he choked when he saw that his floating corpse was decomposing! And so was everyone else's - - Leanna's most of all!

"We have to go now!" Paul screamed, who all of a sudden remembered that they were still lost. "How do we get outta here??" he hollered, looking in every corner of the room.

"This way!" Leanna shouted, who spotted an opening at the other end of the mosque.

"How long were we in Madame Levine's chamber?" Paul cried, sprinting a few paces behind Leanna. "Our floating bodies shouldn't be decaying this fast!"

"I don't know!" said Samol, who was not too far behind him.

"I bet that ol' dirty witch altered time while we were in there!" London howled, now running faster because she was pissed off.

"QUICK!! This way!" said Leanna heading for the dark egress.

They ran through a long, high-ceilinged hallway that was carpeted with a strip of blue velvet. Large, gothic archways leading to hidden parts of the Freedomcorpse castle aligned the walls.

"Let's go through that door!" said Leanna, pointing straight ahead, charging full speed. She yanked at the ice-cold, metal doorknob with all of her strength, yet it was harder to pull than she expected. The four of them pulled together. Nothing.

"Maybe this door doesn't open," said Samol, breathing heavily, looking for another one.

"Why is the door handle so cold??" Paul said, breathing just as hard.

"Let's try again - - on three," London instructed. "One — Two — Three!"

They pulled with all of their strength. The door cracked open ever so slightly, which gave way to a cold gust. After a few more grueling seconds of what felt like tugging at an eighteen-wheeler, the large rickety door opened just enough for the four of them to slip through. What they saw next left them puzzled, yet again.

They were in another long hallway. It was bright and glamorous; carpeted with red velvet and its walls were aligned with portraits of more Aryamites next to bright candles that somehow added no warmth to the frigid room.

The problem was that at the end of the lengthy hall was a door that was not only much bigger than the one they just opened, but it was caked with ice too! Without exchanging a word, the four of them sighed unanimously and thought, 'here we go again!'

Leanna broke the cold silence when she said, "The cold air means that we're getting close to the heart of the castle. Let's keep going," she said, shivering between every word. The large, metal-hooped handle was so cold that it almost felt hot when she grabbed it!

"Ouch!" Leanna screamed when she gave it a swift tug.

"Maybe if we breathe on it, it'll warm up?" London suggested.

"Samol, you've got devil breath! Blow on it!" said Paul, shoving him towards the door.

"With that breath, he might melt <u>through</u> the knob!" London joked.

"All the way back to hell!" Paul added.

"Shut up, you guys!" Samol joked, breathing on them both.

He huffed heavily on the doorknob and it actually worked! Eight hands quickly clasped the handle and yanked. To their surprise, this door was much lighter than the previous one. It flew open and they all fell to the ground. Everyone broke into a hearty, thirty-second laughing spell. Trying to stand to their feet, they were greeted by a large, frozen, white, marbled staircase. The first half of the staircase led to a large window that was wide enough to fit a plane through. It was glazed with hundreds of ice figurines. The second half of the staircase led to the very heart of the Freedomcorpse castle.

"Finally!" Leanna sighed thickly, dashing up the stairs.

"Where are we?" Paul asked, who was rather close behind her.

"The Freedomcorpse foyer!" Samol and London said together.

229

"Hey! How'd you —" London began to ask, before she gasped excitedly. "Oh, my gosh! The potion is working!"

Actually, it hadn't. Samol just remembered seeing this when he entered the castle with Silas. However, he kept quiet to let her have her moment.

"That's right, the potion!" Leanna whispered to herself. From her pocket, she subtly pulled a tiny, glass vile no wider than a pencil and drank it.

"Come on you guys, hurry up!" said Paul, who'd passed them all.

The four of them had a breathtaking view of the very heart of the Freedomcorpse castle at the top of the stairs. Large, gothic archways, which were shaped like humans, scaled the walls. There were sixteen halls that veered from the foyer, leading to unknown places. Paul was craning his neck around the corners to see where they led. At the very center of the foyer was a large, green hourglass with jet black sand that formed odd shapes, creatures, and statues as the sand fell through the middle. They couldn't believe their eyes.

The arctic air cut through them like a knife. "Come on, let's keep moving!" London shivered, looking for the closest way out until she laid eyes on a large, wooden door. She tackled through it like a linebacker and in an instant they were outside. Alongside the castle walls were dead trees and a blanket of snow covering the ground. Samol grew wordlessly angry when he realized that Silas could've brought him in through this entrance!

"This way," said Leanna, with a demanding whisper as they began trudging through the beginnings of the dark, thick Genesis Forest.

"Ouch! You stepped on my foot!" London yelled at Paul, who was notoriously clumsy.

"Well, you're allowed to walk faster than my grandma, ya know!" he snarled back noisily.

"We're going to see Maven, right?" Samol asked, dodging the thorny, low-hanging branches.

"Yes," said Leanna.

230

"Are you sure he'll even be there??" Paul asked, yanking a thorn from his side.

"I don't know, but it's all we've got," shrugged Leanna. "I know he has a small cabin near the center of the forest."

The forest was darkening by the second. The dead trees were growing higher and thicker. With every step, their troubled souls grew wearier. Thick branches smacked them in their faces and sharp thorns tore through their calves and ankles! It was clear that Aryamites were not meant to be traveling this way. After a painful and frightening ten minutes, they'd reached the Freedomcorpse entrance. The electrical mist was barring them from exiting until they said the password aloud.

Samol began to hear voices again; whispering prayers just as he'd heard when he entered into the castle's estate, only these prayers were hateful as though all love had been flipped backwards: *Murder....Destroy....Rip...Kill!*" The voices whispered sharply and grew so loud that Samol dropped to his knees and he covered his ears.

"What's wrong, Samol??" London hollered, crouching next to him.

"These voices!! I keep — I CAN'T —" he couldn't finish and the voices took over.

"Fire.... Burn... Blood...HELL!!!"

"Samol! Can you hear me??" London screamed, shaking him violently because he'd stopped moving. "HELP!" she screamed desperately.

"SAMOL!" Leanna yelled, staring at his motionless body.

"What's happening??" Paul panicked.

"I don't know!" London shouted, sounding as though she were trying to control her panic, but couldn't. "He fell on the ground saying that he's hearing voices!"

"I bet it's that potion Madame Levine gave him!" Paul said angrily.

Suddenly, Samol's body began to quiver as though he were possessed.

"We have to get him out of here! NOW!" Leanna shouted.

His convulsions worsened.

"What's the password to get into Freedomcorpse?" Paul jittered.

"I don't remember!" Leanna hollered.

"Umm — umm — oh, shoot!" said Paul, scratching his head, snapping his fingers, trying desperately to jog his memory.

"Hurry!!" London screeched when she saw Samol foaming from the mouth.

"Ummm….Freedom, affair!" Leanna shouted aimlessly.

"Freedom…will care? Freedom, declare??" Paul said to himself, walking in circles.

"Freedom, aware?" London said dramatically. "No, freedom…BEWARE! That's it! Freedom, Beware!!!"

She shot up from the ground, shoving Paul and Leanna out of the way. Standing in front of the electrical mist, she confidently proclaimed, "FREEDOM, BEWARE!"

The mist still hadn't vanished because they could still hear it. It seemed as if London's mistake only infuriated the mist! It grew louder. Hotter. Deadlier.

"I don't understand — THAT'S THE PASSWORD!" London shouted frustratingly.

"We've got to do something, quickly!" Leanna hollered nervously, staring at Samol whose back was now arched off the ground as though he were in terrible pain.

"Answer me…answer me…" Paul mumbled under his breath.

"What?" howled the girls.

"SHHH! I'm thinking!" he said. "Answer me, answer me or you will be captured….the only way out is if the mansur is backwards. That's it!"

"What's what??"

"The only way out is to say the password backwards!" said Paul, shoving them aside. He stood inches from the mist and quietly whispered, "eraweb, modeerf."

A quiet, swirling wind swooshed the nearby dirt into a vortex that quickly died away. The faint sound of what might've been screeching bats were heard in the distance. The voltaic mist swirled no more.

"Thank God," the three of them sighed heavily.

Now, all eyes were on Samol. He was still being tortured by voices that only he could hear. Suddenly, he came to and was gasping for air as though he'd been held underwater for a long time.

"Are you okay??" Paul asked hyperly.

"What…happened to me?" Samol asked as if he suddenly couldn't remember anything all over again, struggling to stand to his feet.

"We don't know," London said truthfully. "One minute, you were fine. And then you — you said you were hearing voices, but we couldn't hear anything!"

"We have to keep moving," said Leanna, who was growing highly suspicious of the quietening forest.

Paul and London helped Samol to his feet. After a few minutes of walking, they found themselves at the center of the Genesis Forest; the beginning of it all. This was where they were first sorted into Zebrastone together, rather close to where they'd fought that hellish spider together, right where Leanna fell in lust and London fell in hate. Oh, how far they'd come.

Suddenly, London spotted a crumbled, moss-covered, brick shack in the far distance. "Over there!" she pointed. It was nearly impossible to see because it was so dark. A tiny candle sitting in a small window was the only thing that made the shack somewhat visible. Dead trees had fallen through its caved-in roof. The front door hung loosely from its hinges. Mold grew from every corner. It almost appeared that even in this world, the dead experienced poverty. With a closer look, they felt somewhat bad for the mean, old man.

233

Maven had been reduced to living in a shack that was half his size! London courageously went to knock at the collapsing door when something caught her attention - - a voice. It was an angelic voice singing an old Euphod hymn so beautifully that it couldn't have possibly come from a human, only an angel. London leapt from the front door to peek through a side window. When she saw who it was, her eyes nearly popped from her skull!

CHAPTER FOURTEEN

SEEK HER LIKE SILVER

"Do you know the tale of Jym Reapyr?" – Samol

It was Maven!

The same creature whose voice was as raspy as his body was jagged. The same tyrant who didn't even flinch when he made Eoghen Kraw, one of the sweetest people anyone had ever met, cry during this last Thanksgiving. All four of them were now peeking through his window, wondering how could this angelic voice spawn from such a cruel mouth??

London turned to her friends with a look of disbelief in her eyes. Paul mouthed, "Go in!" giving her a swooping gesture with his hand. London took a deep breath and knocked at the door. Three pounding footsteps came crashing towards the craggy door! It flew open and behind it stood an angry, old, rocky man glaring at them with one icy-blue eye and his large, wooden staff ready to attack!

"WHAT DO YOU WANT??" he yelled so loudly that the nearby ravens fled from the trees.

"We-we-we're just here…ummm…" Paul stuttered nervously.

"Our friend has been cursed and we really need your help," London said bravely.

"I don't have time for this! I'm on page seventy-four of *'OK, Euphod!'* Come see me in your next life!" Maven howled rudely and slammed the door.

"It's about the Roscarian Hoggenspit Curse!" said all four of them, freezing Maven dead in his tracks.

"The Roscarian Hoggenspit Curse?" said Maven, slowly opening the door. "Why, there's no such thing…any-more!" he said. "And how did the four of you get out here anyhow??"

"Dumb…luck?" Paul smiled sheepishly.

"DON'T TOY WITH ME!" Maven hollered, his one eye nearly popping from its socket.

"Okay!" Paul hollered submissively, nearly soiling himself again. "We figured out a way to reverse the Freedom-corpse password to pass through the entrance trees."

"Pass through??" Maven hollered hoarsely. "PASS THROUGH?? Why would any of you need to get out of the Freedomcorpse castle? Aryamites clamor at the mere chance to get sorted into that castle! You're all supposed to be there preparing for your next lives!"

"Yes, but it's complicated," London intervened.

"I told you brats once before…I-DON'T-HAVE-TIME-FOR-THIS!!" Maven belted as his jaw popped in and out of its socket.

"Gross!" Paul mumbled, turning his face away.

"Please, sir," Samol said humbly. "Do you really think we would have traveled all this way, through the forest, if it wasn't serious? Please, Maven. We need your help."

Maven paused. For just a second, the slightest bit of sympathy pierced his bouldered heart. He studied all four of them sharply, his eye darting especially between the boys.

236

"...Come in..." he said falteringly as though he didn't want to, but knew he shouldn't leave four children in a dark and dangerous forest.

The inside of the small cottage was just as ugly as the outside. It was made up of only one room; a messy kitchen with a large tree that had grown through it, a bed, and a tiny living room with a table for two.

"Have a seat," said Maven, leaning his staff against the front door as though it were a fastened umbrella.

Paul, with a proclivity for laziness, had no problem making himself comfortable and sat in the rusted, yellow chair.

"No thank you, Maven. We'll STAND!" said London, staring wide-eyed at Paul, which meant he better get his butt up - - now!

Reluctantly, he did so.

"Tea?" Maven offered, sounding almost as though it were out of habit. He was hunching all the way over because if he stood up, he'd tear his roof off! "It's made with Euphod rose petals - - high in antioxidants and luck for your next life...How about some chocolate?" Maven blurted in the same thought.

"No, thank you," they said and Samol's face curdled at the mere mention of *"rose petals."*

"I'll have some chocolate," said Leanna, whose stomach growled as though she hadn't eaten in days.

"What's this all about?" Maven sighed heavily and sat down, still taller in his seat than they were standing.

"I don't know why and I don't know how but...I've been cursed," Samol said sadly.

"Go on..." said Maven, sipping his tea.

"Well, I haven't been able to review any of my past lives before I go to the next one," he explained. "And I—"

"And...he didn't even recognize us when he saw us," Paul interjected. "His memory was totally obliterated!"

"Well, that's nothing!" Maven laughed carelessly. "Many Aryamites have problems reviewing past lives!"

"And memory? Forget about it! You try living three and four hundred lives, you'll start forgetting stuff, too!" Maven said, chuckling hoarsely.

Samol elaborated, "When I tried to see my last life, I heard these creatures calling me by another name. I think they were…the names of the people I've lived as in past lives…"

"But, that's no Roscarian Hoggenspit Curse," said Maven, who sounded for a second as if he were somewhat intrigued by what Samol had to say. "Trust me. That curse has been gone since — well — centuries!"

"So the curse does exist?" Paul asked.

"Did."

"Can you…kill a curse?" Leanna asked, chomping away at the delicious chocolate bar.

"Well, of course you can! It's not easy, but it can be done!" Maven said candidly.

"How?" asked Samol.

"Through spell Euphanasia," he said. "You kids these days have it easy! You only have to deal with a quarter of the curses we had when I was coming up!"

"What are you talking about?" London asked curiously.

"Any Aryamite who was born and/or became an Aryamite after the Death Day Ball that took place three hundred seventeen years ago was vaccinated for all such curses," said Maven. "Those vaccinations made you all immune to many curses and one of them was the Roscarian Hoggenspit Curse."

"Then, how did I get it?" asked Samol.

"You don't have it!" Maven squabbled, spilling a bit of tea on his leg.

"But Maven, blood runs from me!"

Maven spat out his tea altogether! He shot straight out of his seat, banging his head on the already crumbling ceiling, chipping away more pieces! He muddled a few expletives and rubbed his head angrily.

238

Samol and the girls were visibly concerned. Paul, on the other hand, was trying not to laugh. Maven calmed himself. He hobbled towards Samol and stood two inches from his face, which was nearly ten times as big as Samol's, and asked him seriously:

"What do you mean blood runs from you?"

"Well...when I see blood, it sort of recedes away from me as if it can't stand to be around me," Samol explained the best way he could.

"But...how would you have come to the conclusion that this was the Roscarian Hoggenspit Curse? Who've you been talking to?" Maven asked in a slightly accusatory tone. "You must have gone into Euphod's restricted fi—"

"We went to see Madame Levine," Leanna blurted, finishing the last of her chocolate bar.

"MADAME LEVINE??" Maven howled angrily.

"...Yeah," Samol began slowly, somewhat afraid of Maven's outburst. "She gave me a potion and I have thirteen days to undo whatever needs to be undone in one of my past lives. She said it would end the curse!" he said with a flicker of hope in his voice.

Maven began angrily, "Even if you DID have the Roscarian Hoggenspit curse, thirteen days is not NEARLY enough time to go back and undo what needs to be done! In order to get through one — just one —" Maven said, holding up his large, pointing finger, which was as big as Samol's whole foot, "Of your past lives, you need to live your next one in full, first! That one single life could be years!"

"That fugly witch was a hoax! I knew it!" London screamed heatedly.

"You were misdiagnosed," said Maven, who turned around to pour himself another cup of tea.

"Guys, he's telling the truth. He has to be!" Samol whispered to his friends.

"Are you still believing that Galoony-bin girl?" London sneered, rolling her eyes.

"Galena!" Samol whispered back sharply.

"Whatever! Looks like she needs a beat down too — for filling my best friend's head with bogus!" London said protectively, rolling up her sleeves as though she'd leap up that instant and go find her.

"If you're so sure he can't lie, let's put him to the test," Leanna challenged.

"Like what?" he asked.

"Ask him…" Leanna paused for a moment and then stood to her feet, her knocked knees nearly bashed into one another. "Is Agetha Bloodwig morbidly obese?" she asked.

"What?" said Maven, still fumbling with a few chamomile petals.

Is it or is it not true that Agetha Bloodwig is a fat, nasty hog?" Leanna asked loudly.

"Well, you've got eyes, don't you?? Of course that woman's huge! Hell, you don't even need eyes to see that!" he said, adding that last sarcastic remark under his breath. "Why do you ask?" he said, now peeling a few blue rose petals.

"Oh, nothing! I'm just…checking something," Leanna said cleverly and sat back down with the rest of them and whispered, "Somebody else give it a try."

"Good one, Leanna!" said Paul, giggling like a little boy.

"Good one?" said London as though she could do much better. "Really, girl?"

"What?" Leanna whispered submissively. "I thought it was funny!"

"I'm gonna ask him something that we all want to know the answer to," said London, who confidently stood to her feet.

She cleared her throat importantly and spoke:

"Is Harragett Jaede, ruler of Zebrastone, a man or a woman?"

"OUCH!!!" screamed Maven, holding his face.

"What happened?" she asked, studying his head for even the slightest blister or burn to erupt.

"Damn, I gotta get that fixed!" he said, realigning his broken jaw.

240

"Stop stalling!" London demanded. "...Is Harragett Jaede a man or a woman?"

Maven was still realigning his jaw and he finally said, "Truth is, that depends on the situation!"

"Depends on the situation...." London restated with a somewhat gossipy tone in her voice. "If you say so."

She sat back down.

"You ask him one, Samol," London said, snickering with the group trying to conjure up more questions.

For nearly a full minute, Samol didn't move. His friends were too busy giggling amongst themselves to even notice that he was in such deep thought. He cautiously stood to his feet as though he would bump his head on the ceiling like Maven. He'd been suddenly struck with two burning questions:

"Do you know the tale of Jym Reapyr?" he asked strongly.

An abrupt silence smothered the room.

"What?" said Maven, who stopped stirring his tea and his face grew as serious as it was when they first arrived.

"Jym Reapyr," Samol restated with his head held high. "Madame Levine said that there were only six other people who've had the same symptoms that I have - - Jym Reapyr was one of them. What do you know about him?" Samol asked coldly, as if he already distrusted Maven's answer before he even spoke.

Without warning, the top of Maven's head began to smolder! He screamed terribly! Paul, London, and Leanna shot to their feet not knowing what to do!

"Tell me what you know about Jym Reapyr!" Samol howled, sounding half angry and half afraid because he wanted to get the truth out of Maven quickly before he melted away or something.

"Samol, stop it! You're burning him!" Leanna hollered.

"No! He's burning himself!" Samol screamed desperately. "TELL ME THE TRUTH!"

"Samol! He obviously isn't telling you because he wants to protect you from something!!" Leanna pled. "You're burning him to death!!!"

Samol thought wildly for a second and spat out his second question:

"Is Madame Levine an honest witch or a liar?"

"AN HONEST ONE!!!" Maven shouted in the midst of his agony.

The burning stopped.

Maven dropped to the floor. Paul and the girls raced to tend to his injuries. Samol, however, stood in the corner, simmering in his own deep thoughts. 'What if Leanna was right? What if whatever happened to Jym Reapyr was so bad that Maven was willing to fry rather than tell me what was to come?? If Madame Levine is, in fact, an honest witch, then why did she give me the wrong potion?'

Poor Samol was left to the grips of his own darkening thoughts. Suddenly, he remembered the tiny piece of paper he'd found at the bottom of the potion's empty glass. He pulled it out of his back pocket. It was crinkled and still had the lingering, god-awful stench.

"Maven, can you read this?" Samol said, holding out the paper.

"Samol!" Leanna barked. "He just nearly burned to death and all you can think about is him reading some stupid piece of paper??"

"No, no. It's fine," said Maven, breathing heavily and holding his scalp. "To be honest, I would've done the same thing if I were in his shoes."

Leanna fell silent, looking almost sheepish.

Maven took the tiny slip, which in his large hand looked no bigger than a snowflake. He stood to his feet and stared at the tiny cursive words, dusting himself off, and began to read aloud:

"Death chooses its victims wi—"

242

"Wait…so you <u>can</u> read this?" London interrupted seriously.

"Yes," said Maven, who grabbed his head again. "I may only have one eye, but I'm not blind!"

"Told you," Samol mouthed silently.

London said nothing.

Maven continued, *"Death chooses its victims wisely. Sometimes it creeps like a thief in the night. Other times it greets you as an old friend. Death is a strange melody in which he sings to seduce a new home. However, knowing when to let him in and when to shut him out is wisdom to our world. With this curse, you will need to seek her like silver because you may wa—"*

"Seek her like silver…" Samol mumbled to himself.

"What?" said Leanna.

"That's what Madame Levine said right before she disappeared - - *seek her like silver,*" Samol said as though he'd had an epiphany.

"Wisdom…" London said quietly because she somehow understood that this is what it meant. "The 'her' she was talking about is wisdom…"

"What does the rest of it say, Maven?" Samol asked anxiously.

"With this curse, you will need to seek her like silver because you may want to invite death upon yourself. Doing so will doom you to a crooked eternity; one in which you were not meant to live. If you cannot unlock the horrors of your past within thirteen days, then you must do the following: find the Whispering Will, pass through the Death Shrine, and seize Time's Death Certificate. Remember, on your journey, watch what you think.

Thoughts become things.
- Madame N.J. Levine"

"Oh, no," Samol cried.

"We are not leaving your side!" London reassured him again, even though she didn't understand half of what Maven just read aloud.

"There's something on the back," Paul pointed.

Maven flipped it over and finished reading aloud:

"I can alter your future and build from your past,
I was here before you were without being asked,
Life is my best friend and yet secret killer,
I am not death, but a must-see thriller.
I have a thankless job without any praise,
Yet every last one of you abide by my ways,
I'm forever touched without you even knowing,
Yet without my presence you cannot keep going."

"What does that mean?" Samol asked.

"I…honestly don't know," said Maven studying it again.

"So — we have to find the Whispering Will, pass through The Death Shrine, and then get Time's Death Certificate, right?" London asked, counting on three fingers, pretending to know what all of that meant.

"That's what it says," said Maven, still scrutinizing the pint-sized paper from front to back.

"And…exactly how do we do all of this?" she asked.

"No idea," Maven shrugged truthfully. "However, I do suggest two things: First, help Samol retrace every last step he took from the moment he got his memory back and went to… Verstandfall, was it?"

"Zebrastone," they answered quickly.

"Start from Zebrastone," said Maven.

"Got it!"

"Secondly, remember that many things that are of evil may seem good; whether it be a person, animal, plant, or even a liquid. Take extra precautionary measures in whatever you say, think, do, or touch - - especially you, Samol," Maven instructed. "Oh and Samol…you're gonna need this," he said,

244

pulling out a small, dingy, crème-colored cloth from underneath a purple vase under his kitchen table.

"…What is it?" Samol asked, examining it confusedly.

"You don't need to know what it is…only when to use it. And before you ask…you will know when to use it," Maven said surely.

Samol stuffed it in his pocket and the four of them headed out the broken door on their terrifying adventure. Leanna was the last one out and was hit with one last minute concern.

"Umm, Maven?" she began softly. "I found a Blister-wick Albino Beetle in my hair earlier. Should I be worried?"

"A BLISTER-WICK ALBINO BEETLE??" he howled. "You damn right you better be worried! One scent of yours and a whole family of them will slither into your ears and chew through your eardrum while you're asleep in your next life!"

"Oh — oh — shi…" Leanna panicked, holding her ears as though one of them had already popped her eardrum!

"For the rest of your lives, go to sleep with cotton balls in your ears!"

Leanna stood paralyzed.

"What were you doing near an Oryx Beast anyway?" he asked with a piercing look.

"A what?" London intervened, who'd doubled back the moment she heard, *Chew through your eardrum.*

"An Oryx beast!" Maven said again. "That's the only creature they're known to be around!"

"Uhhh…thanks, Maven! We've gotta go!" said London, whose eyes were darting between Paul and Samol, yanking them both.

"PAUL, LET'S GO! NOW!!" she demanded, gritting her teeth in a loud, parental whisper that a child might hear when they're misbehaving in public. The four of them ran off into the woods. Although, London knew that they were in danger, she hadn't a clue as to how bad it really was.

CHAPTER FIFTEEN

THE WHISPERING WILL

"Oh, no! That's Bloodwig!! - - SHE'S COMING THIS WAY!"
– London

"AN ORYX BEAST??" London screamed at Leanna. "Really, girl??"

"What??" said Leanna not even knowing what she was pissed about.

"They're one of the most vicious creatures in our world!" London explained as they trudged through the thick shrubbery.

"Hey, don't look at me! I had no idea that thing was near us!" Leanna said in a troubled tone.

"What's an Oryx beast?" Samol asked innocently.

"It's a big, ugly, but intelligent creature that never forgets the sound of your voice. If it ever hears you, it sends its venom towards your voice to kill you in your next life!" she whispered as though one of the creatures were listening.

"Is it just me or is the Vreek expression, 'YOLO,' sounding good right now?" Paul chuckled, trying to diffuse the tension.

No one laughed.

Leanna, whose eyes had been bouncing from one tall, dead tree to the next, saw the frightening site of her floating body foaming at the mouth and nose! Time was rapidly running out! To make matters worse, Samol had dropped to his knees again. A deafening wave of a thousand conversations from his past lives had rushed over him at once! Every conversation he'd been banned from hearing since he was first cursed, hit him like a sonic boom! Madame Levine's potion had begun to slowly take effect.

"Samol! What's wrong??" London shouted nervously, kneeling beside him.

"I hear voices - - again!" he said, covering his ears in an airy voice, struggling to fight through it.

"Samol! Can you still hear me??" London shouted, shaking his shoulders.

He could not.

The deafening voices were as loud as a jet engine! Samol coiled up in the fetal position and heard several different voices say aloud:

"Amir, you belong to me!"

"The recludet! Get the recludet spell!!" shouted a familiar voice.

"We can't go in there! It's forbidden!" shouted another voice.

"How did you find this castle??" said a stern old man.

"The painful past, hidden present, and memories of the future!" stormed a final voice.

The voices stopped and he was left in a familiar, dark quiet.

"Samol! Are you okay? Can you hear me??" said London, sounding like a panic-stricken mother.

"I — th — I heard them again," he said, struggling to get up.

"What did you hear?" Paul asked, who seemed more afraid than Samol.

"...Voices from one...or...several of my past lives," he replied. "Is this normal?"

"No," all three of them said collectedly.

"Okay, Samol you've got to think," said London, getting even closer to him. "Think back to anything you can remember. Did you tou—"

"Where do we start?" Paul blurted.

"Maven said for us to retrace our steps," Leanna said calmly. "Let's start there."

"Samol, think about what you saw in Freedom-corpse," said London. "Was there anything that stood out?"

"Well..." he paused. "The last thing I can remember (before I fainted) was being with Silas in the spiritual room."

"Did you hear anything out of sorts?" asked Paul.

"...No," said Samol, still thinking.

"What about your last life?" London asked slowly. "Was there anything in particular that was unusual?"

"HA!" he laughed painfully. "Everything! I was the son — well — stepson of this terrible woman that I swear must've escaped from the pits of hell!"

"What did she look like?" Leanna queried as though she might've known who this woman was.

"I don't know. I was blind in my last life."

The three of them fell silent, trying to think of the right questions to ask. Paul almost asked, 'What was your father like in your last life?' but realized it would help nothing.

"Let me see your death certificate," said London, holding out her hand.

He pulled the cockled, blue piece of paper from his back pocket. It was practically illegible by now and reeked of body odor.

248

She studied it for a few seconds and saw that the last letter of his name on his death certificate was an 'R.' Instead of asking him outright, she pondered what his name might've been on her own.

"Ru…Rah…Ri…"

"Ryan," he said.

"Hmmm…" London grunted as if the name meant something.

"What about Zebrastone?" Paul pondered.

"What about it?" Samol questioned.

"Did you hear, see, or experience anything out of the ordinary?"

"Umm…" he said, finally able to stand to his feet, but couldn't recall a thing.

"How about the De—" Paul began.

"WAIT A MINUTE!!" Samol screamed with his eyes bulging like baseballs. "I do remember something!"

"What??" said everyone, leaning in just a tad bit closer to him.

"The mirror!" he said. "The mirror in the Zebrastone common room!"

"What mirror?" Paul asked confusedly.

"There were mirrors on the double doors outside the Zebrastone Maze. Nobody saw them but me," he said.

"I remember!" London suddenly gasped.

"What did you see?" Paul asked.

"I saw myself in what looked like three parts, depending on where I stood. I saw myself as I am, currently, and two misty versions of myself on either side of that. I think it was 'me' in a past and a future life."

"Let's go!" London said, almost violently yanking him by his hand.

They ran wildly for the Zebrastone pathway as if coyotes were biting at their heels! Finally, they'd reached the castle's black and white entrance trees, who stood tall and almost proud looking. The sky was darker than usual, because there were barely any souls being shot off into the cold sky.

This made it nearly impossible to see anything. However, they heard the horrible sound of the invisible barrier of high voltage between the two trees.

"Oh, no! What's the password again?" Samol asked, scratching his head.

"I can't remember it either!" said Paul, who was just as forgetful as Samol.

"Oh, move over!" London shoved the two of them aside. She crouched closely to the left tree and said, *"Your mystery is backwards."*

Like magic, the voltaic wall had vanished and they passed through. The four of them ran down the Zebrastone pathway when suddenly, Samol stopped as if an invisible rope had yanked his neck.

"What is it?" said Paul, who sounded like he would take off running if Samol told him something scary was coming.

"Don't you remember what happened last time?" Samol whispered frightfully.

"….No," he said.

"That — that huge, freaky spider tried to eat us!" Samol said, looking through the dark forest as though it were crouching in a ditch, just waiting to attack them.

"Oh!" said the three of them, fearfully backing away as if they'd all forgotten.

"I don't know if this is such a good idea anymore," said Paul.

"We can't stop now!" London said bravely.

"She's right, Samol," said Leanna, who'd been quiet until now.

"Everyone stay close and stay alert!" London instructed.

The four of them tiptoed through the forest as if they'd stolen something. The closer they got to the castle, Samol grew jittery. His mind raced with the distressing memories of slithering snakes, massive hornets, and the horse-sized spider! There was a slight wind. And then, they saw it.

A figure. The shadowy outlining of a man wearing a hooded cloak was moving in the far distance. He was slowly slinking from tree to tree as though he'd been following them.

"Who is — what is that?" Paul asked, squinting heavily through the trees.

"I can't tell," said London, squinting just as strongly as Paul.

"What is that god-awful smell??" Leanna asked, turning her face away.

"Let's just...keep moving," said Samol, hiding his fear.

And there it was. The Zebrastone castle emerged from the darkness as though it had been waiting for them. The upside-down fortress was terribly quiet and there was not a soul in sight, aside from these four troubled children, who unanimously thought how huge the castle looked now that no one was there. At last, they entered.

"Where is everyone?" Samol asked.

"I was thinking the same thing…" London said. "I don't think I've ever seen a castle this empty!"

"Oh, no! Maybe it's a trap!" said Leanna, who'd been on edge ever since they'd arrived at Maven's cottage.

"Let's just keep mov—" Samol began, suddenly paralyzed by Paul's sudden jump, who saw something or someone lurking in the corner of the castle's foyer.

"What is it??" Samol whispered.

"I think I just saw….Bloodwig!" Paul whispered, taking another look.

"That's not good," said Leanna.

"We've gotta get the hell out of sight! Now!" London whispered quickly.

The four of them slinked against the castle's walls, slithering about like secret agents who were trying desperately not to be killed by the hungry, goblet-shaped woman! Leanna seemed especially cautious. The four of them slipped into the Zebrastone Common Room as a collected bundle of nerves.

251

"Made it!" Paul gasped.

Samol, however, was still uneasy because the mirror was gone!

"Well, do you see it?" Leanna asked him when she saw him staring at the door.

"It was right here - - I swear!" Samol pled, pointing madly.

"Dang IT!" London screamed.

"I don't understand," he said to himself.

"Okay, think!" London spouted. "Let's think back to — to —"

"To The Death Day Ball?" Paul suggested.

"Yes…Yes!! The Death Day Ball!" London said excitedly. "During the Death Day Ball, you and I were together, Samol. Did you see anything unusual?" she asked.

"Well…besides Paul's butt," Samol joked, punching Paul in the arm, "I don't remember seeing anything out of the ordinary."

"This is serious!" she hollered as though she were the one cursed. "When you and I were there, do you remember anything you heard? Any conversations that stood out?"

Samol combed through his memories of the Death Day Ball:

He recalled the mounds of food lying in the caskets; the endless alcohol and debaucherous drinking games; big, festive costumes; the blonde, leggy celebrity and…more alcohol. 'What else was there?' he thought as his eyes swam about the common room. He remembered hearing the question, 'So, when did you die?' almost a hundred times and a woman's dumb, phony laugh and that old man who —

The voice in his head silenced when he suddenly remembered three random things:

'"You've gotta watch that Whiskey Nick. He steals booze from the parties and blames it on the kids…or says it's his friend, Tiff! He got three Aryamites in hot water last year with the administration! The jerk did nothing but laugh about it!"'

252

"'…Some believe the locket is trapped in the Ver-standfall Illusion Room. Nobody has made it out alive, but if you do I heard you have to quickly look into the invisible mirror…It shows the words that describe our gifts — backwards!'"

"'He's so weird! And probably stupid, too! I heard he sleeps in Jym Reapyr's coffin! I heard he died three times in one day — on purpose! We think he's…'"

"Looking for something," Samol said out loud.

"What??" they all said together.

"Who's looking for something?" Leanna questioned intensely.

"London!" Samol called her name strongly. "When we were at the Death Day Ball, do you remember someone saying there was a man sleeping in Jym Reapyr's grave?"

"Vaguely…" she answered hesitantly. "I was too busy making sure nobody put <u>you</u> in a grave!"

"Who was sleeping in Jym Reapyr's grave?" Leanna pressed on strongly.

"I don't know," said Samol. "I don't remember hearing a name."

"Mother, you have terrible hearing too!" Leanna said to herself.

"What?" said everyone.

"I…just don't remember hearing any of this," Leanna explained.

"Of course…maybe she meant a *grave* instead of a *casket?*" London gasped with a great epiphany.

"A grave?" Samol asked.

"She?" Paul howled.

"Who are you talking about?" Leanna asked.

"Honestly, don't you three pay attention to subtext clues?" London said in a swatty tone. "I think Gabriella was trying to tell us something!"

"GABRIELLA??" they all asked with contorted faces.

253

"What does that midget have to do with any of this?" Paul said boldly (only because Gabriella wasn't around).

"Samol, when we were on the tour of the Zebrastone castle, don't you remember when Gabriella said, *'Big things come in little caskets...Samol,'* when she was actually talking to Paul?" London asked.

Samol's eyes locked into Paul's as if the two of them were lost and wordlessly communicating.

"Oh, come on!!" London roared, relieved that she might've been onto a clue, but annoyed that she'd have to explain her thoughts all over again.

She sighed and began, "When we all were here last, in the Zebrastone Common Room, Paul was confused as to how Gabriella always knew what he was going to say before he even said it. Remember?"

"Okay..." Samol said slowly as if a light bulb was beginning to brighten.

"And she was talking to Paul, but then she said — 'Big things come in little caskets...*Samol*."

"Okay..." Samol said once more, a little brighter.

"I could be wrong, but I think Gabriella might be able to see into the future! That would explain why she knew what Paul was going to say and I think she was giving you a clue about something that she probably couldn't say in the presence of everyone else...if you know what I mean," she said.

"Big things come in little caskets...big things come in little caskets..." Samol repeated to himself, trying to make sense of it. "Where do we go off of that?"

"I don't kn—" Paul began to say.

"GULLAVIN'S GRAVE!!" Leanna blurted very loudly.

"SHHHH!!" Samol and Paul yelled, looking around to see if anyone else heard.

"Do you want us to get caught by Bloodwig??" said Paul, now more paranoid than ever. "I think she's right, though!" London whispered. "This way!!"

"No, this way!" said Leanna. "I know a shortcut."

In a dark corner of the Zebrastone sanctuary was a door that was disguised by paintings of the ghouls and ghosts. Leanna leaned closely to a smooth surface on the wall that one might've missed unless they looked for it. She whispered, *"Mystery is my maker."* A section of the wall, no bigger than a small window, began to shimmer and they crawled through. On the other side was a garden full of dead flowers and withered plants. Beyond the morbid and depressed-looking garden was Gullavin's Graveyard, which was surrounded by a thicket.

The sky was still pitch-black and it was nearly impossible to see. Leanna, who was once again leading the pack, had the hardest time because she could barely see two feet in front of her in broad daylight — let alone now! Samol wondered why there were barely any souls being shot into the air like before. In Gullavin's Graveyard, there were hundreds of swaying tombstones covered in dragon skin, viper skin, and tarantula skin. Some tombstones were blank and others were covered in the skin of tiny, albino creatures (which Samol and his friends now knew what they were). A few of the gravestones were even humming. Just like before, there were blue-eyed, black cats and bats surrounding the tombstones, violently hissing and screeching at the four strangers encroaching on *their* territory.

"What are we even looking for?" Samol asked London.

"We have to find Jym Reapyr's gravestone," Leanna answered for her, who was already reading the names on the moving gravestones closest to her.

Samol, too, picked the row of tombstones closest to him and began carefully inspecting each one.

"Reapyr… Reapyr… Reapyr…" he said aloud, going from one gravestone to the next.

"It's not organized by last name," Leanna explained. "The whole graveyard is alphabetized by the month they died."

255

"When did he die?" asked Paul, who was standing in front of a row of grave sites near a large, dead tree.

Leanna placed her hands over her face, struggling to remember. Suddenly, she broke out in a song, "…April through August death is its hottest…"

Paul and London slowly joined in, "…December through February replenishes the cemetery. January, July your emotions will die…."

Miraculously, Samol joined his friends, "…June turns to March when Jym Reapyr is parched!"

"He died in March!!" Samol shouted excitedly.

"SAMOL!! YOUR MEMORY IS COMING BACK!" London shouted and true to form, hugged him too tightly.

"I can't breathe…" he gasped, trying to wiggle free.

Still smiling, she let go.

They ran for the latter part of the cemetery to find everyone who had died in March. The sea of swaying tombstones moaned and sang as they passed them.

"Edgar J. Witchcoff…Karris A. Dottfried…Horus H. Whodweller," they read aloud.

"REAPYR! Guys, I found it!" Paul screamed excitedly, who was standing in a corner by himself. The grey headstone was draped with bushy, tarantula legs. The other three rushed over as though he'd found a treasure.

Samol read aloud, "Jym W. Reapyr; born 'June 17, 1943; died March 23, 1856?'"

"Why is there a question mark on his death date?" London asked.

"I don't know," said Samol, distracted by the bulky spider legs.

"Maybe he's…not dead?" Paul suggested.

"Maybe…" Samol said quietly.

"Let's start digging!" Leanna said, sounding almost too excited.

"Digging??" Paul hollered as though he were above such dirty work.

256

"We can't dig up anything in Gullavin's Graveyard! It's too dangerous!" Paul added.

"Well, you don't expect whatever it is we're searching for to just come looking for us, do you?" Leanna asked sarcastically.

"Well…yes, actually," Paul said honestly.

"Dig!" Leanna ordered, sounding more like a bully than someone who liked him.

Using just their hands, the four of them clawed away at the thick mud of Mr. Jym Reapyr's grave. After a full hour, they'd only dug three feet! Tiresome and fear thickened over them. Samol feared finding the unknown parallel to his curse. London feared getting caught by the administration; as they all were in violation of nearly fifty Euphod rules! Paul was…being Paul and Leanna, however, seemed most pressed for time above all. She'd been dead the longest among her friends and her floating body was turning from green to red.

After a second treacherous hour of digging, London's hand hit something metal. "Guys! I think I found something!" she screamed. "Help me pull!" The four of them yanked and yanked as hard as they could, yet they couldn't move whatever it was. London brushed the dirt from the top of the foreign object and they saw odd symbols; three looped circles and an 'X' meeting its edges. The shapes were twisting, even more so than the fat, white worms that slithered on top of it! What they had found was a tiny, black, metal casket that looked as though it were made for an infant.

"EWWWW!" they shouted and backed away, staring at the oversized, wiggling worms.

"What do the markings mean?" asked Samol.

"What do they mean??" Paul shouted rhetorically. "You mean, 'why are they moving??'"

"Shhh! Keep your voice down!" said Samol, peeking his head above ground to see if anyone (or anything) had heard them.

"Was Jym Reapyr a child?" London asked, in an all-joking-aside tone.

257

Everyone's eyes darted between one another's and then they shrugged and said the closed-mouthed version of, "I don't know." A three-second silence followed as though everyone wanted to blurt a million questions at once, but no one said anything.

"Let's open it!" said Leanna, thirstily digging at the latches. "It's locked!!"

"There's gotta be a way to open it!" said Samol.

"I'm gettin' outta here!" said Paul, who tried to run away again. Per usual, he was yanked back by London.

"London!" Samol said strongly. "Punch the latches with all your might!"

"Punch it?" she said.

"…Like how you did Leanna's face," Samol said, trying to get in her head.

Leanna rolled her eyes, which had healed quite well, actually.

London was tough, but not stupid. She was acutely aware that any injuries suffered in Euphod would go with her to her next life (or however long it took to heal). Yet, her friend's life meant more to her than a potentially broken hand. With trepidation, she balled up her pale fist and swung.

'BOOM!' She pounded the side of the coffin. 'Eek! Eek! Eek!' Whatever was inside screeched angrily! It sounded like bats or spiders or perhaps both!

"Oh, shoot! Oh, hell no!" said Paul, trying to run away again.

This time Samol grabbed him.

"Hit it again!" Leanna grinned slightly.

'BAM!' She hit the latch a second time! Her knuckles felt like they were on fire. The first latch broke loose and revealed the tiniest sliver of the coffin's blackened insides. Leanna pried her thin, bony fingers into the opening and began to pull. After she pried it open far enough, the others cautiously slipped their fingers inside, fearing that the lid would suddenly clamp down on their fingers and crush them! When they finally tore it off, they almost died…again.

258

Large, veiny, black, beating hearts filled the inside of Jym Reapyr's casket! The charcoal-colored organs secreted a thick, gluey residue giving each one of them a glassy look. Not only was it a site straight out of a nightmare, so was the horrible smell!

"What the hell is this??" screeched Paul, feeling almost as frightened as he did when that old man tried to stab him and they ended up in the mailroom.

"I don't like this either!" said London, covering her nose.

"Maybe...the whispering will is in the midst of the hearts?" Leanna suggested.

The four of them looked to see if they could find anything lodged between the beating hearts when suddenly two skeletal hands shot through the pulsating pile, yanking two of them deep inside the coffin! Samol and London screamed terribly when they saw their two friends ripped away in the blink of an eye! Their hovering bodies dropped down low under the dirt as though their floating corpses, themselves, sensed that danger was coming!

And then, there came a terrible voice.

"WHO'S OUT THERE??" barked a raspy voice of a woman who already sounded ugly.

"Oh, no!" London said, carefully peering above ground, her hands clasped at the edge of the dirt, which was just inches below her eyes. "It's Bloodwig!!"

"Oh, no!" Samol cried as his whole body went numb.

"We have to go in after them! SHE'S COMING THIS WAY!"

London took Samol's hand and dove into the festering pile of slimy, thumping hearts! They screamed loudly. Bloodwig turned red when she saw that Jym Reapyr's grave had been dug up! The beefy broad waddled fast enough to catch a glimpse of Samol's foot just before it sunk into the hunk of hearts. This, however, was one foot too many!

The casket was a bottomless pit. The hearts grew bigger, furrier, smellier, veinier, and beated faster the deeper they plunged! Globs of slime and broken pieces of the nasty hearts got into their eyes and mouth! Both of them gagged terribly and almost cried, yet London did not let go of his hand. Finally, they plopped to the ground and found themselves in a vault-like dungeon where Leanna and Paul had been anxiously waiting for them. Aside from Samol scraping his knee, no one was seriously hurt!

Caged doors that looked like the entrances to old, jail cells lined the walls. Directly behind them was a crooked, wooden door that looked as though it led somewhere dangerous. Right in front of them, at the center of the dungeon, however, was a mountain of black and blue trinkets and jewels cloaked in cobwebs that looked as though they'd been hidden there for centuries. "Where are we?" Samol asked, gazing about the strange dungeon. A few seconds had gone by and there was no response from anyone. He asked again, "What is this place?" To a terrible surprise, he turned around to find London, Paul, and Leanna screaming at the top of their lungs, yet he heard nothing! Everyone had suddenly gone deaf.

"I CAN'T HEARRRRRR!!!!!" Samol screeched, clasping his ears as though he were trying to hear himself, but couldn't.

"Can you hear me??" Paul panicked. "WHY CAN'T I HEAR MYSELFFFFF??"

"This is not good!" Leanna said to herself.

Adjacent to the treasures was a large, blank parchment that shined bright like royalty. Leanna was the first to spot it in the midst of this hearing-impaired crisis. She tapped Samol on the shoulder and mouthed dramatically:

"Look over there!" she said, pointing to the end of the room with almost too much expression.

"Where? What??" Samol shouted back, trying to read her lips.

260

"IT'S THE WHISPE—" she began, but yanked him across the room when she realized that mouthing was of no use.

Paul was most frightened of all. He was fearfully mouthing to London, "How do we get the hell outta here??" The two of them had no clue that they'd been left behind by Samol and Leanna. Yet, London snatched Paul by the hand and barreled across the dungeon floor when she noticed that they'd been left.

At last, they'd found it! The Whispering Will stood almost as tall as Maven. Its dirty, gold edges were inscribed with some strange calligraphy that read, *'dna yb ruoy nwo ecnegilletni lla efil lliw eb enodnu, s'evolegdirb sterces era tnavelerri won efil dna htaed era eno.'* Right now, written words were all they could use for clues to figure this thing out! They hadn't a clue as to what it meant and stood desperately in front of the giant parchment waiting for it to show something - - anything! Samol, especially! A few seconds turned into minutes. Still nothing.

"What's going on??" London mouthed dramatically, leaping nearly a foot off the ground. "I don't know!" Leanna mouthed back with just as much expression. Suddenly, the slightest shimmer of bright, gold writing emerged from the white parchment. Soon, there were hundreds of names, birthdays, and death dates whirling vigorously about the page! And then the Whispering Will suddenly went pitch black. What was once bright gold ink now turned blood red! Samol went numb, because he was reminded of the Death Scroll he saw in Madame Levine's chamber. The four of them backed away. London feared that the large parchment would spit at them just as the portraits did in the Freedomcorpse Memorial Hall!

Names, birthdays, and death dates raced by even faster now. Letters continued to appear, then disappear. Appear and then disappear, again and again, as if something in another dimension was toying with Samol and his friends.

Finally, it read:

'I am but a moment in time, thus you must pay close attention….'

'If you can see me….'

'You cannot hear me…'

'Should we meet again…'

'It will not be with sight…'

'Yet, with sound…'

'However…'

'By then, it will be too late…'

'Therefore…'

'I must present you with this final ode…'

'Freedom rises when your ashes fall, I wish to be broken so you can stand tall. Although I may die, let it not be in vain; as death is but a second in which we'll permanently reign.'

'Dear child...'

'Although, you have thirteen days...'

'What I've revealed shall serve you long after such term is obsolete...'

'However...'

'I am filled with the utmost regret....'

'At this time, that is all that I can reveal...'

'Unfortunately...'

'...Someone else is in the room....'

The four of them panicked in the loudest, silent-hysteria ever! Everyone manically looked around the dark dungeon, afraid to catch another set of eyes glaring at them from behind the jail cell bars, or someone who'd crept behind them with a hatchet or something! Suddenly, the vault was overtaken by a brilliant orange. The Whispering Will had self-ignited and all that was left was its charred, gold frame! As it burned away, their hearing returned.

"...od please! I'll nev—" Paul pled, until he realized that he could hear himself.

"Hey — HEY! Can you hear me??" Samol shouted as if he were still deaf.

"YES! Can you hear me??" London said, whose face began to brighten into a smile.

"Man! It's good to hear your voices!" Paul leapt. "What was that all about??"

"I don't know," said Leanna, looking around the dungeon, still holding her ears. "Let's not find out. We've got to keep moving," said Samol.

A long hallway that was hidden behind the tall Whispering Will revealed itself. At the end of the hall was a stairway and a door. The top of the stairs were boarded shut (this time they noticed). From behind the door, however, was the unnerving sound of growling spirits or vicious dogs or something. Unfortunately, there was no other way out.

CHAPTER SIXTEEN

THE DEATH SHRINE

"Don't look them in the eye! If you do, you'll become a prisoner, yourself, and they'll control your soul for the next three lives!"
– Leanna

"Let's go in!" said London, taking the lead.

"I don't think I wanna know what's behind door number one!" Paul cringed.

London carefully placed her ear to the door. Whatever these creatures were, they were speaking some sort of strange language. After almost thirty seconds with her ear placed at the old, wooden door, she could tell that there were hundreds of them!

"What are they?" Leanna asked intensely.

"They're creatures…or monsters…or some sort of wild animals and it sounds like they're trying to communicate with one another," London explained to the best of her abilities with her ear still pressed to the door.

"Let me listen," said Leanna, placing her ear against the door, happy that she weren't deaf anymore.

"Do you hear it?" London asked. "What are they sa–"

"SHHH!" she shushed her and flung her hand in the air authoritatively.

Leanna listened intensely for nearly two whole minutes. Suddenly, she jerked her head from the door and said, "Let's go in…"

"Are you sure about this?" said Paul, who was standing behind everyone.

"We have no choice," said Samol, masking the terror that tore through him.

Leanna cracked open the door. A sudden gust cut through them like a dagger. Not to mention, it was stinking! They found themselves at the top of a large, coiled staircase that split off into three ways; each one was headed by a menacing, ten-foot, gargoyle statue. The four of them stared at the scary statues, wondering if they were the ones making that growling noise. The statues stood still, almost too still, as though they were actually alive waiting for just the right moment to lunge at them! Everyone quickly ran passed them (Paul, the quickest) and they finally saw what lay before them.

They were in a large cave with dilapidated walls aligned with tall, skinny candles made of clear wax. Its fire burned blood red and at the heart of the cave stood many terrible-looking beasts who had the body of a man, covered in the fur of a lion, and the head of a rhinoceros! The creatures were up to their knees in a pool of boiling, acidic blood and were aligned six rows long, six rows wide, and six rows around! Every one of them was asleep, standing up, gently swaying back and forward like the gravestones in Gullavin's Grave, grumbling an unrecognizable language as though they were sleep-talking!

"OH, SCREW THIS!!!" Paul hollered, who began running again.

"SHHH!!" Leanna shushed him, finally getting a turn to yank him back. "These are Furvix Demons!" she whispered strongly. "You do <u>not</u> want to wake them!"

266

Samol was intensely examining the creatures and asked, "Why are they swaying…and what are they saying??"

"According to Euphod history, they sleep standing up. The swaying is believed to soothe their souls," Leanna explained. "In regards to what they're saying, Euphodologists have never been able to figure it out. There were only two who ever have and both mysteriously died within three days of each other!"

"What's with the boiling blood?" London asked quietly, her eyes fixed on the menacing creatures.

"That…I don't have a clue," Leanna said honestly.

Suddenly, there was a crash behind them where the Whispering Will once stood that sounded like an empty pail had fallen to the ground.

"Someone's coming! We have to move!" Leanna said fear-stricken.

"HOW DO WE GET ACROSS??" Paul hollered.

"SHHHH!!" said everyone and in that moment, Paul found four hands clasped over his mouth and two around his body so he couldn't run. He wiggled free from his three friends, but kept panicking. "There's no way out! THERE'S NO WAY OUT!"

"PAUL!! SHUT-YOUR-MOUTH!!!" London said, gritting her teeth, with a wide-eyed, crazy look in her eyes.

"We have to somehow get around it!" Samol instructed bravely.

The four of them divided amongst the three coiled staircases. Leanna hurried down the staircase to the far left, London down the middle, Samol and Paul down the right. Paul, of course, still wouldn't shut up and had to be shushed nearly ten times. When they reached the bottom, they saw that they were trapped! The girls arrived before the boys and were met with a gorge of boiling blood at their toes.

Leanna and London panicked, hopping up and down like they had to pee very badly. Yet, the moment Samol finally reached the bottom of his staircase, the pool receded. He suddenly remembered that blood runs from him and whispered,

267

"Everyone, follow me! Hurry!" Samol parted the red sea as though he were royalty and kept a sharp eye on the demons. The four of them tiptoed past the beasts, which were three times taller than they were!

"Ouch!" Paul screamed, feeling the sting of the hot ground on the soles of his feet.

"Shhh!" his friends hushed him yet again. They, too, were in terrible pain. After all, the blood was boiling! However, they dealt with their discomfort quietly.

Then, it happened.

"Uh, guys?…" said Paul, walking briskly with his eyes locked onto the beasts. "I think we should pick up the pace…."

"Keep your voi—" London began to say, when she noticed it too.

The Furvix demons all had stopped swaying. In the corner of the cave, a set of piercing, red eyes had opened. A subtle, yet dangerous growl issued from its throat. Two red eyes became four. Four became twenty. Twenty became eighty! Now, there were hundreds! The beasts snarled at the smell of fresh meat who so willingly wandered into their home. Samol and his friends froze in a deadly silence, hoping that if they didn't move they'd be fine. Oh, how very wrong they were...

The demons roared at once, sounding like a thousand lions! "RUNNNNNN!!!" Samol screamed, dodging razor-sharp teeth and bear-sized claws! On the other side of the cave sat a single staircase that led up to a door. The four of them screamed and scattered! London was running towards the stairs when a demon cornered her. Operating off of fear and adrenaline, she hurled back and punched the creature in the face with all her strength! 'BOOM!' It was knocked back nearly twenty-five feet! Paul wasn't having such good luck. Two were gaining on him! He was running as fast as he could, but it wasn't fast enough. "HELP!" he hollered.

One of them caught him and bit his shoulder and drew blood! Even though the creature tore off most of his sleeve and some skin, he managed to pull away. The problem was that these creatures loved blood more than sharks. One drop drew a flock. Paul was in trouble.

The four of them dashed up the stairs! Once they reached the last step, they found a small door that looked as though it were made for midgets or toddlers! It was nearly impossible to fit through! Leanna, who was the first one to reach the door, tugged on it vigorously. It was locked!

"Now, what're we gonna do!!!" Leanna screamed.

"GIRL, MOVE!!!" London shouted, running up the stairs away from three demons and drop-kicked the pint-sized door. It flew open like it had been bombed!

Without questioning where it led, she quickly shimmied through the tiny opening. Then, Leanna. Then, Samol. Finally, Paul who locked the door behind him! The demons clawed angrily, desperate to get through! Luckily, aside from Paul's bitten shoulder and a few rattled nerves everyone was okay.

London was the first to see where they were; another large, dark room. Dead trees had grown through the shattered windows. Its walls were littered with worms and larva. There was rotted wood, broken chairs, and shattered glass. The room looked as if something or someone had just destroyed it, almost like it was being searched for something. Aside from the sound of the beasts trying to burst through the door, it was rather quiet. The chamber's presence was so eerie that it could've even curdled the faces of their floating corpses.

"Where are we?" London asked with balled fists, ready to swing at anything that moved.

"Oh, no!" said Leanna. "We have to get out of here!"

"What is it??" Samol and Paul said at the same time.

"This is…a death chamber!" she cringed.

"OH, HELL NO!" said Paul, looking for somewhere to run.

"…But I don't see any pri—" Leanna froze when she saw it.

Her words, just like Paul's nerves, were shattered when her eyes met the bulky silhouette of a man standing in a doorway, who was holding a chain. None of them could see his face, and he kept totally still as though he were trying not to be seen. Suddenly, six more men crawled from an opening directly above them. They, too, were quiet and weren't seen yet, until it was too late.

"PRISONERS!!!" Leanna screamed.

"AHHH!!!" they hollered and scattered.

"Don't look them in the eye!" Leanna ordered sternly. "If you do, you'll become a prisoner, yourself, and they'll control your soul for the next three lives!"

Screaming terribly, they checked the ceiling to see if any more creatures had crawled out! Without warning, two burst through the rickety floorboards and bit London's leg, tearing out chunks of her flesh! She screamed and kicked the zombie's head off! It flew across the room like a soccer ball! Then, almost a dozen more zombies came out of the hole in the floor!

"LONDON!" Samol hollered, fighting off three zombies. "Are you okay??"

"Just keep going!" said London, whose run had become a limp and soon she fell to the floor.

"LONDON!!!" Paul shouted. "HELP HER!" he called to the others.

'Thump! Thump! THUMP!' The creatures ran and crawled faster and faster! If her friends didn't rescue her quickly, London would be their next bit of nourishment in more ways than one. Paul spotted a large log on the floor. He picked it up ready for battle. Leanna snapped a leg off a nearby stool, its edges were now sharp like spikes. Samol grabbed a long piece of shattered glass from the floor. The three of them corralled around London to protect her. By now, there were at least fifty drooling monsters, whose desires ranged from food to sex! This battle seemed hopeless.

270

How could they win a fight with creatures they couldn't even look in the eye?? Not to mention, each zombie had a weapon of their own! Samol, Paul, and Leanna circled around, with their eyes fixed on the creatures' rotted feet, watching for any sudden movements.

For a few seconds it was silent, until there was a terrible growl, and then a large, silvery-eyed mummy, missing all of its skin, teeth, and nose lunged for Leanna with a horrible lust lurking behind its eyes. Leanna saw the creature advancing towards her, but couldn't look up! Paul, standing beside her, had a better view. Keeping his head down, he swung in the nick of time and pummeled the creature so hard that it burst into flames! Many of the zombies backed away.

The fire had created a division between them and the creatures. Yet, this complicated the battle because now it was impossible to see who was coming! The zombies screeched angrily and continued to retreat. Careening towards them was a screaming, disfigured, female zombie who dashed through the fire! All of her rotted flesh had fallen from her body and so had most of her moldy hair. Her eyes were bloodshot. Nose disintegrated. One tooth left. From her bottom lip hung a piece of pulsating muscle that had fused itself to her chin!

Her demented eyes were fixed on Paul. She charged lustfully. "Not my man!" Leanna screamed shoving the wooden stool leg through her neck! The creature died instantly. Unfortunately, Leanna's only weapon was now lodged in the smelly throat of a zombie. The dead creature fell back into the fire, which ignited it even brighter. More of them retreated into the far corners of the chamber. However, the fire was growing dangerously close to the four of them, especially the immobile London.

Then, it came out.

A large, hulking beast. Its three heads were camou flaged by its monstrous shoulders, each were the size of boulders. Its oversized biceps were terribly scarred. The creature's abdomen was ripped open, revealing a second set of pulsating flesh. Its oversized back had a large, twisting, circular mouth that revealed its second set of pointy, razor-sharp teeth. Scariest of all was its forty-four red eyes that were asymmetrically scattered amongst its heads, back, shoulders, and stomach. This creature was made for battle and had almost every one of its eyes locked onto Samol.

The four hundred pound meaty monster ran through the blazing fire as if it were nothing more than a puddle of water. Samol kept his head down and had to rely solely on his hearing, timing, and best friends. When the beast was inches from Samol's shaking body, both he and Paul struck the creature with their weapons as hard as they could. 'BOOM!' The beast fell and landed on its back, popping two of its eyes! It squealed as three voices in one, sounding almost like that horse-sized-spider that attacked them previously!

The monster squirmed in a fiery rage and came back twice as fast, twice as loud, and twice as angry! By now, London had regained the slightest bit of strength in her legs. Next to her was a large piece of broken glass. She grabbed it and stood up weakly, trying not to fall into the flames. The creature was getting closer. At the last second she, Paul, and Samol pummeled the creature again. 'BOOM!' It screeched even louder than the first time. Two sharp pieces of glass punctured two more of its eyes, which shot a venomous, black pus when it landed on its back!

Samol kept his head low, fearing he'd catch only a glimpse of one of its eyes. What he did see, however, was the small cloth that had fallen from his pocket that Maven had given him. Not knowing if it would even work, he picked it up and dangled it in mid-air. To his surprise, the beast and other zombies backed away! The muscular monster, along with what sounded like an invisible woman who lived in the sky, let out a terrible cry!

The beast and other zombies ran away and they were safe. Everyone exhaled heavily and hugged one another. Yet, that woman's scream rang constantly in Samol's ears. He wondered where he'd heard that scream before. 'Was it from a past life? Or was Madame Levine's potion working? And where had I seen a cloth like this before? Wait a minute!...I remember Harragett flashing the same cloth in that freaky spider's face! But what was it about this cloth? Was it magical? Holy? Cursed??'

"London, are you all right?" Paul asked gently.

"I'm fine," she said, caressing her leg wounds.

"Samol, what was that — that thing that was after you??" Leanna asked as if she were more afraid than he was.

"I don't know," he said honestly.

"It came after only you - - three times!" cried Leanna.

"Oh, I remember," he said, somehow able to laugh a little.

"Ew!" Leanna screamed, manically brushing something from her shoulder.

"What??" everyone hollered, still very much on edge.

"One of its fingernails got on my shoulder," she said, brushing it off as if it had a disease.

"We have to keep moving," Paul said cautiously, looking all around the room to make sure that there were no more zombies. "I'm hoping we can just find what we're looking for and get to our next lives, quickly! I've had enough!"

They exited the open door on the other side of the chamber.

Paul continued fantasizing, "Hopefully, it'll be a nice life where I can relax on a beach with a few babes and have not a care in the world," he smiled widely.

"Oh, shut up!" London joked, who'd gained back her spirits. The four of them, happy to have escaped a final death, were even happier to have each other. Now standing in a graveyard, they found something odd. There were hundreds of wailing, withered Aryamites chained to their own tombstones!

It was a site that could have made even those with a heart of stone shed a tear.

"This is horrible!" cried London. "Where are we?"

"I've never seen this place before," said Leanna, who was also suddenly teary-eyed.

"Oh, these poor people," said London, fighting back more tears, slightly turning her face. "Is there any way we can free them??"

"I don't think so," said Paul, biting his lip.

"Oh, no," Samol said sadly, staring at a pale woman with stringy hair who was wailing loudly.

"Look at this!" said Paul, pointing to a glowing tombstone in the middle of the cemetery.

"That's strange..." said Leanna, drying her eyes.

"It's the only gravestone here without anyone chained to it," said Paul.

"Ludwig von Tassell..." London read aloud, wiping snot from her nose. "Why do I know that name?" she asked herself, carelessly throwing her hand over her shoulder.

"Hey! Watch it!" said Leanna, who was standing right beside her.

"What?" said London.

"One of your loose fingernails just hit me in the head!" she said.

"Oh, I'm sorry," said London, checking all ten fingernails (none of which were broken or even chipped).

"Man...with the kind of luck we've had so far, I'm surprised nothing has jumped out or tried to kill us yet!" Paul joked, but was actually serious.

"Let's not jinx it. Just keep mo—" Samol began to say, when suddenly he and his friends began to sink into the ground.

"Oh, come ON!" Paul roared, who was now almost too tired to even be scared.

It was the graveyard's quicksand! The tombstones, however, remained above ground like a tooth to its receding gums.

274

"Guys! Do-not-panic!" London ordered. Her demeanor had suddenly shifted from mushy to militant. "If there's anything loose or heavy on any of you, throw it! Now! You'll float better!"

No one had anything to throw.

"If you're near a tombstone or anything sturdy or rooted in the ground, grab hold of it! NOW!" London instructed. She, herself, kept sinking, but remained calm.

Leanna, who'd begun to panic, was able to grab hold of Ludwig von Tassell's tombstone.

Paul and Samol, however, weren't so lucky.

London further instructed, "If you have nothing to grab hold of, lie flat on your back! If you stay standing, you'll sink."

"Lay on my back??" Paul hollered, who began splashing and thrashing.

"DO IT!" she demanded. "And stop splashing! That's what'll make you sink!"

"Guys! HELP!!!" Paul panicked, sinking further.

"PAUL!! LIE FLAT ON YOUR BACK!!!" London screamed.

The harder he fought the quicker he sunk. The quicksand was now up to his chin! His arms flailed a million miles an hour! Luckily, Leanna was near him. She managed to grab one of his thrashing hands and held onto him until he stopped panicking.

"PAUL, LISTEN TO ME!" London said sternly. "I almost died in a quicksand accident four lives ago and I learned how to get out of it. You must do exactly as I say!"

Suddenly, Leanna's hand slipped and the both of them fell into the endless mud pit, but she quickly grabbed hold of the gravestone again. Paul, once again, wasn't so lucky.

"PAUL! LEAN BACK AND PUT YOUR LEGS UPWARD!!" London said sternly.

Surprisingly, without panic, he did exactly as she instructed and slowly began to float.

"Do everything slowly!" she ordered. "You too, Samol!" who managed to somehow remain calm this entire time, even though the quicksand was inching up to his mouth!

"Take deep breaths and float on your back. I want you both to swim to your left!"

Leanna was still trapped at the center of the graveyard. She carefully let go and followed behind them, doing exactly as instructed. London, herself, swam on her back towards the end of the graveyard.

"Everyone, use your hands to very, very, very slowly paddle your way to the end of the cemetery. It's not that far away," said London. "No sudden movements! You're doing great!" she was sure to compliment them, which quite naturally improved their swimming.

London perched her head up to check on Paul who, to her surprise, was swimming perfectly. Samol, on the other hand....

"Samol, don't submerse your hands all the way in the quicksand. It creates more traction," she corrected gently. "We're almost there!"

Quicker than they expected, they'd reached the end of the pool of quicksand. It was now shallow enough for them to stand up. Covered in mud, sticks, and a finger or two, they were once again simply thankful to be all right.

"London, thank you!" Paul said, hugging her. "You saved my life! Well — my second life — my —"

"I know what you mean and...you're welcome!" she smiled.

Leanna and Paul walked ahead of them, making sure to get as far away from the quicksand as possible.

"I didn't know you almost drowned in quicksand," said Samol, walking past a large, dead tree, rubbing mud from his hair.

"I didn't," she winked. "I saw it on TV four lives ago."

"You little sneak!" Samol snickered, nudging her gently.
276

"Oh, come on! You and I both know that if I would've told him that, then we would've lost him!" she giggled truthfully.

"Yeah...you're right," Samol snickered again.

Just beyond the graveyard was a small, grey cottage. The moment Samol laid eyes on it, he wondered if it was the graveyard ruler's home (if there was such a thing). Or if this was where the person who slept in Jym Reaper's grave was hiding! He was too exhausted to even be afraid anymore. More importantly, he knew that they'd made it through the Death Shrine. However, he was still somewhat cautious, to say the least. Who wouldn't be if they saw a tilted shack with a bright, flickering light that only shined around the edges of its front door and nowhere else...

CHAPTER SEVENTEEN

TIME'S DEATH CERTIFICATE

'"I die when wisdom falls"' – Samol

In front of a tiny, crooked, grey shack was where they stood. There was a nothingness in the air that sent shivers down their backs and all that was around them was very still. It's safe to assume that in the past few hours, these four dead teens might've experienced more than the living do in a full year! The deceased were supposed to be lying stiffly in a casket, six feet under, the entrée of maggots and all the like. Oh, how far that lie from the truth for Aryamites.

It was beautiful that Samol had three good friends to help him through such turmoil. They were like family now; covered in quicksand together and still very much on edge when coming close to nearly being devoured by demons! If someone were to ask them if they loved each other, they would've unanimously said, "Yes." Together, they were determined to conquer Samol's third and final task.

"Well...here we go," Samol said, reaching for the black door knob.

Leanna, Paul, and London humbly hung their heads to the ground in a delicate silence as though they were pleased to say, "We did it."

"Thank you," Samol said with a gracious smile.

Paul and London tilted their heads to the side and grinned at him beautifully.

"You all have put your lives in danger for me when you really didn't have to," he said.

"Hey, that's what friends are for," said London, still smiling.

"All right — enough of this gooey stuff!" Paul hollered, which totally ruined the charming moment. "Let's get this over with! We don't have a lot of time!" he said, suddenly realizing that they were after the death certificate of the very thing they didn't have much of.

Fear iced through Samol's body. He slowly turned the doorknob as if another zombie was waiting on the other side. Cautiously opening the door, it squeaked louder the further he opened it. Inside, there was a bright room that was deceivingly ten times bigger than the whole outside of the tiny, crooked cottage! Many hallways branched from the long, high-ceilinged foyer. At its center, was a large statue that was half angel, half demon. From its muscular back sprouted two monstrous wings, both of which spewed a mist that covered its face. Strangely, its wings had the same symbols found on Jym Reapyr's casket; three looped circles and an 'X' meeting its edges.

"Are we — supposed to be in here?" Paul asked, sounding scared again.

"I've never seen this place before," said Leanna, who looked wide-eyed like a kid in a candy shop.

"Me either," said London, who was nowhere near as enthused as Leanna.

All of a sudden, the four of them were surrounded by bright blue mists! They began swatting and running, just like when they were attacked during the wasp-spider-snake attack! However, the mists felt gentle, almost good on their skin and began showing them secrets of their past:

Before London, stood an abusive, male figure. She couldn't quite see who it was, but she had a good idea. Before Paul, appeared two of his darkest secrets, which took the form of two scrolls that began writing something. He quickly fanned them away and looked to see if anyone saw, which they hadn't. Samol saw a vengeful, evil-looking creature that was not human. It was trying to swat and bite at him through metal bars! He backed away, not knowing if it were real or not.

Leanna's secret was strongest of all, because it physically changed her. She began sprouting grey hairs and her skin began to wrinkle. Her cheeks sunk into her face and her eyes began to wither as if time was aging her right before their very eyes! Samol, Paul, and London saw this and began screaming, when suddenly everyone's mists disappeared.

"What in Euphod's name is this??" Leanna screamed in a very raspy voice that didn't even sound like hers, now looking like a ninety-year-old woman.

"I was gonna ask you the same thing!" said London, fanning away the last of the smoke.

"Were those memories of a past life or…something from the future?" Samol asked with a tone of worry in his voice.

"Past life!" London shouted the same time Paul hollered, "Future life!"

"Maybe it was neither…." Leanna suggested, who began to look and sound like herself again.

"Well, regardless, we need to find that death certificate!" said Samol. They searched the walls, high and low, front to back, corner to corner. The walls were aligned with mirrors that were all shattered in the same spot; the bottom, right corner.

280

It looked as if someone had shot every last mirror with a bee bee gun in the same spot, as though they were either trying to hide something or they were looking for something but couldn't find it. Other parts of the walls had burned fragments of what appeared to be old poems. One in particular was written in the most beautiful, gold cursive Samol had ever seen; *'Time is to blood as future is to life.'* Although the rest of it had been burned away, Samol knew that he'd either seen or heard this somewhere before.

"Hey, look at this!" London said, who was standing in front of another gold-framed poem across the hall.

"What is it?" Samol asked.

"I think — I think it's a prophecy? My aunt told me about this," London said, sounding unsure of herself, but kept reading.

"Your aunt?" Paul said as though he already had a million sarcastic remarks waiting at the tip of his tongue.

"Yes, Paul! My aunt!" London said harshly.

"We're getting close, mom," Leanna whispered to herself.

"What?" said the other three.

"I said…we're getting close now," Leanna said quickly, with the last of her grey hairs finally gone.

"What does the poem say?" Samol asked, now staring at the same poem that London had pointed out.

London read aloud:

"'*In the last days, I will reveal one of my most hidden treasures; the thirteenth month. It is a part of me that cannot be seen, yet will surely be born once every spirit is unclean. During this time, Euphod will experience famine and war, and terrible tremors from its core. Diseases and plagues are only the beginning, to a terrible time when winds will be spinning. Fires will sprout from the very ground, while millions of Aryamites will be drenched and drowned…*'"

281

"I can't… continue reading this…" said an over-whelmed London.

"Oh, move over!" said Leanna, shoving London out of the way and finished reading.

"*'Because iniquity will be multiplied, love shall wax cold. Yet, he who is righteous shall be untouched, pure as gold. You will seek for my sister, yet she will be gone, and you'll beg for my brother but he'll be withdrawn. I am not a Divine Power, yet all things exist through me. Do not seek me. Seek only the person you were created to be.'*"

Leanna fell into a confused silence. "I don't get it," she said.

"It was probably written by one of London's aunt's psycho Epscovian friends!" Paul made fun again, bursting with laughter.

"PAUL!" London hollered.

"Oh, come on!" he begged condescendingly. "Don't tell me you believe in all that stupid stuff!"

"Guys, we need to find that death certificate! We don't-have-much-time…" Samol said. The last four words fell from his mouth as though he suddenly understood that this might've been what everyone was warning him about from the moment he got to Euphod.

With no time to lose, they split up in search of any documents that looked important. They found nothing but more burned and shredded poems on the walls. A few of them even had specific words torn out. There was a single parchment, in particular, that caught Samol's eye. It was written in the same gold cursive as the last one that caught his eye and it read, *Pictures of the future reveal the ___ of your past.* Samol scrutinized the torn papyrus wondering if it was a clue when all of a sudden, his deep thoughts were shattered by a terrible scream.

"AHHH!!! WHAT IS THAT??" Paul hollered, pointing shakily at the ceiling.

"What are y — WHOA!!" shouted the other three, who ducked as if someone swung an ax at their heads.
282

Above them was a massive, hairy, blue eye that squirmed slimily and retreated the moment it had been seen! A blinding, blue, lightning bolt thundered over the big hall. The four of them were knocked to the ground and the room was silent.

"All right, guys! I've seen enough of this!" said Paul, once again scurrying for the exit.

"Haven't you learned by now you're not going anywhere!" London blared, this time yanking him back by his pants, giving him a nasty wedgie.

"Wh — w — what was that thing?" Samol stammered, still breathing heavily.

"Let's just keep going before it comes back!" said Leanna, still covering her ears from the booming lightning bolt.

"Wait!" Samol stopped them, breathing just a tad bit slower now. "Has anyone found anything even close to what we're looking for yet?"

"No," replied an irritated Paul. "Just these stupid poems...oh, I'm sorry, London ... I mean prophecies!" he scoffed.

"This is serious!" Samol shouted. "Maybe we're looking in the wrong places! Or maybe asking the wrong questions. Or..." he paused as if he'd been struck by a terrible thought and said, "...Maybe I'm meant to go this journey alone."

"What are you talking about?" said London as if he'd offended her. "What do you mean *alone??*"

"Think about it," he said. "I'm the one who can't view any of my past lives...I'm the one who can't be around blood...I'm the one who's got this curse...Maybe Euphod wants me to fight this battle alone. I've put you all in enough danger, as it is!"

"You wouldn't last one second out there by yourself!" London belted. "Did you NOT just see all those demons we just conquered...together? As a GROUP?? That's what family is for. Whether you like it or not, you're stuck with me!"

"Mother, be quiet!" Leanna whispered to herself.

"What?" cried the others, wondering if Leanna was losing her mind.

"I said it's rather quiet…" Leanna said quickly.

With Samol's current state of hysteria and Paul being…well, Paul, Leanna was able to scathe by the two of them. London, however, from then on kept a close eye on her.

"All right, you guys, here's what we'll do…" Samol began to instruct. "When we walked in, I noticed several hallways branching from the foyer. Let's each take one and see what's in it and if there's trouble, we'll call each other for help. Sound good?"

"Yes," said Leanna and Paul at the same time London hollered, "No!"

"What's wrong?" Samol asked.

"Did you miss what I just said about sticking…*together?*" London sassed.

"Oh, right!" he said. "New plan! Leanna, you and I will go together and London…"

"Will keep an eye on Paul, I know." London said as if Paul needed a constant babysitter.

"Hey! I'm no punk!" Paul spouted angrily.

"Then act like it, dweeb!" she said, yanking him by his hand.

Off they went. London and Paul, who already began arguing, journeyed down a long, thin hallway. Within seconds, a greyish fog mushroomed in front of them showing them important memories of their very first lives:

London saw Bridgelove; the first castle she was ever sorted into. She was a baby-faced girl who'd just lived her first life, which sadly, was filled with much abuse. Paul saw Culomund and was a scrawny, awkward boy who always looked nervous as though he had many secrets. The two of them saw many memories of Death Day Balls pass by and they stood in a daze for several minutes. Interestingly enough, Samol and Leanna had also run into their own set of distractions.

Leanna and Samol were running down a long hallway filled with more portraits and parchments. Some were portraits of heroic Aryamites. Some were old drafts of the Euphod Constitution of Aryamite Rights and others were sonnets and prophecies. A few gold frames laid empty as if thieves had stolen whatever was once inside. They kept searching.

"Death certificate…death certificate…where are you?" Samol said to himself, carefully examining each and every frame.

"Samol, are you sure we're looking in the right place?" Leanna asked, who was also looking aimlessly at each enclosure.

"No, but let's keep looking anyway!"

"This makes no sense!" she cried. "If we're looking for time's death certificate…then that means that time, itself, has died — which would mean that it no longer exists, which can't be!"

"Not necessarily true - - someone could say the same about us!" he said.

They reached the end of the hall that forked into three separate ways. Samol chose the hallway closest to him.

"Quick, this way!" he said.

When they turned the odd, sharp corner, they were met with an odd distraction, similar to the very thing that arose in front of Paul and London. A mist with every feeling that they'd ever deemed significant appeared. The smoke looked like shimmering holograms and was accompanied by beautiful music.

"What is this?" Samol giggled stupidly, sounding as though he were suddenly intoxicated.

"I don't know…" said Leanna, sounding just as sloppy. "I think the better question is — is —"

Her eyes dimmed and her mouth cracked into a lazy smile. The mist had suddenly intoxicated her too. They both felt tingly and light-headed. Samol couldn't stop giggling until he suddenly saw horrific creatures taunting him in

285

nightmares of a past life. He even saw himself being burned and then awakening into a new life! Samol heard footsteps thumping up a staircase and then watched the image of a man carrying a butcher knife bigger than his own head and then he relived the pain of his murder!

And then a bittersweet memory appeared.

He felt his stomach disappear when he reunited with his best friends who, to him, were nothing more than mere strangers that he couldn't remember. He suddenly felt terrible! Samol heard the sweet music that swirled in his head when he had the dream, living life as Ryan and then it was crushed by that despicable Victoria! The ash-covered breakfast. Her halitosis! Being beaten to death by the metal bat!

Still smothered in the intoxicating mist, Samol turned to Leanna to find that she, too, was paralyzed in a daze of her own past. Mothballs, knitted sweaters, and living in hiding was what she saw, strangely. Skin and a voice that was not her own appeared in front of her. Without any sense of warning, the images and sounds evaporated as quickly as they came.

"What the -- are you…all right?" Samol asked her hesitantly.

"I'm fine," she said sadly. "Samol, there's something I have to te—"

"THERE IT IS!" he hollered, pointing to the end of the hallway.

"What?" she said confusedly and then she gasped when she saw it.

At the end of the hall was a large, black death certificate encased in a twisted, silver frame behind a glistening glass with bright green words. Samol let out the heaviest sigh his lungs would allow.

"PAUL!! LONDON!!!!" Samol roared, "I FOUND IT!!!!!"

Their nostalgic moments were shattered by Samol's squeal. Paul was rather upset actually, because the memories of him having a few romantic endeavors in past lives was still being shown to him.

"LONDON!! PAUL!!!" Samol shouted again.

The two of them hurled towards the sound of his voice and wheeled around the odd, sharp corner. Even though only Samol (and strangely Leanna) could see it, London and Paul could not. The black parchment read:

Time's Death Certificate
Birthdate - When He said 'Go'
Death date - I die when wisdom falls

Samol leapt for joy! Below its three-lined-title were many paragraphs of illegible fine print that was too small to read. Even if it were like the fine print of Madame Levine's seemingly crooked contract, it didn't matter to him in that moment. Samol Doscow had completed his third and final task!

"I don't see anything," Paul said, as his eyes scanned the entire brick wall.
"What?? It's right there!" Samol said, pointing energetically.
London and Paul stared at each other once again, but didn't say a word. Paul broke the silence and said:
"I'm glad that you found it and all, but it's not good that you're the only one who can see it. What if it's not real? Or a trap??"

Samol's happiness was suddenly crushed. He truly began to worry that he was losing his mind…and wondered if it was all a trap from the very beginning…

"Why does this keep happening to me?" Samol said in a sorrowful voice.

"Just read aloud what you see on the death certificate and we'll do our best to interpret what it means," said London.

"All it says is: 'Time's death certificate; Birthdate - When He said 'go'; Death date - I die when wisdom falls.'"

"I die…when wisdom falls…" London and Paul repeated to themselves three and four times as if they were trying to make sense of it, but couldn't.

"Is there anything else?" London asked.

"No," he said. "Well…yes, but it's too small for me to read."

"I die when wisdom falls," his friends continued to mumble to themselves.

"I've got nothing," said Paul, who quickly gave up.

"What if — what if this is just like the Whispering Will?" London suggested, who sounded very unsure of herself.

"What are you talking about?" Samol asked.

"Remember how the Whispering Will told us something that was meant for the future?" London said gently. "What if this is also meant for the future?"

"RAAAAAAHHHHH!" Samol howled, scaring all three of his friends. "I'm sick of this!! I'm not cursed in the future! I'm cursed right NOW!! I don't need answers in the future…I need them NOW!!!" he screamed, carelessly flinging his hands to his head.

"Hey! Watch it!" Leanna barked.

"What?" he said.

"You hit me in the eye with a loose fingernail!" she said, rubbing her eye. Samol stood with an apology seated at the tip of his tongue and he checked all ten fingernails (none of which were chipped or broken).

288

It was then that he knew. He turned to face Leanna when all of a sudden a tooth dropped to her shoulder.

"LEANNA! YOU'RE DECOMPOSING!!" London shouted, pointing at her floating corpse.

"We have to get you reincarnated into your next life! NOW!!!!!!" Samol shouted.

He quickly shattered the glass and snatched the Death Certificate from its frame, not even caring if it were real or not. Off they went. The four of them hurled around corners like speed racers, their hearts thumping loudly!

"LEANNA!! RUN!!!" Samol screamed, who saw a few more teeth fall.

The body parts of Leanna's floating corpse that dissolved, ripped away the corresponding parts of her actual body. An eye for an eye. A tooth for a tooth. A leg for a leg. The knees of her floating body had dissolved, which ripped away her actual knees, leaving her bones exposed! She screamed terribly as she trembled on the ground.

"AHHHHHH!!! HELP!!! PLEASE!!!" Leanna screamed, already missing five teeth.

"OH, NO!!" screamed Paul, who couldn't believe what he just saw.

"Grab her arms and torso!" Samol instructed loudly. "I'll carry her by her legs!"

The three of them quickly and carefully picked her up.

"AHHHHHHHHH!!!" she cried in a blood-curdling scream.

It hurt so badly to even be touched, but they had to keep moving her withering body. She kept hollering. "Leanna, you're going to make it! You're going to be all right!" said London, feeling more sorrow than she could bear. Seconds later, the torso of her floating corpse had liquefied and fallen, ripping her in two, and everyone fell to the ground holding only portions of her body. Leanna wailed even louder than before! In Samol's hand was a piece of her leg. London had a part of her arm and withering ribcage. Paul held her heart.

The rest of her floating body began to dissolve away into nothing and so did she. Samol crawled next to her and could do nothing but watch her poor head twitch as tears cascaded down her withering face. Her eyes were losing every bit of fight and curiosity that once lived behind them. The brown eyes of so many peculiarities were now falling into a deepened abyss of nothing. She painfully parted her decaying lips and softly said, "I'm sorry, mom." She died. Her suddenly green eyes were fastened into Samol's.

What was once a quirky quartet had now become a tragic trio. Holding on to what was left of her withered body, the three of them wept. They didn't care about getting to their next lives or even how they would get back to the castle in which they were sorted. They just wanted their sister back. Leanna's body was now nothing more than dust and memories. From her remains arose a tiny, glowing, lavender spirit that hovered, there, ever so gently. In that moment, the skies let out a massive downpour as if they, too, were sad to lose a daughter they'd watched over for the past thirty-two lives. May she rest in peace.

CHAPTER EIGHTEEN

THE FUNERAL TO NEW BEGINNINGS

~ Euphod would like to dedicate a moment of silence to Lean na Elizabeth Rosewright ~

Grievance is one of life's strangest phenomena. It's an animal that we've all encountered at one point or another. Some are struck with this ghastly affliction on a daily basis, while others scathe by only hearing about it second-handedly through news or by watching others suffer. Truth is, people who've been pounded with such malady, day after day, should have their heads held high because they are strong. Yet, in that very moment, Samol, Paul, and London were the furthest thing from feeling strong.

The three of them continued to weep terribly. It seemed as if time, for just a moment, was kind enough to fall at a standstill and let grief take its course. Their shoulders shrugged as they all hugged. They gnashed their teeth and tears came streaming down their faces. No one could even talk, yet their emotions clamored: 'I miss my sister. I miss my friend.' Samol gazed down sadly at Time's Death Certificate, which was still crinkled in his hand. Although his third and final task was complete, it meant nothing to him because the one who truly led him there was gone.

Suddenly, something strange happened. Around Leanna's bright, hovering soul grew a bright purple mist that smelled of lilacs, lilies, lavenders, and new life, which almost smelled like a newborn baby. The mist cloaked their shoulders and necks as if it were hugging them, apologizing for taking their friend. In an instant, they were whisked away to a never-before-seen part of Euphod; one that was reserved for only the saddest of occasions.

They opened their eyes and found themselves on a grassy beach aligned with hundreds of the tallest weeping willows they'd ever seen. Although it had stopped raining, the skies were still a deep dark grey, as if the sun were setting behind thick clouds on a summer dusk. Behind the rows of weeping willows was Euphod's Dead Sea; an ocean that extended miles beyond what could've ever been imagined.

"Where are we? London asked, looking all around, wiping snot from her nose.

"I don't know…" Samol said, drying his tears, who also began looking around.

"I think this is…Vebelamourn?" Paul said, sounding more like he were asking a question than giving a response.

"What??" they said.

"I know – It's a mouthful…" Paul said, laughing a bit in hopes of easing the tension. "I think this is where Euphod holds its funerals for Aryamites who have died a final death."

"I don't think I've ever seen this place," said London, drying the last of her tears.

"You wouldn't," Paul said. "You'll only remember the person you've lost."

"How is that possible?" Samol asked, wiping a small tear from his chin.

"Well, according to what I've read in Euphod's library (the funeral section), once you leave Vebelamourn, Euphod only leaves you with the memories of the person who has passed on, not the funeral itself."

"Wow," Samol said, thinking to himself how much of a loving gesture that is.

"Funerals?" London questioned. "When did you read this?"

"*When?*" Paul frowned, as though he thought it were a stupid question.

London nodded.

"A few days ago, when I found out that Samol was in the Freedomcorpse hospital wing," he replied sheepishly, feeling terrible that this was the honest-to-god truth.

"You thought I was going to die - - again??" Samol said and his mouth fell wide open.

"You looked pretty bad, man!" Paul laughed weakly. "Anyway, let's do what we came here to do," said Paul, whose eyes had drifted to one of the weeping willows.

"Where is Lea—" Samol began to ask, but froze when he saw her.

Off in the distance, was all that was left of Leanna; her hovering, bright, lavender soul. She was being lovingly wrapped in large willow leaves by twelve Euphod pallbearers; tall and strong men dressed in hooded, silk, purple cloaks. Although they looked menacing, built somewhat like the giants who guarded the entrance to the Death Day Ball, they were exceedingly loving and rather sensitive. Each and every one of them cried after every burial.

Surrounding the pallbearers was everyone who was touched by Leanna. There weren't many. Yet, the few that were there wept terribly, saddened by her tragic and untimely, final death. "Hey, there's Maven!" said Samol, pointing emphatically. Samol, Paul, and London waved and Maven gave them a weak half-smile. He, too, was heartbroken. "Who's that woman standing next to him?" Samol asked.

Aside from the puddle of tears that Maven so desperately tried to conceal, was a tall, sobbing, curvaceous woman dressed in an elegant, black gown. She towered high enough to crane her neck over a two-story-building, standing nearly eye to eye with Maven. The shapely, giant woman had long, luscious, emerald green hair that was long enough to climb. She continued weeping into her black handkerchief as though Leanna was her own daughter.

"Oh, no," said Paul, feeling suddenly guilty.

"What's wrong?" Samol asked anxiously.

"That's Jerboa Galorian; ruler of Bridgelove," London answered, who also then felt guilty.

"Bridgelove?" said Samol, who was confused again, "But I thought sh — wait — Leanna wasn't sorted into Freedomcorpse like the rest of us?"

London and Paul kept silent.

"What am I missing here??" Samol begged nervously.

London revealed, "Leanna was initially sorted into the castle of Bridgelove and was supposed to be preparing for her next life…"

"Instead, when she heard that you were in danger she came and found London and myself so that she could help you," Paul finished.

Samol's eyes glazed over with a million apologies. He could never forgive himself! He burst into tears and collapsed to the ground.

"Samol," London said sternly, tightly grabbing his face. "This is not your fault."

"See…" his voice quivered. "I told you this was my battle. I TOLD YOU THIS WAS MY BATTLE!" he wept loudly, feeling responsible for an unnecessary death.

"Samol, Stop it! Stop it RIGHT NOW!" London hollered. "THIS IS NOT YOUR FAULT! DO YOU HEAR ME??" she bellowed, shaking him so violently that anyone watching would've thought she were attacking him.

"I will not have you blaming yourself because deep down, I know that any one of us would have done the same."

By now, the pallbearers were waist deep in the waters, humming a beautiful hymn in unison, gently carrying Leanna like she were a newborn baby. They delicately pushed her out to sea, which was when London finally noticed it.

"So I guess the myth is true," she said.

"Myth?" Samol asked thinly.

"The Euphod Dead Sea really is bright lavender because of the little pieces of Aryamite souls who've died a final death," London said, grinning smoothly as though she were actually at peace that her sister was in a better place.

The purple ocean was breathtaking and they stared silently, watching their loved one peacefully float away. Its waves crashed against the sand, leaving behind trails of thick, lavender silt. Paul moved a bit closer to the edge of the sea.

He was overtaken by such a spiritual moment and was ready to say his final goodbyes.

"The mother of all seas," Paul sighed warmly with a smile.

"Mother…" London whispered under her breath as though she had another revelation.

"What?" said Samol.

"Mother!" London said a bit louder, sounding almost manic. *"Mother, be quiet… Mother, you have terrible hearing…We're getting close, mom…"*

"What are you talking about?" said Samol, now studying her as if <u>she</u> were the one losing her mind.

Paul took notice as well.

"Let me see your death certificate!" London demanded.

Samol, not knowing what she was up to, quickly pulled it from his back pocket and she began to investigate wildly.

"Oh, my gosh, Samol…" she said with her eyes widening almost as much as her mouth.

"What??" he said, looking closely to see what she saw.

"I think you've completed your purpose," she smiled, giving it back to him.

"What? What do you mean?"

And then, he read:

Death Certificate
~ *The kingdom of Euphod would like to formally welcome you to a blissful eternity* ~

Name - S.T.R.A.D.O.O.R.
Birthday -- '..ir… …f.. d…'
Death Date: December 17 – 3 days 1 hr 23 min 16 sec
Life purpose – X
Obstacles/disabilities/challenges – X
Gifts/talents/capabilities – X
Scar – X

Hidden Purpose – Show Elizabeth L. Rosewright The End of Time

"I still don't get it? There are x's everywhere!" he said half confused, half panicked.

"Because you've fulfilled both your life purpose and your hidden purpose!" she said.

"How do you know?"

"First of all, when you're reincarnated into another life, you'll only die once your life's purpose has been fulfilled. However, your hidden purpose is something that can only be completed here in Euphod! Once both have been fulfilled, everything on your death certificate, except for your name and death date, will have x's through it."

An eavesdropping Paul walked towards them and pried Samol's death certificate from his fingers. He, too, grew wide-eyed but for a different reason.

"We still haven't figured out your curse!" Paul gasped. "You have thirteen days, remember??"

"Relax," London said calmly. "We've completed all three tasks. Samol's gonna be fine."

Paul's mouth fell open as though he were going to ask 'Are you sure?' but instead asked, "Who is this Elizabeth L. Rosewright, anyhow?"

Samol gasped. His eyes met London's, who looked as though she'd already figured it out.

"Was Leanna living as…?" Samol began to ask when he, then, figured it out.

"Whoa," said Paul, the last to figure out that he'd been getting hit on by Leanna's mother this entire time! He walked away and stood by his lonesome to say his personal goodbyes at the edge of the sea.

Samol and London stood side by side, watching him, and looked almost as if they were about to hold hands, but didn't.

"Ya know, I think my memory is starting to come back," Samol grinned gently.

"What do you mean?" London asked.

"Oh…I don't know…" he sighed and began to sing:

"Throw, throw, throw your hope..."

He stopped and waited for London to finish the rest.

She gasped, throwing her hands over her mouth. Her eyes glassed over with tears of joy. London was practically unable to speak - - let alone sing! Quiveringly, she finished the verse:

"In the death machine..."

They began singing the rest together:

"Merrily, merrily, terribly, wearily,
Life is but a scheme..."

The two of them locked hands, dancing in a circle, and continued singing other songs that suddenly came back to Samol's memory:

"We've lived lives of luck,
Hid-den in dis-guise,
Where-ever, how-ever,
You-get-her, be cle-ver,
Grace is in the skies..."

"...Six-teen lives below,
se-ven-teen above,
At thir-ty three,
He died for me,
I'm co-vered in His love..."

The two of them sang and harmonized happily for hours. London was more ecstatic that Samol got his memory back, even more so than he was! These were songs that the two of them used to sing after enduring hard lives. Up until this moment, said songs remained as nothing more than an *unspoken rhyme;* yet they were now being sung freely. Oh, how joyous the two of them were!

The evidence of Samol's curse seemed to have gone away. However, later on that night, he had an inquisitive dream. In this dream, he wondered how he'd completed three tasks based off of a misdiagnosed curse - - and yet he was cured? Maybe he wasn't cured! Or maybe it was because of Elizabeth L. Rosewright; a woman who'd been secretly living under a spell that allowed her to live in the body of her daughter, Leanna Rosewright, but see and hear through her own eyes and ears for the past three lives, who made the ultimate heroic act of sacrificing her own needs to help Samol and died in the process, which cured him of his curse?... It's strange that Samol Doscow could figure out more truth in a three minute dream than he could in one hundred forty-two days.

Till our next life.

If you could come back in another life - -
What would it be? When would it be? Where would it be?

_____

_____

_____

_____

_____

_____

_____

_____

_____

_____

_____

_____

_____

_____

additional thoughts....

~Thank you for imagining with me~

Made in the USA
Columbia, SC
19 August 2017